# NEW SWAN STONE

### Book 1: Lizzie's War

### Kevin O'Regan

**Core Books**

Julia
With warmest thanks for
your support.
Kev.
xx

*for Carrie*

# CONTENTS

# WHAT READERS SAID ABOUT
# NEW SWAN STONE

*A page turner! I particularly liked the strong female lead character. I also liked the sub-plots and the increasing tension as it reached the climax.*  Fred

*The trickle down of clues and creation of the WWII setting are excellent as are the domestic scenes with Jenny's family and the whole fuel scam sub-plot.*  Patrick

*This book is a gripping read with an unexpected ending; I enjoyed getting that jolt. I appreciated the research, the war context and the inclusion of a woman pilot in that macho society. I loved it.* Brenda

*The multiple, parallel stories create intrigue and drama. Lizzie is a strong, credible, central character, a good, powerful, female role model.*  Mark

*It's a great plot with interesting characters. I really liked Lizzie, Patricia and McBane. I thought the flying scenes were particularly good and the identity of the culprit cleverly hidden.* Jane

# ACKNOWLEDGEMENTS

I first came across the important role that the Air Transport Auxiliary (ATA) and especially its female pilots played in World War II after reading 'Spitfire Women of World War II' by Giles Whittell. It is an account of the real women who flew aircraft from factories to operational air bases and who flew other non-combat missions. I am very grateful to Richard Poad of the ATA Museum based in Maidenhead for his help with specific questions as I am to the staff at the history section of the RAF Museum, London. Both museums are well worth visiting. Thanks too to David Bush for sharing his RAF experiences.

The ATA was sometimes unkindly referred to as Ancient and Tattered Aircrew or, as they preferred, Anything to Anywhere. We are all indebted to them and especially the women pilots who were true pioneers for the emancipation of women.

Once again, I am indebted to Fred Lockwood, Patrick Sanders, Brenda O'Neill, Mark Kenny and Jane Wilkinson for their very valuable comments on an earlier draft. I also thank my wife, Carrie, for her patience and encouragement.

# PROLOGUE

Time falls like dust upon the past, settling, obscuring, covering. Colours fade, edges blur, definition falters. Treasured memories of course appear fresh, constructed anew with each re-telling, accuracy and truth sacrificed to entertain or re-assure. Not so those things that damaged and hurt; however much they seem buried by time's falling, however much we tell ourselves their destructive power is spent, they linger like cunning spies, corrupting our present, clouding our future, awaiting only the slightest of fortune's capricious winds to lay them bare.

# PART 1: MONDAY 15TH FEBRUARY 1943

# CHAPTER 1

The wind was screaming past the cockpit as the big bomber hurtled towards the ground. Lizzie was shouting but there was no one to hear. "Come on, come on, lift your nose." She was braced backwards, the joystick pulled into her stomach, the huge Merlin engines roaring but the ground was expanding into ever greater detail. "Oh God, not like this."

Suddenly her view was changing, the field that had a moment before seemed an inevitable and untimely crash site slipping underneath and …at last… the horizon, appearing like heaven in the cockpit windscreen. She was shaking and could feel sweat cold on her forehead and in her armpits. She brought the heavy plane level and snatched glances above and behind her as far as she could see.

She was not out of danger. The Shrike would be back, its guns blazing, the pilot keen to add another kill to his list.

It had appeared from the clouds, suddenly, on a different course but it had veered round as soon as its pilot had seen her and it had dropped like a hawk, machine guns rattling and bullets ripping through the fuselage. She had banked quickly to port and fortunately, the Shrike had banked to starboard. In the precious seconds before it could line her up in its sights again, she had dived. Get closer to the ground and hope that the Wellington's camouflage would blend with the countryside. If she could lose him for a while, he would give up and turn for home. No fighter had a sufficient range to stay around for long.

Her head was already composing her report. Attacked by a Focke-Wulf 190 at - she glanced at her wristwatch – nearly 1500 hours. It was a day raider, Hitler's latest tactic in the war against Britain. They sneaked in low over the coast trying to avoid the radar and attacked anything they thought might be worth destroying. A new Wellington bomber was a worthy prize. This Shrike was well inland now and would have to turn back soon...surely?

The Wellington galloped over the ploughed fields, a small tractor harrowing the ground like a toy crawling beneath it. Each mile took her closer to safety but every sinew in Lizzie's body was tensed, ready to make the next manoeuvre. At the sound of a different engine on her starboard side, she flung her head round. The Shrike's pilot was clearly visible as he flew beside her. He raised his hand in a wave. What was it? A gesture of friendship or just a horrible game to terrify her? While he was there beside her, he was ironically no danger as his guns could not swivel. She watched for a few seconds and then eased the joystick back slightly. The big plane again lifted her nose and began to climb but the German aircraft climbed with her.

This was a strange game. She was heading North, taking him away from his route. Surely he must realise that and turn back? Again he waved. "You're smiling aren't you? This is fun for you." She knew she was at his mercy. The Wellington could not match the Shrike for speed nor agility. At any moment, he could roar upwards, bank to starboard and come round behind her when he would get her in his sights and fill her plane with bullets, probably ripping the tail out so she lost control. "Stay calm and watch," she muttered. On the horizon, she could see woodland. Fly over it so that if he does attack, he might lose her against the trees, even in their winter nakedness.

Suddenly, the Shrike veered off to starboard and rose

out of her vision, exactly as she had predicted. She banked hard to port as she started to fly over the woodland and kept the turn on until she was heading south - back the way she had come. If he had turned to come down on her as she anticipated, she would, with luck, be directly underneath him so he would have to turn again. She looked up through the cockpit perspex and sure enough, she saw him above her travelling northwards.

"I can keep this up for hours matey."

Her jaw was clenched in defiance but fear stalked her, the silent presence always in one's head. She had plenty of fuel but she needed to try to get a sighting. If he turned back again, he could attack her as both planes flew South. She had to be ready to turn through 180 degrees again. Sure enough, she caught sight of him banking into a cloud. He would come roaring down behind her in a minute or two. She turned sharply to starboard once more, the heavy plane tilting, the starboard wing tracing a curve on the landscape, the familiar hollow in her stomach. As the compass needle crept towards the north, she straightened up at a bearing north by northwest and levelled off.

A dot dropped from the cloud ahead. It grew bigger and bigger and she knew without a doubt that it was the Shrike returning for the kill. He had obviously flown north in the cloud out of her sight before turning south and heading straight towards her. This was a game of nerves then. Who would turn first and would she be alive to manage the plane if his machine guns smashed into the cockpit? If she banked too soon, he would be able to follow her and give chase. She wished now she had climbed as high as the Wellington could go as the Shrike was not so good at high altitude. But she knew it was not really a solution: it would still be more agile than the heavy bomber, though were she higher, she could have bailed out.

"Why don't you let us have at least one gun armed and someone to fire the damned thing?" she yelled aloud. And then her mouth, dry with the bitter taste of fear, set in a tight line and her eyes narrowed on the target. She would hold her course and dare him to destroy her and himself.

The two aircraft charged like raging horses in a joust. She had no weapon, but she had size. Both aircraft would be destroyed but it would be one day-raider less for Hitler.

Her hands gripped the joystick, her brain working so rapidly, thoughts were mere flashes. She could see the cockpit of the Focke taking shape, the head of the pilot. What was going through his mind. Did he want to die for the glory of the Fatherland? He had some nerve, she had to give him that. And then suddenly, the Shrike veered to starboard and roared past her port side, creating enough turbulence to shake the Wellington. She breathed. He had not fired. Perhaps his ammo was spent, or he wanted to play.

She kept low and held her course. She would have to get her bearings once she thought she was out of danger and pick up the road she had been following. But there was still a risk. He might come back and take her out. She looked from side to side and above her, scanning the sky for any sign. After about a minute, he was suddenly there, alongside her. She could see him clearly. He took off his mouthpiece revealing a small, dark moustache and a huge smile filled his face. He saluted, not the Heil Hitler salute, but the British services salute. She was wearing no mouthpiece as she had no radio. She smiled back, nodded and then saluted, unwilling to allow him to believe she had been afraid.

He smiled again, put on his mouthpiece and surged ahead. The wings of the Focke dipped to starboard, to port and then the fighter banked to starboard and curved away from her, heading south-east. She let out a huge breath. Surely now he was heading home?

She did not relax however but maintained her nervous vigil for several more minutes before gradually coming to accept that the threat had diminished. Strange how someone could try to kill you and then give a smile and a salute. She guessed he had been impressed by her flying, out-smarting him, but she knew, had he really wanted to and with sufficient ammo, he could have brought her down. The threads of chance are slender.

She had lost sight of the A5 which she had been following. Her map had fallen to the floor of the cockpit so she retrieved it, turning it over and around until she had it the right way up. She could no longer see the road but guessed it might be over to starboard.

Not for the first time, she cursed her Air Transport Auxiliary boss for not letting her have a navigator.

"It's daytime," Commander Trueman had said, "it's good visibility, the weather's fine. A storm is forecast for later but you'll be there well before it hits. You'll be able to follow the A5 which takes you almost directly to RAF Silverstone. No need for a navigator."     It was crazy, risking a brand new bomber by having just a pilot on board. When operational, it would have five crew and some versions six.

She turned the heavy aircraft slightly to starboard and scanned the ground. Soon she saw a road snaking north-west across the landscape and she flew over to take a closer look. It certainly looked right. She should pass Dunstable before too long; the A5 ran right through the middle of it. She glanced at the map now hanging from the curved frame member in front of her. Dunstable was on a crossroads with factories to the right and the old Priory Church near the cross. Her eyes searched ahead. Villages emerged like mushrooms blooming on the landscape and disappeared from view behind her until she saw a town approaching.

The crossroads became visible first, the vast roofs of the factories appearing at the same time and then, a little later, the squat tower of the ancient church. She was back on track. Another thirty minutes or so should see her touching down at Silverstone. There was another RAF airfield at Turweston, just a few miles south of Silverstone, which was also used for bomber training. She must land at the right one. With gradual relaxation came enjoyment of the flight. On her port side, she could see high, hazy cloud paling the blue of the sky, the harbinger of the coming storm.

She had wanted to fly ever since, at the age of about five, she had seen her first aircraft. It was a bi-plane and she remembered vividly how it had crawled across the vast sky, passing in and out of the puffy white summer clouds that drifted across the Surrey countryside. Oh to be up there looking down, free like the birds, soaring gracefully.

It had of course been different in reality. She remembered her first ever flight in the little, single-engined Tiger Moth. It was the cold she remembered most. The open cockpit of the Moth gave little shelter and she was thankful for her thick flying jacket. But the thrill of it, the way it gripped her stomach when the engine roared in response to the throttle and the nose lifted from the ground. In front was just the sky, huge and inviting. She remembered looking down and gasping at the miniature scene beneath her, growing smaller every second. Passing through the first cloud was strange, the sudden fog, losing sight of the ground, no sense of direction. But then the glorious blue expanse when one emerged, the sense of freedom, the excitement; nothing she had ever experienced before could match it.

Taking flying lessons had been prompted by her older brother, Ralph, becoming a pilot in the RAF. A legacy from her grandmother had paid for enough lessons to qualify as a pilot on light aircraft though there had been constant sniping from her parents who did not consider it ladylike. They could not prevent it, however; it was her money.

She remembered then the conversation with her parents in late 1940 when she announced she was joining the Air Transport Auxiliary.

Her father had frowned. "What will your duties be... presumably administrative?"

She had taken a deep breath and, as lightly as she could, replied, "No, I'll be flying."

Her Mother stared at her. Lizzie was not sure if it was

surprise or alarm – probably a combination.

"Women can't fly warplanes. What on earth is going on?" her father blurted.

Lizzie had nearly exploded at her father's statement but, with forced calm, she explained that the RAF was so short of pilots for combat duties it had recruited disabled, older and foreign men to transport aircraft from the factories to air bases. This was still insufficient so they were inviting young women to do the job. "There are other women pilots already. They're experienced flyers but some, like me, will need more training."

"But...but it's dangerous." Her mother's hands were clenched together as if by doing so she could prevent her daughter taking this rash course of action.

"I've dealt with plenty of danger...at the Hunt ball...all those Hooray Henry's chucking me about on the dance floor!"

"Don't be flippant, Elizabeth. This is serious. You might be killed."

"It will only be flying in this country. It's not like Ralph doing missions over enemy territory." Ralph was already an experienced fighter pilot. "Sometimes, we have to transport important people around the country. Maybe I'll get to meet Winston Churchill. Perhaps he'll ask me to be his personal assistant...light his cigars that sort of thing."

"Your Mother has already told you not to be flippant, Elizabeth. I wish you'd rid yourself of that habit of treating everything as a joke. War is not a joke."

The discussion rumbled on, her father making telephone calls to various people before grudgingly accepting it. Her mother remained baffled as to why any young woman would want to do such a job even in wartime. Lizzie smiled at the memory.

She glanced at the dials in front of her and her heart began to pound. The port side fuel gauge had dropped alarmingly. Glancing out of the port window, she could see a faint mist of fuel coming from somewhere beneath the port wing. "Damn," she shouted. A bullet must have ruptured the tank. What should she do? Would she have enough fuel to run both engines until she reached Silverstone? Should she cut the port engine to conserve fuel and reduce the risk of fire? She knew the Wellington could fly on one engine without a heavy payload of bombs on board but she had never flown a heavy aircraft on one engine. Would it be manageable? Could she land it like that?

She kept glancing nervously at the port wing expecting any moment to see a burst of flame. Cut the engine or press on hoping the fuel would last and fire not break out? "Make a decision...now," she shouted at herself.

# CHAPTER 2

The frown on Robbie McBane's forehead deepened. How could a training base with that number of personnel and that number of ground vehicles be using so much fuel? He went through the figures again. "They must be driving to bloody Aberdeen every week," he muttered to himself. He rose from his chair, the piece of paper on which he had written his notes held firmly in his hand, and wove a path through the desks at which his two colleagues laboured. He tapped on the door of the next office and stepped in.

Flight Lieutenant Richard Belding looked up from his desk. "What have you got Robbie?"

"Well, Sir, it may be nothin' but…"

Belding laughed. "How many times have I heard you say that? No doubt your infallible Scottish instinct has caught a whiff of something suspicious."

"Aye, Sir, it has. I've been looking at various aspects of some of our air training bases here in the South and one o' the things I've looked at is fuel use…you know how concerned the ministry is aboot fuel conservation, Sir, what with rationing and all."

"And rightly so, Robbie, rightly so."

"Well, Sir, the new training base - No 17 OTU up at Silverstone - seems to be getting through a helluva lot of petrol and also stores of all kinds. For that size o' base with that number of personnel, they certainly use a lot of stuff."

Belding stretched out his hand and McBane put the paper into it. Belding's shrewd eyes perused it, flicking quickly over the figures. Robbie McBane knew that, even in what appeared a cursory glance, his boss would be taking it all in, assessing, calculating. Belding's face remained expressionless;

his clean cut good looks and charming smile were a trap for the unwary for Belding's quick grasp and insight were legendary.

"I've put comparative figures of other bases on there, Sir, so ye can see what I mean."

Belding lowered the paper to the table and looked directly at McBane. "Good God. They must be drinking petrol and feeding the five thousand every week but with a lot more than a few loaves and fishes."

"Aye, Sir. Ah think you're right."

Belding motioned McBane to sit in the chair in front of his desk. "Worth looking into, d'you think?"

"Definitely, Sir."

Belding nodded. "Ok, but let's go in softly-softly at first…routine check that sort of thing. Go on your own. Can you be ready to go tomorrow?"

"No problem, Sir."

"Great. I'll phone the commanding officer now. Who is it by the way?"

"Group Captain Lovell, Sir."

Belding groaned. "Oh God. You'll need to tread carefully, Robbie. He'd be only too happy to watch us mess up."

McBane smiled. "Aye, Sir, ah'll tread as light as a fairy."

Belding laughed at the idea of the six foot, athletic, red-haired, rugby player in front of him treading like a fairy. "Right, you get yourself sorted for tomorrow and I'll tackle the ogre."

Some ten minutes later, the phone on Belding's desk rang and Daphne Morris, Belding's secretary in the office next to his, informed him in her clipped, efficient voice that Group Captain Lovell was ready to take his call. Belding looked out of the window at the dark sky rolling across the Buckinghamshire countryside; he smiled and prepared his most cheery voice.

Thirty minutes later, Robbie McBane threw a kit bag on the bed in his quarters. He wouldn't need much but he needed to be ready for one or two nights away. He put a finger to his lips as he contemplated the chest of drawers. Clean underwear, socks, spare pair of trousers, a couple of shirts. One advantage of uniform was not having to make decisions about what to wear. He had never been good at that and had relied on Catriona's judgement.

Catriona. He stepped over to the bedside cabinet and lifted the picture frame from it. He gazed at the photograph tenderly. So lovely. That smile which seemed to light her whole face, the softness of her eyes, the way her hair bounced when she walked. He never really believed his luck that such a beautiful young woman could love him.

He sat on the bed and allowed the memories to transport him to another place. Glasgow, before the war, the dance hall where he had first set eyes on her. He had been a young airman, home on leave and she, he discovered, was from Edinburgh, staying with her aunt and cousins. He smiled at the anxiety he had felt approaching the three young women; his gaze was focused only on her.

"May I have the pleasure of this dance?"

There was the slightest pause before she replied, a pause in which he underwent the pangs of anticipated rejection, saw the fleeting looks between the three girls that he assumed was derision, until she looked at him and smiled. "I'd love to," she said, standing and putting out her hand to be led onto the dance floor.

Carefully, he laid the photograph between the clothes in his bag. He wanted her with him, always, even though now he would never see her again, never savour the fragrance of her perfume, never feel her soft touch. He shuddered, the horrors of that night exploding once more in his mind. On the second of two nights of carnage on the Clyde, one bomb had obliterated her aunt's house and all its occupants, including the girl he had planned to marry. March 14th 1941, a day engraved on his heart like the lettering on her gravestone.

He looked around his bachelor quarters. Not much

to show for his life. After her death, he needed something different and his commanding officer had told him about the RAF Police. It had not been a difficult decision. The only drawback was that he was not contributing so directly to the war effort. He wished he had been able to become a pilot and bomb Germany as they had bombed Glasgow, London and countless other cities in an attempt to destroy factories, ports, anything that might help Britain's military campaign. But he had reconciled himself to that; he was still doing something.

"I'm a bachelor and will always be," he said grimly into the mirror on the back of the wardrobe door. There could never be another who could make him feel as she had done.

Lizzie made a decision. She cut off the port engine and, as the prop slowed, she could feel the big plane trying to slew to port; she pressed the port prop feathering button to reduce drag. She knew from her training that in asymmetric flying she had to keep the rudder over to counteract the pull of the one remaining engine on the starboard side. She must concentrate, she told herself, fly the plane as economically as she could. The fuel should hold out with only one engine operating but the port wing tank was draining all the time.

Disappointment, irritation, even anger filled her. She prided herself on delivering aircraft in impeccable condition and this would be the first time she would arrive with a damaged plane. But at least she had stood up to the Shrike, especially when he had come straight for her. "Manage your fear." Her English teacher, Miss Blackwell's words came to her mind. It was advice that had stood her in good stead in many situations and, when it was given, it had helped her to stop the bullies who were making her life a misery. She had learnt then at the age of thirteen that there is only one way to deal with a bully – stand up to them even if one is hurt as a result. She refused to allow herself to be intimidated; fear was real – she felt it often – but she was determined she would never let it dominate her.

After passing Dunstable, the A5 began to curve to the North West, like a scar on the landscape, passing villages in Bedfordshire and then Buckinghamshire. She glanced at the map. She needed to head due West when she approached the smoke from the iron oxide works at Deanshanger. She could see heavy smoke blowing almost at right angles from a tall chimney and decided to make the turn as soon as she had passed over it. With the wind driving the smoke across the ground, she would be high above it when she passed.

That course should take her mid-way between the two airfields of Turweston and Silverstone and she should be able to see both from her current height. Sure enough, they came into view at almost the same time.

"Just as well the clouds haven't thickened yet. I'd have had to lose height to get beneath heavy cloud and perhaps would have missed them." Speaking to oneself was an occupational characteristic of the solo flyer.

She turned the heavy plane to starboard to fly due North. This would enable her to make her approach into the wind. As she turned, the aircraft notes which she had hooked on the metal frame in front of her slid sideways, hit a bracket and tumbled off, resting precariously on the floor beside her.

"Damn." She reached down to retrieve the folder but her fingers could not quite grasp it. As she stretched, she moved the joystick and the plane lurched further to starboard. She watched in frustration as the folder slipped out of her section and fell into the bomb aimer's position in the well beneath her.

"Blast," she yelled. "What do I do now?"

There was no hope of retrieving it – it was far too risky to leave the controls and let the plane fly itself. She levelled the plane and looked to port and ahead where Silverstone airfield lay spread out ready for her landing, a neat cross made by the intersecting runways with buildings on one side and the control tower projecting above it all. It looked peaceful in the hazy afternoon light – that might change if the undercarriage would not lower!

She remembered something from the notes about how to get the wheels down if there was not sufficient hydraulic pressure for the safety catches to release automatically. But she could not bring that section of the notes to mind. "Blast you," she shouted at the Shrike pilot. She knew it was the stress of that encounter that had temporarily wiped her mind.

Praying fervently, she pulled down the lever to lower the wheels. Nothing happened. No familiar rumble as the mechanism engaged, no extra drag as the wheels were caught in the airflow.

Desperately she searched the controls in front of her. Three red lights glowed beside the lever. That meant the safety lock was still on. The safety lock release must be somewhere close. She was running out of time.

She banked to port and turned the Wellington so that it lined up with the runway. The wind sock, streaming at almost ninety degrees from the pole was now clearly visible. The big plane yawed as it rode the wind. She still could not see the manual safety lock release for the undercarriage control. "It must be right in front of my eyes. Look, you idiot, look."

She was reducing height but knew that if she did not get the wheels down soon, she would have to abort. In panic, she shouted, "What do I do if I can't find it? I can't put a brand new aircraft down on its belly." With fuel leaking, fire was a certainty, bringing the destruction of the aircraft and her death, burned alive until she lost consciousness.

She could see details of the airfield now, the fire truck, fuel bowsers parked near the buildings, even one or two tiny figures close to the vehicles. Closer and closer. Again, that time at school when she had been bullied flashed into her mind and the quiet voice of Miss Blackwell. 'Think Lizzie. Don't let your fear take control. There is always a way.' There must be a way – she just needed to think.

She stared hard at the three red lights and the switches close by and suddenly shouted at herself. "Oh God, Lizzie. Sort it out."

# CHAPTER 3

"What the bloody hell is he doing?" Group Captain Lovell watched the Wellington swooping over the airfield and heading close to the control tower in which he stood surveying his domain. He flinched slightly as the Wellington passed overhead, its engine rattling the glass in the control tower windows. "Port side engine is not operating. Sound the alarm and get the fire trucks out ready," Lovell barked.

"Is he trying to land?" Flight Lieutenant Dearing screwed up his face in disgust.

"Well he damned well missed whatever he's doing. He'd be better off with his wheels down!"

The metallic sound of the tannoy echoed around the buildings of the air base as the Wellington came into sight again on the north side of the airfield, flying low. The two officers watched it, barely visible, making a distant circle in the dark sky. "Have you had any radio contact?" Lovell snapped at one of the controllers.

"No Sir. Nothing at all."

There was a tense silence as the dot on the horizon slowly grew and took the shape of the bomber. "He's coming down this time by the look of it – his wheels are down." Dearing's voice was an arrogant drawl betraying his background and public school education.

"Well let's hope he brings it down in one piece without taking out one of our buildings."

The big aircraft slowed and dropped, seeming to hang in the air. Its wheels touched the tarmac of the runway, sending a little puff of smoke from each as the rubber briefly burnt. Fire trucks gave chase, bells ringing and lights flashing. The aircraft's tail lowered gently and the plane slowed to taxiing speed. Turning off the runway it headed towards the apron in front of the hangars, only one propeller still turning, the fire trucks still chasing.

"I want to see that pilot in my office as soon as he's off the plane." Lovell's jaw was set firm and the words were a low growl.

Flight Lt. Dearing dispatched Airman Andrews to the apron to escort the pilot to Lovell's office. He would like to be a fly on the wall but would probably have to make do listening outside. He had witnessed a dressing down from Lovell a couple of times and it was a sight worth seeing – provided you were not on the receiving end. He looked out now at the apron, keen to get a glimpse of the pilot who, unknowing, was to be Lovell's victim. Andrews hovered at the nose of the plane waiting with the fire team and ground crew who had already put chocks each side of the main wheels and were spreading sand on the ground beneath the dripping wing tank. The starboard propeller had slowed to the point where you could see each blade.

Dearing waited for the hatch under the belly of the aircraft to be opened and the ladder to come down. This was out of his sight. Eventually, one figure appeared from under the plane and the ground crew saluted. Where were the others? There must be more than one person on the bomber. He waited, a frown deepening on his forehead. The single figure in the flying suit removed goggles and helmet and a shock of fair hair cascaded out. She, for it really was a woman, shook her head and the hair bounced before being swept sideways by the freshening wind.

Dearing's mouth fell open and he smoothed his black hair down with his hand in an habitual gesture. He saw Andrews approach the figure and there was a conversation. Andrews was looking at the plane, clearly asking for the pilot. The woman pointed at her herself and laughed. She was pretty, he could see that even at this distance. She and Andrews began to walk towards the buildings and Dearing decided to intercept them before they reached Lovell's office.

He met them in the corridor by the Officers Mess. "Well hello…"

She saluted. "Second Officer Barnes, Sir, delivering your Wellington bomber."

"You're the pilot?"

"Yes Sir."

"But…but…"

"Yes, I'm a woman, Sir." She smiled, pleasantly but with just a hint of amusement at his expense thought Dearing. Her eyes were bright, aquamarine, intelligence radiating from them. "I understand Group Captain Lovell would like a word with me, Sir, so, if you'll excuse me…"

"Yes, yes of course. I don't want to hold you up." He stood watching Andrews and the pilot as they continued along the corridor. Even dressed in a flying suit, he could see that she had a good figure. "She should brighten the place up," he murmured. "I wonder how long she'll be here?"

Lizzie could feel Dearing's eyes on her, knowing he was assessing her figure. She was tempted to turn around and say something but bit her tongue. She did not want to make enemies. After climbing some stairs, her guide halted outside an office.

Lizzie and Andrews heard the phone being slammed down inside and the muttered expletive. Andrews waited a few seconds before knocking sharply on the door and going in when he heard Lovell's menacing command to enter.

"Second Officer Barnes, Sir," he said standing in the doorway. At Lovell's signal, Andrews stood aside and let Lizzie pass into the room but she could not fail to see the smirk on the airman's face – cocky, insubordinate, a barrack room lawyer.

Lovell was writing something at his desk. Lizzie guessed it was a favourite tactic; let them wait for a while - it would make them uncomfortable. Without looking up, Lovell suddenly put his pen down and said, loudly, with an icy edge to his voice, "What on earth were you playing at when you first approached the airfield?" He looked up suddenly and his mouth fell open. He stared at Lizzie, who could see shock clearly written on his face.

Lizzie saluted and stood to attention. She expected him to tell her to stand at ease but he did not. "The undercarriage lock would not release, Sir, so I had to check the notes. I had to go round again." She watched the anger drain from his face, replaced by a comic surprise. It was an unremarkable face, regular, fairly handsome, topped with dark hair slicked to the side but with a bald patch on the crown.

"What do you mean, you needed to check…?"

"Well, Sir, I've not flown a Wellington before so I had to check the notes but unfortunately the folder fell off the frame into the bomb aimer's well as I was approaching Silverstone and I couldn't retrieve it. I couldn't find the manual safety lock release for the undercarriage and then I was too close. But, by revving the starboard engine as I went round, it generated enough hydraulic pressure to get the wheels down."

Lovell stood, shakily, propping himself on his desk with both hands. Lizzie could see anger returning, smouldering slowly beneath his urbane exterior. She smiled brightly, hoping to soften that face. It seemed to have the opposite effect. He glared at her and she let the smile fade.

His voice was low, threatening, but rising with each word. "I asked for a Wellington bomber to be delivered here to train pilots and aircrew for missions against Germany and someone has seen fit to let a young woman, who has never flown one before, fly it up here. Are you sure you flew it here or was there a pilot on board?"

Lizzie resorted as usual to humour. "I didn't see any one else on board, Sir, so I think I must have flown it by myself."

Lovell's face twisted in a snarl. "You came in on one engine. Why in God's name didn't you radio ahead to let us know?"

"I tried, Sir, but it's quite difficult without a radio…the Ministry don't think we need to talk to anyone."

Lizzie saw a rebuke forming in Lovell's mouth but it stalled at a knock on the door. "Enter!" he shouted.

"Sir, I felt you should know that the tail of the Wellington is damaged...some bullet holes apparently and the port wing tank has been punctured." Dearing looked sideways at Lizzie and smiled. She could not decide whether the intention was malicious or unctuous. Either way it was unwelcome. She looked at him more carefully, his dark pomaded hair smoothed back into perfect tidiness. There was something vaguely familiar about that look in his eye. Had she met him before?

"Thank you Flight Lieutenant Dearing." Lovell nodded at him to dismiss him but as he turned added, "Oh Dearing, I've had a call from Belding - RAF Police. They're doing some kind of routine check on use of stores, fuel that kind of thing so he's sending a..." he looked down at his desk, peering at his notes, "Sergeant McBane up here tomorrow to have a look. Usual waste of time, they should be out fighting the bloody Hun not getting in our way."

Lizzie saw Dearing's face stiffen, the enigmatic smile fading immediately. Lovell did not appear to notice. When the door closed, he walked around his desk, propping his behind on the front of it and folding his arms. His tone was sarcastically pleasant. "So Flight Officer Barnes, can you offer some explanation as to why you have brought me a damaged aircraft?"

"I was attacked on the way up by a stray German fighter, Sir. It will be in my report when I write it. I suspect he was out of ammo or I wouldn't have made it."

"I will read your report with great interest. Is there anything else you want to say now – we will of course talk again when I've spoken to your commanding officer on the telephone."

"With the storm rising, Sir, I won't be able to get back to White Waltham tonight so I wonder where I should stay."

Lovell looked at her, seemingly baffled by the question.

He was clearly unable to deal with having a woman on an air base designed only to cater for men? Finally he said, "I will have someone check with Matron in Sick Bay – she may have a bed in the nurses' quarters. Wait outside and I'll arrange that." The irritation was plain in his voice and the way he grabbed his pen from the desk. It was unusually slim, blue with gold rings. Strange how one noticed such trivia.

Lizzie saluted again and left the office. "You're a bit of a Hitler but it's bluster; I've met your type before," she muttered to herself as she stood outside the door. There was something oppressive about the base, an impression formed not just from her interview with Lovell. She could not say why she felt that but feel it she did.

She had left her overnight bag, which she always brought with her just in case, on the aircraft. She would need to retrieve it once she knew where she was going. She waited for what seemed an age, increasingly conscious that she needed a visit to the lavatory.

Eventually, she heard brisk, light steps approaching and, turning the corner in the corridor, a young nurse approached her. The stiffly starched uniform was crisp and the nurse's upright posture spoke of efficiency. Some wisps of dark hair had escaped from her hat. Her face was slightly concave, the chin protruding, giving her a severe look but this impression was instantly dispelled when she broke into a sudden smile that was warm and full, tiny creases appearing at the corners of her soft brown eyes. About my age, Lizzie thought, perhaps a year or two older.

The nurse extended her hand. "Patricia O'Flynn."

Lizzie took it and looked in the other woman's eyes. "Lizzie Barnes," she said, returning the smile. Lizzie trusted her instinct a great deal and felt this was someone she liked and would probably trust far more than the two male officers she had already met though, in making that judgement, she had registered the slightest reserve on the part of the nurse.

"You want a bed for the night then?" There was an Irish

lilt in her voice.

"Yes please but first I need a toilet and then I must get my bag…it's still in the aircraft."

"Ok. Loo it is." Patricia smiled and turned on her heel to head back the way she had come. Lizzie fell into step. "Good flight?"

"Fine apart from the stray German fighter who tried to take me out. It was strange though." Lizzie explained what had happened and the German's final salute.

"I 'spose some of them are gentlemen. No reason why not." Having left the building they were in, Patricia led the way into the adjacent building, along a corridor which smelt of hospitals and stopped by a door. She nodded to it. "There you are. Toilet for the use of, as they say."

When Lizzie came out, she was led back outside that building, in front of the first to the apron where the Wellington sat motionless and silent on the concrete. Several men in RAF overalls were examining the tail, one on top of a step ladder. "Shouldn't be too hard to fix," he called to the others. "Bit of a shame though – brand new plane and all that."

"Pilot's a bloody woman. Not surprising really."

Lizzie was tempted to retaliate but thought it was pointless; as she climbed the ladder into the belly of the aircraft to retrieve her bag, however, she saw Patricia approaching the group. "You'd have done better would you?"

"Well I reckon…"

"Do you know what happened?"

"No, no I don't."

"Well perhaps you should find out before you make judgements about women pilots. As it happens, there was an attack from a stray German fighter. The pilot of the Wellington was on her own and the guns not armed. 'Tis a testament to her skill that she got the plane here at all with so little damage."

Lizzie re-appeared in time to see Patricia turn away from the group after firing her volley of words. "Thanks," she said to Patricia, "but there was no need. They're not to know."

"They're too quick to blame us because we're women. I'd like to see one of them fly this thing solo."

◆ ◆ ◆

The blue Bedford truck shuddered to a halt by the fuel tanks and two airmen jumped down. On one side, the wind bellied the canvas against the frame; on the other, it ballooned outwards. The two men worked in silence. With furtive glances towards the hangar beside the huge tank, one took the pump from its holder and thrust it into the Bedford's fuel filler. The other, eyes also flicking frequently towards the hangar, was taking empty metal jerry cans from the back of the truck and lining them up beside his colleague.

When four tanks were on the ground beside him, the first one transferred the filling pipe to each in turn. "Not too many at once," hissed the first as more tanks were brought out. The other halted and waited until the first two tanks had been filled. Then as the next two were being filled, he lifted one of the full ones, leaning away from it with his arm outstretched to counter balance the weight and hoisted it into the back of the truck.

"Take two at a time, you weakling."

"What and drop 'em? That won't do us any good."

More empty tanks were lined up and duly filled until a dozen stood in two neat rows across the back of the truck. The filler was replaced on the pump and the first airman, whistling nonchalantly as he read the gallons on the pump dial, went into the hut to record it. "Sixty-five gallons," he said and smiled.

When he rejoined the truck, he walked to the back. "Nice and secure, I 'ope."

"Of course. What d'you think I am?"

"By the way, I put your initials on the sheet." He laughed

at the cross expression on his colleague's face. "Keep hidden, that's my motto."

The February afternoon was curling into twilight, hastened by dark clouds, as the engine roared into life and the heavy truck lumbered forward. It turned onto the perimeter road for the short distance to the gate. One of the guards strolled towards the cab and watched the window wind down. The driver, his arm on the door, looked down at him.

"Alright Smiffy? Got to collect some stores from Brackley."

The two men shared a smile and the guard waved to his colleague to open the barrier. The truck slowly drew through it and onto the road.

Lizzie stood at the window of her room watching the lorry drive through the gate. The airbase going about its normal work she supposed, though it did seem quite late to be going out now, especially in this weather. With her characteristic attention to detail she made a mental note of the lettering on the truck: RAF 142031.

# CHAPTER 4

Lovell picked up the telephone handset. "Group Captain Lovell here, No 17 OTU Squadron." His voice was steely, ready to employ his most cutting sarcasm. "Trueman, I ordered a Wellington bomber for our training of aircrew. It arrived today, the tail shot full of holes and piloted by a young woman, with no crew, who tells me she has never flown one before."

"Yes, Group Captain. That'll be Lizzie Barnes. Superb pilot. What made the holes in the tail?"

"She tells me she encountered an enemy fighter on the way up who fired on her. She assumes he ran out of ammo or he would have finished her off. Tell me Trueman, is it your habit to have untrained pilots, women pilots, deliver heavy bombers without any protection? She overshot the runway and had to go round again because, she said, she had dropped her notes on the floor and couldn't remember how to get the wheels down."

"As you know, pilots are in short…"

Lovell exploded. "You can spare me a lecture on the supply of pilots, I'm busy here trying to train them to address that issue. We can't do it, if the planes arrive full of holes. I need a temporary pilot instructor on Wellingtons until I can find someone to do the job permanently but I can't use a woman."

"No reason why not, Sir, she's excellent."

"She's only flown the bloody thing once and she had to use notes to do so."

Trueman held the earpiece away from his head and let the tirade burst from it without taking any notice. The raging voice stopped and he was about to put the phone to his ear when it started again. He waited. At last, when he judged Lovell's ire to be spent, he spoke again, calmly, as if talking to a child with a tantrum.

"Please let me explain the situation, Group Captain. As you know, we have lost a large number of pilots, young men who have given their lives for the war effort. We need every able-bodied young man who has the right aptitudes to fly aircraft on combat missions. That leaves us with the disabled, the foreign and women to deliver planes to operational bases, take them to be repaired and ferry important people around the country. I am proud of what our pilots have done. We train our pilots on groups of aircraft. Once they have qualified in one aircraft from that group, they are deemed able to fly any type from that group. We give them notes to cover the particular controls of that aircraft." He paused.

"Do go on please," Lovell sneered, "I've nothing better to do than listen to your excuses."

"These are not excuses, Group Captain, they are necessities created by the situation we are in. Lizzie Barnes is one of several young women who have been trained to fly and have graduated to larger aircraft. She has flown numerous successful missions and is a truly gifted pilot, able to adjust to new aircraft very rapidly."

"And do pray tell me why you deemed fit to send her on her own."

"The route is very straightforward. She simply had to skirt London and pick up the A5. There was no need for a navigator. As I am sure you're aware, the Air Ministry does not allow aircraft guns to be armed when being delivered, so there is no point in sending a gunner. You will probably also be aware that radios are not fitted to aircraft until they reach their destination and we do not of course train our pilots to fly on instruments. That's quite a set of restrictions to place on them but they do the job anyway and it's a job that is vital to the war effort."

"Humph! So you seriously think I can have your young woman train my recruits on flying a Wellington?"

"Surely you already have pilots who have been taken off combat operations to do that?"

"A couple but not enough."

"Lizzie Barnes will do an excellent job if you want to use her. She's intelligent, resourceful, personable and has a natural poise that commands respect. Anyone who sees her at the controls of an aircraft will have no doubt about her capability. But of course if you do not wish to use her in that capacity, please send her back as we have plenty of work for her to do."

Lovell put down the telephone without the courtesy of a farewell.

❖ ❖ ❖

With a weary sigh, Albert Sumser hung his overcoat on one of the hooks in the small entrance hall of his home. He looked at his face in the mirror hanging on the wall beside the hooks, noticing as always the grooves scouring ever deeper.

"Good day Dear?" Enid, his wife came through from the kitchen wiping her hands on her flower-patterned apron.

"Much the same as usual." He kissed her lightly on the cheek. "Wind's strong – we'll have a lot of rain before the night's out I think." He tucked the newspaper he held under his arm and rubbed his hands together. "Gor, I'm ready for some grub I can tell you that."

"It's nearly cooked. You go in and make yourself comfortable."

Their daughter, Jenny, ran lightly down the stairs. "Hello Dad."

"You'll take a tumble one of these days, coming down the stairs like that."

Enid tutted. "I keep telling her but she won't take a blind bit of notice."

"That's the way with the young these days. In too much of a hurry to get somewhere else."

"You can't blame us. We may all be dead tomorrow."

"You shouldn't say such things Jenny." Her mother

retorted as she returned to the kitchen muttering about the war.

Dinner – one sausage each, some mash potato and cabbage - was eaten in near silence. As always at family mealtimes, the absent member seemed to hover in the room as if waiting to sit on the empty chair at the table. George, whose picture, taken at his passing out parade when he was nineteen, graced the mantelpiece in the sitting room. George, killed two and a half years ago in Northern France as the allies withdrew, the son and brother who would never return, never kiss a sweetheart in the pictures, never stand at the altar rail waiting for his bride to join him.

Enid Sumser coughed and took a drink of water.

"Alright Dear?" Her husband touched her gently on the arm, watching her face keenly. She recovered her composure and nodded.

Jenny laid the cutlery on her plate and, keeping her head lowered, looked carefully at her mother. She felt George's loss too, the older brother who could be relied on to look after her, though there had been times when they had found each other irritating.

"D'you remember when he brought home those frogs?" Enid chuckled. "Always up to mischief but a good boy, heart of gold." She lifted her hand to her mouth and her brow furrowed.

"It doesn't do to dwell, Love." Albert put his hand on her shoulder and gently slid it down her back.

"No...but sometimes...I can't help thinking..."

"I'll do the dishes," Jenny announced abruptly and stood to stack the plates.

"Thank you Dear. You're a good girl too. I don't know what we'd do without you." Enid sniffed and Albert led her into the sitting room.

Jenny was brisk about clearing the table and washing up. The kitchen was very small and her mother kept it tidy and spotless. Jenny washed and dried, putting the plates away in the cream cabinet on the wall and the pots in the cupboard underneath it. She made sure to wipe the draining board, the top and around the rings of the gas cooker before hanging up the dishcloth but she left the frying pan with the fat congealing in it ready for using again. Waste not want not, that was what her Mum always said.

She ran upstairs and into her bedroom, closing the door behind her. The evening was her time. Pulling off the top and the slacks she had worn to work, she slid open the top drawer in her wardrobe. Rummaging underneath the thick stockings and underwear she kept there, she felt the two packets she wanted and smiled to herself. The first contained expensive nylon stockings. She took them out carefully and let them flow from her hand, feeling their smoothness with the other. Laying them on the bed, she placed the contents of the other packet, a pair of pink silk knickers, beside them.

She lingered over dressing, slowly sliding the pink suspender belt around her waist and sitting on the bed to roll each stocking up her leg. When she had drawn on the knickers, she looked at herself in the long mirror on the back of the wardrobe door, turning one way and then the other, bending one leg slightly, pushing out her hip, admiring the lace that fringed the knickers and the slight sheen of the stockings. She was proud of her figure. She pushed her bust out and pouted her lips like Rita Hayworth on the poster for her latest film with Fred Astaire, *You Were Never Lovelier*. Jenny tossed her head so that her long brown hair cascaded onto her shoulders and down her back a little. One day she would dye it auburn like Rita had in another film. She smiled at herself.

Reaching behind her, she unclipped her brassiere, shrugging the straps off her shoulders and catching it when it slipped down her arms. Stretching into the drawer, she selected a pink one; it was not an exact match for the knickers but was close enough. Finally, she stepped into a dress and pulled the zip up the back. Just hair and make-up and she was ready.

Ten minutes later, Jenny stepped softly down the stairs

in her stockinged feet, holding her shoes in one hand and her bag in the other. In the hall she put on her coat, tied a scarf around her hair to keep it tidy from the wind and pushed open the sitting room door that was always left slightly ajar. Her father was flopped in his armchair with the newspaper, discarded earlier by a railway passenger, and her mother was in the armchair opposite knitting. A small fire burned brightly in the grate, the coal supplied from Albert's work on the railways. The wireless was playing music quietly.

"I'm off out," Jenny said brightly. "I won't be late but don't wait up."

"Have you got your key? We have to lock the door these days – you never know who might be about…a German spy or someone." Enid Sumser did not look up from her knitting, the needles clacking rapidly like a telegraph machine.

"I don't think German spies would be interested in our house Mum."

"Well the door'll be locked anyway."

"I've got my key."

Mr Sumser suddenly lifted his head from the newspaper. "It says in the paper here that Orde Wingate – strange name that - with 3,000 Chindits crossed the Chindwin River on Saturday on their march into Burma…that's Saturday just gone." He flicked the top of the newspaper back to look at the date. "Today's Monday the fifteenth so Saturday was the thirteenth of April. That's great. Take the fight to the Japs is what I say."

"That's good Arthur. Where are you off tonight?" As Enid Sumser asked the question, her husband's head swivelled towards Jenny and then back to the paper.

"Oh not sure. I'll meet up with Maggie and Rita and we'll think of somewhere to go."

"You be careful." Enid stopped knitting for a few seconds to look at Jenny.

"I will Mum. Bye." She turned rapidly and left the room before they could detain her longer. Similarly, she was quickly out the front door, pulling it closed behind her, listening for the click of the Yale lock.

◆ ◆ ◆

Maggie was huddled against the wall of the Town Hall, their agreed meeting place, but Rita had not arrived by the time Jenny, head bent into the wind, struggled up the wet paving slabs to join Maggie. Brackley Market Square gleamed dully in the last of the daylight and Jenny twisted her nose at the familiar farmyard aroma left from the cattle market.

"Wild night!" Jenny shouted into the wind.

"I hope so." Maggie's eyes flashed in a sudden smile.

"I've got those nylons on. They feel really sexy."

"Let's have a look." The two girls giggled as they turned to face the wall and Jenny opened her coat. She lifted the hem of her skirt until the tops of the stockings showed. "I can hardly see in this light."

"They feel lovely. Got them on Saturday. I could see that nosey old bag, Mrs Norris in the shop, was dying to ask how I could afford them."

Rita, tall and slim, joined them. "Bloody hell. I nearly got blowed off me feet."

"Ya need to put some weight on ducky. A man likes a bit of flesh." Maggie poked Rita's side.

"Leave off. I don't wanna get fat."

"Not much chance of that with the rationing. One sausage each we had for our tea."

"Great night on Saturday wasn't it? I do love a dance." Rita's flat voice did not reflect the enthusiasm of her words.

"You could at least sound a bit excited Reet," Maggie laughed.

"I said it was good didn't I?"

"Did you…you know…score?" Even Rita allowed a smile to crack her impassive face.

"That would be telling wouldn't it?"

The three girls stood with their backs to the Town Hall wall, seeking what protection they could from the wind, and looked up the hill in front of them. Brackley High Street was dead. No lights, no one about. They were used to that now though.

"Ok so how many Valentine cards did you get yesterday?" Maggie looked sideways at her friends.

"Hundreds me. How about you Jenny?"

"I got a couple. At least I'm being honest."

"A couple. Who are they? Come on tell."

"Dunno do I? That's the point of Valentines...they're secret."

After some more ribbing of each other, they fell silent again until Rita spoke. "Where shall we say we went tonight... to our parents and stuff?" Rita's voice had an edge to it as if she were always cross.

"There's some dance class or something on at the WI Hall. That'll do. No one they know is likely to go."

"Sounds a good idea, Maggie. The WI Hall it is then." Jenny shivered. "Ooh, I think someone just walked over me grave."

"You ain't goin' nowhere yet." Rita let out a short bark of a laugh. "You got work to do first."

"I can't wait to see the new Fred Astaire and Rita Hayworth film. I've seen the posters. She looks fantastic in them. It should be coming soon. I do love Rita Hayworth."

"We'd never have guessed."

Jenny slapped Maggie playfully on the shoulder. "Aw shut up you."

They heard the engine before it came into sight, the low grumbling roar unmistakeable.

"I think this is our chauffeur, girls." Rita lifted her forearm and circled her hand in a royal wave.

"It don't sound like they've sent the Rolls this time though."

# CHAPTER 5

Ronald Dearing turned up his collar and hunched his shoulders against the strengthening February wind. The first spits of rain stung his face as he struggled to the main building, heading for the Officers Mess. There would be no flying tomorrow with the storm rising and low, dark clouds scouring the land. The mess was filling up with the trainee pilots having a convivial drink before the evening meal. It was a requirement to be in dress uniform and there was, as always, an atmosphere of warm camaraderie. He leant nonchalantly against the bar and ordered a double scotch with ice.

Stevens, the barman, placed his drink carefully in front of him. "Going to be a rough night I think, Sir."

"And a rough day tomorrow."

"No flying then tomorrow, Sir?"

"I should doubt it." Dearing turned away, bored already. He surveyed the room, the trainees laughing heartily, joshing each other and, at one table, leaning forward conspiratorially, no doubt talking about their exploits with women. At twenty-six, Dearing felt a good deal more experienced than the trainees though, in some cases, he was only two or three years older. That's what dozens of combat missions did for you. Those hours in cold bombers lumbering across the Channel to devastate German cities and positions, ack-ack bursting around you, fighters screaming like banshees. This was a better posting, but....

The mess door opened and Flight Lieutenant Edward Driscoll, his fellow instructor, entered slowly. He always looked somehow apologetic, thought Dearing, a trait that engendered feelings of contempt in himself. The problem was that he was too nice, always excusing sloppy work by the trainees. He was from a different class of course, the grammar school boy made good. His father was probably a farmer or school teacher. Dearing smiled at the thought, the comfortable little home in some village or small town, respectability, smallness, dull, dull, dull.

Driscoll approached the bar close to Dearing and ordered half a pint of beer. "Quite a storm shaping up."

"Yep. Quite a storm."

"I doubt we'll be flying tomorrow. Best do some classroom work. I've got some stuff on enemy aircraft capability which it would be good for the chaps to know."

"Of course you have."

Driscoll looked at Dearing sharply, sensing the derision in his voice. "Do you have a better suggestion?"

"No...no...no. We'll go with that. To be honest, I don't really care what we do. The important bit is making sure they can fly."

"Of course but if we can't fly tomorrow...."

"We'll teach them about enemy aircraft. Good idea." Dearing tapped his empty glass on the bar and Stevens re-filled it.

The mess suddenly fell quiet, a few voices loud in the silence until they too stopped in mid-sentence. Lizzie, now changed out of her flight suit into her dress uniform, stood by the door, smiling broadly at the room. She took a step forward and at first no one moved. Then one of the trainees, Flight Officer Perkins, rose to his feet and took two steps towards her.

"Excuse me Miss, I'm afraid this is the Officers Mess."

Lizzie turned her smile on him. "Yes...I gathered that."

"I'm afraid Miss that this is for gentlemen officers only."

"Oh...it doesn't say so on the door."

"No...I think it's an assumption....you see, there are no lady officers here."

"Until now."

Driscoll had stood at the bar, glass in one hand and mouth open. The sight of a young and very attractive woman had frozen his arm halfway to his mouth. Now he gathered his wits rapidly and stepped forward. "It's fine Perkins. Do please come in Miss. What can I get you to drink?" He approached her, his hand outstretched.

She took it and looked at him keenly, so keenly that he dropped his eyes from her face. "Thank you. I'm Lizzie Barnes. I delivered your new Wellington today. A sherry would be lovely."

He put his hand gently behind her elbow and led her to the bar. "I'm Flight Lieutenant Driscoll. This is Flight Lieutenant Dearing."

Dearing had been combing his hair, using the mirrors behind the shelves at the back of the bar. He turned, leaning his back against the bar, his elbows resting on it. "We've met already. Found some quarters?"

"Yes, I'm with the nurses. I thought one or two might be in here actually."

"Now that's definitely not allowed. Matron would have a heart attack at the thought that her girls would be prey for us chaps." He turned his head towards Driscoll. "Mine's a double scotch if you're buying."

Driscoll's mouth tightened but he clearly did not want to make a scene in front of a lady. He handed the sherry to Lizzie.

She lifted the glass towards his and they chinked together. "Thank you and cheers." She turned to Dearing to do the same but he did not raise his glass and said nothing. His cynical eyes met her own.

Driscoll invited her to join them for dinner. It was not a comfortable affair. Despite attempts by herself and Driscoll to make conversation, Dearing's presence was like the leaden sky which scowled outside now the last of the daylight had faded. It was raining steadily and it was a rain that lashed the buildings, driven by a buffeting wind. Dearing was drinking wine, draining his glass frequently and becoming louder.

"Well what do you think of our lady pilot, Driscoll? We

should have more of them…brighten the place up." He leaned over towards Lizzie, his mouth twisting in a grin. "You are rather gorgeous," he added quietly, glancing down at her chest.

"My Mother always said never to trust the compliments of a drunken man." Lizzie looked at him straight in the eye for several seconds until he averted his gaze. She was cross and she could see that he was too at her unexpected rejoinder. It would probably cause her trouble: she was a guest here and probably should not be dining in the Officers Mess at all. But…she was not going to allow Dearing or anyone else make her a target for lewd suggestions.

She turned and smiled at Driscoll, asking him where he had grown up. As he answered, she studied his face. There was a slight nervousness about him, a reserve, almost a boyish shyness that she found attractive. He was a very different man to Dearing; Driscoll seemed to make no assumptions about his value and yet was probably worth a good deal more.

After dinner and coffee, Lizzie excused herself and rose to leave. Perhaps too pointedly, she thanked Edward Driscoll for his kindness and invitation to dinner and said she should return to the nurses' quarters so she did not disturb anyone.

Edward had stood as she rose from the table. "May I see you back to your quarters? It is dark now and…"

"Thank you that would be very kind but I don't want to interrupt your evening."

"There's nothing to interrupt. Another drink then back to quarters for an early night. That's my evening."

Dearing watched them go. "You puny specimen Driscoll," he whispered to himself. "It needs a man." He drained his brandy and stood up, resting a hand on the table for a moment to gain his balance. He watched the door swing closed behind them and then left the mess, bumping into another table as he tacked across to the door.

"Thank you so much for your kindness and your company." Lizzie turned to face Edward Driscoll as she spoke. She looked at him…handsome, slightly boyish still, his smile brief, his eyes wandering away from her gaze. Shy or secretive, she wondered?

"The pleasure was all mine. I'm sorry about…you know Dearing. He really needs to lay off the booze."

Lizzie smiled. "There's nothing for you to apologise for. It's sad isn't it? What war has done to people. He would probably have been a very nice young man if he hadn't seen what he has seen, done what he has had to do."

"Perhaps but…well others have had similar experiences but not become like that."

"True. I suppose it affects people differently."

"I think you're a very kind person."

She laughed. "Perhaps you should wait until you know me better before you make that judgement."

"I hope I do get to know you better…" he stopped and coughed. "I'd better be getting back to my quarters. I'll say goodnight."

"Goodnight, Edward." She hovered a moment, wondering if he would give the customary kiss but he seemed frozen like a man about to walk a tightrope. "And thanks again for a lovely evening." She flashed a warm smile at him, spun round, her hair swinging out around her head and opened the door. When she turned to close it, he was still standing there, looking mesmerised. She gave him a little wave, another broad smile and shut the door quietly, listening to his fading footsteps as he descended the stairs.

She looked at the room under the harsh light of the single, central bulb. It was bare, functional but it was a bed for the night and what could one expect in the middle of a war? The window was a dark square of heavy blackout curtain; she turned off the light and crossed the room to it, pulling the heavy material sideways enough to peek out. Drops of rain streaked the glass but, though the wind was driving against this side of the building, she could see the scene clearly enough. Two guards were at the barrier as before, rifles slung over their shoulders. The entrance was well lit and she pitied them being out in this weather though their greatcoats were no doubt snug.

She took out a book from her overnight bag and flopped on the bed. She would read for a bit and then sleep. Would she get back to White Waltham tomorrow? Certainly not by air. Maybe there would be a vehicle heading that way that could provide a lift. If not, what would she do all day? Then she thought of Patricia. There would be plenty of work to be done in the Sick Bay – cleaning, helping the patients. She would make herself useful.

She was lost in her book so the banging at the door startled her. She thought there must be an emergency and, leaping off the bed, pulled the door open. Dearing was standing there, his hand on the wall to steady himself. His face broke into a leering grin. "Thought I'd come and keep you company."

He moved forward as if to come in the room and Lizzie put her hand on his chest. "That's not a good idea, Flight Lieutenant."

He grasped her wrist with one hand and suddenly jerked her hand downwards so that they stumbled together. "Just want a little chat...no harm in that is there?"

She wriggled away from him. "It's late and I'm going to bed. You've had too much to drink and shouldn't be here."

"Here is exact...exactly where I should be...with a sexy young woman." He lunged forward quickly, his arm slipping round her waist, and pulled her towards him. She managed to free the wrist he had grasped at first and, with both hands, pushed hard against his chest. The smell of drink on his breath was strong.

"Let me go... now."

"We should keep each other company. It's a lonely time in war." He looked at her mischievously. "They say young women are very keen on sex nowadays...it's the effect of the war. We may be dead by tomorrow so we should live for today."

"That may apply to some but it does not apply to me." She whipped one hand away from his chest and slapped him hard across the face.

He winced with the sudden pain. "You bitch." Anger blazed in his eyes and, for a moment, Lizzie thought he would hit her back. She prepared herself to duck but no blow came. "I don't forget an insult," he spat. And then he turned and headed unsteadily for the stairs. Lizzie shut the door quickly and locked it before he changed his mind. She stood inside, trembling, straining to hear the sounds outside. At last she heard his heavy steps on the stairs, retreating. She had made an enemy but what else could she have done? No gentleman would ever have put her in that position.

She returned to her bed but could not concentrate on her book. Dearing's leering face kept forming in her mind. A memory flashed across her consciousness - a Summer party somewhere...she was wearing her new dress...it was the first adult party she had been to. Her parents were there and she had been allowed one glass of champagne. Something unpleasant had happened...beside the terrace. A young man, boy. Was that where she had seen Dearing? It was the look in his eyes, an expression of disdain.

She would make sure she left Silverstone the next day and not have to face him again. Why are some men such animals? She knew it was her past again, sliding stealthily beneath the surface, threatening, like a submarine. She thought of Dearing's public school drawl, his arrogant expression, the way he had treated Edward Driscoll as if the latter were his inferior. She had met plenty of those already, often at the instigation of her parents trying to arrange a husband they thought suitable. But she had no intention of marrying anyone as yet and maybe never. She had an important role whatever some people thought. The Air Force could not do their job if the planes they needed were stuck at the factories.

She tried to read but without much success. Gradually, however, she calmed enough to feel drowsy and she glanced at her watch. Ten o'clock. Time for bed. As she was unhooking her stockings from her suspender, she heard the rumbling of a truck. Again, she switched off the light and pulled the heavy blackout curtain aside to peer out, her face close to the glass. It was the same truck but not, as she had expected, returning to the base. It was leaving again. She frowned. Definitely odd that.

# PART 2: TUESDAY 16TH FEBRUARY 1943

## CHAPTER 6

In better weather, Robbie McBane would have enjoyed the drive from his base at RAF Burnham to Silverstone but the rain lashed the windscreen and the wipers were barely able to keep it clear making the journey tiresome. The Humber Super Snipe he had been issued for the trip was comfortable and plenty powerful enough in these conditions. He was quite grateful not to have more power under his foot as with roads this wet and the wind buffeting the car, the temptation to speed was best avoided.

From Burnham, buried in the beech woods of Buckinghamshire, he headed North through Beaconsfield and Amersham to Aylesbury, splashing through the centre of the town and on towards Bicester. A bye-road took him to the A43 where he headed North, through the sleepy town of Brackley and on to Silverstone. The RAF base at Silverstone was about a mile east of the village centre and, with a fairly early start, he had covered the sixty odd miles by nine o'clock. The car purred as he stopped at the gate, like a cat well pleased with itself.

He wound down the window when the guard approached and held out his identity card. "Sergeant McBane, RAF Police Special Investigation Branch. I'll need to speak with Group Captain Lovell to start with."

The guard peered at the pass, stood to attention and saluted. "Morning Sir. I'll open the barrier."

"Thanks. It's a wild day."

"You can say that again, Sir. You just need to drive over to those buildings. The Group Captain has his office in the one on the right - with the control tower on top."

The barrier was raised and Robbie McBane gave a wave as he drove onto the base. He drove slowly across the perimeter road towards the building indicated. Three huge hangars stood defiantly against the elements to the right of the control tower and a line of huts stretched into the distance on the left. Beyond those, a line of immense trees spread skeletal fingers upwards, scraping the clouds as they swayed. He parked by the door into the two-storey brick-built building which boasted the control tower on its roof. Clutching his briefcase and coat in one hand, he hurried, head bowed, into the shelter of the lobby. An airman was waiting to escort him to Lovell's office.

The one word 'Enter', shouted in response to the airman's knock, seemed a fierce challenge rather than an invitation and Robbie McBane prepared himself to encounter the ogre within. The office was spartan, a desk behind which Lovell sat and a few chairs arranged at the side. A low shelving unit was fitted along one wall beneath the windows that looked onto the airfield but there was little on the shelves. Lovell's desk was tidy, just the document he was reading in front of him, a telephone, a wooden tray containing pens and a photograph standing on the opposite corner to the telephone, facing Lovell.

Remembering his boss's instruction to go softly-softly, Robbie McBane stood in front of the desk and saluted smartly. "Morning Sir. Sergeant McBane from RAF Police Special Investiga..."

"I know who you are. You'd better sit down"

"Yes, Sir." Robbie McBane pulled a chair from the side of the room, positioned it in front of the desk and sat down. "It's just a routine call, Sir...you know...a check on fuel use, stores and so on as this is a new base."

"As if we haven't got enough to deal with, you people

come here poking about, worrying about use of stores. We're not going to beat Jerry by counting toilet rolls you know."

McBane crossed his legs and smiled. "Quite so, Sir." He could see Lovell drawing himself up in his chair as if ready to explode.

"So why the blazes are you here?"

"It's like this, Sir. There's a huge black market in all sorts of goods which are being pilfered from service bases – not just RAF bases of course. The spivs are out trying to beat rationing. If we don't keep an eye on it and stop it where it occurs, we'll mebbe no have enough food to keep our troops going and not enough fuel to keep our planes in the air. That'll play right into Jerry's hands…Sir."

"Aircraft do not use petrol, Sergeant."

"I'm well aware of that, Sir. I was ground crew before I joined the RAF Police. We have to import all our crude oil, Sir. The more we have to refine for petrol, the less we have for aircraft…."

"Spare me the sermon, Sergeant." Lovell snapped. "Alright, get on with it…see Dearing next door…but don't get in our way. We've an important job to do."

"Of course not, Sir." McBane turned to leave and then hesitated. His voice was calm, casual. "If there's anything to report, Sir, will I be able to find you here later this afternoon?"

"Yes," Lovell barked, turning back to his paperwork before McBane had left the office.

Robbie walked a little way along the corridor from Lovell's office and stopped at the next door. Flight Lieutenant R. Dearing was the legend printed in gold lettering. He knocked and waited. A gruff "Enter" was called from within.

"Sergeant McBane, Sir. I'm here to do a…"

"I know why you're here. We do talk to each other you know."

"Of course, Sir." He smiled and looked at the figure crumpled in the chair behind the desk, nursing a cup of coffee. "I'd like to start by checking fuel use for ground vehicles, Sir. I need to see the storage tank records, vehicle log books and…"

Dearing had already lifted the telephone and dialled a number. "Send Davies up to my office would you?" He dropped the receiver back on its cradle. "Davies can show you the books. Bloody waste of time if you ask me."

Robbie McBane simply smiled again, ignoring the provocation. "I'll wait outside and let you get on, Sir. I know you have important work to do." McBane looked at the empty desk and at Dearing slumped behind it but the latter did not seem to notice the barb. Instead, he scowled through the window at the heavy mass of dark cloud spilling rain on the airfield.

◆ ◆ ◆

Patricia introduced Lizzie to Matron. She was a short, solid, strong-looking woman in her forties and stood with legs slightly apart but her face was handsome. Her handshake was firm, very firm and Lizzie flinched at the grip. Matron Agnes Fisher had all the features one associated with Matrons: no nonsense, forthright, severe, an unsmiling face with penetrating blue eyes. Lizzie admired those qualities. No one would willingly confront her, though perhaps at another time, in another place she would be warmer.

"We have men here from the base at Turweston as well as from this base. Fortunately not many at the moment but the RAF has made provision for the bases to grow in the future. Let us hope we will not have too many wounded men to deal with." Lizzie assumed Matron's last remark had been made out of concern to avoid suffering but was it partly annoyance that her workload may increase?

"I'm stuck here on the base because of the weather and thought I would make myself useful. I'm happy to do anything."

Matron's eyes narrowed slightly. Lizzie watched her

heavily powdered face as the older woman scrutinised her. "Well Miss Barnes, perhaps you could take Trainee Officer Saunders for his morning walk. He must exercise his leg to get it back to full use."

"Of course...if that would be a help."

"It would be a great help." Patricia smiled. "He's a bit of a character. Don't take any nonsense."

" I won't. Don't you worry." She strode confidently into the ward and stopped at the foot of one of the beds. Trainee Flight Officer Brian Saunders was lying fully clothed on it propped up against pillows, reading a magazine. His dark hair, swept sideways, nevertheless flopped on his forehead almost touching his dark brows. The eyes beneath were bright, framed already in a fine web of smile lines.

He looked up and grinned. "Hello. Who are you?"

"Lizzie Barnes. I'm having to spend the day here as I can't get back to my base...weather's no good for flying. So I'm making myself useful...I'm taking you for your morning walk."

"Nice! Though maybe it would be better just to have a chat – it's very windy and wild out there. I might get blown over. You might be blown away." He grinned again. "So why don't you just sit down beside me on the bed..." He tapped the blanket beside him.

"Now that won't help you recover will it? Exercise, I'm told, is what you need. So up you get, coat and shoes on and let's go."

Saunders groaned and slowly swung his legs over the side of the bed, wincing theatrically as he did so. He stood shakily, looking as though he was about to fall. Lizzie stepped quickly to his side and he grasped her arm. "Thank you, thank you," he mumbled as if an old man. "You saved my life."

"Bit of an actor are you?"

He looked at her and smiled mischievously. "You've got to have some fun you know. Lying here all day is no good at all."

She helped him with his shoes and coat. "So why are you

in here?"

"Had a bit of a turn – some bug or other – which made me feel woozy. As I climbed down the steps from the plane, I fell the last few and did something painful to my leg. The quack is not sure what but prescribed rest and recuperation. Main thing is I do have to exercise it. It's amazing how quickly your strength goes when you've been sick in bed. But, thank God, I'm nearly ready to resume my duties, give Hitler a bloody nose that sort of thing."

They walked slowly down the ward, past the stores and offices and out of the building. Saunders had not done up his coat and the wind whipped it away from him. "Whoa, boy, whoa." He turned his back to the wind and fumbled with the buttons. "Maybe you could do these up for me?"

"I'm sure you can manage them on your own." Lizzie spoke firmly but turned away and smiled. He was certainly a bit of a character.

Progress was slow but they left the two main buildings behind, one which housed the Sick Bay and nurses' quarters and the other the offices and Officers' Mess. These were the only two-storey, brick-built buildings on the base, apart from the commanding officer's house, and on the top of the office building squatted the control tower. Slowly, they were passing the line of huts that stretched away from the main buildings. Between each, the wind moaned, threatening to blow them over. Lizzie walked close beside Saunders, anxious to prevent him stumbling, though she wondered how much of his slow progress was an act.

When they reached the last hut in the line, he wheezed, "I'm going to need to rest a bit."

"Can we go in this building here?"

"If it's open. Sometimes is, sometimes not. I don't think it's used yet to be honest."

The door was unlocked and yielded with a firm push. Like sailors entering a sheltered harbour, they savoured the relief from the wind. They were at one end of a corridor that ran the length of the building down its centre; Brian Saunders opened the first door they came to. It looked like a meeting room or mess, chairs arranged around a square of tables. They flopped onto chairs and Saunders exhaled. "Blimey. That's better. Thought at one point I wouldn't make it."

Lizzie ran her fingers through her hair. "I must look frightful."

Brian Saunders turned to look at her. "It looks lovely… wild…free."

"I'm not sure I want to look wild but free I'll settle for."

"Forgive the corny line but what's a nice girl like you doing in a place like this?"

"I delivered a plane yesterday. I'm in the ATA."

"Ah an Ata-Girl. What plane?"

"A Wellington bomber." Lizzie smiled at the surprise on his face.

"And who flew it here with you?"

"No one. I flew myself." Lizzie was enjoying the stir she was creating at the base. Here was another man who supposed that women could not fly. "I can see you look surprised."

"Well yes…not because I doubt what you say but I'm wondering why you didn't have a co-pilot or navigator or someone else in case something went wrong."

"We don't have enough people. Simple as that." She stood and walked over to the window which looked out over the airfield. There was no rain but it was clear from the clouds that the storm was far from done. "I can't get a ride back until this storm passes so I'm stuck."

"That's nice…for us. Maybe we could have dinner together tonight? Shall I pick you up at say 7 o'clock. I'll bring the Rolls…you'll like that. Smart car for a smart girl."

Lizzie laughed. "In your dreams. You'll be dining on the ward and I doubt very much whether you can afford to run a car like that."

"One day…one can but dream." He sighed. "I just want to get out and resume flying training again."

Lizzie left the room to explore the building. After several yards, there were a series of doors on both sides of the corridor. She gently opened the first. An office – it looked unoccupied as it contained just bare furniture, a desk, two chairs, an empty bookcase. The room opposite was also an office, smaller than the first, but the third she entered had curtains drawn and she took a moment to adjust her vision to the gloom. It looked like a bedroom. She stopped and listened intently. No sound. She was able to pick out a bed and on the other wall, a chest of drawers, a desk or dressing table. She walked carefully across to the window and opened the blackout curtains enough for some daylight to enter the room.

When she turned, she froze. Her mouth was open but no sound issued.

# CHAPTER 7

As the base leadership had, Davies made it clear that he felt McBane's inspection was an unwelcome intrusion; the studied nonchalance with which he escorted him from one vehicle to the next and his slouched posture while Robbie was examining the log books made it plain. They arrived at a Bedford truck.

Robbie McBane flipped through the log book until he reached the last entry. Corporal Davies was leaning casually against the side of the truck apparently paying no attention. He was short but powerfully built, a former rugby player like himself probably. Robbie hoisted himself easily onto the step and leaned into the cab, peering at the mileage counter on the dashboard. He checked it against the last entry in the log book. "Corporal, can you think of any reason why there would be a discrepancy between the mileage on the truck counter and the last mileage recorded in the log book?"

"No idea. I don't use this truck."

"Twenty-eight miles more in the truck than in the log book. A journey of fourteen miles return or two journeys of seven miles each way. Where would that take you?"

"Could just be driving around the airfield, Sir."

"The truck was last used according to the log book in the morning to go to Brackley. That's a lot of driving around the airfield."

Davies shrugged. "Fourteen miles takes you somewhere past Towcester almost as far as Northampton and seven miles takes you to Brackley..." Davies then added, "or Buckingham."

"Does it?" mused McBane. "Ok, I'd like to look at the fuel storage tank records now please."

"Follow me, Sir." Davies walked away, his short frame

swaggering with each step.

The fuel ledger was where it should be in the small office beside the storage tank. The last entry was for late the previous afternoon. Sixty-five gallons put into RAF 142031, the truck he had just inspected. The initials beside the entry were indecipherable. Davies said he could not make them out either. McBane's terrier instinct was roused. "I'd just like to take another look at that truck we last checked, Corporal. Davies shrugged and swaggered away with Robbie in pursuit. "I'll need the ignition key." Robbie was losing patience with Davies's attitude and knew that he would snap at him at the slightest further provocation.

Davies sighed and retrieved the key from the office at the entrance to the hangar where the truck was parked. He dropped it as if into Robbie's hand but missed. There was a distinct smirk on Davies's face as the key clattered on the concrete floor. Davies made no move to pick it up and no apology was forthcoming. Robbie waited, his hand out, his eyes narrowing. Davies did not move.

"Pick it up Corporal and hand it over without any more games...unless you want to find yourself on a charge."

"Yes Sir." Davies grabbed the key and placed it with studied care into Robbie's outstretched palm. "Will that suit you...Sir?"

Robbie exploded, his voice ricocheting around the hangar. "I've had enough of you, Davies. That's your last chance. Any more insolence and I'll march you back to Group Captain Lovell."

Davies said nothing, but Robbie knew that all he had done was ensure more opposition and even enmity. Davies would be entertaining his chums with accounts of that little incident and Robbie would doubtless be greeted with dumb insolence by all his cronies. Interesting to see, he thought, how many of those at the base would treat him like that. It may be that they would all be resistant to any kind of scrutiny. Perhaps Lovell had created that ethos. But perhaps there would be a divide: those who were keen to keep scrutiny away for reasons they would not like discovered and those who had no reason to frustrate his attempts to establish exactly what was happening.

He focused his attention on the truck again, turning the key enough to bring on the display but not starting the engine. He watched the needle of the fuel gauge creep up slowly and stop well below half full. He frowned, tapped the glass of the gauge. The needle did not move. He jumped down from the cab.

"Fetch a stick, Corporal. I want to check the fuel level in the tank manually." Whilst Davies swayed off to fetch a dipstick, Robbie reached for the log book again. Sixty-five gallons late yesterday afternoon. That would definitely fill the tank and probably make it overflow.

His finger traced the entries of journeys to the last fill of fuel. Four days before, last Thursday, with sixty gallons. Even if the truck did as little as ten miles to the gallon, it should have done about 600 miles since the last fill. He added up the distances. Most of the journeys were into Brackley or around the base. The total was ninety-eight miles. He carefully examined the end mileage for each entry and the start mileage of the next. All tallied except the first. Again there was a discrepancy of twenty-eight miles. He went further back. Every week, twice a week, there was a similar fill of fuel and almost exactly the same discrepancy in mileage immediately after the tank had been filled – or so the log book claimed.

Robbie allowed himself the merest flicker of a smile but removed it as soon as Davies came into view, whistling and swinging a stick.

"This any good?" Davies held up the stick. "You should be able to tell from the fuel gauge…Sir."

"Yes, but I need to be sure the fuel gauge is working properly. Take off the cap and put the stick in." As Davies did so, Robbie saw immediately that he was trying to put the stick in at an angle to suggest the tank had more fuel than it did.

Before the stick had gone in even six inches, Robbie put a hand on Davies's arm, guiding it firmly so that it entered vertically.

Davies shook off the hand. "I can do it by myself."

"So I noticed." Robbie stared hard at him and Davies met his gaze for a moment. Both men knew that Davies had revealed something he would have preferred kept hidden.

When the stick was withdrawn, it confirmed that the gauge was correct; there was less than half a tank of fuel. "Well Corporal, how do you suppose that sixty-five gallons of fuel have disappeared from this tank?"

"No idea, Sir." Davies half turned away and avoided Robbie's gaze.

"I hope, Corporal, for your sake that you truly do not know. But believe me, if I later find out that you do know, I will make sure you pay the penalty for obstructing an investigation."

Davies swivelled back to face McBane and his little eyes burned with hostility. "I'm obstructing nothing alright." Robbie felt that he was about to spit on the ground to indicate his utter disrespect but he did not do so. He stood, glowering at McBane's feet. Robbie told him to replace the fuel cap and return the stick.

"Sergeant McBane?" The voice belonged to an airman who had entered the hangar. He looked shaken but gave a rapid salute. "AC Andrews Sir. Group Captain Lovell would like to see you in his office now, Sir."

"Thank you. I'll be along shortly."

"He was very definite that he wanted to see you right now, Sir." Andrews looked as though he wanted to run back to the office building.

"Very well. I'll come now. Corporal Davies," he called, "we'll resume this after I have seen Group Captain Lovell." He could not be sure but he thought he saw a look pass between Andrews and Davies. Was that a warning? It was definitely not amusement. He followed Andrews, holding the truck log book in his hand and refusing to move any faster than at a brisk walk.

Enid Sumser hesitated when she reached the building. Its honey-coloured natural stone spoke of solidity, formality, things that Enid found a little overwhelming. She had never set foot inside before and, not for the first time that morning, wondered whether she was making a fuss about nothing. They would have more important things to do. A metal semi-circular frame projected above the door and from it hung the lamp, blue with white lettering: Police.

She forced herself to enter. The heavy oak door swung closed behind her with a soft swish and a final thud. She looked around her uncertainly, shifting her weight from one foot to the other but not at first moving forward. She approached the counter slowly and waited. No one appeared though she thought she could see at least one figure behind the screen of frosted glass separating the counter from the rest of the office. The walls were plastered with war posters: 'Dig for Victory'. Her Arthur had certainly done that. He was just starting to sow seeds in his greenhouse that would later go out into the carefully tended veg patch.

Beside it was one she had not seen before though she had seen plenty with the same message. An elegant young woman in a red dress with a deep vee at the front of the neckline which showed her figure to advantage sat on a stool, legs crossed with just a glimpse of thigh showing. The legend above it declared 'You forget – but she remembers' and then lower down, beside her slim legs, 'Careless talk costs lives'. She wore a red headband on her blonde hair, red shoes and an expression that was hard to read – aloof, scheming perhaps. Enid Sumser shivered. You could never know who might be a spy.

She looked at the bell on the counter and wondered if

she should ring it. 'Please ring for service' announced a note stuck to the counter beside it. She pressed the knob on the top and recoiled at the sound. A chair scuffled in the office and the figure loomed tall behind the screen. A few seconds later, a burly police officer with a sergeant's stripes appeared behind the counter.

"Mornin'. And what can I do for you Madam?"

"Oh…I'm sorry to bother you but I'm worried about my Jenny…she didn't come home last night see and that's not like her…she was out with her friends, she often goes out of a night but in the week she's always back by about eleven as she has work next day …today that would be…but she's not come home and I'm so worried…."

The Sergeant held up his hand. "Now, now, steady on. I'm sure there's a perfectly innocent explanation." He lifted the flap of the counter, opened the small door beneath it and stepped up to her. "What's yer name?"

"Mrs Sumser…Enid."

"Right. Well Enid you come through here with me, we'll sit down and we'll get some details and then we'll know what we're dealing with."

He led her by the arm through the opening in the counter and round the screen to the office. The sergeant helped her remove her wet coat and she released the scarf that bound her hair. It was dark brown with a few streaks of grey, cut neatly and fairly short. She accepted the chair gratefully and sank into it, resting her elbow on the desk beside it. She dropped her forehead onto her hand and sighed deeply.

"My name's Sergeant Bailey. Now how about I get you a nice cup of tea and then we'll get to the bottom of this."

"Thank you Officer, that would be nice." Enid Sumser looked up and smiled weakly at the young officer working at another desk. He waved cheerfully but she felt too burdened to reciprocate.

When the tea was steaming in front of her, Sergeant Bailey asked Mrs Sumser about herself and family and especially about Jenny - her age, job, who her friends were. "So what kind of girl is she...I mean does she like to go out having fun or is she someone who's happiest at home...that sort of thing?"

"She's a good girl, she does her jobs at home, she works hard – up at Bronnleys - she's always on time but...she does like to enjoy herself with her friends. I mean she's nineteen and she wants to have some fun. That's quite normal isn't it for girls these days?"

"I suppose it is Mrs Sumser. I think a lot of young people think they must have some fun while they can. Will they still be here tomorrow? That's the way many of them look at it. Enjoy yourself while you can."

"Exactly...and who can blame them? But...I do wonder a bit about her friends...you know...whether she's too influenced by them. I mean I don't want to speak ill of anyone but that Maggie Bennett, she's a bit of a tearaway. She was walking out with boys even when she was still young – fourteen, maybe even earlier."

Sergeant Bailey was making notes in his pad. When Mrs Sumser at last fell silent, he looked up. "Now Mrs S...Enid, have you been round this morning to the homes of any of Jenny's friends? She may have decided to stay the night with one of them."

Enid's eyes brightened. "No I've not done that." She blushed. "I should have done that before coming here shouldn't I?"

"No, no. Always best to let us know early on but either you or one of us needs to check that. If she's not stayed with a friend, we need to know as we'll need to talk with those friends to see what they know. But let's hope that's what has happened. And if so, you can tell her off from me for not coming home early this morning. She could have saved you a lot of worry."

Enid Sumser smiled and struggled to her feet. She thanked the Sergeant for the tea and his understanding and noticed the gentlemanly way he helped her with her coat. In the foyer, she pointed to the poster of the woman in the red dress. "That's a new one isn't it?"

Sergeant Bailey looked at it a moment, his eye following the legs from the red shoes. "It is, yes. Very important to get that message across you know. Spies don't go round looking shady. They look normal, like anyone else, fit in so you wouldn't even think what they're up to. Clever and cunning."

"It's a worry...you don't know who you can trust."

Now dressed to contend with the weather, she left the Police Station, optimistic that there was a simple explanation for Jenny's failure to return the night before. She decided to go home first before visiting Jenny's friends in case her daughter had returned.

# CHAPTER 8

Andrews knocked on the door. Immediately, the command to enter was issued and he turned the handle, stepping aside to allow Robbie McBane in.

"That will be all, Andrews. Thank you."

"Sir."

The door closed quietly behind Andrews and Robbie looked at Lovell; he was pale, shocked, perched on the front of his desk. A young woman sat on an armchair a little distance from the desk. Her face was also pale and she was dressed in what looked like flying clothes, though not an RAF uniform.

"Ah McBane. Allow me to introduce Second Officer Barnes who delivered a Wellington bomber to us yesterday. She is with the ATA. This, Miss Barnes, is Sergeant McBane of the RAF Police. He is here on a routine inspection but that is fortuitous. I'm afraid this morning Miss Barnes has had a terrible shock as indeed have I. Miss Barnes, please tell Sergeant McBane about your discovery this morning."

She stood and, taking a pace forward, offered her hand which he took. "Please do call me Lizzie. I was walking with one of the patients from the Sick Bay this morning and we stopped to rest in the hut at the far end of the line. Hut Fifteen. Inside, I made a horrible discovery. The body of a young woman, lying on a bed in one of the rooms."

She stopped abruptly but her face, though pale, remained impassive. Robbie McBane could not but feel admiration for the dignity she displayed, the concern. Her fair hair, falling in waves, swayed gently around her head as she moved and set off the delicate lines of her face. He looked away quickly as he felt a stab of pain in his chest. There was too much about her of Catriona and, as with Catriona, he felt an immediate attraction.

"Naturally, I thought we needed to involve you, McBane. This is clearly an RAF Police matter."

"Who is she?"

"That needs to be established. The only women we have on the base are Matron and her nurses who are all where they should be...and of course Miss Barnes temporarily."

Robbie turned to Lizzie. "Did you see anything that made you think her death might be...suspicious?"

"She was wearing very little and lying at an awkward angle but I don't know if that is suspicious."

McBane nodded. "We need to secure the scene and I need to take a look. Miss Barnes, would you feel able to show me where the body is?"

"Andrews can show you," Lovell said quickly.

"It's quite alright, Group Captain. I am willing to show Sergeant McBane where..."

Lovell nodded. "I need to make a telephone call to my superior. Oh and McBane...let's keep this in house shall we? Don't want the civilian police trampling over everything. Mustn't let the public get wind of this."

"That will depend on what I find, Group Captain. If I suspect foul play, I have a duty to inform the local police. We may need a post-mortem of course which only they can arrange."

"I'm sure it's just an unfortunate accident. She must have got onto the base somehow... perhaps had drunk too much."

"Mebbe. We'll see. We need the scene to be preserved so please arrange a guard."

"Already arranged," Lovell said curtly.

Lizzie led the way out of Lovell's office and McBane closed the door. Andrews was standing at ease beside the door, hands behind his back, though it looked as though he had just moved into that position. "Should I escort you back to the vehicles, Sir?"

"No thank you, Andrews. I have something else to look at right now. Perhaps you would let Corporal Davies know that I will not be back for a while so he can get on with something else."

"As you please, Sir." Andrews saluted and walked smartly down the corridor.

As they left the building, Robbie looked at Lizzie keenly, trying to read her expression. "It must have been quite a shock finding the body."

"Yes. It was." They walked side by side in silence for a while and then she added, "I didn't want to say anything in front of Lovell in case I was wrong, but there were marks on her neck. She may have been strangled."

He turned his head to look at her. The face remained calm but there was the slightest crease in her brow. This was not someone showing callous disregard for the loss of life but a young woman who was maintaining a professional quiescence while feeling the horror of her discovery. Walking in silence, they emerged between the two main buildings onto the airfield apron.

To their right, Andrews was walking quickly towards the first hangar where Robbie had left Davies. Before turning the opposite way to Hut Fifteen, Robbie and Lizzie heard raised voices. Davies, gesticulating with one arm in which was an unlit cigarette, was shouting at Andrews but stopped abruptly when he saw them.

Charles Lovell replaced the telephone receiver carefully in its cradle, ensuring that the flex was not twisted. He was meticulous about this as he hated seeing a twisted coil of flex hampering the easy movement of the handset. He had constantly had to untangle it when the children lived at home and were allowed to use the telephone. Now it was therapy. He had dreaded having to make the call to his superior in the RAF command structure and had been horrified when the call had been passed directly to Air Commodore Mitchell who was like a starving rottweiler at the best of times.

There was a history of course to the antagonism with which Mitchell always greeted him, the way he always made him feel he had failed. Things had been fine before the war when he had been flying, commanding a squadron based in Suffolk. Life as an officer was easy, the job was clear, they were good days. He could not help but remember the dinners in the officers' mess, the occasional dinner dances to which ladies were invited. Those were times when he loved Marjorie, he loved his life, felt in control.

Then the war came and everything changed. His squadron – No 9 based at RAF Honington was tasked, along with Squadron No 149, with carrying out a bombing raid on the German fleet which was anchored at the entrance to the Kiel Canal in Northern Germany. It was the first British bombing raid of the war – September 5th 1939, a date he would never forget. Two of his Wellingtons had been lost with all five crew killed on each. Even now, in his own mind, he protested that it was not his fault. They could do nothing to protect themselves from the ack-ack that greeted them. The only way to save everyone would have been to abort the mission. Even then, they may have lost some aircraft to enemy fighters.

Someone had to be blamed. Of course it was reported in the papers as a great success, ships damaged and sunk and so on, but he knew they had caused little harm. No amount of training prepares you for flying in those conditions when the plane is being rocked with shells exploding around you, when you can't see where you're going because you're blinded by the flashes of light. Most of the bombs had fallen harmlessly in the sea.

He could still taste the fear in his mouth, feel the panic that had threatened to make him turn his aircraft back before reaching the target area. He had tried to explain this to his commanding officer – Mitchell – but his words had fallen on a distinctly unsympathetic ear. He had known that he could not face that fear again. He had been forced to carry out a few more missions which he found equally harrowing before he was deemed unfit for flying after repeated visits to the medic about his nerves.

In his heart, Charles Lovell knew he was a coward. One had to present oneself in the way that people expected. He had succeeded in that in the non-combat role he had been given after leaving the squadron which came with promotion to Wing Commander. Now he had been awarded this posting which he did not want going belly-up. He must get this business sorted quickly. Any delay would certainly reflect on his leadership in Mitchell's eyes and he held the power.

Unaware of his commanding officer's troubled thoughts, Edward Driscoll knocked on the office door. The instruction to enter was uncharacteristically tame and Driscoll raised an eyebrow to Dearing who stood beside him. They entered wondering why they had been summoned.

Lovell was slumped in the chair behind his desk. He waved vaguely to indicate his two senior officers should find seats. "Bad news, gentlemen. Very bad news. I am still struggling to believe this. The body of a young woman has been found in Hut Fifteen, you know the one at the end of the line of huts – one of those we do not as yet use." Dearing and Driscoll stared at him. "She was found this morning by the ATA pilot, Flight Officer Barnes. It would be a visitor wouldn't it?"

"Who is it? One of the nurses?" Driscoll felt a cold hand on his heart and he knew his voice expressed not merely bafflement but shock, fear.

"No one from the base I think. She's in civilian clothes."

Relief flooded through Driscoll. "What was she doing here then? I mean how did she…?"

"I've no idea as yet Driscoll. I just know we could do without it." Lovell wiped his hand across his brow and slowly sat up straight. "A new training base and an unknown girl decides to come and die here. The World has truly gone mad."

Driscoll was sitting in a chair opposite Lovell and Dearing was perched on the low shelving unit in front of the window. "There must be a simple explanation for it, Sir." Driscoll's face, despite this sentiment, was creased with concern.

"Driscoll's right, Sir. There will be a simple explanation. We've just got to find it." Dearing stood and looked out at the rain hammering again on the tarmac below. "Can we trust McBane, Sir. I mean is he experienced enough to deal with something like this? Shouldn't we just handle it ourselves?"

"He's involved now, Dearing. Besides there would have been no way of keeping it away from the RAF Police. That was the first thing that Air Commodore Mitchell said when I phoned him just now. He was happy that we had someone on site already."

"So you think, Sir, that she must have found a way onto the base?" Driscoll looked at the tired face of his commanding officer.

Lovell spread his hands. "I can't think of any other explanation."

"But what was she doing here? Why come onto an air training base?"

"Let's hope we discover that soon." Lovell sighed deeply.

Dearing turned back from the window. "Perhaps I should organise a thorough check of the perimeter fence. She may have got in somewhere."

Lovell looked up, a drowning man clutching for anything. "Good idea Dearing. Do it as soon as you can."

"What should we tell the trainees and other staff?"

"You get the trainees together, Driscoll. Tell them that we are investigating a matter and may need to ask some questions. Leave it at that for now. You tell the ranks the same thing Dearing." The two officers turned to leave. "And thank you gentlemen. It is reassuring to know I have such dependable senior officers...who understand the need for... discretion."

Lovell looked down at his desk and coughed. Not used to paying compliments, thought Driscoll but clearly relieved to share the burden.

The two officers exchanged the briefest of nods outside the office door and Dearing hurried away down the corridor to organise the perimeter fence inspection. Driscoll watched his brisk steps; how unusual it was to see Dearing hurrying. His gait was normally an arrogant stroll, as if he was so important the whole World could wait for him. Why be in such a hurry about a perimeter fence inspection? It needed to be done soon but the fence was not going anywhere.

Driscoll made his way to Hut Five. He and Dearing had left the trainee pilots and navigators with the work on enemy aircraft. They were to test each other on recognition, capabilities and so forth, what they had covered in the first two hours of the morning. He pulled his greatcoat on before leaving the office building and buttoned it firmly even though it was not a long walk to the briefing hut.

A babble of excited noise greeted him when he entered the briefing room. There seemed to be much hilarity at some of the answers being given and it was clear that some of the trainees had departed from the subject altogether. Driscoll coughed to clear his throat and then stood in the middle of the room to gain their attention.

"A word chaps, please." The room gradually fell silent and Driscoll waited until he had full attention. "There is a matter...something has happened on the base which will need to be investigated. You may have already come across Sergeant McBane who is with us from the RAF Police Special Investigation Branch. He is based at RAF Burnham. If he or any other officer investigating this matter wants to ask you questions - whether you saw anything unusual for example – please give him your full co-operation. Thank you. Now let's see where you've got to."

Uncomprehending glances were exchanged between the trainees at this announcement but Driscoll did not elaborate nor invite questions. He moved straight to the job in hand. Pairs of trainees were invited to give full details of each enemy aircraft covered in the exercise he had set. As they came to the front and spoke, Edward Driscoll sat at the side and made a few notes. His mind was elsewhere however, wondering who the young woman was and what she was doing on the base. His thoughts constantly wandered to the young woman who had become so important in his life. He could at least be certain that the dead girl was not her.

And then his mind settled on Dearing. He had suggested the perimeter fence inspection and was clearly very keen to get it done. There was something in his manner which troubled Driscoll beyond the usual arrogance that he disliked so much. Did Dearing have something to hide? He had seen him outside the previous night, later on, after that embarrassing display of drunkenness at dinner with Lizzie Barnes. Where had he been going on such a wild night?

# CHAPTER 9

"She's in this room here." Lizzie indicated the door.

"No need for you to come in Lizzie. I can take it from here." Robbie opened the door and stepped into the room, leaving it slightly ajar. He did not open the curtains which Lizzie had instinctively shut earlier before reporting her find to Lovell. He switched on the light instead just in case there were prying eyes outside. When Lizzie entered the room, he turned his head at the movement. "There's really no need for you…"

"It's ok…I'm ok." Lizzie closed the door behind her.

It was the body of a young woman, a girl really, probably late teens or early twenties at most. Her face was heavy with make-up though the lipstick was smudged making her mouth look unnaturally large. Luxuriant bronze hair flared from her head, seeping over the pillow on either side and her face was pale as marble. The body lay half on its side and half on its back, twisted, with the legs splayed. Her skirt was up around her hips, her knickers still on but pulled sideways. One stocking was still hooked to her suspender; the other had been released and was crumpled above the knee. Her blouse was unbuttoned, revealing her brassiere and the curve of her pale breasts.

Lizzie wanted to adjust her clothing and reached forward to pull the skirt down but McBane held her arm and shook his head. "We need to wait until we have photographs for the record and the body has been examined." He leaned forward, examining the neck. There were distinct marks on either side that looked very much like finger marks. "I think you're right about strangulation. I'll need to report this to the local police so they can arrange a post-mortem. They'll need to examine the scene. Did you touch anything previously?"

"The door handle, the curtains, but nothing else."

"Good. They may want to take your fingerprints just in case."

They stood side by side at the foot of the bed. "She has no dignity like this."

"No... but it is necessary."

"I expected to feel the shock that I felt when I first saw her but...I think no one can hurt her now...she looks quite calm. I've never seen a dead person before."

Robbie McBane swallowed hard and turned away as if looking around the room. "There is a strange quietness, peace about the dead. As you say, no one can hurt her now but how terrible that a young life has been cut short."

The catch in McBane's voice drew Lizzie's attention but she could not see his face to read his thoughts. Some memory uncovered. "I could imagine her laughing, perhaps out dancing with her friends, a young man's arm around her. Her poor family."

"I feel all those things too but I also feel anger. Someone did this to her, someone took her life. I imagine the fear when she felt her life ebbing from her, struggling with her attacker, unable to fight him off. I am determined...determined to find the animal who did this."

Lizzie turned to look at him again, surprised by the anger that had momentarily overcome him and the resonance it had with her own stifled feelings of outrage. She leaned forward. One of the girl's hands, her right, was lying on the bed beside her body. She looked carefully at the fingernails, long and quite sharp, painted bright red to match her lipstick. She peered beneath them.

McBane saw her and understood immediately what she was doing. "The pathologist will examine everything in detail," he said.

"Yes, I'm sure he will. But her attacker may well have a scratch somewhere." She pointed to the tiny piece of flesh trapped beneath the fingernail of the index finger. "Might be something to keep an eye out for."

As she turned to go, Lizzie noticed a tan coat draped over a chair in the corner of the room. She pointed to it. "Probably hers. Stylish… all the fashion nowadays. Must have cost a bit."

McBane nodded and, spotting something on the floor, reached a little way under the bed. He withdrew a comb carefully with index finger and thumb. "Interesting. I wonder who owns this?"

A faint bell rang in Lizzie's mind but nothing came. "There's a short hair there – it'll be a man's comb – the hair looks dark in this light…a couple of spots of dandruff."

"Looks like it's made of bakelite."

Lizzie looked at it closely. "No…that's tortoiseshell… expensive."

They checked all the other rooms. It was Lizzie's sharp eye that spotted it, a small flash of silver half under a bookshelf in the office next to the room in which the dead girl lay. "What's that?"

Robbie McBane picked it up carefully using his handkerchief. It was a cigarette case…not heavy enough to be pure silver, probably plated. He turned it over and then opened it. Six cigarettes were still inside and, on the lid, the initials: RD. "Who might RD be I wonder?"

"Ron Dearing?"

"Could be." Their eyes met. Could Dearing be the killer?

McBane folded the case in his handkerchief. As he did so, Lizzie peered into the waste basket sitting next to the desk. There was only a large, crumpled envelope which she straightened carefully. In the top left hand corner was written 'By hand' and in the centre an address: 'New Swan Stone', 7 Acacia Avenue. Her eye was drawn to the way it had been written – the letters seemed almost indented on the paper. The flap of the envelope was torn.

"Curious," she said. "Worth keeping?" She looked at Robbie who took it.

After another look around the office, they left the building. As he closed the door behind them, McBane spoke to the guards. "No one - and I mean no one - is to go into that building until the Police have finished with it. Understood?"

"Sir," they replied in unison and straightened their backs to indicate the seriousness of the task. Their faces smarted in the stinging rain and their greatcoats glistened with droplets of water.

"I must report to Lovell and then call the local police though he has made it clear he does not want them involved. We have no choice."

"I'll be back in the Sick Bay if you need me."

"When were you planning to leave Silverstone?"

"As soon as the weather improves and I can get a ride back to White Waltham."

"I'm afraid I must ask you to stay here until the investigation reaches a suitable point." He smiled at the shock on her face. "Don't worry. You're not a suspect. It's just that I or the Police might need to question you about anything else you've seen or heard. You seem to be very observant. You might be useful to the investigation."

"Thank you. I'd be happy to help if I can."

"Oh and, by the way, please say nothing to anyone until we have announced it."

She nodded "I'd like to say it will be a pleasure to stay but that's not how I feel about it. How long do you think it will be before the news is given to the base?"

"I hope later today if the local Police respond quickly."

They parted between the two main buildings, two figures holding coats close about them, bowing into the wind.

❖ ❖ ❖

Enid Sumser approached the house cautiously. This was the other side of town, the council houses, and some of them showed serious signs of neglect. The Bennett's was no exception. An old armchair was dumped in the front garden. It had clearly been there for some time as grass was growing long around it. The cushions were mildewed and the seat sagged alarmingly. This was very different to her own trim gardens which her husband, Arthur, tended with great care. There were no flowers here, just overgrown grass up to the fences. Snowdrops were already in full bloom in her own garden though this driving wind and rain may ruin them. Daffodils were also poking up from the soil.

She wondered if she should go to the back door but decided to knock at the front. Inside, a woman was shouting, presumably at a young child or children. The door was wrenched open and Mrs Bennett stood before her.

"What is it?" Her apron was dirty and hair was escaping from her scarf.

"Hello, Mrs Bennett. It's Enid Sumser…Jenny's mother. I wonder if Maggie is at home."

"She's at work…as you'd expect at this time of day."

"Oh…of course. Well the thing is Mrs Bennett, my Jenny hasn't come home from last night and I wondered if Maggie might know where she went. She didn't stay here did she?"

"Not that I'm aware of." She turned suddenly and bellowed back into the house. "Keep the noise down you two." The instruction had no noticeable effect. When Mrs Bennett turned back, she must have noticed at last the anxiety on Enid Sumser's face and she softened. "Where did she go last night?"

"I don't know but I assume she went out with Maggie and their friends like they usually do."

"Perhaps, but I didn't talk to Maggie last night nor this morning. I was in bed when she came in and she's always right grumpy in the morning so I leave her to it."

"Of course. I'm sorry to have troubled you."

"Have you tried Rita…Rita Polesworth? They usually go round together. She lives on the Wayneflete, number thirty-two."

"No I haven't tried there but I'll go now. Thank you."

"I'm sure she'll turn up, love. These young girls get up to all sorts these days."

McBane replaced the receiver carefully, feeling vindicated. He had been quite right to inform his own boss, Flight Lieutenant Belding, who in turn would inform his superiors. Lovell had of course wanted no one else to know but that was not possible. Belding was absolutely in agreement that McBane should inform the local police despite Lovell's desire to keep it all in house. Is he trying to cover something up? Robbie wondered as he started to dial the number he had been given for Brackley Police Station.

"Brackley Police Station, Sergeant Bailey speaking." The voice was slightly pompous, someone who enjoyed his position.

"My name is Sergeant McBane from the RAF Police... Special Investigation Branch. I'm at Silverstone Air Base at the moment and we have a serious situation which you chaps need to know about."

"Oh yes? Someone stolen one of the planes have they?" Sergeant Bailey was in jocular mood despite the dreary day.

"No Sergeant. We have found the body of a young woman in a room at the base and I believe she has been murdered. It appears she is a civilian as she is unknown on the base."

"Stone the crows. Murdered?"

"It looks as though she was strangled. Can you get someone up here as quickly as possible. You need to send a pathologist and there should be a post-mortem. It needs to be a senior officer that comes."

"I'll call Towcester and ask Inspector Fletcher to come over. He usually deals with serious crimes."

That changed his attitude, Robbie thought grimly. And now we must wait until they arrive. He was still holding the log book from the truck and the notes he had made. He decided to see Lovell again while he was waiting for the Police.

Lovell was pacing his office. Robbie up-dated him with the phone calls he had made. "Sir, we need to make sure that no one leaves the Base at least until the Police give the all clear. We will have to interview everyone. Someone might have seen something."

Lovell sighed deeply. "Very well. How on earth are we supposed to train pilots for the war effort when we have this kind of thing going on? It's just as well there was no flying today anyway."

"Yes Sir. It's very frustrating." Robbie's icy tone was lost on Lovell so he held the log book in front of him. "Before this happened, Sir, I was checking vehicle log books and fuel consumption. There is something unexplained." Lovell looked puzzled.

"You see, Sir, every three or four days, this particular truck is being filled with enough fuel to fill the tank to overflowing but the mileage recorded is nothing like enough to warrant that fuel usage...unless there is a serious leak in the tank. Furthermore, twice per week, there are twenty-eight miles unaccounted for – that's a regular discrepancy between the miles recorded in the log book and the mileage on the vehicle's distance gauge."

He paused and Lovell stared at him. "We have just found the body of a young woman on the base whom you believe was murdered and you're talking to me about a bit of fuel that might have leaked." Lovell erupted. "Do you seriously think I've got time to worry about fuel when I've got this on my plate?"

"I thought it best to report it, Sir. I can do nothing more on the other matter until the local Police arrive."

"Well go to the Mess and put your feet up. Don't bother me with this...trivia."

"Fine, Sir." Robbie MacBane turned smartly and left Lovell's office, determined to investigate the fuel discrepancies fully; there could be a link with the young woman's death. One never knew.

He decided to find Lizzie. She had a good mind and was calm. He felt he could use her as a sounding board. She was not in the Sick Bay. "I sent her to lie down for a bit. She's had quite a shock." Nurse O'Flynn lifted the sheet she was holding and flipped the top half over, making a neat fold.

"You've done that a few times I think."

She smiled. "More times than I care to remember."

"I'll leave you to it." Her face lights up when she smiles, he reflected. The smell of something cooking made him look at his watch. Almost noon. Time for lunch soon.

# CHAPTER 10

Inspector Fletcher pulled his shoulders back as he strode beside AC Andrews. When he entered Lovell's office, he marched directly to the desk with his hand out. Lovell was still seated but he stood and took Fletcher's proffered hand, wincing slightly at the strong grip. Fletcher's shrewd eyes rapidly assessed the other man.

"Inspector Fletcher, Sir. Northamptonshire Police. I understand you are in charge of the base."

"Yes. Group Captain Lovell."

The corner of Fletcher's mouth turned up at the emphasis Lovell had placed on his rank. He had met his type before, business owners very conscious of their senior positions, that sort of man. "I understand you have found a body?"

"That's right Inspector. A young woman found by a visiting ATA pilot in one of our rarely used buildings. We have with us a Sergeant McBane from the RAF Police SIB - Special Investigation Branch - who happened to be on the base and who felt you should be notified though I imagine you'll be happy to leave it to him. Must have lots to do."

"It sounds as though the girl might have been murdered, Sir, so we need to be involved especially if she proves to have been a civilian."

"Yes, yes, Inspector. It's just that we have an important job to do here and we can do without the disruption of a major investigation. Not good for public morale if it were to get out... I'm sure you understand."

"Yes, Sir. I do understand. My time in the army during the last war gave me a very good impression of how senior ranks like to keep things quiet."

Lovell looked up sharply. "I'm not asking you to cover it up, Inspector, just to let us get on."

"I'll do what I can but we will have to interview people, carry out inspections and so forth. I will need to look at the scene now and afterwards I would like to speak with yourself, Sergeant McBane and anyone else whom you think I should talk to at this stage."

"Good. I'll arrange for McBane and my two senior officers, Flight Lieutenants Dearing and Driscoll to come here at...." He consulted his watch..." shall we say fourteen hundred hours - two o'clock? That gives you an hour. Is that enough?"

"Plenty, Sir. We will need to set up an incident room and will need access to a phone somewhere private."

"There are some vacant rooms, a couple of offices, in the same building as the body. I'll have someone check that the phone over there is working. Andrews can escort you to the scene now."

As Inspector Fletcher walked with AC Andrews towards the building that housed the dead girl, he reflected on his experience of the services. He had been in the army as a young man during the last war and carried to this day the resentment at what the rank and file soldiers had endured because of incompetent leadership. The generals had sat well behind the front lines ordering troops over the top, knowing they would be mown down in their thousands. He had seen carnage, horrors that occasionally haunted his troubled nights. He had no interest in sweeping things under the carpet and he did not trust Lovell who clearly wished to do so.

Lizzie was lying on the bed, trying not to think about the dead girl. It was hopeless really; she'd be much better off doing something...like flying...something that did not allow time for thought. The tap on the door surprised her and she hoisted herself into a sitting position before swinging her legs off the bed and padding over to the door.

"I hope I'm not disturbing you. Nurse O'Flynn said you'd come to lie down. I wonder if I can run a few things past you."

She was surprised that he should wish to consult her but opened the door wide for him to enter. She motioned to him to sit on the one chair in the room and she perched on the side of the bed. He was a big man, athletic, but his voice was rounded, softened by his accent.

"Are you sure you're ok to talk about this?"

"I am not so easily shaken, Sergeant. I would much rather be doing something useful but Nurse O'Flynn was determined I should come to my room."

Robbie smiled and dropped the log book on the floor beside the chair. He saw her eyes follow it. "It's just a log book from one of the trucks. I'm here to check the consumption of provisions, fuel, that sort of thing. I certainly did not expect to be confronted with a body."

"Nor I. That poor girl." Lizzie turned her face away from him but then looked him in the eye. "So was it someone who works on the base I wonder?"

"Mebbe but it's too early to speculate about that. I wanted to ask you whether anything struck you about the girl...her appearance, clothing...that sort of thing."

"She was out for the night. She had made up her face and the clothes she was wearing I suspect were some of her best. She had put on stockings too – nylons, quite expensive I'd guess." Lizzie hesitated, feeling a slight embarrassment at the remark she was about to make. "I did notice her underwear... her knickers."

He looked at her intently for a moment and then looked down, the faintest blush colouring his cheeks. "Do you mean how they were on her?"

"No. They were quite expensive...maybe even silk but certainly not what you'd wear every day." He looked up puzzled so she continued. "You'd put on underwear like that either to feel very good on a special night or because you thought someone might be seeing it."

"Ah...I see." He looked at the floor again. "You are observant."

"Not sure about that but a woman would notice some things a man would not."

"Quite so. Did you notice anything else?"

"I didn't see a handbag. A girl out for the night would take a handbag...it's what we do. It's probably somewhere. Otherwise, apart from what looked like flesh beneath her fingernail, no I don't think so. One wonders who she is and what she was doing here."

"Indeed. I need to check how she might have got on the base – maybe a lapse in security. I think Lovell has asked Dearing to arrange for the perimeter fence to be checked." He smiled. "I probably should not be telling you this...you might be a suspect!"

"Yes, but I probably would not be strong enough to strangle someone unless I had drugged her first."

"True. I guess the autopsy will tell us that." He smiled again. "Well, if you think of anything else, do please let me know. I daresay the police will want to ask you some questions."

"Naturally." She watched him pick up the log book from the floor and stand. The number on the cover was clearly visible. "By the way, that log book. Can I check the number please?"

He held it up. "RAF 142031. Why?"

"It's a truck isn't it? I saw it leaving the base yesterday afternoon quite late...about seventeen thirty. I didn't think too much about it but wondered where they might be going at that time on such a foul day. What surprised me though was that I heard it going through the gate again at about twenty-two hundred hours and what was really odd, was that it was leaving again, not returning."

"Interesting. Thank you for that. It is these small details

that often lead somewhere. You'd make a good detective I think."

She laughed off the compliment. "I'll keep my eyes peeled."

"Please do. I think I'm going to need all the help I can get."

Lizzie watched him walk down the stairs before closing the door. He was very unlike Dearing in his manner and she guessed his nature was more like Driscoll's though she would not use the word secretive about him. There was something lurking behind those eyes, determination certainly, but something else. There was a sadness she felt sure.

Lizzie chuckled briefly. "Nothing so intriguing to a woman than a sense of something hidden in a man," she said softly to herself as a warning. But then, she was very unlikely to fall in love as she had no intention of establishing a serious relationship at this stage of her life. That could wait until the war was over and she was replete with excitement and the need for adventure.

And always there was that issue hovering like a spectre in the shadows of her mind.

"We've found a section of the perimeter fence that has been cut through, Sir. Davies and Andrews made a start checking it. It's been cut – how long ago we don't know – but maybe people have been coming on to the base through it... perhaps to steal, maybe something even more sinister. Sorry Sir."

Lovell had stood up abruptly as soon as Dearing had started talking and he listened intently. Relief, the feeling of the first sips of his evening whisky, settled in his chest. "That is not going to go down well with the top brass – we're supposed to check such things. But at least it probably means we're not looking at one of our own for this murder."

"I think that's right, Sir."

"Ironic isn't it? At any other time, I would have been furious to know we have such a security breach but now…"

"Of course, Sir." Dearing paused a moment. "The other thing we should think about, Sir, are any maintenance contractors that come onto the base. One of them could be involved."

Lovell looked at Dearing keenly. "That is a distinct possibility – I didn't think of that. Do we have a log of when they come onto the base and leave?"

"Of course, Sir. It'll be in the gatehouse. I can fetch it."

"Do that Dearing. We need to be ready when Inspector Fletcher and his local bobbies come and we need to be able to head off that troublesome Scotsman, McBane. Be back here at fourteen hundred hours sharp. I'm bringing them all together. Got to try to keep control of things."

Dearing saluted wheeled around and left the office at a smart pace. Lovell was surprised; 'languid' was the word he would use for Dearing's usual movements but now his stride was purposeful as he headed for the office door and his steps rang in the corridor.

Lovell absent-mindedly re-arranged the items on his desk, pushing the phone a little to the right, straightening his desk pad and setting the new pen carefully in front of it. He looked at the photograph of his family. Two children, one boy, one girl, both gainfully occupied in useful occupations though Michael, the boy, had disappointed him by refusing to join the RAF. Still, a scientist working on God-knows-what fiendish devices to help win the war was a worthy task.

He looked at the photograph more closely, his eye resting on his daughter, Valerie. She would have been about twelve when it had been taken, before the War had disrupted everything. He was proud of her becoming a nurse, proud of everything about her. She was always a pretty girl and now turned heads. Lucky blokes who were nursed by her.

It had not been the best of marriages. He and Marjorie had drifted together without any great love on either side. It was somehow expected. Part of him regretted that, always wondered what it was to have a passionate relationship with another person. But then he was not a passionate man, he knew that. Reason and rationality were his watchwords. Marjorie had given him two fine children and had been an excellent mother; for that he was grateful. But it was definitely now a marriage of convenience, going through the motions, loveless. Neither of them was at fault – just one of those things.

A tremor of excitement started in his breast and crept down his body; there may be some compensation! He smiled, thinking of the night to come. He had no grounds for complaint about his life. This posting was a good one, no difficult decisions to make, out of the firing line. He wanted to hang onto it for the duration... provided this business could be sorted out.

Seven miles away, an elegant lady climbed the stairs of her large home, pausing briefly on the half landing to look out of the window at the grey mass of cloud fleeing across the sky. She walked purposefully along the landing and entered a room that, had the window not been covered by a blackout curtain, would have given a commanding view of the rear garden. Checking that this blackout curtain was fully drawn, she flicked on the main light in the centre of the ceiling and then a strong lamp that spread a pool of brightness on the desk.

She sat down at the desk and, taking a key from the pocket of her skirt, unlocked one of the drawers. She took from it a slim folder and a small Minox Riga camera. With deft finger movements, she inserted a new film into the camera and laid it aside while she spread two documents from the folder under the pool of light. She examined them intently, bending over them and using a magnifying glass to peer more closely. They were drawings, one a rough, hand-drawn map and the other a complex technical drawing.

After lengthy and careful scrutiny, she looked up and smiled. She lifted the camera and, standing to achieve the best shots, took several photographs, covering the technical drawing in sections and the map in one shot. The camera whirred as she wound the film to the end before extracting it. She turned off the desk lamp and moved to the side of the room opposite the window where a table was laid with trays and chemicals and a line stretched above it.

The flick of a switch brought a red glow to the room which intensified when the ceiling light was extinguished. She busied herself pouring a fluid into a tray and then, carefully, unrolled the film and dipped it into the prepared chemicals. She left the room.

Some thirty minutes later, she returned and extracted the roll of film which she held up for inspection in front of the main ceiling light. She nodded to herself with satisfaction and rolled the film tightly, packing it into a small metal cylindrical case the size of a thimble. She would need to take a train to London soon to deliver this precious cylinder to her contact.

The telephone rang in the hall. Her brow creased with concern; she knew who would be calling.

# CHAPTER 11

Lizzie stood with Fletcher and Robbie McBane outside Lovell's office with Andrews guarding the door like a faithful dog. They had been there only a couple of minutes but Lizzie could see Fletcher did not like being kept waiting. Andrews consulted his wrist watch and rapped sharply on Lovell's door. "The Group Captain likes absolute punctuality," he said in explanation and, when he heard the command, threw open the door.

Lizzie followed Fletcher and Robbie into the room.

"Oh, I didn't think there was any need for Miss Barnes to come." He was the kind of man, Lizzie guessed, who would want a 'gentleman's agreement' probably to sweep everything under the carpet. Another example of male attempts to dominate or was it insecurity, a nervousness that a woman might show them up?

"I took the liberty of asking Miss Barnes as she found the body and Inspector Fletcher may wish to ask her some questions." Robbie McBane smiled innocently. "Miss Barnes, Inspector Fletcher and I have introduced ourselves already."

"Well, well, fine. Do sit down gentlem…do sit down. Tea anybody?"

They all declined.

Lizzie noticed how, subtly, Fletcher's manner indicated he was in charge. "Right, Sir, I've visited the site of the crime and I've made the necessary phone calls. The pathologist is on his way and I have a small team of my officers also coming to take statements. I'm afraid that will be a lengthy job but we must interview everyone. I or one of my colleagues will be contacting the local police stations in a fifteen mile radius to see if any young women have been reported missing. We may be able to identify the victim like that. Sergeant McBane, anything to add?"

As he spoke, Lizzie watched the Inspector. There was a steely aspect to his demeanour. He would not be taken in by anyone nor would he be intimidated. If she were being cross examined by him, she was sure she would blurt out whatever information she was holding. She guessed he was mid-forties, the lines on his face already well formed and his dark hair streaked with grey. His voice was even, no melodrama nor shock. How terrible to be so used to dealing with such crimes that one could speak with so little sentiment. McBane was listening to him carefully, respectfully, and sat forward slightly when invited to speak by Fletcher.

"Miss Barnes noticed three things when we visited the body that may be of significance I think. The first was a tiny piece of flesh beneath one of the fingernails, the second was that there was no handbag to be seen and the third was that she was dressed…at least her underwear suggested she was expecting it to be a special night."

Fletcher nodded slowly and looked at Lizzie. "Very observant, Miss. So if we can establish who this young woman was, we will have more chance of understanding how she came to be here and who would want to…to do this."

"Flight Lieutenant Dearing has just reported to me a breach of our security. It seems a gap has been found in the perimeter fence. She may well have come in through that though for what reason I've no idea."

"We'll need to take a look at that then after this meeting." Fletcher caught McBane's eye who nodded agreement.

There was a knock on the door and Dearing strolled in carrying a large book which he held up to show Lovell. "The log of entries and exits from the Gatehouse, Sir." He opened the book and laid it on Lovell's desk, pointing with his finger. "The last maintenance visit was yesterday just after fifteen hundred hours. Plumber, Sir, to fix a leaking tap apparently."

"Who was it? Staples…does he work for someone or is

he a one man operation?"

"I'll have someone check that, Sir." Fletcher made a note of the name in his pad.

As if struck by a sudden thought, Dearing said, "Of course, Sir, this means that there was someone else on the base yesterday afternoon. The young woman could have been brought in by him, smuggled herself in or come in through the gap in the fence. This Staples chap might of course be the culprit." Something in his voice alerted Lizzie; he seemed too keen to press that line.

"Either way, it probably means this death has nothing to do with anyone on the base." Lovell looked at each of them in turn but only Dearing met his gaze.

"May I take a look at that, Sir?" Robbie approached Lovell's desk and held his hand out for the book, making it difficult for Lovell to refuse. Even so, Lovell was reluctant to let him see it. The conversation continued with Lovell and Dearing pushing the theory that the whole thing was down to outsiders while Robbie scanned the entries. Lizzie could read them from her position next to him. There was no entry for that truck leaving on the two occasions she had seen it, once in the afternoon and once in the evening. The entry relating to the visit of the plumber was in a different colour pen and different handwriting – nothing necessarily significant in that but…

"Right, Sir, we'd best leave you to your work and I'll get on with mine. Perhaps your man can show me where the gap in the perimeter fence is."

"Thank you Inspector Fletcher. Do please keep me informed of developments."

"Naturally, Sir."

The three visitors left the office and, accompanied by Andrews, left the building. The wind was still strong but the rain had stopped and shafts of sun, breaking between the clouds, angrily sliced across the airfield like swords. They walked in silence, the two men holding their coats closed;

Lizzie had fastened her flying jacket.

Two cars were entering the base and as they drew close, Fletcher flagged them down. He gave instructions to the occupants of both and they drove on, one towards the building where the body lay and the other to the building they had just left.

"That's the pathologist and my team arriving. They'll get on without us for the time being," Fletcher said.

Andrews led them along the fence to a point close to the building which housed the victim. Rooks swayed at the top of the trees nearby like hooded monks, their raucous calls scratching the air with gossip. He stopped and pointed to the fence some three yards away which had been cut vertically and a gap opened by pushing away the sides.

"Looks like they came in there, Sir." Andrews stood awkwardly, unsure what to do with his hands. "We've made a temporary repair." He pointed to the wire used to sew the fence together.

"When was this discovered?"

"Just this morning, Sir. Flight Lieutenant Dearing asked Corporal Davies and me to check the whole fence. We made a start and found this. Hopefully there won't be others."

"Thank you, Andrews." The airman did not leave, but thrust his hands in his pockets and shuffled from foot to foot. "We can find our own way back. Thank you."

Andrews hovered a moment longer, clearly reluctant to leave, but then turned and walked away whistling with rather studied nonchalance.

When he was out of earshot, Fletcher said, "Do you notice anything?"

"That wire looks freshly cut to me." Robbie McBane took a step forward but Lizzie laid a hand on his arm.

"Look at the grass before you go any closer."

"The grass? What's wrong wi' the grass?"

"Look at the way it's completely flattened on this side of the fence. It's what you'd expect if several people were coming through. Now look outside the fence."

"Nothing at all," said Fletcher with an admiring smile to Lizzie.

The three of them stood and stared at the long grass outside the perimeter fence. It was wet and some long stems had flopped over but there was no way anyone had walked over it. The flattened grass on the inside of the fence revealed no useful evidence; no individual footprints would have made discernible impressions in it. Attention turned to the fence itself.

"That looks to me like it's been cut recently. No sign of rusting," Robbie said.

"I agree," responded Fletcher. "What does that suggest to you?"

"It was cut from the inside by people who want us to suspect that the victim and or her attacker came onto the base through it," Lizzie said.

"Precisely. I think Group Captain Lovell and his sidekick Dearing seemed very anxious to divert our attention away from the base."

"Definitely." Robbie McBane nodded vigorously. "My instinct tells me that the unexplained miles on the truck and it's two trips out yesterday late afternoon and night are connected with this. When I looked at the gatehouse log in Lovell's office, the truck was not mentioned at all and I think the entry of the plumber was added later."

"I noticed that…sorry, I was reading the entries over your arm." Lizzie smiled.

"What's this about the truck?"

Robbie McBane explained to Fletcher the discrepancies in the log book, the huge consumption of fuel and the two occasions on the previous day when Lizzie had seen the truck leaving the base. "We really need to establish who was driving that truck and where."

"We can fingerprint the steering wheel though it may have been wiped by now. We would of course need to take fingerprints from any RAF chaps who drive it. Might be quite tricky but we can try."

"Presumably there is a way of checking with this plumber whether he was indeed here or not yesterday?" Lizzie looked at Fletcher.

"We will certainly do that tomorrow. Sergeant McBane, may I suggest we work together on this. I have the manpower to take statements from everyone on the base. We'll establish where everyone was, whether anything unusual was seen, that sort of thing. Broadly speaking, I'll handle things outside the base and you handle things within until we have more definite information. You'll want to interview some particular people from the base I imagine."

"I'd be happy to work with you Inspector and I'd be mighty pleased to have your advice. I've no handled a murder investigation afore."

"Procedure, Sergeant, that's what's needed. Methodical, careful checking of all angles, all lines of enquiry. And evidence. It's all very well for these sleuths in books to have wonderful brain waves but courts can only convict on evidence."

"Quite so, Sir. But of course I have a very powerful weapon in the search for the answer."

"And what's that?"

"I have my very observant assistant to help me." Robbie McBane turned to Lizzie and smiled at her.

Fletcher did not smile. "As long as that will not put you in a compromising position, Miss Barnes."

"I'll stay discreetly in the background, picking up what I can. And do call me Lizzie Inspector." Fletcher nodded in acknowledgement.

Charles Lovell closed the front door quietly and

shrugged off his greatcoat. It felt heavy as he lifted it onto the peg in the hall and it glistened with rain drops. It wasn't just the rain though; he knew its weight was caused by his own weariness. Running through his mind all day since the discovery of the body was the thought, 'What will Mitchell make of it?' As he had told himself numerous times already, it was bad enough as it was but it needed to be sorted quickly otherwise the proverbial would fall on him with serious questions about his management of the base.

He walked slowly into the drawing room and crossed to the sideboard. He was lifting the decanter of whisky to pour himself a large shot when Marjorie bustled into the room.

"Charles. What is going on? I needed to go into Brackley today for my hair appointment and was told at the gate that no one is being allowed off the base."

Charles Lovell finished pouring his whisky and set the decanter on the silver tray carefully before replying. "That is correct, Marjorie...police instructions. Today, the body of a young woman was found on the base and there is now a murder investigation going on."

"Young woman...on the base. Was it one of the nursing staff?"

"No. Her identity is unknown. What she was doing on the base is also unknown but no one can enter or leave the base apart from the Police."

"But, but...how long will that last?"

"I don't know. Until they sort it out I suppose. An Inspector Fletcher from Northamptonshire Constabulary is on the case and we have a Sergeant McBane from the RAF Police Special Investigation Branch as well – he came this morning about something else but is staying on."

"So what am I to do about my hair appointment? I had to telephone to cancel and I said I'd ring tomorrow to arrange another time. It's most inconvenient."

Lovell's voice was laden with sarcasm. "Yes, dear, most inconvenient. I'll ask Inspector Fletcher when he discovers who her family are to tell them it was very inconvenient her dying on the base."

"There's no need to take that tone, Charles."

Charles Lovell could not face an argument. He wanted sympathy, understanding. "I'm sorry, Dear, but I've had a helluva day. We lost one day of training because of the storm and now we'll lose tomorrow as well. Bomber Command are breathing down our necks for more pilots already." He took a large sip of whisky and felt the sharpness in his mouth. When he swallowed, there was that wonderful fire down his throat and in his stomach. It cheered him a little.

"Surely you can authorise my leaving the base? I mean I have nothing to do with this business and you are after all in charge."

Lovell was wondering whether that was the case. It didn't feel like it today however much he asserted his authority. His eyes strayed to the closed curtains and the comfort of the room. Theirs was the only house on the base and, until today, he had seen that as a real perk of the job. Perhaps it wasn't so good after all.

His wife looked at him for a moment and then with a curt "Supper will be at six-thirty," left the room.

Lovell relaxed into the armchair, leaning back and closing his eyes. Perhaps tomorrow this would be sorted and they could get on with the job and tonight ...tonight he would need to go back to his office for...something. What reason could he give Marjorie?

# CHAPTER 12

Enid Sumser had decided to wait until Rita would be back from work before going round to see her. The rain had mercifully stopped so at about five o'clock, with the light already draining from the sky, she made her way to Wayneflete Avenue. She felt tired. She knew it was the worry, all day asking herself what had become of Jenny, the same question and answer endlessly. Had she run away? But why would she do that? She had nothing to run from.

Mrs Polesworth answered the door. "I wonder if I could have a word with your Rita? Only my Jenny didn't come home last night and I was wondering if she was with Rita."

"Come in." Mrs Polesworth's brow furrowed and she called up the stairs. "Rita. Someone here to see you."

The two women sat in the front room and waited. Enid Sumser noted that the furniture was in good condition. The front room looked rarely used. Three china ducks were on the wall as if flying, a small one, a larger one and an even larger one. They were the latest fashion. She noticed the clock on the mantelpiece was slow, only reading quarter past four but it was working - the second hand was moving.

Mrs Polesworth saw her eyes on the clock. "Oh that clock is slow again." She went into the kitchen to check the time, returning a moment later to adjust the clock. There were heavy footsteps on the stairs.

"Oh hello," Rita looked at Enid Sumser without recognition. Her lips pulled back in an attempted smile that had no warmth. Enid stood up.

"This is Mrs Sumser, Jenny's Mum. Jenny didn't come home last night. Was she with you?"

Rita coloured. "No...no she wasn't. We didn't see her last

night."

"Who were you out with then?" Her mother's voice had a slight edge.

"Just Maggie, that's all. We went to the WI Hall...they had a sort of dance class there. It wasn't up to much to be honest but we had a bit of a laugh."

"So my Jenny wasn't there?"

"No...no we didn't see her all night."

Enid Sumser felt her legs start to buckle and she slumped back onto the settee. "I don't know what could have happened to her. I'm worried. She's not the kind of girl to go off without saying anything. Something bad's happened, I'm sure of it."

"Now, now, don't go fretting. I'm sure there's a perfectly reasonable explanation. Does she have any other friends she might have gone to...an aunt or a cousin perhaps?" Mrs Polesworth wiped her hands again on the tea towel she was holding.

"We don't have any other family in these parts. We moved here from Rugby for my Arthur's work, see. He's on the railways, works at the top station." Enid Sumser looked at Rita, trying to control the fear that was gnawing inside her. "I wonder Rita...if you're out tonight, would you keep an eye open for her please?"

"Course."

Rita did not look at her as she was leaving the room . "She's a hard one...you wouldn't get much out of her," Enid muttered to herself as she walked wearily down the path on her way home. This had gone on too long. Something must have happened to Jenny. She felt an ache in her chest and her whole body was tensed with dread.

❖ ❖ ❖

Thankfully, the wind was dropping though Lizzie

noticed Robbie McBane still held his coat tight around him. He did not speak until they had reached the Sick Bay building.

"I think the storm is through, Lizzie, but we do need you to stay around here. Is that ok with your boss?"

"It'll have to be won't it? To be frank, much as I love flying and my job, I feel a need to help catch that poor girl's killer."

"Is there anything else you can think of that it would help me to know. Anything you've seen or anything that has occurred to you?"

"Well...I feel somewhat embarrassed to mention this but perhaps I should. Last night, I had dinner in the Officers Mess with Flight Lieutenants Driscoll and Dearing. The latter drunk far too much and was quite unpleasant. Edward Driscoll, in a very gentlemanly manner, escorted me back to my quarters and we left Dearing in the mess. A while later, Dearing turned up at my room wanting...you know...trying it on. It was quite frightening but I put him in his place and sent him packing. Thankfully he left but I suspect I've made an enemy."

"I took an instant dislike to the man. What ye tell me is no surprise. He's the sort who believes he can do what he wants. Born into privilege, always had what he wanted, probably a spoilt brat as a child. What time was it he came to your room?"

"It would have been at about twenty-one hundred hours... nine o'clock."

"What did you make of Driscoll? He seems to be in the shadows a bit."

"He is a gentleman, quite shy I think or perhaps...maybe a little secretive. He avoids direct eye contact."

"I think I'll start with him in the morning. Right now I need to find somewhere to stay. I'd rather not stay on the base."

"That sounds a good idea. Let's hope though the murderer is not looking for another victim tonight!"

"Are you afraid?"

Lizzie laughed. "No Sergeant, not me. I'm perfectly capable of looking after myself."

"It's Robbie, by the way. Do take care won't you... someone who can strangle another human being is a serious threat. No snooping about looking for suspects...that sort of thing. I can't afford to lose you...your powers of observation that is."

"Goodnight Serg...Robbie." Lizzie dropped her head to hide the smile on her face. Could it be that this rather serious Scotsman had feelings for her? The smile faded quickly, wiped by the turmoil she felt. Always there was that anxiety; she liked him but could she free herself enough to allow him in?

She watched him struggle to his car, head bent into the wind, then hurried inside the building. It was a relief to be out of the elements. She ran briskly upstairs to her room and let herself in. With a sigh, she tugged off her flying trousers and put on her suspender belt. Pulling her skirt on, she glanced in the mirror and saw her hair was a complete mess. She brushed it vigorously to untangle it and shook it so it fell into place. She sat on the bed and slid each stocking up her leg, the action giving her a small tingle of pleasure. Lifting the hem of her skirt, she attached the stockings to her suspender belt.

"That's better," she said to herself, feeling more civilised. "Now for something to eat." She had missed lunch and was hungry. She decided not to go to the Officers Mess as she did not want to see Dearing. She would eat in the nurses' small staffroom. Food was brought over from the kitchens. It would be what the airmen were given rather than what the officers ate but she was sure it would be wholesome and well cooked.

Patricia was in the nurses' staffroom. "Well now, look at you. How are you feeling?"

"I'm fine thanks Patricia. I've been busy with the investigation. I think, you know, that male detectives don't always see what we see. We women are natural detectives I think."

"We are surely. 'Tis because we're so nosey." Patricia's eyes flashed merriment.

Lizzie took in the room: it was small with a solid wooden table against one wall and a few armchairs on the opposite side. As with everything else, it was functional rather than comfortable.

"The food'll be over soon. One of the kitchen fellas brings it on a trolley." Patricia's voice became casual. "What can you tell me about the…investigation?"

"I don't think I should say anything…sorry…but you know how things are."

"Of course…I shouldn't have asked."

"It's natural to want to know. I can't help thinking about her family, the people who loved her. There's so much misery in the World with the war, no one needs any more."

"You're right. What did you make of Sergeant McBane? He's quite a dish I'd say."

"Probably spoken for I should think though he wore no wedding ring. He's fine."

"Ah maybe 'tis you have someone special."

"No…no one special. How about you?"

"Ah well, there's no time for that with the War. Matron would not allow any such thing." Patricia blushed and stood to look out of the window. "Where's that food. I'm getting ravenous."

"I always think when someone changes the subject that they're hiding something," Lizzie teased. "Come on now, you can tell me. I promise to keep it to myself."

"Well there may be someone…but…I couldn't confirm that."

"You're being very mysterious. It must be someone on the base."

"Stop fishing. You wouldn't tell me about the murder so you'll not get anything more out of me on that subject."

Before Lizzie could probe further, the door opened and Matron strode in. The severity Lizzie had noticed in her expression that morning had not disappeared. Her manner was brusque, evident in the way she pulled the chair back from the table and sat down. Lizzie had half risen from her seat, a sign of respect drummed into her as a child but Matron did not seem to notice.

"I wonder what delight they'll serve us up tonight?"

"I don't care what it is, I'm famished and I'm on duty tonight. I need a good feed to keep me going. You must be hungry too, Lizzie – you had no lunch."

"Today's events rather dulled my appetite but I am ready for something now."

Matron turned her penetrating eyes on Lizzie as if she could see what she was thinking. "I hear it was a girl and not fully dressed."

"I'd rather not talk about it, Matron, if you don't mind."

"Probably some young hussy, too ready to spread her legs for any man. This war is destroying the morals of the young in this country. No backbone."

Patricia looked down at the table but said nothing. Lizzie was not going to let that go unchallenged. "That may be true for some, Matron, but it is certainly not true for all of us. I know I've retained my morals and I'm sure Patricia has too."

Matron clearly did not like being challenged and the three sat in awkward silence for some minutes until the food arrived, the young man barging the trolley noisily through the door and bustling about.

Sergeant Bailey lifted the telephone receiver and glanced at the clock on the wall as he did so. Five forty-five. It would soon be going home time for him and PC Grant as the station was not manned overnight. He was ready to put his feet up but hometime always made him jocular.

"Brackley Police Station, Sergeant Bailey at your

disposal. What can I do you for?"

"Inspector Fletcher here. Your humour is somewhat mis-placed Sergeant. I could have been someone in desperate trouble."

"Oh sorry, Sir. Didn't mean any harm. Just like to keep people smiling…so much bad news what with the war."

"Quite. I've just come from Silverstone RAF base. You'll remember there was a report of a body found in one of the buildings. We need to check whether any missing persons have been reported recently. The body is of a young woman. Have you had any reports of a young woman missing?"

"Blimey! I have as it happens, Sir. This morning, a Mrs Sumser said her Jenny had not returned home last night. She went out with friends, is always reliable and comes back at about eleven o'clock but she didn't last night and was still not back this morning. I told the lady to check with her friends in case she stayed with one of them, went straight to work this morning that sort of thing."

"What was she wearing?"

"Well she had an overcoat on and a scarf on her head… oh you mean the daughter. Can't say, Sir. We didn't get that far."

"So have you been to see if this girl has turned up since? Have you checked her workplace?"

"No…no Sir, I've not. I expect she'll be back home by now. You know what young people are like these days… gadding about, no thought for their poor parents."

"You need to visit the home and find out…right away."

"Yes, Sir, of course Sir."

"And 'phone me back here at Towcester to let me know one way or the other. And, if she's not back, get a description of her and what she was wearing."

"Of course, Sir. I'll get back to you." Sergeant Bailey replaced the receiver and swore softly under his breath. Another late night. Why couldn't people just stay at home? PC Phil Grant was sorting some paperwork at his desk. "I've got to go and check on a missing girl. You're in charge now. Lock up at six. See you tomorrow." He shrugged his cape on and lifted his helmet from the stand. "It's all I need traipsing round the town on a night like this."

"It's not raining now Sarge."

"Thanks for nothing. I'd rather be at home tucking into me dinner."

"Hey Sarge, did you hear about Hitler and Goering standing on top of the Berlin radio tower surveying the damage after a bombing raid. Hitler says 'What should I do to cheer up the Berlin people?' Goering said, 'You could jump mein Fuhrer.' Good one eh?"

"Where do you get these from Grant?"

"Wireless last night, Sir."

"Let's hope they do some funny ones soon."

"Bye, Sarge. Cheer up." Phil Grant grinned.

# CHAPTER 13

Robbie McBane let the car roll to a stop on the road outside The Silver Swan inn. The sign bearing its name hung from a large iron frame above the door and was swinging in the wind. Though the clouds were thick, some moonlight was penetrating, giving everything an unworldly sense of mystery. When he had slammed the car door shut, he stood for a moment listening to the creaking sound from the sign. Had he been a believer in ghosts and such nonsense, he would have found it eerie, attached as it was to a low, two-storey building made of old grey stone. Due to blackout regulations, there was no welcoming porch light. He hefted his bag in his right hand, using his other to push open the heavy door.

He was immediately greeted by warmth and he saw with pleasure the log fire crackling cheerfully at one end of the room. The floor was flag stones, the walls stone with horse brasses and pictures of country scenes. The smell of cigarette and pipe smoke hung in the air, not unpleasantly, adding to the impression of a place of relaxation. Two old men were sitting on stools at the bar. They both turned to look at him but then resumed their positions facing the optics shelves at the back of the bar and saying nothing. A classic country pub and a welcome escape from the dreary base where he was clearly viewed with suspicion.

"Would the landlord or landlady be about?" he asked.

The old man nearest to him nodded. "Ah." He made no move to fetch him nor any attempt to call him.

Robbie McBane waited a few seconds and then called "Hello" loudly

A minute or so later, a tall man in his fifties came through to the bar from a doorway into the back. He had a full stomach which he projected almost proudly in front of him, holding his shoulders back and his head up. Looking down his hooked beak of a nose, he regarded the newcomer with a degree of suspicion.

"Evenin'. What can I get you?"

"I was wond'ring if you have a room for the night?"

The landlord looked surprised. "You from the base?"

"I'm visiting there t' do some work." Robbie McBane could see the landlord was puzzled. "I prefer to stay overnight off the base."

The landlord nodded. "We have rooms. Is it just the one night?"

"Well it's definitely tonight but I may need it another one or two nights. I'm not sure how long things are going to take. Is that possible?"

"Of course." The landlord seemed to be a bit more cheerful now and Robbie put that down to the prospect of some income from letting a room. "I'll show you up now."

"Can you provide an evening meal?"

"Naturally. I'll show you to your room and then if you'd like to come down, the missus'll let you know what's on offer."

"Thank you." Robbie looked at the two old men but neither moved. They watched him with sidelong glances but said nothing.

The room was comfortable, sparsely furnished, but he needed very little – a bed and a chair would serve but a heavy Victorian wardrobe and chest of drawers skulked against the wall. Floral print curtains which rather clashed with the floral wallpaper, were drawn to cover the blackouts at the window. A little way along the corridor was a bathroom which again was fit for purpose. The accommodation would do him very well and meant he would not have to make conversation with the ranks on the base who would almost certainly be after information. He needed to keep them at arm's length as they were all suspects until proved otherwise.

A short while later, McBane returned to the bar where

the two old men were still sitting, nursing the same pints of beer by the look of it. He ordered a pint and as it was being poured, the landlady, Mrs Rogers, came into the bar. She was completely unlike her husband, immediately friendly, welcoming and garrulous. She was short, probably not much over five feet were she in bare feet, and rather rotund; she laughed frequently at nothing in particular and was clearly disposed to chatter. She seemed much more suited to the job of running an inn than her husband.

"Oooh, it's horrible out there isn't it? I expect you'd like something to warm you up. Oh, by the way, before I go on, do you have your ration coupons 'cos obviously I'll need them to replace the food we use. It's terrible isn't it this war? I mean it's so embarrassing asking people for coupons when they want something to eat."

Robbie McBane reached into his jacket pocket and extracted his ration book. They quickly agreed which coupons she would need and what his meal would be. That settled, he relaxed onto a stool at the bar and took a long pull from his glass of bitter. It tasted good and he felt himself calming. The events of the day had put him on edge, making him feel out of his depth never having handled a murder investigation before. At least he had Fletcher for guidance.

"D'ye get many chaps from the base in here of an evening?"

"We do." Again Mr Rogers looked a bit more cheerful. "Mondays and Thursdays is quieter. I think some of them must have things to do those evenings but otherwise we get a good number."

Robbie McBane's attention was aroused by the mention of Mondays and Thursdays. Yesterday was Monday and that was when the girl had been murdered. If none of them had been here, he would know that any attempt to give that as an alibi was false. "So you had no one from the base in last night?"

"We did have a couple but not many. Like I said, Mondays tend to be quiet. We had these two old rogues though."

The two old men chuckled, a sound that started as a cackle and ended with wheezing.         "We're always here, ain't we Bert?"

"We are that Sid. Reckon the master of the house makes a good bit from us."

"It costs me more to keep the fire going than I make on what you two drink."

Robbie McBane was disappointed. If a couple of the men from the base had been here, that would provide an alibi. He reminded himself that he needed to relax, switch off. He addressed the landlord again. "The opening of the base has been gud for business?"

"Certainly has. I suppose there are some benefits to the war. We should be getting some of 'em from the base a bit later."

Robbie hesitated, wondering whether to say anything. "Most are confined to base tonight." The landlord looked surprised. "Probably something to do with the weather or... something."

Once again, the landlord's eyes lost all lustre. No good takings tonight then. Mrs Rogers bustled in with a tray and set it down noisily on one of the tables. Robbie thanked her and sat down before it, the smell of the sprouts reminding him that he was hungry. There was a good mound of mashed potato and a plump leg of boiled chicken all smothered in a rich gravy.

"That's one of our own chickens and the sprouts and spuds come from one of the farms in the village," she announced proudly.

"Lovely. Thank you."

The landlady hovered by the table. "So you're up visiting the base then are you?"

"That's right."

"I expect you're doing some training? Are you a pilot? Oooh it must be ever so hard flying one of them things and all that flak they have to go through when they go bombing

Germany."

"No…I'm not a pilot. I don't actually fly. I have a ground job." Robbie McBane was self-conscious when he was eating. To have someone so near him scrutinising every mouthful he took was very off-putting.

"You're a sergeant ain't you?"

"That's right. Mmmm this is lovely. Thank you. I don't want to keep you…"

"Oh you're not keeping me. It's so quiet I've nothing else to do."

Robbie McBane's heart sank. He just wanted to enjoy his dinner without the questions. He was sure they would become more intrusive as the conversation continued so he decided he would take the initiative. "Do the chaps from the base have much to do with the locals?"

"We see some of them in here of a night and there's been occasional things. Course it's not been open long. But they did have a dance on Saturday in the village hall for Valentine's night you know. Quite a do it was. My Albert did a bar for them and all the villagers were invited though it was mainly the young'uns went…the girls really. There aren't that many girls in the village – it's quite small you see – but they put on a coach from Brackley and Buckingham and quite a few came from there."

"That was a good gesture. It went well I hope."

"So I believe though I was stuck here. I'd have liked to have gone…not much chance of dancing round here, what with the war and all." She paused, a wistful look in her eyes. "Still I'm sure there'll be plenty of other events. I mean the base hasn't been open long. They were building it last year and I think it officially opened beginning of January." She turned to the bar and called to her husband, "Albert, was it January the base opened?"

"Yep. Right at the beginning, though there were people there last year building it and so on."

The landlady rattled on only pausing to take away his

dinner plate and come back with a very welcome serving of apple pie and custard. The apples were from their own garden, stored in the outhouse since being picked in the Autumn apparently. They were good. The pie and custard were excellent and it was clear to Robbie McBane that food was easier to come by here in the country than in the towns. There was a good trade in bartered goods, he was sure, and he wondered whether his food coupons were really needed. His meal was finished with a cup of Camp coffee, the bitterness of the chicory welcome after the sweet pie.

A few locals came into the bar but Robbie did not feel like chatting. He had picked up as much local information as he was likely to on his first night. Perhaps more would be revealed when he was less of a newcomer. He bade the hosts goodnight and retired to his room.

Enid Sumser heard the front door close and her husband do what he did every night – put his coat and hat on the stand, sigh and clump through to the back room for his dinner. She braced herself, wiping her face once more with her apron, trying to remove the evidence of her tears, before joining him.

"What's up, Love, you look terrible?" He stepped close to her and laid a gentle hand on her shoulder.

She could say nothing but burst into tears and it was some time before, his arms around her, he could quieten her enough to speak.

"It's our Jenny. She didn't come home last night and she's still not back now. Something's happened to her, I know it."

"Now steady on, steady on. She probably went to a friend's last night."

"I went round to Maggie Bennett's and to Rita Polesworth and they both said they didn't see her last night.

So who was she with and where is she now? She wouldn't have just gone off would she? Not Jenny? She's not like that."

"We should inform the police, Love. They'll keep a lookout for her."

"I did, I went to the station this morning. The nice sergeant said I should check her friends which is why I went round."

"We need to tell them then that she's still not back and we don't know where she is."

The loud knock on the door startled them both. "Perhaps that's her," Enid said clutching her hands together."

"She's got a key, Love. She wouldn't knock. If she'd lost her key, she'd come round the back."

Arthur Sumser approached the front door cautiously, as if there may be danger lurking outside. He took a step back when he saw the burly police officer in the porch, seeming to fill it.

"Mr Sumser? It's Sergeant Bailey from Brackley Police. I'm just checking on whether your Jenny has turned up."

"No Sergeant, she hasn't. I've just got home from work and been told by my wife. You'd better come in."

Sergeant Bailey's cheery manner disappeared as he perched on the edge of the slightly-worn, moquette settee with his notebook and pencil, asking questions and noting the replies. He knew he had to be thorough or incur the wrath of Inspector Fletcher. The description of Jenny was easy enough, height, hair colour and so on, but when it came to what she was wearing, the Sumsers could not say.

"She had her coat on when she came in to say goodbye so we didn't see what she was wearing. Besides, I was knitting and Arthur was reading the paper. We just checked she had her key and off she went."

"What sort of coat was she wearing...what colour?"

"Well I suppose you'd call it beige, tan, something like that. She was very proud of her coat. Saved up for ages to buy it. I think it was called the Hollywood style. She desperately wanted one like that…she was really into the films and film stars. You know the sort of coat, Sergeant, big lapels, thick belt of the same material. It was wool…expensive." Enid Sumser stopped suddenly.

"I'm not too familiar with ladies fashions but I'm sure there'll be other officers who will be able to recognise it. Hollywood style is the key and the colour."

"What are you able to do, Sergeant?" Arthur Sumser's voice was not challenging but practical.

"I'll alert all patrols, we may talk with her friends again, check pubs and so on to see if anyone saw her last evening. If you think of anything, anything at all, you must let us know." Sergeant Bailey stood up as did the Sumsers. He shook hands with each. "Now don't you worry Mrs Sumser. She'll turn up I'm sure."

Enid Sumser's eyes began to fill with tears again as Arthur closed the door. In the space of a few hours, her world had collapsed just as it had done when they received the telegram about George, her first born. She could not bear the loss of her remaining child.

# CHAPTER 14

After removing his shoes, Robbie lay on the bed thinking through the key information gleaned from the day and worrying like a dog with a bone at the connection there may be between the fuel use, log book discrepancies and the awful death of the young woman. Was fuel being sold on the black market, or perhaps traded for some kind of favours? Or was there a simple and legitimate explanation? Was the young woman at the dance on Saturday? Had some kind of arrangement been made?

Amidst these serious thoughts, McBane remembered he had not arranged a time with the landlady for breakfast. He slipped on his shoes and stepped slowly down the dark stairwell to return to the bar. The door into it was ajar and light spilled down the corridor onto the bottom steps of the stairs. As he approached the door, he heard a voice he recognised. A Welsh accent, a surly tone. He stopped and listened.

"So if anyone asks, I was here last night. Got that?"

"Why would anyone be asking?" It was the landlord.

"Just in case, alright."

"Fine. You were here. We've got a fella staying here from the base tonight. D'you know him? A Sergeant McBane."

"McBane. I met him alright. He's the one who may be asking. Just watch what you say look."

"Alright. Don't get in a lather. You should know me by now. Mum's the word."

"Good. You wouldn't want to lose a good supply of provisions now would you?"

"There's no need for that kind of threat. I know which side me bread's buttered."

Robbie waited until he heard the steps on the

flagstones and the door close noisily before strolling with deliberate nonchalance into the bar. He sorted out breakfast arrangements with the landlord and returned to his room. No one should have left the base tonight but he knew who that was. Davies. Preparing his alibi. Why would he need to do that if he were not involved?

Lying on the bed, questions started to roll around his mind, merging with each other but his thoughts kept returning to one image: the face of Lizzie Barnes. He swung his legs off the bed and rummaged in his kit bag, tenderly lifting out the picture of Catriona. He held her for a long time, gazing at her beautiful face. But as he scrutinised it, the face of Lizzie Barnes floated over it. In many ways they were so similar. Both had a fineness and gentleness in their features, the delicate nose, the soft cheeks, the line of the jaw. But it was the eyes that drew him. Lizzie had the same intelligence, vitality as Catriona and she had a playfulness of manner that reminded him so much of the woman he had lost.

Robbie set the picture on the bedside cabinet. Could it be that he may be able to love another? Was that a betrayal or a reasonable thing? Would Catriona approve a relationship with another? Was he ready for that?

The wind was no longer rattling the windows, the storm slowly departing like a lingering and unwelcome guest, but Lizzie could not sleep. Every time she closed her eyes, the image of that poor girl appeared and then her mind churned with possibilities. She could not help feeling that Dearing was somehow responsible for her death though she had absolutely no evidence.

She tossed in her bed, turning every few minutes but unable to get sufficiently comfortable to induce sleep. In the end, she swung her legs out of bed and crossed to the window.

Pulling back the blackout curtain, she looked out. Two guards were huddled inside the sentry box. She felt for them…it was a cold duty, even though the worst of the storm had passed.

"I'll go and talk to Patricia," she whispered to herself. "She'll be bored on her own in the ward."

She slipped on her skirt over her nightdress and pulled a sweater over her head. Turning the door handle slowly, she stepped outside in her bare feet, the wooden floor chilling her toes, and groped her way along the wall in the darkness to the top of the stairs. With great care, she negotiated each step until she arrived at the corridor that led into the ward. A light was burning further along by the office where she assumed Patricia would be.

It was easier now she could see but, when she arrived at the office door which was ajar, there was no sign of Patricia. A single bulb illuminated the small office, a desk with a solitary chair and a cupboard that was secured with a padlock and which presumably contained medicines.

Lizzie assumed she would be on the ward so she continued along the corridor and into the ward, pushing open one of the green swing doors. She stopped and peered from bed to bed. There were only humps on three beds presumably the occupants she had seen in the morning. Patricia was nowhere to be seen. As she turned to leave the ward, she noticed the clock on the wall; it was eleven minutes past eleven. Lizzie decided she would have to forego a conversation with Patricia and do her best to sleep.

Lizzie returned along the corridor and, as she passed a door marked 'Store', was sure she heard murmurs, voices, very quiet. She stopped and listened. Two voices, one male and then one female. She recognised it as Patricia's. She was about to knock on the door and open it when she stopped, listening intently.

The male voice: "We just continue being careful, that's all."

Patricia: "But the Police will be snooping about…they're

bound to find out."

"They won't have any interest in us so just calm down."

Lizzie was sure she recognised that voice. She had heard it before. Definitely not Dearing but perhaps...

"What if they find out about your brother?" Patricia again.

"What if they do? I'm doing my bit...he's back in Ireland. He didn't as far as I know do anything. It's just what he believed at the time."

"I'm still nervous."

"I can see that but there's no need to be. It's Matron you need to be careful of. Come here."

The voices stopped. Lizzie heard the sound of kisses, a stifled giggle. She felt suddenly embarrassed to be spying on such an intimate moment. She stepped away hurriedly in case the door opened and re-traced her steps swiftly to the foot of the stairs. So this was Patricia's secret lover, a relationship that matron would not sanction. She wondered whether to hover there and perhaps check her suspicions as to the identity of Patricia's lover but she decided to return to her room.

"Will the body be there still, Corp?"

"Course not, you idiot. They took it away late this afternoon. Got to do a post-mortem on it."

The two figures crept along the rear of the huts, hugging the shadows where the arc lights did not shine. When they reached Hut Fifteen where the body had been discovered, the first one took a bunch of keys from his greatcoat pocket and unlocked the outer door.

"You stand there and you give me a shout if you see anyone approaching. Don't let 'em see you right."

The first figure disappeared inside and, without turning on a light, crept along the corridor to a room. He stopped and took a breath before turning the handle and slipping in. Drawing back one of the blackout curtains allowed dim light into the room from the distant floodlights. Systematically, he checked under the bed, in every drawer, inside the empty wardrobe. Nothing. Producing a torch from his greatcoat pocket, he closed the curtain and left the room. The torch made a small pool of light on the corridor floor and he checked the full length of it. Nothing.

Each room along the corridor was checked in turn, the beam from the torch piercing the darkness like a miniature searchlight. Nothing at all. At the end of each search, the word 'shit' was hissed in an angry whisper.

He returned to the outside of the building. "Nothing at all. Either it wasn't dropped in there or it's been found."

"If it's been found, that's a problem isn't it?"

"Too right it is. And if you'd done your job properly, there wouldn't be this problem."

"It's not my fault, Corp. What was I supposed to do? I asked if everyone was in…no one said anything so I banged on the back and off he went."

"Just make sure you keep your trap shut, right?"

"You can rely on me Corp. I'll not say a word."

"Hopefully they'll be looking to pin it on Staples. As long as Smiffy and Webster keep quiet, we might be ok. What a bastard thing though."

"I guess that will put a stop to things won't it?"

"Until the dust settles. We lay low, keep our heads down. If everyone keeps their nerve we should be ok."

The two figures slunk back in the shadow of the buildings towards the residential huts.

❖ ❖ ❖

Reaching the landing, Lizzie glanced down the corridor which, as on the ground floor below, ran along the centre almost the full length of the building. At the end was Matron's room – she assumed rather larger than those of the nurses – and a crack of light showed around the door. Matron was either still up or she kept the light on overnight. Should she investigate? What could she say if she knocked on the door and a ferocious Matron flung it open?

Discretion was clearly a better path than valour so she opened her own room door. As she stepped inside, she heard Matron's door open. She closed her own silently and listened to the steps, barely audible, as Matron walked on tip toe down the corridor. Should she go out and stop her, perhaps make a big noise so that Patricia would be alerted? Her instinct, however, told her to wait and watch. Lizzie's own room light was still off and she waited until she heard the steps on the stair before easing the door open enough to see out.

There was only just enough light from the hospital corridor to reveal that Matron had reached the half-landing and was turning to descend the second section of stairs. She was wearing a dark overcoat, perhaps a cape, it was impossible to tell but she was dressed to go outdoors. Where could she be going? Should she follow her? But she would have to dress and put on stockings and shoes to follow her outside. By the time she had done that, Matron would probably have disappeared.

It may be quite innocent. Perhaps she had been called to a sick airman? Perhaps…on the other hand…

Lizzie closed her door softly and sat on her bed, digesting these latest revelations. What did Patricia mean about his brother who was back in Ireland? What might that brother have done? Where was Matron going at this time of night? She must tell Robbie McBane about all this in the morning.

Robbie McBane…a good-looking chap with his fine physique and strong features; she could forgive him his red hair. His accent was attractive, not the harsh, guttural sound of some parts of Scotland, though she suspected it had been modified by being in the South for a few years. He was intriguing too. It was that look in his eyes, something remote as if he were determined to hold everyone at bay, do his job, never really engage.

She remembered the look on his face when he had seen the dead girl, a look that had been full of pity as though he wanted to take her in his arms and cradle her. And then anger, that fierce determination to find the killer. He was driven by something, some tragedy she guessed and he would find that killer of that she had no doubt. She would try to play her part, keeping her wits about her. For a moment she pictured Dearing being arrested, handcuffed, led away to the waiting police car, before reminding herself that she must not jump to conclusions.

She returned to the bed and tried to clear her mind. Eventually, sleep claimed her, a troubled sleep in which killers lurked in cavernous aircraft hangars and grinned savagely like a distorted image of the German fighter pilot the previous day.

# PART 3: WEDNESDAY 17TH FEBRUARY 1943

## CHAPTER 15

"Now here's a test of your local knowledge, Grant. Where would I find Staples the plumber? He's definitely a Brackley man 'cause I've seen his van about."

"No idea Sarge. You could try the phone book."

"I've got a better idea. You try the phone book, you ring the number and find out where he is. Then I'll go and see him."

"I could see him if you want Sarge."

"No I'll do that bit. You'll end up telling him jokes instead of asking the right questions. Oh and by the way, when I'm out, make sure everything is ship-shape. Fletcher's coming later…we've got to see that couple…you know with the missing daughter."

"Have they found her, Sarge?"

"Maybe."

Phil Grant established that Andy Staples the plumber was working in one of the big houses at the top of the town. Sergeant Bailey swore, swung his leg over his bicycle and adjusted his cape so it covered his legs. The last thing he needed was cycling up that hill. He set off, wobbling slightly until he had gained a bit more speed. He arrived at Acacia Avenue quite breathless and pedalled slowly along to number seven. The number was on one gatepost, the house name, 'New Swan Stone' on the other. Leaning his bike against the garage wall, he took his time removing his cycle clips, wondering why such a strange name had been chosen. The green van with "Staples Plumber" emblazoned on the sides was parked in the driveway.

Sergeant Bailey took his helmet from the saddle bag and straightened his tie before ringing the doorbell. He stood in the porch looking out at the gravel drive sweeping round to the gate, mature trees gently swaying in the much-reduced wind. The door was opened and when he turned, he saw an elegant woman in a tapered skirt, blouse and an expensive-looking cardigan.

"Hello officer. What I can do for you?"

Bailey's eye rested on the string of pearls around her neck while he tried to identify what it was about her voice or what she had said that surprised him. It had a clipped tone; she looked thoroughly home counties...very attractive too. "I believe Mr Andrew Staples the plumber is working here. I need to ask him a few questions. Perhaps..."

"I'll call him. A new bathroom he's fitting. Do wait there, officer."

There it was again, an unusual word order. But Sergeant Bailey dismissed the thought. Perhaps he was imagining things...German spies even in a small Northamptonshire town! This war did make you suspicious of everyone.

"Hello." Andy Staples' eyes flicked rapidly over Sergeant Bailey and away again. "You want to ask me some questions?"

"Yes, Sir. Nothing to worry about. I understand you do work at the Silverstone RAF base sometimes."

"That's right...yeah I do. Quite often actually – I did a lot when it was being built."

"And were you called to go there yesterday afternoon... three or four o'clock time?"

"No. I was working here. Why?"

"Can anyone vouch for you?" Even as he asked the question, he thought it sounded daft.

"I'll call Mrs Chalmers, the lady you just met." He disappeared and a minute later came back with the woman who had answered the door. She looked annoyed."

"Mr Staples was working here all the day yesterday until about five o'clock. Is that what you need to know, officer?"

"Thank you, Madam. We just need to eliminate people from our enquiries. You know how it is."

"Right. If that is all, officer, perhaps Mr Staples can the job continue."

Sergeant Bailey returned to his bicycle. He was disappointed. He always liked to see how the other half lived and a cup of tea sitting on a comfortable sofa would have been very welcome. He sighed. "Que sera..." At least he could report to Fletcher that Staples was in the clear.

Robbie McBane had made an early start in the morning. The wind had dropped to a fresh breeze and greyish clouds raced across the sky but with nothing like the fury of the previous day. When he stepped out of his car, he heard again the raucous calls of rooks sitting at the top of the tall trees like spiteful old men in black laughing at him.

He had obtained the rota for gate sentry duty and identified AC Smith and AC Webster as having been on duty late afternoon and evening of Monday, the day Lizzie had seen the truck leave the base on two occasions that had not been recorded in the log. He had commandeered the other office in Hut Fifteen, the hut where the body had been found, so that he was close to Fletcher's operations base. A calendar block sat on the table and, being a stickler for accuracy, he changed it to read Wednesday 17th February 1943.

AC Smith sat bolt upright in front of him, defiance in every sinew of his body.

"Tell me AC Smith, what is the usual practice for signing vehicles and personnel in and out of the base."

"Simple, Sir. We write 'em dahn in the log." Smith's

London accent was even more pronounced than his own Glaswegian.

"Is this the log?"

"Looks like it, yeah."

"I understand you were on gate duty from sixteen hundred hours on Monday of this week. Is that correct?"

"Yep."

Robbie McBane's eyes narrowed. He was alert to the slightest sign of insubordination and was already ready to snap at the cocky individual in front of him. "Was there anything out of the ordinary that day, any unusual visitors, any unexpected departures?"

"Can't rightly remember. Anything that 'appened will be in th' log."

"You were on duty with AC Webster. Which of you wrote the entries in the log?"

"What d'you mean?"

"The question is plain enough, AC Smith. Did you write the entries on Monday or did AC Webster?"

"I guess we both did."

"How many times did you have to open the gate?"

"Just when it says in the log."

"So just the once then?"

Smith leaned back in the chair and looked out of the window. "Can't really remember."

"You can't remember only one occasion when the gate was opened? Who was it that came in or left?"

Smith cleared his throat. "Can't remember."

Robbie McBane snorted. "Can't? Won't is what you mean." He flipped the log book open and leaned forward to hold it in front of Smith. "One entry for Staples the plumber who came onto the base at 4.30 pm. No further entries. So Mr Staples never left. Is that correct?"

"Well, yeah, if that's what the log says."

"And who wrote that entry about Staples arriving?"

"It's not my handwriting."

"That's not what I asked. Who wrote that entry? Was it Webster or perhaps someone else?"

Smith's head thrust forward, his voice belligerent. "You'll have to ask Webster. It wasn't me."

"I may well want to talk with you again, AC Smith, and indeed the Police may want to talk to you."

Smith shrugged and rose. "Can I go now...Sir?"

"Aye, ye can."

Robbie McBane watched him swagger out of the room. He had already arranged for Webster to be brought to another, empty room in the building so that the two could not confer though he realised they may have done previously. He put his head round the door of that room and asked Webster to come with him. The airman sat on the chair, legs apart and leaned forward with his elbows on his knees. He was gripping his hat between his hands, passing it from one to the other.

McBane went through the same preliminary questions. Webster's answers were far less sure, mumbled, evasive. Robbie's instinct was aroused. This one would tell him something.

"It's Stanley isn't it? May I call you Stanley?"

"Stan...I prefer to be called Stan"

"So, Stan, I imagine you don't record absolutely every movement through the gates...I mean, when you get regular trips out by personnel you know, there seems little point."

Webster shuffled in his chair and twisted his hat, the knuckles of his hands whitening.          "We record just about all movements."

"Yes but not absolutely every one."

Webster lowered his eyes. 'No Sir, not every one."

"So the two trips out and presumably return of the truck on Monday were not recorded because they happen every Monday?"

"Um...I think...sometimes they don't...don't get recorded."

"And were they recorded on Monday of this week?"

116

"I couldn't say without looking at the book, Sir."

"You see, Stan, I have a witness who says that the truck numbered RAF 142031 left the base at about seventeen hundred hours. It must have come back in at some point because it was seen leaving again at about twenty-two hundred hours. Would that be right?"

Webster's face twisted in agony. "Sir, please don't tell 'em it was me who said. It would be bad...you know."

Robbie leaned forward with the log book open in front of him. "Did you write that entry about Staples the plumber?"

Webster shook his head. "No Sir. That's not my writing."

"Did AC Smith?"

"I can't say for sure but we used a black pen. If you look where we've signed our names when we came on duty."

"Thank you Stan, That will be all for now."

"And you won't say, Sir...that I said anything about..."

"No need for me to. We've got an eye witness."

AC Webster stood up and exhaled deeply, relief in every muscle of his face.

Lizzie took the sheet from Patricia and made the last fold in it whilst Patricia picked up her end of the next. "Lots of sheets to fold."

"Yep. At least we don't have to wash and iron them. The ladies should really fold them too but they're too busy. And I don't mind...rather be busy than sitting around idle."

"As if you'd get the chance for that with Matron."

"True."

The two young women worked for a while in silence. Lizzie was wondering how she should broach what she had witnessed the previous night. Should she say anything to Patricia about the man in the store room and about Matron's nocturnal ramble...wherever it was she went? In the end she decided to broach at least the first.

"Last night, I couldn't sleep at all what with you know... I came down here to see you...thought a chat might help."

Patricia busied herself with a pillow case, her head bent. "Oh yes."

"I couldn't find you."

"I must have been with a patient."

"No...I checked the ward." Lizzie paused but Patricia said nothing. Her movements were becoming more rapid and Lizzie could see her neck colouring. "I did hear you though...I think you were in the store. There was another voice."

Suddenly Patricia looked up, alarm on her face. "Lizzie, please...it's nothing but ...Matron mustn't know. I know I shouldn't..."

"It's ok Patricia. I'm not going to tell anyone." Lizzie paused, wondering whether to go on. "You know, Patricia, Matron is just a bully. Perhaps you should tell her straight about it and let her say what she likes."

"It's easy for you to say that but she has some power and she'd have no qualms about using it. She could easily get me re-assigned elsewhere and then where would that leave me?"

"Yes...I suppose she could."

Lizzie's mind flashed through the situations she had encountered, starting with that time at school when she had been bullied. It was Abigail Weston who had been the ringleader, stirring up a little gaggle of other girls when they had all started at boarding school. She had not confronted her physically but had dug around until she had found out something about Abigail that she wanted kept secret.

"There must be a way of finding out something about her, something that would give you some leverage," Lizzie mused aloud.

"That would be grand but I've no idea how one would do that."

"In the meantime, I think you should be more careful. I could hear the other voice was a man's but I couldn't be sure who it was. Perhaps it was that special person?"

"Ok it's someone on the base but I'm not saying who."

"That's fine...I'll just speculate then." Lizzie's eyes sparkled with mischief but she did not pursue it. She changed tack. "You may not have realised but, last night, Matron was out on the prowl."

Patricia's eyes opened wide with alarm. "What d'you mean out on the prowl?"

"When I went back upstairs to my room, she came out of hers in a cloak or big overcoat went down the stairs and out of the building."

"What time was this?"

"It would have been about half past eleven."

Patricia's brow furrowed. "Wherever was she going at that time I wonder?"

"Perhaps she has a secret lover. Maybe she's having an affair with Lovell."

The two young women giggled like schoolgirls. "God sure that'd be a sight."

A sudden presence in the doorway made them both jump. "Sorry. Didn't mean to startle you. Just wondering if you know what's for lunch. I'm starving already." Brian Saunders stood grinning at them boyishly. "Perhaps you would care to join me for luncheon Second Officer Barnes. I know Nurse O'Flynn will be too busy."

"Are you in the Rolls today?"

He shook his head. "Sorry, 'fraid not but," he broke into song, " you'll look sweet on your own two feet or on a bicycle made for two." He attempted to turn in a circle as if dancing, hopping on his one good leg, but fell against the shelving.

"God sure you'll injure your other leg, you eejit and then we'll never be rid of you."

"Nurse O'Flynn has such a lovely way with words. It's the Irish blood you know. They may not have given us the ports but they've given us Nurse O'Flynn."

"On yer way before I give you a clout on the ear."

Saunders turned to Lizzie. "She models herself on Stalin, you know, whereas Matron emulates Hitler. Not sure there's much difference."

"Out."

Brian Saunders grinned and hobbled away from the store room.

# CHAPTER 16

Flight Lieutenant Dearing lolled back in the chair. "You do realise, Sergeant, that we need to start flying again as the weather has improved. We have an important job to do. Commander Harris will want aircrew to bomb Germany soon I'm sure. We can't leave it to the Americans."

The public school drawl, the patronising smile, the arrogant tilt of the head backwards angered McBane. "I realise that, Sir. But this is a murder. Firstly, please talk me through your movements on Monday evening."

"My movements?" Dearing gave a hollow laugh. "Well I went to the toilet at about… oh, I see, my movements."

McBane did not flinch. He waited for Dearing to go on.

"Well let me see. I went to the Mess at about eighteen hundred hours. Had a couple of drinks, had supper…with Driscoll and that ATA pilot as it happens so you can check that…and left at about twenty hundred hours. I then went back to my quarters, read a book and went to bed at about twenty-two hundred hours."

"Do you recognise this, Sir?" McBane laid the comb on the desk between them, watching for the slightest narrowing of Dearing's eyes that would tell him he did.

Dearing gave him a sickly smile. "It's a comb, Sergeant. Civilised people use them to keep their hair in order."

"Do you own a comb, Sir?"

"I own several. If you're asking me whether it's mine, frankly, I've no idea." He shrugged. "Could be but there again, maybe not."

"Thank you, Sir." Robbie McBane took the cigarette case, still wrapped in his handkerchief, from his pocket and laid it on the table. Again he watched Dearing's eyes carefully as he folded back the handkerchief to reveal the case. He was surprised that there was no flicker of recognition in Dearing's eyes. A doubt crept into his mind but Dearing could be a practised liar. "Do you recognise this, Sir?"

"No. At least I don't think so. I might have seen it before but it doesn't ring a bell."

McBane opened the case carefully, using the handkerchief to prevent his own fingerprints disturbing those already on it. "As you see Sir, the initials are RD."

Dearing lifted his eyes from the case to McBane's face. He smiled and then scoffed derisively. "Oh I see. So I suppose you found this somewhere incriminating and because it has initials matching my own, you decide I'm the killer. You'll have to do better than that Sergeant. That case is not mine....from here it looks cheap. I don't smoke...not cigarettes anyway, perhaps the occasional cigar. But if I did, I'd have a better quality case than that."

Dearing's arrogance was on full display and McBane knew it was a criticism of himself, a put-down.

"There must be plenty of other people with the initials RD anyway," Dearing added and looked out of the window as if bored by the whole process.

McBane wrapped the cigarette case in the handkerchief and replaced it in his pocket. "You said that after dinner, you went straight back to your quarters. But that isn't quite true is it, Sir?"

"What d'you mean?" Dearing was suddenly aggressive.

"I am told by Miss Barnes that you visited her at her room at approximately twenty-one hundred hours – nine o'clock - in rather a poor state."

Dearing's mouth narrowed and fear or was it anger flashed in his eyes but he very quickly recovered his composure. "Oh that. Yes, I'd forgotten...must have been the drink. I thought I'd keep her company. Must be lonely being on a strange base where you know nobody."

"And where did you go afterwards?"

"Back to my quarters as I said."

Robbie McBane looked at Dearing who returned his gaze unflinchingly. He noticed the faintest scratch on Dearing's left cheek and leaned forward to get a clearer look. "You appear to have a scratch on your cheek, Sir."

"Do I? Which cheek?"

"Your left one, Sir."

Dearing rubbed the fingers of his right hand across his cheek. "Oh, I hadn't noticed. Must have done that shaving this morning."

"It's quite a long scratch for a shaving cut, not the sort of nick one normally makes."

Dearing stood up suddenly. "Good God, Sergeant. I know you've a job to do, but this sort of Hercule Poirot stuff is ridiculous. I know nothing about the death of this girl and I resent your petty attempts to link me to it."

Robbie McBane stood too. "Right, well thank you, Sir. I do have to explore every avenue. No one can be above suspicion – that's the way it is. That will be all for the moment." When Dearing had closed the door after him, McBane swore under his breath. "I know you're hiding something and I'll get you... arrogant bastard."

Sergeant Bailey heaved his bulk into the front passenger seat of Fletcher's Wolseley. "Right, Sir. We turn left at the end of the road into the High Street and then up to the top and turn right. I'll tell you where."

Inspector Fletcher nodded and the black car eased away from Brackley Police Station. Fletcher was not looking forward to this. He was certain that the dead girl was Jenny Sumser and to bring that news to her parents was not an easy task. Worse, he would have to ask at least one of them to attend the mortuary at Tranters to identify the body.

"Shame you didn't think to get a photograph of the girl, Bailey. That would probably have made it certain."

"Sorry, Sir but with everything else…you know how it is."

"Pathologist said the time of death was probably between eight and ten o'clock on Monday evening but of course he can't be absolutely sure."

"Killed on the base was she or dumped there?"

"He said there were signs that she had not been killed in that room. He suspects her body had been dragged from somewhere close and positioned on the bed. You have to wonder why she was left like that."

The car turned down the hill into Brackley Old Town and slowed to a stop outside the house that the sergeant indicated. The two officers climbed out slowly and walked to the door. "Let me do the talking, Bailey."

"Of course, Sir."

Mr Sumser answered the door. He had stayed home from work he said because Jenny had not re-appeared. He led the officers into the sitting room and called his wife. As soon as Enid entered the room and saw the two officers, her legs buckled and she sank onto an armchair.

"I'm sorry to disturb you but we need to ask you some questions. Do you have a photograph of Jenny?"

Mr Sumser lifted a framed photograph from the mantel piece. "It was taken a couple of years ago…we don't have anything more recent."

Inspector Fletcher looked carefully at the photograph which showed the top half of an attractive young girl: a faint smile, confident, the eyes warm and brown, her chest and head slightly forward. The colour in the photograph had probably been added but was well done. She could be – could have been - a film star or a model.

"And this is our son." Arthur Sumser held up the photograph of George for Fletcher's inspection.

"Serving somewhere still, no doubt?"

"No...he was killed in action...Northern France...just before Dunkirk."

"I am sorry." That just made it harder. "I'm afraid I will have to ask you to come with us. We have found the body of a young woman and we need you to identify...see if it is your daughter."

Enid Sumser let out a wail and her hands leapt to her face. "I knew it, I knew it."

"Please Mrs Sumser, it may not be Jenny. We need to be sure."

Arthur Sumser had sat on the arm of the chair beside his wife and hugged her to him. He looked up. "Where did you find her?"

"At Silverstone RAF base."

"Silverstone! Whatever was she doing there?"

Enid Sumser suddenly stopped crying. "That can't be Jenny. She would have no business up at the base. How would she get there anyway?"

Bailey and Fletcher exchanged a glance. "If it is Jenny, that is something we need to establish."

When Mr and Mrs Sumser had prepared themselves, put on coats, scarves and gloves, Sergeant Bailey and Inspector Fletcher escorted them to the car, where they sat in the back in dignified silence during the journey to the mortuary. Enid Sumser gave a small, choking cough, when she stepped out of the car and looked at the entrance to the building. Her face was a picture of dread.

With her husband's arm around her, she entered the mortuary, looking at the row of cabinets against the wall. Mr Tranter, the funeral director, in a black suit and highly polished shoes turned to the Sumsers, his grey face an expressionless mask.

His voice was little more than a whisper, slow, careful, bringing a serenity to the bare room. "The process of laying out has not been fully completed. The deceased is covered with a sheet and when you are ready, I will draw it back to reveal only the face."

Arthur Sumser's voice was cracked. "We're ready."

Mr Tranter opened a door in the cabinet and pulled forward the rack. The contours of the body moulded the sheet, the feet projecting slightly upwards, the small mounds of the breasts, the point of the nose. Mr Tranter turned to the parents again and Mr Sumser nodded. The sheet was folded back revealing the face.

Arthur Sumser stepped forward to look. He clenched his jaw tightly, refusing to allow the anguish inside any outlet. Enid knew already that it was Jenny. She began to sob, deep convulsions that shook her small body. She forced herself to look and this, surprisingly, calmed her. Jenny was as pale and still as marble, as if her face had been carved. It was beautiful, the nose and cheekbones perfectly formed and the thin line of the lips just right. But it was a statue, there was no life and never would be.

"Why?" she said. "We've lost our son and now we have to lose our daughter. Why us? Why my Jenny?"

Arthur's arm closed around her shoulders again and he pulled her into himself. As he did so, he looked at Fletcher and nodded. "It's her...our Jenny. You will find him, won't you, the animal that did this to her? Give me five minutes alone with him and I'll make sure he never does it again to any other girl."

"Thank you, both of you. I know how hard this is for you and I am so sorry for your loss. We will leave no stone unturned to arrest this man and he will face the full force of the law."

◆ ◆ ◆

Flight Lieutenant Driscoll was a different case to Dearing, Robbie McBane decided as he invited him to sit down. He was earnest, trying to help, concerned about the girl. "It's important we get this sorted out as soon as possible...we need to get flying again. Group Captain Lovell is very anxious about the loss of flying time."

McBane ensured his voice remained neutral. "I understand that, Sir, but until we've interviewed everyone, we can't allow that. Could you please tell me your movements on Monday evening." As Driscoll talked, McBane made an assessment of him. His fair hair had a slight wave, his blue eyes spoke of sincerity but Lizzie was right, there was a shyness, perhaps nervousness about him.

"Certainly. I went to the mess soon after eighteen hundred hours, spoke with Flight Lieutenant Dearing at the bar briefly and then we had dinner with Miss Barnes, the ATA pilot. After dinner...about twenty hundred hours I'd say...I escorted Miss Barnes back to her quarters and then went back to my own. A bit later, maybe an hour or so, I scratched my hand on a spring sticking out of the armchair in my room, so I went over to the sick bay for a plaster. Then I went straight back to my quarters."

"You scratched your hand?"

"Yes." Driscoll raised his hand to show the bandage and looked puzzled at McBane picking up that detail.

"Who supplied the plaster?"

"Nurse O'Flynn."

"How long do you estimate you were there?"

"Oh only about five or ten minutes."

"And on your travels to and from did you see anyone, notice anything unusual?"

"Well nothing especially unusual but...on the way back from the sick bay, I did see Flight Lieutenant Dearing walking towards the huts further down the airfield...at least I think it was Dearing. It was difficult as his head was bowed against the rain and wind. I'm sure it has no significance."

"Is there a reason why Flight Lieutenant Dearing would be heading that way?"

"Well...I'm not sure...I supposed he had been to check the hangars were firmly closed against the wind or something of that nature and was on his way back to his quarters."

"What are the men saying about the discovery of the girl's body, Sir?"

"I've not really picked anything up. I'm sure they are all horrified and, like all of us, mystified. I mean what was she doing here? Who is she?"

"We do not have the answers to those questions as yet, Sir, but, rest assured, Inspector Fletcher from the Northamptonshire Constabulary is investigating that as we speak."

"We do need to get flying again, Sergeant. This war will not wait."

"Yes, Sir. Thank you for your time. That was very helpful." The two men rose from their chairs but something was niggling Robbie McBane, something he could not put his finger on. Perhaps it was the way Driscoll did not look him directly in the eye. What had Lizzie said, shy or secretive? On the spur of the moment he asked another question. "Do you have a middle name, Sir?"

Driscoll looked surprised. "Well, yes. It's Roger."

Robbie McBane stopped suddenly. Roger Driscoll...RD. He slipped a hand into his pocket and withdrew the cigarette case. "Would this be yours by any chance?"

As with Dearing, Driscoll showed no sign of recognition, no concern at all. "Not mine. I've never seen it before."

"Thank you , Sir. I won't keep you any longer."

Robbie McBane stared at the door after it had closed behind Driscoll. Dearing was definitely a liar, he had caught him out on his movements and he had not mentioned walking to the hangars after seeing Lizzie. That slight mark on his cheek. It was faint but it was nearly forty-eight hours since the murder and could have been a scratch made by the dead girl. Dearing must be kept in the frame.

And what of Driscoll? He was far more difficult to fathom. His answers were straight enough but McBane could not avoid the feeling that Driscoll was hiding something…and that scratch on his hand…a piece of metal from an armchair or a fingernail?

# CHAPTER 17

Robbie McBane heard the tap on the office door and glanced at his watch...almost mid-day. He called "Come in" and the door was pushed open. Lizzie poked her head around it.

"Hello...I hope I'm not disturbing you."

"Not a bit...come on in." Robbie McBane motioned to a chair and Lizzie sat down. The softness of her skin, the faintest colour in her cheeks, the brightness in her eyes stirred something in McBane's breast which felt like a betrayal of Catriona.

"There are a couple of things I wanted to let you know about...things that I saw last night."

"Oh aye? Please go ahead."

"Well last night I couldn't sleep, thinking about that poor girl so, just after eleven, I went downstairs to the Sick Bay for a chat with Patricia, Nurse O'Flynn, as I knew she would be on night duty. But there was no sign of her. Then, as I was passing the store, I heard voices. Patricia was one of them, the other was a man. I think it might have been Driscoll. I asked Patricia about it this morning but she wouldn't tell me who it was. I think she's afraid of what Matron would think about it."

"In a store cupboard? Interesting. Presumably they are courting?"

"I think so...if it was him. Otherwise she's with someone else. But the thing that was strange was that she said something about people finding out about his brother in Ireland which he then dismissed but I thought...you know...it sounded as though there was something to hide."

"Curiouser and curiouser. A brother in Ireland... something to hide. I need to follow that up."

130

"That's not all. When I went back to my room, I saw Matron come out of hers in a greatcoat or a cape and go downstairs. She must have been going out of the building dressed like that." Lizzie laughed, a soft tinkling sound in the drab office. "Patricia wondered if she's having an affair with Group Captain Lovell."

"God help the man if he is!"

"God help her too."

"Aye…fair point. You had a busy night then."

"I did."

"Lizzie, you do need to be careful. I'm very grateful for the information but you must not take risks. There is still more than a possibility that the killer was someone on the base."

A smile made Lizzie's mouth twitch and danced in her eyes. "Well Sergeant, I'm very touched that you care about my safety."

Robbie McBane flushed. "I'm just giving you sound advice and I hope you will give it due consideration."

"I will do that, Sergeant." She became brisk again. "Well that's my news. How are things going otherwise?"

Robbie McBane was relieved to get back on solid ground. The attraction he felt for Lizzie unnerved him a little. "I've interviewed the two airmen on the gate on Monday evening. One was stony-faced and admitted nothing. The other told me that not all movements were written down and that Staples had not been on the base. The truck did go out but he doesn't know where or who was driving."

"There's something very suspicious going on then."

"Certainly is. I interviewed Dearing and Driscoll. Neither of them recognised the cigarette case and I think they were genuine but Dearing was not honest about his movements. He also had the faintest scratch or something on his left cheek. He claimed he must have done it shaving but I'm definitely suspicious about him. Driscoll said he saw him walking towards the building where the body was found probably just after he had visited you."

"The mark on Dearing's cheek…could it have been made by a slap?"

"It could have been I suppose but you noticed the flesh beneath the girl's fingernail suggesting a scratch."

"You know I told you about Dearing coming to my room, I'm not sure I mentioned that I slapped him across the face, hard. I'm right handed so I would have hit his left cheek and I was wearing my grandmother's ring that evening."

"Ah. He never said you'd hit him. I wonder why that was?"

"His pride would not allow him to admit that he had been rejected so definitely."

"Hmmm. That rather undermines my theory but, if Driscoll is right, Dearing could have been in the right place at the right time."

There was a sharp rap on the door which was pushed open without invitation. Inspector Fletcher strode into the room and stopped abruptly, the small dimensions of the office leaving him nowhere to go. "Ah McBane. Good morning Miss. I hope I'm not interrupting anything."

"No, no Inspector. Miss Barnes was just letting me know about a couple of things last night. Quite curious."

"I've arranged to meet Lovell in fifteen minutes to up-date him with progress. He's keen that they get flying again. We can't give him all details but we can tell him a few things such as about the fence and so on. We need to up-date each other on the way."

"Right…I must be getting back." Lizzie rose from her chair and, smiling briefly, left the office.

"A smart young woman I'd say." Fletcher looked approvingly at the closed door.

"Aye she certainly is that….in more ways than one."

Fletcher's eyes narrowed just the slightest amount. "She could still be a suspect Sergeant, so keep your mind open."

"I'd stake my fortune on her being absolutely above reproach."

"That'll be your baronial seat in Scotland will it?"

"Something like that."

As they walked across to the administrative building where Lovell's office was housed, the two men speedily brought each other up to date with the progress of their separate investigations. They took scant notice of the three Wellington bombers which dominated the apron in front of the hangars beyond the admin block. Ground crew were busily working around the tail of one.

"Can we let them resume flying do you think?" Fletcher turned to look at McBane as they walked.

"I need to conduct a couple more interviews which I'll do this afternoon so they could probably start tomorrow but I'm not sure about Dearing. If he's our main suspect, we may need him on the ground."

Once inside the building, the two men marched along the corridor to Lovell's office and McBane knocked. The usual instruction to enter was barked but when Lovell saw who it was, his voice lost its imperious tone. They were invited to sit and Lovell offered them coffee which they both declined.

Fletcher started. "We have discovered the identity of the murdered girl. Her name was Jenny Sumser and she lived in Brackley. As yet, we do not know how she got here or what she was doing here. The pathologist gave the time of death as probably between eight and ten o'clock on Monday evening. There was some alcohol in her system and she had had sexual intercourse at some time in the few hours before her death. She was strangled." He nodded at McBane who took up the account.

"Inspector Fletcher and I inspected the perimeter fence where it had been cut. The grass inside the fence was flattened but there was no trace at all of any footsteps on the outside of the fence. We can be certain that no one came in that way. Worryingly, the wire looked very recently cut and we must assume that it was cut from the inside."

He paused, watching Lovell make sense of that.

"So what you're saying is that it was someone on the

base who cut the fence. But why would they do that?"

"Why indeed, Sir?"

"There was an entry in the gate log for the plumber Mr Staples on the afternoon of the murder but Mr Staples was working all day at a house in Brackley. We confirmed that with the lady of the house." Fletcher waited for Lovell to say something but he sat behind his desk with furrowed brow, clearly trying to make sense of what he was being told.

McBane took over. "One of the airmen on gate duty on Monday confirmed to me that sometimes entries in the log were not made, especially for regular trips. He had no recollection of Mr Staples coming through and did not recognise the handwriting of the entry that was made. One of the trucks left at about seventeen hundred hours and again at about twenty-two hundred hours. Neither exit was recorded in the log."

"So Group Captain, with that information from Sergeant McBane, it is clear that someone on the base is trying to hide something. We will keep our minds open of course but I think we will be looking for our murderer from amongst those who work on the base."

All Lovell's bluster was gone. He looked stunned, staring at the two men in front of him as though he did not recognise them at all. Slowly he regained some composure, sitting up in his chair and desperately trying to appear in control. "We need to get flying again...we must train pilots for Bomber Command. Is there any reason why we can't?"

Robbie McBane almost pitied the man. "If you can hold off for the rest of today, that would be appreciated, Sir. We can carry out the other interviews this afternoon and you can resume flying tomorrow. But we must have no one leaving nor entering the base."

"Really. Still need to enforce that? You know I can't believe that anyone on this base can be involved in this... murder for God's sake! The only people we want to murder are German soldiers and air crew."

Robbie McBane was on the verge of telling Lovell his suspicions about Dearing. But he decided to withhold the pleasure of watching Lovell's reaction for when his precious senior officer was arrested. Instead, he returned to the subject of the missing miles on the truck and the fuel consumption.

"Is there any reason, Sir, why a truck would leave the base and not be signed out?"

"None that I can think of. The personnel on gate duty are required to log all movements."

"Quite so, Sir. We have a reliable witness who says the truck with the number RAF 142031 left the base on Monday at the rimes I mentioned earlier. Would you have any idea where that truck would have gone at those times?"

Lovell looked at McBane as though he had gone mad. "Why should I know about truck movements? Good God, Sergeant, I'm a Group Captain...I don't deal with truck movements. Ask Corporal Davies."

"Thank you, Sir. But does it strike you as unusual that a truck would leave twice and not be signed out either time?"

"What are you driving at Sergeant?"

"I'm not completely sure, Sir, but I know I am not getting straight answers from some of your people. There are some miles every week on that truck unaccounted for as well as a significant consumption of fuel. I will get to the bottom of it and I am certain that it is connected to the murder."

Lovell suddenly sat heavily back in his chair. "What is the World coming to? I am sure there is a simple explanation for the truck's movements and the fuel consumption. Why you think it is connected to the murder of this girl, I can't imagine."

"I guess it's instinct, Sir."

"Instinct? Evidence is what you need Sergeant."

"Of course, Sir, and I will find the evidence."

There was a tap on the door and, after Lovell's summons, a young airman walked briskly into the office. He handed him a piece of paper. "Message just through from headquarters, Sir. Thought you might want to see it."

Lovell picked up the piece of paper, unfolded it and read. A smile broke on his face and he waved the paper in the air. "The Russians have re-taken Kharkov...yesterday...that was the sixteenth. So the Germans only held it for a few days. Good on the Ruskies. The more Hitler is occupied over on the Eastern Front, the less trouble he'll be causing us."

"That is good news," offered Fletcher.

Having been restored to his usual blustering confidence by this news, Lovell ushered his two visitors out of his office. "Thank you gentlemen. I must get on. Must sort flying out for tomorrow."

◆ ◆ ◆

Clouds were still punishing the landscape, driven by a blustery wind, appearing to scrape the bare fields beyond the garden and threaten the house. She lifted the telephone receiver in the hall and dialled the number, a number that allowed a direct connection without the need to go through the operator. Whilst she waited for it to be answered, she fiddled with the string of pearls around her neck.

"Hello."

"Hello. The weather here worrying is. What it is like with you?

"Clear now...the storm has passed."

"I may need to come to see you soon...and bring a friend."

"Has the storm caused specific damage?"

"No more than I've already told you but...more may be discovered...you know how it is."

"Stay calm. It's important not to do anything different to normal. I guess you'll use the train as usual if you come."

"If we can. I let you know. But maybe, we need to go away further from the storm."

"I'll be ready to arrange that."

"Thank you. I have present for you – I bring it if we come."

"How nice. I look forward to it."

"Goodbye for now."

She replaced the receiver and sighed. She had become rather fond of this place, this house, but she knew where her duty lay and there were other places she could make a contribution.

# CHAPTER 18

"We need to establish how Jenny Sumser got to the base on Monday evening and why she went there. So, Bailey, I want you to interview the two friends that she usually went out with...I know they told Mrs Sumser that they didn't see Jenny that night but that may not be true...find out where they went and make sure you verify their stories. You know the usual thing, see them separately, play them off against each other if need be."

"Yes, Sir...I know exactly how to do that." Sergeant Bailey's patience was running thin. After all, he'd been in the force longer than Fletcher.

"And then do some enquiries. Someone must have seen her when she went out, saw where she went, that sort of thing. We need any scrap of information we can get."

"Righto, Sir. Grant and I will get onto it right away."

"Good man. We owe it to her poor parents to get to the bottom of this."

Sergeant Bailey replaced the receiver. More running about. "Grant."

"Sarge?"

"Job for you."

"But I'm busy, Sarge. I've got to check through all these fuel dockets from the garage. You wanted me to make sure no one was getting more than their ration."

"That'll have to wait. I want you to go up the High Street and find out if anyone saw Jenny Sumser on Monday evening early. Some of the shopkeepers may still have been in their premises or just leaving. Take the photo. Try the pubs up there. Someone must have seen her."

"What'll you be doing, Sarge?"

"I need to see Mrs Sumser down in Old Town and get the names and addresses of the friends her Jenny used to go out with and also where they work. I need to see them straight away…find out what they know."

"Right Sarge. Did you hear about the German soldier on the front line when Hitler visited. Hitler says to him if you could have one request what would it be and the guy says I would like to die for the Fatherland with mein Fuhrer beside me."

"From the wireless I suppose?"

"No…that's one of me own." PC Grant grinned boyishly.

"Stick to the day job Grant. You'll never make it as a comedian."

Sergeant Bailey glanced at his watch - one-thirty - went outside to the shed and, having just managed to swing his leg over his bicycle, wobbled away. Struggling up the High Street, he wondered why he couldn't have a car like Inspector Fletcher. There was no justice. He was grateful when he turned off the High Street and was able to coast downhill into Old Town. The house looked the same. He was not a philosophical man but he wondered how it could look the same when something so devastating had happened. It should be like a bombed house for the loss of their daughter had devastated the lives of the Sumsers as cruelly as any missile.

Mrs Sumser opened the door. Her face was expressionless, pale, and her sunken eyes were vacant.

"It's Sergeant Bailey from…"

"Come in Sergeant."

"I'm sorry to disturb you so soon after…Is Mr Sumser in?"

"He's gone to work. No point in hanging around he said."

"No. I wonder my dear if I could have a look in Jenny's room. There may be something that gives us some clues about why she was at the base. If I could also have the names of the friends she normally went out with…you know the ones you visited on the Tuesday."

"Maggie Bennet and Rita Polesworth. You'll be wanting their addresses too."

"And where they work if you know it."

"That's easy. They worked with Jenny at Bronnley's."

After writing the names and addresses in his notebook, Sergeant Bailey trudged up the stairs behind Enid Sumser who opened the door of a room and gestured to him to enter. She did not wait while he examined the room but returned down the stairs. Sergeant Bailey took in the room. Small, quite tidy for a young girl, a bed, a hefty looking polished wood wardrobe, a dressing table with drawers topped by a mirror. A hairbrush and some make-up were lying on the dressing table, probably where Jenny had left them after getting ready to go out on Monday evening.

There were two cards standing up on the dressing table too. Frank Bailey lifted one . A valentine card. The message inside was simple: 'From your secret admirer," followed by numerous kisses. The second had a little verse in it.

My love is a fire, my heart for you will burn,

Never doubt my desire, never doubt my return."

"Quite the poet," he said quietly, wondering if at least one of these young men was on active service somewhere, dreaming of returning to a lovely young woman, thinking of a life together, children. Perhaps he would not know of Jenny's death until he came back, hurrying down the street, barely able to contain his excitement at the prospect of seeing the girl he loved. It was cruel, this war; Jenny's death would affect not just her parents.

Frank Bailey thought about his own daughter, now in her twenties. How would he and her mother cope if she were taken from them, especially as a result of violence? He turned his attention to the wardrobe, opening the door and seeing the dresses and blouses. It felt wrong to be going through her clothes, raking through her life, but there may be something that would yield a clue. He touched the soft fabric of a summer dress, a dress she would now never wear again.

There were drawers inside the wardrobe and he gently slid each open in turn, feeling underneath the underwear, stockings, socks and other small items they contained for anything that might provide that elusive clue. Nothing there.

The drawers in the dressing table were small. The centre one contained make-up, a hair brush, comb, nail scissors and nail files and other bits and pieces. A diary and some letters were in one of the side drawers and Frank Bailey scanned one or two of the letters. They were from a friend – female – or relative, just chatty girlish stuff. Another of the drawers yielded, underneath an assortment of miscellaneous items, an envelope. Five and ten pound notes made it bulge and when counted, it proved to be over one hundred pounds. Bailey whistled softly. That was a lot of money for a girl of Jenny's age to have stashed away.

Frank Bailey at last stood up and looked around the room again. A magazine was lying on the bed, the edges slightly curled so obviously already read. He picked it up and flipped through the pages – all about films and the stars in them, the sort of thing that would interest a young girl. There was nothing that explained why Jenny had been at Silverstone and nothing to explain her disappearance. There was just the money. He stood with one hand on the door handle and surveyed the room for the last time.

It had all the signs of a life suddenly and unexpectedly stopped.

His tread on the stairs was heavy as he descended and Enid Sumser was in the hall when he reached the last steps. "Would you like a cup of tea?"

"No thank you, my dear. Just a couple of questions. Did Jenny have a steady young man, someone perhaps away in the services?"

"No. Oh she has some admirers – she is quite..." Enid Sumser stopped and clutched her face with her hand.

Frank Bailey laid a hand gently on her shoulder. "Now,

now. Take your time."

"She...she was quite pretty but she hadn't settled on anyone. She got a couple of valentines cards though."

"So I saw." He cleared his throat. " There was quite a bit of money in one of the drawers in an envelope. Would that be her savings?"

"Was there? Well she liked to save up for clothes and going out but...How much was there?"

"Over a hundred pounds."

"Oh my goodness. I had no idea she had so much. I didn't think she would be able to save that much on her earnings, after paying me some rent and so on."

"Well perhaps she'd saved more than you thought."

"Perhaps." But the frown on Enid Sumser's face did not clear.

After taking his leave, Sergeant Bailey plodded back up the hill to the High Street, pushing his bike. It was far too steep to cycle. When he was on the relatively level ground at the top of the High Street, he swung his leg over the bicycle and pedalled northwards to the edge of the town where the Bronnley Soap factory was situated. At reception, the prim lady behind the desk looked at him over her glasses and clacked away in her heels to find Mr Grainger, the manager. Sergeant Bailey asked to speak to him in private.

"Firstly Mr Grainger, I need to give you some bad news. One of your workers, a girl by the name of Jenny Sumser was found dead yesterday."

"Dead?" Mr Grainger's mouth was open and he stared at the police officer.

"Yes, Sir. Dead."

"But how...?"

"I'm afraid I'm not at liberty to discuss the details with anyone, Sir. I'm here because I need to talk with two of her friends, Maggie Bennett and Rita Polesworth."

"Of course, Sergeant. I'll fetch them for you. You can use my office."

"Thank you, Sir." Frank Bailey looked at the office...tidy, desk with a large swivel chair behind it, two chairs in front, two filing cabinets in the corner side by side and some posters advertising Bronnley products on the wall. Just as one would expect.

The two girls were ushered into the office. They wore aprons and headscarves. One was tall and slim with a rather severe expression, the other, average height and wearing concern on her face. Neither looked directly at him.

"I'm sorry to disturb your work, Ladies, but I must ask you some questions. I understand you are friends of Jennifer Sumser. Is that correct?"

"Yes officer." It was the shorter one.

"And your name is…?"

"Maggie…Maggie Bennett."

"So you must be Rita Polesworth," he said looking at the tall one. She nodded. "I'm afraid to have to tell you that Jenny has been found dead."

He noted the shock on both faces.

"I'm afraid I can't give you any details but I need to establish her movements before she…before it happened. She left her house soon after six o'clock on Monday evening. Did you see her that evening?"

He noted the quick glance that shot between the two girls before Rita replied. "No, we didn't see her at all on Monday. Haven't seen her since Saturday night actually."

"How did she seem to you on Saturday?"

"Her normal self…bubbly…talking about films and film stars…nothing out of the ordinary."

Sergeant Bailey nodded. Maggie, the shorter of the two girls looked a little frightened, he thought but Rita gave nothing away. "Did you two girls go out Monday evening?"

"Yeah, just in Brackley." When Sergeant Bailey said nothing, she went on. "We went to a dance class at the WI Hall actually."

"A dance class. What was the teacher's name?"

"Can't remember."

"Was it busy…lots of people there?"

"Not especially…sort of middling."

Frank Bailey knew evasion when he saw it. Rita's answers were not secure, as if she were making them up. He would have to find out who the teacher had been and check whether he or she remembered the two girls. He had no doubt that they would be remembered …if they had been there.

"Thank you ladies, I'll let you get back to your work."

The WI Hall was just around the corner from the station so Sergeant Bailey took a detour down Manor Road. Just as he had thought, there was a poster among the many on the board outside the hall advertising the Monday dance sessions. That was the term used rather than lessons. He took out his notebook and jotted down the name, Mrs Weatherstone, and the telephone number.

A few minutes later, having unlocked the station, he was at his desk with the telephone receiver in one hand and the index finger of his other hand on the dial. The phone was connected and rang a few times before a cheerful female voice gave the number.

"Mrs Weatherstone? I'm Sergeant Bailey from Brackley Police. I just need to check something with you. I gather you run a dance session at the WI Hall on Monday evenings."

"That's right Sergeant. Are you interested in joining us?"

Bailey laughed. "I think my dancing days are long past. I'm wondering if you had two girls come on Monday evening, a Rita and a Maggie?"

"No, we had no new people at all on Monday, just our regulars and there are no Ritas nor Maggies amongst them."

"You're absolutely sure about that?"

"Absolutely, Sergeant. We had nearly everyone that night…seven couples so fourteen people and myself."

"Thank you, Mrs Weatherstone. That is very helpful. Goodbye."

"You should try dancing, Sergeant. You're never too old

to dance and I'm sure Mrs Bailey would enjoy it too."

Bailey laughed again. "I'll leave it to people who are more nimble on their feet but thank you." He replaced the receiver slowly.

So, his instinct had been right. The two girls had been lying. He'd need to see them again and get the truth out of them. It would be a formal interview, individually, at the station. That would make them think twice about lying to him again.

A little later, PC Phil Grant came into the station, whistling cheerfully. "Hit the bullseye, I have Sarge."

"What you got?"

"There's a shop on the High Street called Brackley Fashions – ladies clothes and so on – d'you know it?"

"Of course…though naturally I do not shop there."

"Not even to buy a present for the missus?"

"Get on with it Constable."

"Well it's run by a Mrs Norris who recognised the picture, said the girl was in buying expensive nylon stockings on Saturday. She wondered how she could afford them. Aaaand…here's the good bit…as she was finishing up on Monday, she looked out of the window to see what the weather was doing and saw three girls – one of them Jenny - huddled by the Town Hall. She was interested given that it was so windy and watched for a bit. Then an RAF truck turned up and they all three got in the back. Not a bad bit of detective work eh?"

"Well done, Grant, well done." Bailey smiled to himself. He would enjoy phoning Fletcher.

# CHAPTER 19

Across the apron, Lizzie could just see the three Wellingtons standing in front of the hangars. She longed to be in one, flying, or at least back at White Waltham preparing for her next job. Now the storm had passed and the wind died to an acceptable level, it seemed a cruelty to be grounded here. She was making herself useful of course, doing various jobs in the Sick Bay which Patricia very much appreciated. Even Matron had given grudging thanks at lunch.

She had been asked to check the stock of bandages, dressings and numerous other items in one of the store rooms and she was noting everything down in a ledger so Matron would know what needed replenishing. It did not tax her mind and hence her thoughts were wandering as she mechanically counted and noted. She was glad to be nearly finished as such dull work irritated her.

Like a frantic painter, her mind was mixing the separate colours again but no clear picture was emerging. How had that girl come onto the base and why? She had not come through the fence, that was obvious from the lack of flattened grass outside the repaired break. That truck, she was sure, was involved in some way. What if the girl had been brought in by that truck; it's movements had not been logged at the gate? Why would she have been brought onto the base? The image of the dead girl with her clothing awry was etched into Lizzie's mind and, with certainty, she knew the answer to her own question. She had come for sex with someone. Was it a romantic liaison or was it a trade? And who was the man...or men?

Dearing was definitely the chief suspect. He had been drunk, he had come to her room clearly looking for sex and, when she had turned him away, he had been seen by Driscoll heading towards the building where the girl's body was found. He had been angry with her. Perhaps he had taken it out on that poor girl because she had sent him packing. There was that something about him that niggled in her mind, some vague recollection, a feeling that she had met him before but she could not pin it down.

Was Driscoll involved in some way? Lizzie hoped that Robbie McBane had followed up the information she had given him about the brother in Ireland. What dd it mean? She knew she could not get anything from Patricia or could she? She glanced at the one  remaining pile of dressings, counted them quickly and, taking the ledger to Matron's empty office, laid it on the desk. Then she walked as casually as she could into the ward and saw Patricia tending to Brian Saunders.

"Do you think I'm going to die, Nurse?" Saunders spoke with slow tragedy.

"Oh without a doubt...but not before yer dinner."

"That's fine then, I wouldn't want to miss out on the exquisite culinary delights I'm sure we'll be served."

Lizzie hovered until Patricia had moved away from Saunders and, other than a brief wave, she ignored the trainee pilot's attempts to engage her attention. "I've finished the stock take. Just wondered if you had a minute?"

"Of course. Matron is off somewhere so no danger of being surprised. Let's go to the staffroom and get a cuppa."

Lizzie waited for the kettle to boil and Patricia to fill the pot before speaking. "You know last night...the conversation you were having with someone in the store...I am curious about one thing you said. It was about the brother of whomever it was you were talking to. Something about him being back in Ireland but he didn't want anyone to know about him."

"It's nothing...a private matter."

"Patricia, a young girl has been murdered. Anything that is secretive might be...."

"It's nothing to do with that at all. 'Tis nothing of importance."

Lizzie looked at Patricia who turned her face away, stirring the tea pot with unnecessary vigour. "I can keep a secret. Perhaps it would be better just to…"

"Can you? can you keep a secret? Or will you be telling that Robbie McBane with his square jaw and bright eyes?"

Lizzie said nothing for a moment, stung by the implication. "If you're anxious about McBane knowing, it suggests that it isn't something unimportant."

Patricia faced her. "It has nothing to do with that girl's murder. I promise you that so please leave it be."

Again, Lizzie left a few seconds of silence hang in the room before saying quietly, "It was Driscoll with you wasn't it?"

"Yes it was. Are you happy now?" Patricia poured the tea, banged the mugs on the table, spilling a little of the liquid and sat with a hand hiding her face in silence. After a few moments, Lizzie saw her shoulders shaking.

"I'm sorry Patricia. I didn't mean to upset you."

"Why are people so resentful of the happiness of others? Why is everyone seeking to destroy it? Isn't there enough misery in the World with this bloody war without…?"

Lizzie walked around the table and put her arm around Patricia's shoulders. "I am sorry." She waited a moment. "Did you meet when you came here?"

Patricia sniffed, took out a handkerchief and re-settled her face before replying. "No. We met when I was nursing at a hospital in Kent and Edward was admitted for a few days – nothing serious. We seemed to hit it off right from the start."

"He is certainly a gentleman…and a gentle man I think."

Patricia turned to face Lizzie. "He is Lizzie…kind, considerate, always anxious for my happiness."

Lizzie nodded. "And you should be happy. How come you both ended up here?"

"As you would guess, 'twas no accident. When Edward

discovered he was being posted here, I applied for a post here too…said my sister lived up here, was very ill and I needed to be close. A little white lie. I think I can be forgiven for that."

"I'm sure you can. But… but surely there's no reason why anyone would be trying to keep you apart?"

"You don't know Matron as well as me. She can be hard and she is determined there will be no 'liaisons' as she calls them."

"It won't be forever and then you can be together."

"There's no sign of it stopping yet is there?"

"No…I'll give you that." Lizzie returned to her chair and said no more until Patricia was calmer. "I think maybe you're being unnecessarily cautious about McBane. He seems to me to be very professional. I'm sure he would be discreet about the relationship. I'm not sure why you are so worried about anyone knowing about Edward's brother."

"It's Edward's privacy I am protecting, not my own. I don't have the right to reveal what he may want to keep unknown."

"Yes, I see. I'm not trying to be nosey, Patricia. I think though that this investigation may bring things to light that people are trying to keep hidden and perhaps it is better to be honest about them from the start."

"I don't think Edward would see it like that."

Lizzie understood that the conversation was over and she excused herself, saying she wanted to check on the Wellington she had delivered. But before leaving she put her arms around Patricia and held her. "I'm on your side, Patricia, really I am."

There was still activity around the tail of the Wellington Lizzie had delivered. A member of the ground crew was putting the finishing touches to the paintwork. No holes were visible and it looked as good as new.

"You've done a lovely job on that. I'm sorry I caused you more work but there's not much you can do against a German fighter when you have no crew on board and the guns are not armed."

"No Miss. I don't suppose anyone could have got away with less." He came down the step ladder and stood back to look at his handiwork, holding the brush in one hand. "All sorted now, though and, thanks to Barnes Wallis, it was only superficial damage."

"Barnes Wallis?"

"Yep. He was the engineer at Brooklands who came up with the construction method. It's called geodetic design. So every part of the aircraft, fuselage, tail wings the lot, has thin metal strips fixed diagonally in two directions on the basic frames creating a whole network of diamonds. It makes it strong, light and it's not catastrophic if some of the strips are blown away. Damage is often just superficial to the fabric covering as in this case. Course if you get too many holes in the tail, it won't function properly and I guess you'd lose control."

"You're very knowledgeable about it." His tall, lean frame was topped with fair hair which was shining in the sun now breaking between the clouds.

"I was always interested in aircraft, even as a boy. Wanted to be a pilot actually but I went to the wrong school."

"That is so wrong. You'd think with the pilot shortage they would be looking to train people like you."

He gave a short laugh. "I'm not officer material and they only let officers fly. Simple as."

"It seems wrong and foolish to me. Anyway, thank you very much for fixing it. I don't feel so guilty now. I'm sorry, my name is Lizzie Barnes...I'm with the ATA."

"Yeah I know, Miss."

"And you are?"

"Langford, Miss."

"Terrible business about this girl isn't it?"

Langford's easy manner suddenly changed. He looked away as if he were being watched. "Yeah, shocking."

"I wonder what she was doing here?"

"No idea, Miss. Well I best be getting on," he said abruptly and turned away.

"Of course, I mustn't keep you." Lizzie watched him disappear, paint brush in hand, into the hangar. He knows more than he's letting on. She walked around the Wellington's tail, admiring the repair, longing to climb into the pilot's seat and get airborne. It was an injustice and another piece of folly that she was not allowed to see active service. She loved her job but to be more directly involved in the war effort would give her great satisfaction. She was gazing up at the cockpit windows when a voice startled her. The drawl was unmistakeable.

"As you can see, they've fixed it."

She turned to see Dearing's sneering face, his eyes saying very clearly that she had failed. "Yes and they've done it very well."

"We'll be flying again tomorrow, thank God."

"I wish I could join you."

"It's best left to the professionals."

Lizzie felt anger rising. What did he think she was? An amateur, someone playing at it? "Have you ever flown one of these on your own with no one else on board Flight Lieutenant?"

"Of course not. Why would anyone do that?"

"Some of us have no choice. If you want an aircraft, we have to get it to you and do it on our own."

"Yeees, but then delivering an aircraft in daylight on home soil is hardly the same as flying at night through flak to bomb a target over enemy territory."

"Of course, but we still do a professional job."

Dearing smiled, an irritating, supercilious smile designed to put her down. She bit her lip, fighting the urge to give him both barrels. She knew that would only persuade him that he had won so she said nothing.

"Will you be joining us in the mess for dinner tonight? We missed you yesterday."

"No...I prefer more civilised company."

Dearing suddenly stepped close to her. He was taller than her and she was initially intimidated by his proximity, the way his face distorted into a vicious mask. "You're so high and mighty aren't you? Think you're better than me? There's only one thing you're fit for."

And then he was gone, striding away from her. But Lizzie was transfixed. His last words, she had heard them before and with a sudden flash of memory, the scene came back to her. It was a large hotel, her first proper evening out. She must have been sixteen and had been taken by her parents to the hunt ball. She had wandered outside to get some air and had stepped off the terrace into the garden, infused with the scent of mock orange - philadelphus the proper name for it - she knew it because they had the shrub in their own garden.

She was enjoying its powerful aroma which seemed to envelop her when a figure came close. A young man, black tie, swaying in front of her face. An arm around her waist, pulling her closer, his breath on her cheek, the strong smell of drink, wine, champagne, whisky she did not know. She tried to prise the arm away but he was too strong. She was being moved away from the terrace further into the garden. She was resisting but was too startled, too afraid to make a scene. He stopped and stood in front of her, his face close to hers. He was kissing her so she turned her face one way and then the next. His hand held her face tight and he planted his lips on hers.

She pushed but he was so close, she could get no pressure on his chest. "No, no," she repeated, the sound stifled by his mouth on hers; he took no notice. And then one of his hands was sliding up her front and rested on her breast. "Come on, you know you want it." His voice was hoarse, full of desire. She began to panic and then felt his hand on her bottom pulling up her dress. She knew she had to act. With a huge effort, she pushed him away and immediately turned to run back inside.

He grabbed her hand and held her. "Leave me go... now or I'll scream."

"You silly little bitch. What's wrong with a bit of fun?"

"I don't call it fun. Let me go."

He flung her hand away. "Piss off then but just remember... there's only one thing you're fit for."

She had not waited to hear any more. Now she knew without doubt that she had met him before. He was an animal, especially when fuelled by drink and an animal who would stop at nothing to get his way. That girl, that poor girl. It was him, she was sure.

# CHAPTER 20

Andrews slouched in the chair opposite Robbie McBane, disdain radiating from him like heat. "Let me ask you again AC Andrews. What do you know about the movement of one of the base's trucks on Monday afternoon...late afternoon and at night?"

"Why should I know anything about it? I've already told you, I don't know nuffin and it don't matter how many times you ask, I still won't know nuffin."

Robbie McBane stifled the urge to correct the man's English. "It appears that this truck makes the same journey or journeys every week. There is a weekly discrepancy which is always the same. What about the weekly fuel discrepancy too? What can you tell me about that?"

"Nuffin."

"Nothing, Sir."

"Nuffin...Sir."

"Do you ever drive the truck with the number 142031?"

Andrews shrugged. "Might 'ave done, sometime. Don't remember. If I have to drive a truck, I just take the one that's nearest."

"Who is responsible for assigning drivers if and when such things as stores need to be collected from the local towns?"

"Corporal Davies."

"I'm glad you do know something." Andrews either ignored or was impervious to the ice in McBane's voice. He slid the log for the fuel storage tank across the table. "This is the log book in which fuel taken from the storage tank is recorded. Do you recognise those initials in the last entry?"

"Nah. Someone with bad hand writin' anyway."

Andrews gave a short laugh.

"Aye, bad enough to ensure no one can work out who it was. It is of course only a matter of time before we find out." McBane withdrew the log book and then suddenly shot another question. "Was it you AC Andrews who drove that truck and signed that fuel log?"

"That is not my handwriting. My initials are easy to work out. Give me a pen and I'll show you."

"So you cannot tell me anything about the driver of the truck?"

"I've already said, I know nuffin…Sir."

"I will pursue this with Corporal Davies then."

"Rightio." Andrews shrugged.

McBane shuffled the papers in his hands and laid them on the desk in front of him. He had arranged to see Corporal Davies immediately after Andrews and had told him to be waiting outside the room from fifteen hundred hours. He listened carefully. He could hear the sound of shuffling feet in the corridor outside the office, shuffling with impatience or nervousness, perhaps both. He glanced at his watch: ten minutes past the hour.

"I gather that you and Corporal Davies found the section of perimeter fence that had been cut?"

"That's right. That girl must have come in that way and perhaps whoever murdered her."

"The thing that puzzles me and indeed the Police is that the grass on the inside of the fence was flattened, indicating plenty of feet had been tramping round there, yet the grass outside the fence had not been flattened at all. If the fence had been cut from the outside and the girl had come onto the base through the fence, the grass would have been flattened on the outside too."

Andrews for the first time in the interview looked uncomfortable. "I don't know nuffin about that. We found it cut and made a temporary repair. That's all I know."

"I do hope you are not withholding information,

Andrews. This is serious."

"If I knew anythin' I'd tell you. But I don't."

McBane looked carefully for several seconds at Andrews who avoided his gaze. Finally he said, "Dismissed." Andrews jumped up from his chair and in the one movement reached for the door handle. Before he could open the door, Robbie McBane said, "Oh just one more thing, Aircraftman. Do you recognise this cigarette case?" He held the case in front of him on the palm of his hand. McBane's eyes were on the face of the other man where momentary recognition flitted before the stony look returned.

Andrews pursed his lips. "Nah, never seen it before."

"Has anyone been asking about a lost cigarette case? It must be special to someone. Look it has initials on it." McBane flipped open the case to reveal the letters RD.

"Not heard of anyone looking for a ciggy case, nah. I'll let you know if I do." As McBane returned the case to his pocket, Andrews grinned and opened the door. Robbie was on his feet and right behind Andrews, looking through the doorway at Davies, watching for whatever sign Andrews was going to give him. To his satisfaction, there was no time for any communication between the two of them.

"Do come in Corporal Davies. Please sit down."

Davies sat upright in the chair, his arms folded in front of him, staring at McBane with apparent indifference. That will change to hostility soon!

"Now you have given the police a statement of your movements on Monday evening and declared that you saw nothing and nobody unusual. You also said that you went to the Silver Swan pub for an hour or two. Is that correct?"

"That is so, yes."

McBane wondered if Davies' manner of speaking was deliberately pedantic or just the result of his Welsh turn of phrase. "The thing that puzzles me Corporal is that you were not signed out at the gate."

"Why would they sign me out? They know who I am

and where I'm going."

"Every movement through those gates must be recorded in the gate log. You know that as do those on sentry duty. That's one thing that's going to change immediately. Sloppy security could lose us this war."

"A little melodramatic don't you think?"

"No Corporal. So you were at the Silver Swan on Monday evening?"

"Yes…like I said in my statement."

"I'm staying at the Silver Swan as you'll know Corporal because I heard the Landlord tell you that when you came in on Tuesday evening." Robbie McBane enjoyed Davies's discomfort. He shifted in his chair, put his hands on his knees, sat forward, looked at the floor. "Of course I also heard what you said to him…about saying that you were there on Monday if anyone asked and a threat about supply of provisions."

"That was nothing to do with this business at all. It was something else."

"I don't care what it was. You were off the base when you had been given a clear instruction that no one was to leave. You were creating an alibi for Monday evening. That points to one thing."

Davies stared defiantly at McBane but said nothing.

"What are you covering up Corporal? Murder? Black marketeering?" Davies said nothing but stared fixedly ahead of him avoiding McBane's eyes. "As you know, Corporal, I came here to investigate the excessive use of fuel and other stores at the base before my attention was diverted onto this awful business. We were, you will remember, in the middle of checking vehicle log books and fuel consumption on Tuesday when I was summoned to Group Captain Lovell's office. Can you tell me anything about that?"

Davies shook his head slowly. "Nothing at all but I'm surprised you're still going on about that when you have a murder to solve."

"There may of course be a connection, Corporal."

McBane again pushed the fuel log book across the table. "Do you recognise those initials, Corporal?"

Davies gave a cursory look and shook his head. "You asked me that before. I can't decipher them."

"Do you think that's an 'L' perhaps?"

Davies shrugged. "Could be…or maybe a C…dunno."

"I understand one of your duties is to assign drivers when a truck needs to go somewhere off the base."

"That's right."

"So how come you canna remember who drove that truck on Monday…afternoon and night?"

"I know nothing at all about a truck being driven off the base on Monday afternoon nor night."

"Where is all the fuel going, Corporal Davies?"

"Into vehicles for the war effort, Sergeant."

"So how come, every week, that truck is filled with sixty-five gallons of petrol but it does nothing like the mileage to use that much?"

Davies spread his hands wide. "Search me, Sir. But perhaps someone is stealing it…coming through the gap in the fence."

"Presumably, they hover over the ground until they get through the fence?"

"What d'you mean?"

"The grass, Corporal, the grass. It was completely flattened inside the fence where the wire had been cut but not a blade was flattened on the outside. Didn't think of that, did you?"

"I know nothing about the fence except that Andrews and I found the cut when we were inspecting it on Flight Lieutenant Dearing's instructions."

Davies was riled and McBane decided to push him. "Convenient isn't it, Corporal. There's a need to explain how that girl came onto the base and next thing a cut in the fence is discovered, a cut that had all the appearance of being newly made. And you discovered it with Andrews."

Davies was fuming but he stared out of the window and said nothing. McBane withdrew the log book and laid the cigarette case on the table, again watching the eyes of the man opposite. There was the slightest flicker of concern before Davies responded.

"You've got my cigarette case. Where did you find it? I've been looking everywhere for that. Lost it last week sometime."

"Have you been asking people if they'd seen it?"

"Course I have."

"Then why did AC Andrews not know anything about it? He said he was not aware of anyone asking about a lost cigarette case?"

"Probably didn't want to get involved."

"Or perhaps knew it was yours and knew that it could be incriminating."

"Incriminating?" Davies pronounced each syllable carefully. "If that's all you've got, you've got nothing. I lost it last week…it means nothing."

McBane opened the case. "Initials RD."

"That's right. Present from my wife. Reginald Davies see…though my friends call me Reg." He leaned forward to pick up the case but McBane's hand closed over it and slid it back to his own side of the desk.

"I'll need to keep that as evidence, I'm afraid."

"Evidence?"

"Yes, Corporal, evidence. Dismissed…for now but I am certain I will need to speak to you again."

Davies stood and looked down at McBane, a sneer on his face, before leaving the room with his characteristic swagger and pulling the door closed behind him with sufficient force to make it slam. Robbie McBane was annoyed. He knew there was a conspiracy of silence. He knew they were lying but Davies was right. He needed hard evidence. His voice was impatient when he responded to a knock on the door but immediately softened when Lizzie appeared.

"Just thought I'd up-date you with a few thoughts and

observations."

Robbie McBane held up his hand. "Wait. I've arranged to have a catch-up with Inspector Fletcher so you can let him know as well."

They left McBane's office and knocked on the door of the one opposite. It was bigger than the room they had just left and had four chairs. Behind the desk was a noticeboard which nearly filled the wall from waist height. The dead girl's photo was pinned in the centre and names were written in large letters on sheets of paper pinned to various parts of the board.

When they had greeted and were seated, Fletcher said, "So what have we got?"

"Lizzie was about to tell me some thoughts of hers and observations so I suggest we start there." Robbie McBane looked at Lizzie.

"Firstly, I've been thinking about the girl and what she was wearing. I'm sure it has occurred to all of us that she was here either to meet an individual or perhaps to provide… services to more than one man."

"Prostitution?" Fletcher nodded slowly. "That's a definite possibility though I'm sure her parents will be devastated if that proves to be the case."

"Secondly, I remembered meeting Dearing once before. I was sixteen, he a few years older." Lizzie hesitated. "He behaved in a completely inappropriate manner towards me and with a degree of aggression. I believe he is quite capable of being violent to a girl. Thirdly, I had a conversation with an airman called Langford. He knows something. He became very cagey when I mentioned the girl."

"But Lizzie, we must have evidence. Dearing may be an unpleasant character and certainly had the opportunity but we've got nothing to link him to the scene. I've got nothing from my interviews with Andrews and Davies except that the latter laid claim to the cigarette case – says he lost it last week."

Fletcher smiled. "We are getting somewhere though. Our chaps in Brackley have picked up some very useful information. The girl, by the way, has been positively identified by her parents. She is Jennifer Sumser, nineteen, worked at Bronnley soap factory in Brackley. She has two friends who claim they were not with her on Monday; they said they went to a dance class. However, they were not there – the Sergeant at Brackley checked – and three girls were seen waiting by the Town Hall. They were then picked up by… wait for it…an RAF truck. The witness, Mrs Norris, owns a dress shop on the High Street; she recognised Jenny as she had bought a pair of nylon stockings on Saturday from her shop and Mrs N had been surprised that she could afford them."

"So I was right. She was providing services to men on the base…presumably all three were."

"Not so fast. It is possible the truck came from RAF Turweston which is just outside Brackley. We tried to get fingerprints from the truck you mentioned Sergeant but there was nothing distinct enough."

"But, as I thought, the key to this is to find the driver of that truck. I can check with Turweston whether any of their trucks was out on Monday late afternoon or night."

"I think Langford might tell us something," Lizzie offered again.

"I'll interview him first thing tomorrow."

"Actually, Robbie, I wondered if it might be a good idea for me to talk with him…informally…he'll be on his guard with you. I can have a casual conversation."

"Miss Barnes is right, Sergeant. It's worth a try. If she gets nothing, you can interview him formally afterwards."

"Has the truck been searched thoroughly? I mean, there may be something that will prove Jenny was in it or something that tells us who was driving it."

"Done. Nothing found at all."

"And don't forget to check the business of Driscoll's brother."

Robbie McBane looked at Lizzie and then at Fletcher. He smiled. "I thought I was running the investigation on the base."

Lizzie giggled. "Of course you are. I'm just making suggestions."

# PART 4: THURSDAY 18TH FEBRUARY 1943

## CHAPTER 21

Bailey and Fletcher looked through the glass in the interview room door. Its stark walls were pale green and the room was deliberately bare apart from the table, two chairs either side of it, the clock on the wall and the picture of the King. The young woman at the table was sitting upright, her hands twisting in her lap. PC Grant had brought her in first thing, before she started work. He said she had been very nervous and her mother had words with her before they left.

Sergeant Bailey spoke quietly. "In Grant's words, she's a bit of a tart. Mrs Sumser did say she was very forward…going with boys when she was only fourteen, that sort of thing."

"Let's see how she deals with what we've got." Fletcher opened the door and marched into the room with Bailey behind him. Maggie Bennett started to rise from her seat but Fletcher signalled her to remain seated. "I'm Inspector Fletcher and this is Sergeant Bailey whom you've already met."

"Is this about Jenny again?"

"It is indeed Miss. May I call you Maggie or would you prefer Miss Bennett?"

"Oh no…Maggie'll do fine. I'm not posh or anything."

"Yesterday afternoon, you told Sergeant Bailey that you did not see Jenny on Monday evening."

"That's right. Me and Rita went to the dance class at the WI Hall and Jenny didn't come. We assumed she wasn't coming out."

"The dance class. Are you sure about that?"

Maggie hesitated. "Ye-es."

Fletcher suddenly became brisk. "How many people were there?"

"About a dozen…I dunno…maybe fifteen."

"Was it a dozen or was it fifteen?"

"I can't remember exactly."

"What's the teacher's name?"

"Umm…I can't remember…Mrs something."

"What dances did she teach you?"

"Well it was sort of swing and you know…dances."

Fletcher said nothing but looked at Maggie sternly. The clock on the wall ticked slowly and loudly in the silence. "You seem to think we are fools."

"No…why d'you say that?"

"Because, Maggie, Sergeant Bailey had the good sense to check with Mrs Weatherstone, the dance teacher, who said she had only had her regulars on Monday night. No young women had attended the class."

Maggie coloured and looked down at the table but said nothing.

"If you were not at the dance class, where were you?"

Maggie looked up. "I can't say, Sir. I don't want my Mum to know and…"

"Well let's start with you Jenny and Rita standing outside the Town Hall. You didn't stand there all night did you…not in that weather."

"No…no…we went to a pub."

"Oh it's a pub now is it?" Fletcher stared at Maggie, his annoyance at her evasion growing. "You got a lift to this pub did you?"

"No…well that is…sort of."

Fletcher leaned forward. "Maggie, you need to consider what we already know and tell us the truth without further delay. If not, I will charge you with wasting Police time. You did get a lift, though not from a car."

Maggie was agitated. "I can't say...they told me not to tell anyone."

"By 'they' I assume you mean Corporal Davies or perhaps AC Andrews?" Maggie nodded so Fletcher pressed the point. "Which was it?"

"Davies. Andrews is usually there...at the base."

So, on Monday, all three of you were picked up from the Market Square and taken to Silverstone. What happened there?"

"Well...you know...we spent some time with some of the men and then they gave us a lift back. But Jenny wasn't in the truck on the way back."

"What happened to her?"

"I honestly don't know, Sir. We thought she stayed with one of the men but...we didn't know what to think."

Sergeant Bailey let a silence hang in the air and then said, "And how much do you get from each man?"

"It's not like that...."

"It's called prostitution, Maggie. It is an offence in our law though it seems to me that the real offence is committed by the men. How much?"

"Corporal Davies pays us at the end of the night depending on how many..."

"The men pay Davies and he pays you, no doubt having taken his cut."

Maggie remained silent. While Fletcher explained to Maggie that they would be interviewing Rita, Maggie looked increasingly anxious.

"Will you have to tell me Mum?"

"If you are charged, she will be told of course."

"Charged? We wasn't doing anything wrong...just a bit of fun. What harm is there in that when there's so much misery around?"

"The harm is in the fact that a young woman is now lying dead in Tranter's mortuary." Sergeant Bailey's voice was as stern as he could make it. The two officers rose and Bailey escorted Maggie to the front door.

Lizzie watched with envy as the aircrews climbed into the two Wellingtons that had been prepared for flying. The third, the one she had delivered and now fully repaired, sat forlornly on the apron as there was no flying instructor to take her up. Lizzie would have been very happy to fulfil that role but Group Captain Lovell was having none of it. Dearing was taking one set of trainees up and Driscoll the other.

The broken cloud and scything beams of sunlight of the previous day had been replaced by an unbroken wash of grey. There was little wind and the cloud was not heavy but lay like a soft, woollen fleece over the landscape. It was a good day for flying – once one rose above the cloud mass.

There was much light-hearted banter between the men. Each plane would have the trainer and two of all the other roles: two trainee pilots, two forward gunners, two rear, two for the centre gun and two navigators. They would have to huddle in the fuselage when not in position and swap over at some point in the flight. The engines of Dearing's plane were fired up first and Lizzie felt a surge of excitement at the distinctive roar which was amplified by the hangar and bounced off the buildings. When Driscoll's engines were started, the noise was almost deafening.

Lizzie stood by the open hangar and watched as the chocks were removed. Then ground crew scuttled back with the chocks, bent over to make sure they did not catch anything on the aircraft. There was a royal wave from Dearing and the engine sound increased as he opened the throttles. Slowly, the huge machine rolled forward and began to turn onto the taxi way. As it did so, everyone watching clutched coats tightly and bowed their heads into the huge blast from the props. It was a relief when the aircraft had made the turn and the thrust was directed along the airfield.

Driscoll's plane followed and the two heavy aircraft rumbled along the taxi way, their wings flexing like the wings of giant birds as the aircraft trundled over the concrete. At the far end of the taxi way, the two aircraft turned slowly onto the runway and waited, Driscoll's behind Dearing's. The tower cleared them for take-off and Dearing's plane lumbered forward, picking up speed. Its wings bent slowly upward as it gained speed and then it was off the ground. Suddenly, the heavy machine looked graceful, smooth, powerful as it lifted effortlessly into the air. It gained height slowly and was followed by Driscoll's aircraft.

Lizzie stood watching until the two aircraft were small smudges against the cloud and near silence had returned to the airfield. She was aware of a figure stopping beside her.

"It would be great to be going up in one of those wouldn't it?"

She turned to see Langford gazing into the distance. "It would. It's where I feel I should be…as no doubt do you."

"Yeah…but it'll never be."

"I wouldn't be so sure about that. There is a huge shortage of pilots and at some point the top brass is going to have to think about how it can boost numbers. Can you not ask for a transfer to aircrew? You could be a gunner or a navigator to start."

Langford gave a short laugh. "I couldn't be a navigator… too much Maths involved in that and I was never good at Maths at school."

"Well, I'm sure it'd be worth trying for trainee gunner and then pilot. Be positive."

"You're very kind, Miss. Maybe I will one day."

"My name's Lizzie by the way. May I know yours?"

"William…Bill. We normally only get spoken to by officers when they want something done. Then it's an order."

Lizzie said nothing and they both turned to walk into

the hangar. The rest of the ground crew had dispersed to other duties and Langford clearly had work to do. Lizzie knew this was the best moment though. "I'm hoping they let me go back to White Waltham soon. It'll drive me crazy if I have to stay here much longer. I'll have to use the train unless perhaps one of the trucks is going in my direction soon?"

"I wouldn't know about that, Miss...Lizzie. Most of the trips are just local...into Brackley or Buckingham, maybe over to Turweston."

"Do you often have to drive the trucks?"

"Sometimes...."

He did not elaborate and Lizzie thought for a moment. How could she explore Monday evening's truck movements without alerting him? "Presumably you have to sign the log book if you take a truck out?"

"Yeah. Usually write our initials that's all."

"So you'd write WL?"

"That's me." Langford grinned and abruptly returned his face to its normal serious expression.

"Those were the initials of the person who filled the truck with fuel on Monday... on the storage tank log." Lizzie held her breath.

Langford looked at her sharply and then turned away, his face hot. He looked afraid. "I know nothing about that."

Lizzie remained silent for a few seconds. "Bill, this is a serious business you know. That truck brought the girl onto the base on Monday. McBane is determined to find out who drove it and if it was you, it would be far better to tell him before he confronts you with it."

"You don't understand...I can't."

"Who are you afraid of Bill?"

Langford picked up a spanner from a rack on the side of the hangar. "I've got to go."

As he turned away, Lizzie laid her hand lightly on his arm. "Bill, please...for your own sake. Do you think they'll let you become aircrew if you're found to have any involvement at all? It'll be the end of your career. But if you were acting on someone else's orders, you cannot be blamed."

"I was told not to enter anything in the log book."

"So it was you who drove the truck on Monday?" Langford nodded, his face contorting with shame and fear like a schoolboy discovered in some misdemeanour. "You went to Brackley to pick up the girls didn't you?" Again he nodded. "Who told you to do that? Andrews...Davies?"

"I can't say any more, Miss, they'll kill me. I've got to go."

"I have to go to one of the accommodation blocks, Nurse. You'll be fine on your own." Matron raised the bag she was holding by way of explanation.

Patricia watched her stride down the ward and through the double doors. She could hear her steps reverberating along the corridor until she left the building. Matron never asked; she told you things. Frankly Patricia was relieved to have her out of her hair. She was still tired after her night shift on Tuesday and any relief from Matron's stern presence was welcome. She did wonder where she might be going and who might need treatment. A smile lit her face at the thought of a possible liaison with Group Captain Lovell. A nice bit of scandal that would be with him married and all. A whisper close behind her made her turn.

"Where's she going? Very suspicious, I'd say."

"You're being very melodramatic, Mr Saunders."

"You can't be too careful these days...you never know... she might be..."

"Just quit your silly speculations. She's gone to attend to a patient I suspect. Nothing sinister about that. You're ready to go back to duties, I'd say. You need something to keep you occupied."

Saunders spoke in his normal voice. "I'm almost ready,

Nurse, I agree. But…I need to take my morning exercise, so if you'll excuse me…" His voice became a whisper again. "I'll follow her and report back." Brian Saunders, already in his coat, followed Matron's footsteps, limping badly like Long John Silver.

"For pity's sake, Brian, stop the acting. You're terrible at it!"

Saunders continued on his way, now mincing effeminately. Patricia shook her head and went back to her duties on the ward.

Some twenty minutes later, Matron returned, her eagle eyes looking for anything that might be out of order. "You've done the morning medicine round, Nurse?"

"Yes Matron." From the corner of her eye, Patricia could see Brain Saunders tip-toeing into the ward behind Matron who stalked off to her office.

Saunders came close to Patricia and hissed, "She went to the officers' accommodation block. Not in there long but long enough." He tapped the side of his nose with his index finger. "Who d'you reckon she was with? Dearing, Driscoll?"

"Don't be ridiculous. She was doing her job and I wish you'd let me get on with mine." Patricia marched away leaving Saunders staring after her.

"Blimey, she's touchy today."

# CHAPTER 22

The faintest murmur in the far distance became a drone, louder and louder until the two Wellingtons came into sight, sweeping low over the fields, returning like wild geese from the morning's training flight. Lizzie watched as they flew past the airfield on the south side, the mighty engines like continuous thunder, and receded into the distance before the first made a wide turn to line up with the runway. The second plane continued on its course eastwards for some thirty seconds before also turning and picking up the same track.

As the first aircraft approached, it veered from port to starboard, each wing dipping and then rising in reciprocal motion, until settling and coming down over the landing lights, skimming the runway. When it hit the runway, it bounced up a few feet before settling back down again and rolling along the concrete. The second aircraft made a better landing.

Lizzie looked at her wrist watch: eleven hundred and thirty hours. She watched as the two planes turned onto the taxiway and returned to the hangars. Ground crew were hovering with the chocks, ready to carry out their usual tasks. One of them swung himself up into the cab of the fuel bowser that was standing ready. Lizzie loved the business, the bustle of the airfield, the excitement it always generated in her, lifting off from one place and soaring over the landscape to somewhere else.

The two aircraft came to a halt outside the hangars and the props slowed. Before they had finished turning, air crew were dropping down the ladders from the underside of the planes amidst much shouting, laughter and banter.

"Bloody hell, Philips. You must have been miles away

when you were landing. I thought I was a goner."

"We got down fine didn't we? Nobody died, we didn't hit the control tower. What are you moaning about?"

"I got seasick, that's what."

"Just stick to firing your gun and leave the flying to me."

Dearing and Driscoll left their respective planes last and stood together between the two aircraft. Dearing raised his voice. "Right chaps. Get yourself sorted with some coffee or something . De-briefing in fifteen minutes in Hut Five."

"I need a stiff Scotch, never mind a coffee."

"We've another training flight this afternoon so leave the whisky till later."

The men dispersed, hanging flying helmets, buoyancy aids and flying jackets in the hangar before trailing slowly along the buildings to Hut Five. Driscoll followed them but Dearing lingered for a few moments. He had taken off his flying helmet and mouthpiece and he now smoothed his pomaded hair down with his free hand. That gesture...Lizzie had seen him do that before. It was the action of a vain man, a man who was always concerned to make sure no hair was ever out of place. She watched as he slipped a hand into his inner jacket pocket and withdrew a hip flask from which he took several sips. So much for avoiding alcohol before the next training flight. The man was something of a liability.

A voice behind her startled Lizzie. "Missing the flying?" It was Robbie McBane.

"Absolutely. You need to hurry up and get this murder solved so I can get back to it."

"We're making progress but I could do with running a few things past you...to untangle my brain a bit."

"Fine. Is Fletcher not available?"

"Not just at the moment. He's having to sort something else out apparently. Probably some black market crook or something. You'd think with a war on that criminals would stop their activities but the opposite seems to be true. With so many people engrossed in the war effort, they seem to think they'll get away with murder....sorry that was unfortunate."

Lizzie became serious. "We need to make sure that whoever is guilty of Jenny's murder does not get away with it." And then the memory that had eluded her before flashed through her brain. It was that first night, in the officer's mess, Dearing standing at the bar when she had approached it with Driscoll, combing his hair. The comb...she was sure it was tortoiseshell.

"Robbie. I think I know who owns that comb we found under the bed. It's Dearing's. I'm sure I saw him use it the first night I was here...in the Officer's Mess."

As they walked to the hut where McBane had set up his office, Lizzie explained in detail the incident. "So Dearing could be our murderer."

"It's certainly looking like that isn't it?"

"We must be careful, Lizzie. This is all circumstantial and there could be an explanation. Dearing showed no recognition of the comb when I showed it to him."

"He's an artful liar I think."

When they reached the office, Robbie McBane sat down with a sigh. "I made a phone call. You know you wanted me to pursue that issue about Driscoll's brother. We have of course access to RAF records and colleagues in the special services. Driscoll is from Irish parentage....his mother and father came here at the end of the Great War - before Edward was born. His family name is O'Driscoll but he dropped the 'O' before applying to join the RAF. Why was that I wonder? But here's the really interesting part. He has an older brother who, when he was eleven, went back to Ireland to help on his uncle's farm as the uncle had been injured in an accident. The brother became involved in the IRA who were cosying up to Hitler at the start of the War because they thought Hitler would, in return, re-unite Ireland...give back the six counties to the South. I wonder where Driscoll's sympathies really lie?"

Lizzie exhaled softly. "That is interesting...yet he seems thoroughly... English."

"He would be. He's lived all his life in England, grew up here, went to school here, then university."

"But how could murdering Jenny Sumser be of any use to the Irish or the Germans for that matter?"

"I don't know but maybe she found out something and he needed to silence her."

"There's nothing to link him with that room nor Jenny though is there? Whereas Dearing…"

"Perhaps. He left a comb in that room at some point and was seen walking in that direction on Monday night. I need something more concrete than that Lizzie to arrest him."

"Perhaps you should search his room. There may be something there that links him."

Robbie McBane nodded slowly in agreement. "I think that will be the next stage. Lovell won't like it."

"Do you have to tell Lovell?"

"Of course…afterwards. I'll get on to my boss before I do, make sure I've got my back covered. Then I'll see Lovell with Fletcher. He should be in later. I'll try and catch Driscoll now before they do the afternoon flight and I must see AC Langford. You're keeping me busy."

Lizzie smiled cheekily. She was growing to like Robbie McBane but he always seemed a bit remote as if he was hiding behind his work. Perhaps he has someone already, she thought as she left the office. It was not that she was after a man, far from it, but she had to admit to herself, she was not averse to a little flirting…but with the right kind of man, someone who was safe.

"I was in the pub with a couple of mates last night, Sarge, and picked up a nice bit of gossip." PC Grant's eager face glowed with triumph. "D'you want to know what it was?"

Sergeant Bailey looked up from the report he was

reading, his glasses perched on the end of his nose. "I've got a horrible feeling you're going to tell me...but, if this is another of your pathetic jokes, Grant, keep it to yourself."

"It's no joke, Sarge, though I did pick up another good one. What's the difference between an ATA pilot and a duck?"

"Just tell me the gossip Grant or I'll have you cleaning the toilets with a toothbrush."

"The difference between an ATA pilot and a duck is that a duck can fly. Good one eh?"

"For all you know, I might have a relative in the ATA and I might find that attempt at humour very offensive. Now if you're not going to give me the gossip, shut up and get on with your work."

"Alright, Sarge. No need to bite me 'ead off. Well we were sitting there just having a chat you know and there were two guys at the next table. You could tell there was something secretive going on between them as they were huddled forward like this." Grant leant forward over his desk, and looked furtively from right to left.

"I suppose you're going to tell me, they turned out to be German spies and were passing on information crucial to Hitler's war effort."

"No nothing like that Sarge. One of them was saying that you could get extra petrol from Wallace's garage up the top of the High Street. He gets a couple of small deliveries a week from the RAF."

Frank Bailey looked up sharply. "Interesting...I suppose you'll know about that because you've been checking the fuel dockets from the garage."

"Um...yeah Sarge...yeah..."

"And?"

"Well, I've not noticed nothing yet, Sarge."

"So you have noticed something?"

Phil Grant looked at his boss with complete incomprehension.

"You used a double negative, Constable. A double

negative is a positive so you have noticed something."

"I'm not with you, Sarge."

"Sometimes I wish that were true, Grant. Forget it."

"But Sarge, if Wallace is selling petrol under the counter as it were, he wouldn't give out a docket for it would he? I mean it would be all hush-hush, no questions asked, nothing in writing, funny handshake, Bob's your uncle, wouldn't it?"

"Maybe. I'll have to investigate. We've got to follow up these things." Frank Bailey put his hands on the desk and pushed himself up out of his chair . "I will once more tackle that hill and go visit Mr Wallace. I wish they had built our police station at least halfway up the hill or they supplied me with a car. Man of my age. You hold the fort and go through those dockets again just in case."

Sergeant Bailey pulled on his cape and left the building to retrieve his bicycle from the locked shed at the side of the station. At least it was not raining and that wind had dropped. As he pedalled away slowly the short distance along Banbury Road to join the High Street, a part of him was excited. If he could find a black market, ration-busting sale of petrol and bring the perpetrator to justice, maybe, just maybe, he might get promoted...or at least have a claim on a car. He tackled the hill with new determination.

There were no cars filling up at the garage when he arrived, blowing loudly. Having propped his bike against the wall, he retrieved his helmet from the saddle bag. He waited for several minutes until his breathing was normal and his heart had stopped pounding in his chest before walking through the large, open doors of the workshop. Greg Wallace was bent over a car, the bonnet of which had been folded back on one side. The usual clutter of equipment and boxes of spares lined the walls. A long rack held new tyres, the black rubber pristine. The smell of oil and grease hung in the air, not unpleasant but strong.

"Mornin' Mr Wallace."

The garage owner, putting one hand on the small of his

back, straightened and winced. "I'm getting too old for this, Sergeant."

"You and me both. What's wrong with this one?"

"Nothing. Just doing a service. It's got to be done regular like...check the spark plugs and adjust the gap, change the oil, that sort of thing. D'you need yours doing?"

"Might do, if I had one but I can do me bike myself."

"You'd think they'd supply you with a car – important job like yours."

"Yes, they should, but then again they may be worried about petrol consumption." Bailey watched the other man's face; there was just the faintest flicker of alarm, the pupils of his eyes contracting minutely. Frank Bailey was beginning to enjoy this detective work and he reckoned he was quite good at it. "D'you ever get people trying to get extra...you know...more than their ration."

"Just occasionally someone tries it on, but not often."

"You won't mind if I check your books?"

"Course not. Come to the office." The office was at the front of the workshop separated from it by a grimy partition, the bottom of which had once been white and the top of which was wired glass. Grubby finger marks and smears of grease were over both. An old green filing cabinet stood in a corner opposite the open door and a desk stood against the front wall. It had a pile of invoices under a large cog that served as a paperweight, a ledger open with a few entries, the corner of each page grubby from greasy fingers. "Here we are, Sergeant. Not the plushest of offices but it serves its purpose. What was it you wanted to see?"

"Let's start by your records of fuel deliveries."

Wallace turned to the filing cabinet and pulled out the top drawer which screeched in protest. He extracted a file and handed it to Bailey. Inside was a wadge of tickets showing fuel deliveries. Each had two scrawls at the bottom which presumably were the signatures of Wallace and the delivery driver. Bailey looked at the amounts...only one thousand gallons each week. "How much have you got in the tank at the moment?"

"I'll have a look." Wallace led the way outside to a dial fixed to the wall. "Four hundred and twenty near enough...it's not absolutely accurate."

"Next delivery?"

"Tomorrow...it's every Friday. The tank holds two thousand gallons but I'm not allowed more than one thousand."

"Thanks. Let's go inside." Back in the office, Bailey looked at the ledger on the desk. It recorded all the fuel sold, the date and the amount. He added up the amounts until the last delivery the previous week. "Well that all seems to be in order."

"Everything above board, Sergeant, that's me. It's not worth trying any funny business."

"No and you wouldn't want to harm the war effort by selling above rations."

"Spot on. There's some that do though."

Bailey waited a moment, saying nothing, until Wallace started shuffling his feet. His question was sudden and he looked Wallace straight in the eye. "Do you ever sell petrol to RAF vehicles?"

Wallace looked away. "RAF...no...no."

"Then why would an RAF truck be on your forecourt a couple of times a week...we have witnesses." A little white lie was justified in such circumstances.

"RAF truck...there must be a mistake, I d-don't know nothing..."

"Come on Greg. I know all about it. How much do they supply you with?"

Wallace's eyes were wide with fear. "I told you, Sergeant, I don't..." and then the bluster left him. "It seemed like too good a chance to miss...a bit of extra money...only a small amount...helps a few local people who need extra..." He tailed off and suddenly flopped into the swivel chair in front of the desk.

"Let's start at the beginning shall we?"

When Wallace had finished, Bailey told him to report to the station to make a formal statement as soon as he could get cleaned up. He was feeling very pleased with himself as he freewheeled down the High Street giving cheery waves to shoppers and gracing them with beaming smiles. He was looking forward to another telephone conversation with Fletcher.

# CHAPTER 23

Lizzie joined Patricia for lunch in the small staffroom by the ward. "No sign of Matron today?"

""Oh she'll be eating in her suite upstairs." Patricia grinned and slipped another forkful of mash potato into her mouth.

Lizzie pushed a small pile of what appeared to be minced meat around her plate with her fork, watching the thin gravy swirl gently around it. She was not sure whether to say anything and, if so, how to start. She decided that being direct was the best way.

"Robbie did some research into some of the staff here… Edward."

Patricia put down her fork, staring at Lizzie, waiting for what was coming.

"He knows about Edward's background and his brother."

"So because he's Irish, it makes him a suspect for murder is that it?"

"No Patricia, of course not. But he has to investigate everything…be able to rule people out."

A hostile silence fell between the two young women as they pretended to continue their meal until it was broken again by Lizzie. "Robbie said that Edward's brother was involved with the IRA and their attempt to befriend Hitler to recover the six counties for Ireland."

"That was at least three years ago. The IRA dropped that plan when they realised that Hitler was not someone you could trust. And anyway, what Edward's brother has done is nothing to do with Edward. For God's sake, Lizzie, he has risked his life fighting Hitler. He flew countless missions before coming here.

He's absolutely committed to doing his bit as are many Irish men and women. I could be back home in Ireland, a neutral country, but I chose to work over here."

"I know, I know…I'm not getting at you…but why be so secretive about his brother?"

"You wouldn't understand it Lizzie, growing up in this country as a fully English person. Us Irish face a lot of prejudice. You must have heard about the signs in the lodging houses in London and places – 'No blacks, no wogs, no Irish, no dogs.' How can we trust people in this country? There's suspicion anyway but since Ireland declared itself neutral and refused Churchill the use of the ports, they're only too ready to condemn us."

Lizzie stared at her plate. "I see. I didn't realise it was so bad."

"No reason why you should…you don't have to face it. I get it every day from that old bag, Matron."

Lizzie looked up sharply. "What does she do?"

"Oh it's not what she does or even says. It's the way she's always so hostile, as if I'm the enemy. Whatever I do is not quite right, she checks everything, she picks holes…"

"I suspect she's like that with everyone though isn't she? She's just a bad-tempered, ageing woman."

"Perhaps. Maybe I'm just getting tired of it. 'Tis only Edward being here that keeps me really."

"But that's a good reason. He's a good man, Patricia."

"Well you've changed yer tune have you not? A few minutes ago, he was a murderer, a Nazi sympathiser, member of the IRA."

"I never said all that Patricia. I just think it's better to be open, then there's no speculation."

Patricia sighed deeply. "I hope this bloody war is over soon and we can start living again."

"We can agree on that." Lizzie smiled and reached her hand across the table. Squeezing Patricia's. She looked up and their eyes met. Patricia gave a tired smile and Lizzie said softly,

"I'm sorry this has come between us Patricia but I think it's better to be straight."

Robbie McBane had caught up with Driscoll before lunch. The meeting ended with surprising cordiality. Driscoll seemed almost relieved to tell him about his brother, about his own determination to do his bit to defeat Hitler. "I'm not my brother's keeper," he said at the end, his blue eyes earnest. He stood, dignified, serious, no trace of cynicism on his face. The two men shook hands, McBane with a new respect for a man who simply wanted to avoid the prejudices against his background. He had experienced enough of that himself to know how it could limit your opportunities.

He had waited until the Wellingtons had lifted from the runway for the afternoon flight and were climbing slowly into the grey sky before he entered the officers' accommodation hut. Most of the rooms were empty and he found Dearing's easily enough. It was not locked and an envelope addressed to Fl Lt R. Dearing was lying helpfully on the chest of drawers. It was, as with all RAF accommodation, uninspiring and only a few personal items gave it any individuality. It was almost a statement of the uncertainty of life: here today, gone tomorrow.

It was unusual, however, in that there was no photograph on the bedside table, no young lady who had captured Dearing's heart as his own had been captured by Catriona. That was perhaps surprising; Dearing was young, clearly from a wealthy background, good-looking but perhaps he knew too much about the tragically short lives of aircrew and did not want any attachments.

There was a photograph on the chest of drawers of two older people that he took to be Dearing's parents. They were smartly dressed and the man stood very erect, looking severe and fairly pompous. The lady was smiling almost apologetically, as if she should not be in the photograph, her carefully groomed hair topped by a small hat. At least Dearing had someone to call his own but Robbie McBane wondered at the relationship between father and mother. What sort of example had his father set to the young Ronald? What lay behind that stern face?

McBane slid open the top drawer in the chest. It contained items for personal grooming. His attention was immediately drawn to a hairbrush and clothes brush. He lifted out the former and held it up so that the light from the window was behind it. Tortoiseshell, without a doubt, probably a gift from his parents, bought by his mother when he joined the RAF. Mothers thought about such things. But no comb. Surely there would have been a comb to complete the set?

Robbie McBane had a growing certainty that Dearing was the man they were after, a feeling of excitement like the rush one had as, clutching the ball, the opposition's line was only paces away and one knew the try was in one's grasp. But he knew he needed something more. The absence of a comb was not proof that the one they had found was Dearing's. He needed something that tied Dearing indisputably to the dead girl.

He searched all the drawers of the chest. Nothing, other than the clothes one would expect to find. Then he turned his attention to the wardrobe, even checking the panels at the back to ensure they were not false. He laughed at himself. What did he expect to find that would need false panels in the wardrobe? Dearing's dress uniform, shirts, a greatcoat – he checked the pockets of that – and felt a card or something in one. He pulled it out and stared at it. His heart raced. This was it. This was the evidence he needed. He put it carefully back in the greatcoat pocket. He needed someone else with him when he 'discovered' it.

◆ ◆ ◆

"How did that idiot Langford not realise he had only two of them in the truck?"

Andrews shrugged. "Search me Corp. He heard the bang on the back of the truck – usual signal for off – so he pulled away."

"This is getting hot but as long as everyone keeps mum, we'll be alright."

"Langford is with Dearing now. I warned him but he's a deep one. He could spill the beans I reckon."

"Shit. If you need something doing, do it yourself," Davies said gloomily. "That bloody meddling Scot, heard me talking to the Landlord up at the Silver Swan. Picked up on supplying provisions too. As long as he doesn't find out what the girls were up here for and how they got onto the base, I reckon we'll be alright. They have to have evidence see."

"So long as no one talks…"

"We'll be ok. Your job is to make sure no one does."

"But if they think one of us murdered that girl…I mean that's much more serious isn't it than just the…you know."

"Course it is. It's a hanging offence that."

The two men sat side by side on a bench in the open hangar looking out at the grey wash of cloud over the airfield. Neither spoke for some time, each contemplating what McBane might know and who might be under suspicion. Davies knew he was. McBane had made that very clear. What he needed to do was throw suspicion onto someone else for the fuel thing and especially for the murder. He was not going down for that.

A figure appeared in the entrance to the hangar, walking slowly, deep in thought. As it approached, Davies and Andrews saw it was Langford. They both stood up. Langford was looking down at the ground and did not see them until he was very close.

He almost jumped. "Alright Corp, Andrews. Didn't realise you were here."

So I noticed...miles away you were. So you've just seen McBane?"

"That's right Corp."

"And?"

"I didn't tell him nothing, nothing at all. He thinks I was driving the truck though and said it was my initials on the fuel tank log. That was you're doing Andrews."

"So what did you say?"

"I told him I didn't recognise the handwriting but it wasn't mine. Said someone must be trying to drop me in it."

"Did he buy that?"

"Couldn't tell but he can't claim it was me when I've said that."

"Quite right boyo. He won't stop though. He'll come back at us all again." Davies leaned towards Langford, his face reflecting the menace in his voice. "Just you make sure you keep quiet, Langford. Keep our names out of it. Got that?"

"You can rely on me, Corp."

"I'm sure I can. You wouldn't want anything to happen to that sweetheart of yours."

Langford stepped back alarm on his face. "You wouldn't. That's not fair...she's got nothing to do with this."

"Not fair...listen to him. There's a bloody war on boyo, what's fair about that?"

"There could be an accident." Andrews wanted his share of the intimidation. "Always things happening on air bases."

"I've not told him anything, right? So leave me alone." Langford walked off rapidly, out of the hangar.

Andrews was going to call him back but Davies laid a hand on his arm. "Let him go. He's got the message. I've got things to do."

Davies walked towards Hut Fifteen where McBane was based. There was a risk of course in what he was going to do but he needed at least to create a smoke screen and hopefully divert attention for the murder elsewhere. He entered the hut and, before tapping on the door, set his face to an expression of genuine concern and honesty. He could do that. he could be anything he needed to be. When he entered, the Sergeant was sitting at the desk making notes.

"Corporal Davies. What brings you here?"

"I've just picked up something that I thought I should pass on to you, Sir." Davies made sure there was no cynicism in the use of the address.

McBane gestured towards the chair and Davies sat down, leaning forward and making sure his face showed concern. "It's about the murdered girl, Sir." McBane nodded. "A couple of the chaps were talking, like, and I overheard the conversation. One of them said that, on Monday night, he had slipped out of his own hut to have a fag and he had seen someone coming out of the end hut - this hut that is – at about twenty-one thirty hours."

"Did he see who it was?"

"He's pretty certain that it was...Flight Lieutenant Dearing, Sir. I don't know what he could have been doing up here but, you know, there could be a connection like."

The eyes that bored into Davies were suspicious, watchful and the corporal realised McBane would be wondering why he was now suddenly being so helpful. For a moment Davies wondered if he had made a mistake bringing this information to McBane which was, after all, untrue. If he was asked who had seen Dearing, he would naturally claim he could not remember. He looked straight into McBane's eyes, hoping his expression of naïve assistance was convincing.

McBane stood up. "Thank you Corporal. You were right to bring this to me but...please do not think it will divert me from investigating what is going on with fuel and trucks and so on."

"Oh no, Sir. I know you've got to do that. And that business on Tuesday night at the Silver Swan. See I was supposed to be meeting a lady in the pub on Monday but I completely forgot. So if she asked, the Landlord could say I was in there but arrived late so we must have missed each other."

"And the name of the Lady?"

"Margaret, Sir, though she calls herself Peggy."

Robbie McBane picked up his notepad. "And her address?"

"I…I don't rightly know. I've only met her in the pub see on account of the fact…. she's married so I can't go round there can I?"

"What a tangled life you live, Corporal. Perhaps I will be able to untangle it for you."

# CHAPTER 24

Inspector Fletcher looked grim, his jaw clamped tight. He stood in front of the pinboard in the makeshift incident room which was covered with sheets of paper. The picture of Jenny was in the centre and names of others written in various positions around it. He looked at Robbie and Lizzie who were sitting facing him with equally serious expressions.

"We've got a lot of catching up to do and we need to be pretty quick. What we have just found in Dearing's room is pretty convincing that he was at least with Jennifer on Monday night. But Sergeant, before we get to Dearing, let me up-date you on fuel and truck movements. You'll be pleased to know that you were right to be suspicious."

"Aye, but I think there's a link to Jenny's murder. I just canna put my finger on it."

"Our Sergeant at Brackley, Bailey, picked up a whisper about black market fuel being sold from one of the garages. He investigated and a Mr Wallace has been accepting, obviously for some cash, two deliveries a week from an RAF truck. It was organised originally by our friend Corporal Davies though Wallace has not seen him since. It's Andrews or Langford that usually delivers. It's not a great deal, twelve five-gallon jerry cans twice a week, so one hundred and twenty gallons. Davies and Co are no doubt making a good bit and Wallace makes a bit on top. Deliveries are Mondays and Thursdays. Sergeant Bailey told him not to expect any more!"

Robbie McBane spread his hands wide to indicate he knew it from the start. "Langford has admitted that he drove the truck on two occasions on Monday night and that he brought the girls back to the base and then took them home later. So, he obviously drops the fuel off and then picks up the girls. A bit smelly in the back of the truck I should think."

"That confirms the witness statement we have from Mrs Norris about the three girls being picked up by the truck." Fletcher drew a line from the names of the three girls at the top of the board to the right and added Mrs Norris's name. "We know from Maggie Bennett and Rita Polesworth that they were working as prostitutes here, again organised by Davies who is charging the men and paying the girls, no doubt keeping a generous percentage."

"So Davies is the mastermind behind selling the fuel and running the prostitution racket?" Robbie could not keep the triumph out of his voice. "That'll put him away for some time."

"Presumably Andrews can also be charged with aiding him?" Lizzie asked, her soft voice surprising the two men.

"Oh yes, most definitely." Fletcher drew some more lines on the board linking Davies and Andrews with fuel and the girls.

"And what about Langford?" Lizzie continued. "He was only involved because he was under orders from Davies and probably threatened. He more or less told me that he would be subject to some kind of reprisal if he didn't comply. It wouldn't seem fair to lay all this at his door."

Inspector thought for a moment. "Let's see how things go. I agree he is less culpable but he could have reported it, indeed he should have."

"Difficult to do that, Inspector, when you are being threatened."

"It may be that we can deal with it through a Court Martial – he'd probably get a reprimand," offered Robbie. "He was very helpful when I did question him and that will count in his favour."

"Good point Robbie," said Fletcher. "That may well be the best way to deal with Langford. You'll also have to deal with the two sentries on Monday who didn't record the truck movements and so on. It's not a criminal offence but definitely a dereliction of duty."

"Aye don't you worry. I'll not forget them, especially that cocky sod Smith."

"What I don't understand," said Lizzie, her brow creasing, "is why they left Jenny there. They must have realised that there were only two girls in the truck. I mean Langford must have surely."

"I asked him about that and he said that he was in the cab and heard a bang on the back of the truck which is the signal to go. So he did. It was whoever banged the truck or maybe it was made by something else, someone dropping something, I don't know. Jenny's friends must have realised. I don't know why they didn't say anything."

"Apparently, they thought she was staying longer with one of the men and would be taken back later. Rita did say that Jenny was with the 'posh bloke' at the end. Who does that sound like?"

"It could have been one of the trainees. There's plenty have what could be called posh voices. But I would guess it was Dearing."

"I'm afraid guesses are inadmissible in court, Lizzie." Fletcher turned back to the board. "Right let's go over the evidence we've got against Dearing. Robbie take us through it."

"Firstly he was seen by two people on Monday night in the vicinity of this hut, though one of those witnesses is second-hand through Davies so not reliable. Secondly we found a tortoiseshell comb under the bed. Dearing has a grooming set in his room which is tortoiseshell but the comb you would expect to find is not there." The comb lay on the desk along with other pieces of evidence. "I think the convincing evidence though is what we found in his greatcoat pocket. Difficult to claim he was not with Jenny when he had her identity card from Bronnley's factory."

"That will take some explaining certainly but it's still fairly circumstantial. It may prove he was with her but it does not prove he killed her. What's his motive?"

Lizzie shuffled uncomfortably in her chair and Robbie McBane looked at her. She nodded. "Lizzie had a visit from Dearing on Monday evening at about twenty-one hundred hours. He clearly wanted…you know…and Lizzie declined. He was drunk. Lizzie also had an experience with him several years ago when he intended to impose himself on her. It adds up to a man who thinks women are there for his gratification."

"He becomes very angry when he is thwarted, Inspector. I know that to my cost. I could very easily see him becoming violent if Jenny had refused the particular depravities he perhaps wanted."

"Sexual violence." Fletcher turned to stare out of the window and, whilst he did so, Robbie McBane reached over and laid his hand on Lizzie's. He smiled at her, a smile she returned, grateful for the comfort he was giving. "We certainly have enough to question him but not, as yet, to charge him. You and I Robbie will go over to Lovell now and tell him we will be taking Dearing in for questioning. I think it best, Lizzie, if you are not with us."

"That suits me. I'll look out for the Wellingtons returning and try to contain my envy that I was not flying one of them."

"That's a good point, Sir. We need to be ready to get him when the training flight lands."

"We'll be ready."

"What about Davies and Andrews?"

"We'll pick them up in the morning, no word about it now. Happy with that Sergeant?"

"Aye. Very happy. Let's get the big fish first."

The two men walked speedily but in solemn silence the length of the huts to the administrative block and knocked on Lovell's door. They did not accept the invitation to sit down and Lovell rose shakily to his feet, alarmed at their manner.

Fletcher did not wait for civilities. "We are here to let you know, Group Captain, that, as soon as he returns from this afternoon's training flight, we are going to take

Flight Lieutenant Dearing to Towcester Police Station for questioning."

"Dearing...questioning? What on earth is going on?"

"There is strong evidence that links him to the murder of Jennifer Sumser here on Monday night."

Lovell dropped back into his chair as if his legs had given way. "But, but...Dearing? That's impossible."

"Why do you say that, Sir?"

"He's an officer... and a gentleman. He went to one of the finest schools in the country...and his father is a judge." Suddenly he was on his feet and shouting. "Good God man. You can't be serious. Dearing would have nothing to do with this sordid business."

"That may prove to be the case, Sir, but we need to question him." Fletcher looked Lovell straight in the eye. "We are letting you know as a courtesy and because you will obviously have to make some arrangements for his duties to be covered. He may be with us overnight and perhaps for some time tomorrow."

"How in God's name am I supposed to run a training base if you take away one of my two instructors?"

"I realise it's a frustration, Sir, but we have to do whatever is necessary to bring that girl's killer to justice. This can't be swept under the carpet with some mis-guided gentleman's agreement. And, I might add, in my experience, the school someone went to and their parentage are no guarantee of their conduct." Fletcher was tempted to add that, in fact, those who had been raised in privileged circumstances were often led by arrogance to be the most culpable. "We will be making some arrests in the morning."

"Arrests? Who are you arresting? I thought you wanted to question Dearing."

"We are doing that, Sir but there are other matters to deal with." Robbie McBane looked carefully at Lovell. He was going to enjoy this. "The fuel consumption and unrecorded miles on the truck I reported to you the other day...Sir."

Lovell looked baffled and the two detectives left him to contemplate the collapse of his little empire. They ambled towards the hangars in silence. Eventually Fletcher spoke again. "I don't like that man."

"Who, Lovell?"

"The same. He's a little man who's puffed himself up and now thinks he's important. He's full of bluster and has a naïve view of human beings. He lives in some kind of fictional world where chaps from wealthy backgrounds are always 'jolly sporting' and the villains are ruffians from poor areas. I mean, telling us that Dearing couldn't have anything to do with Jenny's murder because of the school he went to! My God, he should have experienced some of the things I've dealt with."

"He strikes me as being unsure of his authority. He makes up for it by being aggressive."

"Very profound, Sergeant." Fletcher's usually inscrutable face twisted into a grin.

The low drone of aircraft engines drifted through the still air and soon the two Wellingtons came into sight, flying low as before across the Northamptonshire countryside. The shapes, dark against the low cloud, gradually showed the green and brown of their camouflage. They flew past the airfield on the South side and, as before, turned through one hundred and eighty degrees to approach the runway from the East. In the distance, they looked like vast birds of prey hovering in the air before gliding down to land.

Lizzie came out of the hangar in which the third Wellington, the one she had delivered, stood silent and neglected. "Such a waste to have it sitting there idle. Beautiful sight isn't it?"

"Aye it is that. They'll give Hitler something to think about I'm sure. Now you stay back here Lizzie. We'll talk to Dearing when he's dismissed the crew."

They waited until the aircraft stopped on the apron, the crews were disgorged and the final instructions to meet in Hut Five shouted. As the crews shuffled away, Driscoll had a parting word with Dearing and then the latter was left on his own. Fletcher moved forward with Robbie McBane beside him.

"Flight Lieutenant Dearing."

Dearing looked at the two men approaching but said nothing.

"I'm going to have to ask you to come with us, Sir. We have some questions to ask you."

"Fire away. Ask what you like."

"No, Sir. Not here. You will accompany us to Towcester Police Station."

"Will I now? What makes you think I'm going to do that?"

"If you prefer, Sir, I can arrest you."

"Arrest me?" Dearing shouted. "On what charge?"

Faces turned towards the sound, aircrew who were not yet inside the hangar.

"I suggest, Sir, that you come without making a fuss. No point in giving the trainees something to gossip about." Robbie McBane tried to sound conciliatory though frankly he didn't care if junior ranks saw this particular officer in an embarrassing position.

"What's this about? Why me? Oh I get it. You need someone to pin it on so you've chosen me because I'm from a different class is that it?" Dearing glared at McBane and Fletcher, his jaw thrusting forward aggressively. Then his eye caught Lizzie who was hovering in the entrance to the hangar. "Oh I see…it's that little bitch from the ATA isn't it? What's she been saying? Poisoning you against me?"

"That's enough," Fletcher snapped. "Any more and I will arrest you."

They led him away still grumbling and firing murderous looks at Lizzie who returned them with an unflinching expression though she dearly wanted to fire a salvo back. She watched as he was led towards the block and disappeared around it to where Fletcher's car was no doubt parked. Lizzie breathed out. There was a sense of satisfaction that Dearing had been taken in for questioning. A vile man. But at the same time, a voice of doubt whispered in her head. Had she unduly influenced Robbie McBane and poisoned his mind against Dearing? Could it be that he was innocent and she had instigated this because of her own antipathy towards him?

She began to make her way back slowly towards the Sick Bay and her own room. She was deep in thought, staring at the ground and did not see Edward Driscoll approaching her.

"Lizzie, Lizzie?" She looked up. "Some of the chaps said that Dearing has gone with McBane and Fletcher. Is that right?"

"He's being taken to Towcester Police Station for questioning." Driscoll stood still staring at Lizzie. "It doesn't mean anything but…"

"Then why Towcester? Why not question him here?"

Lizzie shrugged. "I guess they think he may be responsible for…"

"They can't think that, surely?"

"Not everyone is as honourable as you, Edward. Dearing has some very disturbing attitudes."

"I need to see Lovell. What will we do tomorrow? We're now down to one instructor."

"I don't want to take advantage of the situation but I would be happy to stand in."

Edward Driscoll saw the eagerness in Lizzie's face. She was a remarkable young woman and it might be worth raising with Lovell. "I'll explore that possibility."

# CHAPTER 25

Corporal Davies plonked his tray on the table in the mess hut next to Andrews who was already well into his evening meal. The mess was busy, the ranks tucking in hungrily to a good beef stew with dumplings and cabbage followed by treacle steam pudding with custard. Cutlery clattered on tables and the hubbub of conversation bounced around the bare walls, softened only by the heavy blackout curtains. The bitter aroma of cooked cabbage hung in the steamy atmosphere adding to the warmth of the hut.

Andrews sighed with contentment as he picked up his spoon and drew the pudding bowl in front of him. "You wouldn't get this on Civvy Street that's for sure."

"Did you hear…about Dearing?"

"I've heard about nothing else since the Wimpies came back. D'you think he did it?"

"Dunno, maybe he did, maybe he didn't but it takes the heat off us if he's the prime suspect."

"What makes them think he did it? Do they know about him and…?"

"Don't know but shall we say a witness told them he saw Dearing coming out of that hut on Monday night at about the right time."

"Witness? Who was that then?"

Davies smirked at Andrews. "I've no idea."

The penny dropped with Andrews and, thoughtfully, he lifted a spoonful of sponge pudding and custard to his mouth. A blob of custard slipped off the spoon onto his chin.

"For God's sake man, you haven't learned to eat properly yet. Small bites like your mother told you."

Andrews rescued the custard and put it in its rightful

place in his mouth. "What about the other thing. I mean do they know how the girls got here and about the petrol and other stuff?"

"No idea. They've said nothing so perhaps they're still at sea. If Dearing talks though…"

"He won't say nothing will he? I mean if he does, he can kiss goodbye to his career. He'd be busted down to the ranks and he'd never be able to cope with that. Arrogant bastard. Mind you, I wouldn't be sorry to see him court- martialled."

Bill Langford lifted his tray from the serving hatch and looked around the mess. His eyes avoided Davies who was looking in his direction and he walked well away to a table with spaces at the end of the mess.

"Well now. Langford doesn't want to know us. I wonder why that is?"

"Perhaps he thinks he'll stay out of trouble if he's not seen with us."

Davies gave a short, humourless laugh. "He's in it right up to his neck. At least I've got nothing to worry about."

Andrews looked up from his pudding and frowned. "How's that? If they find out about the fuel, the girls…"

"Ah but I didn't drive the truck, I didn't take the fuel from the storage tank nor deliver it to Wallace. I didn't pick the girls up."

"But…you're in it more than us. I mean you arranged it all."

"Oh I've no doubt others will claim it was all my organisation but how can that be proved?"

"You wouldn't let us take the flak for it all. I mean that's not fair."

"You sound like Langford - a kid in the playground. 'That's not fair, Miss. Johnny punched me in the bollocks.' You listen to me." Davies leaned forward over the table and spoke with vehemence. "There's nothing fair about this life, this World. What's fair about kids being blown up by Hitler's bombs? What's fair about some posh gits getting to tell us what to do? It's each man for himself and I intend to survive."

"And let us carry the can is that it?" Andrews finished his pudding in silence, slung the spoon in the bowl and lifted his tray. Without saying a word, he strode away from Davies who regarded him with an amused glint in his eye.

Lizzie, deep in thought, opened the door of the nurses' staffroom where Patricia and Matron were serving themselves the stew and dumplings from the trolley.

"Ah Lizzie, come and help yourself. Stew and dumplings with cabbage. The chaps on the ward were in heaven when they discovered it was treacle sponge and custard for pudding."

"Thanks. It smells good. You can't beat a proper pudding. I suppose we should spare a thought for civilians who struggle to have a decent meal on rations."

Matron sat heavily on one of the chairs but said nothing until Lizzie and Patricia were seated and had started eating. "That Dearing has been arrested then?"

"Well not arrested...just taken in for questioning." Lizzie picked up a tone of satisfaction, pleasure in Matron's voice. Much as she disliked Dearing, there was something about Matron's attitude that she did not care for.

"I s'pose that's the expression they use. It probably means they think he's guilty."

"Perhaps, Patricia, perhaps." Lizzie was not comfortable with the topic of conversation as she did not want to let anything slip that may prejudice the investigation. Matron seemed intent on extracting information from her, however.

"What led them to Dearing? They must have some evidence."

"I'm sure they have. They wouldn't take him away for questioning if not but..."

"I've never liked that man. He's arrogant, looks down on everyone, especially women." There was bitterness in Matron's voice and Lizzie recognised guiltily that she was hearing her own thoughts expressed. Patricia exchanged a surreptitious glance with Lizzie.

"I agree, but that doesn't mean he's a murderer." Patricia offered.

"One leads to the other. He'll be charged, you mark my words. It always comes down to sex, him wanting to do things to that tart she didn't want I suppose. I don't know who is the worse between them. No decent girl would be selling her body like that. Some parents don't know how to bring up children."

"How do you know she was selling her body?"

"It's obvious is it not? What else would she be doing here?"

Neither Patricia nor Lizzie offered an answer and all three concentrated on eating, the absence of conversation filled with the occasional chink of cutlery on plates.

"A child should be brought up properly, become the pride of his parents." Matron's voice caused Lizzie to look up. It was not the blunt tone she had come to expect, but wistful. The older woman's eyes were soft, distant. Perhaps beneath that granite exterior there was a heart, an individual with a history.

"No good comes of liaisons like that...outside of marriage...only heartache," Matron added.

Lizzie wanted to say something to encourage Matron to go further but she saw Patricia's blush even with her head lowered. The door of the staffroom opened slowly and Edward Driscoll peered around it. "Ah Lizzie, I hoped I'd find you here. Do forgive me ladies for interrupting your meal. Lizzie, I had a word with Lovell about tomorrow and he's given the green light for you to take one of the Wellingtons up. If you take Dearing's plane and crew that would be great."

Lizzie had almost jumped out of her chair. "That's wonderful. Thank you so much for asking. Did he take a lot of persuading?"

"Surprisingly not, actually. To be honest I think he's so shell-shocked about Dearing that he can't think straight. But just make sure you bring it and everyone on it back in one piece."

"Of course. Could I take the one I delivered on Monday though? I know they're the same but it looks so lonely sitting in the hangar and I think it would be good to give it a spin... Langford told me it had all been repaired and checked over."

"I didn't realise aircraft got lonely!" Even Matron smiled briefly.

"You know what I mean."

"I don't see why not – take that one. Briefing at zero nine hundred hours in Hut Five and we'll aim to set off as soon after zero nine thirty as possible."

"That's marvellous. Tomorrow morning then."

Edward nodded, hardly looked at Patricia and was gone. Lizzie was beaming.

"I thought those Wellingtons had a fault with the cooling system leaking or something." Not even Matron's cold voice could dampen Lizzie's excitement. Flying at last and a chance to prove her worth to this bunch of men who clearly believed women couldn't fly.

"Apparently the early versions did but that's been fixed."

Matron seemed to lose interest immediately and chewed a piece of meat, her eyes wandering to the side as if miles away. Then she said abruptly, "At least we're rid of that malingerer Saunders. I discharged him this afternoon...gave him his marching orders."

"I'd become quite fond of him. He at least added a bit of fun." Patricia stopped suddenly under a fierce stare from Matron.

"We're not here to have fun Nurse O'Flynn. We're here to do a job."

"Of course Matron. I just meant..." she tailed off and stood to busy herself serving pudding.

◆ ◆ ◆

Dearing had sat in angry silence in the car which suited Fletcher and McBane who did not wish to enter a conversation until they had him sitting in an interview room. It did not take long to reach the police station in Towcester but the light had all but evaporated from the sky by the time they arrived. The station was built of red brick with stone corners and two stone pillars supporting a porch over the front entrance. It was a bigger and grander station than Brackley reflecting the larger town it served.

They escorted Dearing into the building and Fletcher had a brief word with the desk sergeant before leading the way into an interview room. "Please sit down Flight Lieutenant."

Dearing sat heavily in the indicated chair and looked around the room. Robbie McBane watched him carefully, the way his eyes shrank from the coldness of the décor: walls covered with a shiny paint, green bottom halves and yellow top like a public lavatory, a single light with a dusty glass shade like a small Chinese hat hanging from the ceiling in the centre, casting a shadow on the grubby, white ceiling. A picture of the King, looking grave and noble, hung from the wall opposite Dearing as if a reprimand. He flinched at the screech when the plain, metal-legged chairs were pulled out from the table by Fletcher and himself.

Dearing looked at Fletcher. "So what's this about? Why am I here?"

"The general idea, Sir, is that we ask the questions. We have invited you to come in for questioning because we have evidence that suggests you were in the room where the young woman, Jennifer Sumser, was murdered. That room, that hut, is not in use as yet so, perhaps you would explain what you were doing there."

"I've no idea what you're talking about. What evidence

do you have?" The word evidence was given heavy emphasis, almost spat out.

Robbie McBane sat forward. "Firstly, we have two witnesses that say they saw you in the vicinity of the hut, one walking towards it and one who saw you later leaving the hut."

"How do they know it was me? It was dark, stormy, I was wearing a greatcoat and anyone else out that night would have been wearing one too. One person in a greatcoat looks like any other."

"Perhaps, Sir, if I go through all of the evidence and then you can respond." Robbie McBane took from his pocket a brown paper bag and withdrew from it the comb he had found under the bed. He laid it on the table in front of Dearing. "I've shown you this before, Sir, and you denied that it was yours. However, a search of your room revealed a man's grooming set that, like this comb, is made from tortoiseshell. We could not find a comb anywhere."

Whilst McBane had been speaking, Dearing had sat upright and his face became red with anger. "You did what? You searched my room? How dare.."

"This is a murder investigation Flight Lieutenant." Fletcher's voice was loud and ice cold. "We are entitled to do what is necessary to get to the truth. If you had a shred of regard for the life of that young woman, you would be assisting us readily instead of complaining."

"So I'm a suspect then?"

Fletcher looked him in the eye. "Yes, you are. Sergeant McBane do go on."

"Is this your comb, Sir?"

"It might be. I don't know."

"But you did have a tortoiseshell comb that was part of that set I mentioned?"

Dearing nodded, his face sullen.

"And where is it now?"

"No idea. Perhaps you took it when you searched my room."

"This comb was found lying under the bed where the girl's body was lying. It has a short dark hair trapped in the teeth which looks as though it is pomaded. Just like your hair."

Dearing said nothing. Robbie McBane slid his hand into the bag again and withdrew the card. He turned it over so it was face up. "This is Jennifer Sumser's pass for her job at Bronnley soap factory. It was found in the pocket of your greatcoat hanging in your wardrobe."

McBane paused and Dearing stared at the card and then into McBane's face.

"Would you care to explain how it got there?"

"I have absolutely no idea." He stopped and then his face twisted in a sneer. "Oh I get it. You've decided to frame me. You put that card in my pocket. How else would it get there?"

Fletcher remained calm but spoke with the gravity that he had developed over years of policing. "I was with Sergeant McBane when we searched your room, Flight Lieutenant. I can assure you we do not go in for framing people or planting evidence. You're the one who needs to explain how it got there."

"I don't know." Dearing was suddenly on his feet and shouting. "Why in God's name would I want her identity card? If I'd killed her, I wouldn't keep it would I?"

Fletcher waited until he had subsided into his chair. "Sadly, Sir, some murderers like to have a trophy of their victims. I've encountered that several times before."

"A trophy? Do I look like a monster?"

"You'd be surprised at the kind of people who commit murder. You would never guess it by looking at them."

"Well I did not kill that girl, no matter how much you try to pin it on me. And I am not going to answer any more of your stupid questions without a lawyer present. I want to make a phone call...now."

"If you are unwilling to answer any more questions, we will have to keep you overnight."

"Overnight? You are joking!"

"No, Sir, I'm not. You will stay in one of our cells here until we have asked you everything we need. So you can do that now or you can stay here until tomorrow when this interview will resume with your lawyer. I can of course arrange for a local solicitor if you wish."

"I'm not having some country bumpkin representing me. He'd probably just say what you want him to say. I want to make that phone call."

Inspector Fletcher and Robbie McBane escorted a smoking Dearing from the room. Fletcher showed him into his own office and turned the telephone to face him. "I'll tell the desk sergeant you need an outside line." The two detectives left him to it but Fletcher signalled to McBane to follow. He spoke quietly with the desk sergeant who flicked a switch and handed the handset from the desk telephone to Fletcher.

After a minute, Fletcher took the handset away from his ear and, covering the mouthpiece said, "He's calling his father. No doubt a judge will be able to get a high-powered London lawyer here by the morning, one of his cronies. That will be difficult because we don't have a lot to hold him but at least we've rattled his cage and I daresay something will come from it." He replaced the handset on the cradle and added, "I'll give you a lift back to your digs. There's nothing more we can do tonight."

# PART 5: FRIDAY 19TH FEBRUARY 1943

# CHAPTER 26

The briefing room took up much of Hut Five. Aircrew were entering in twos and threes ready for the morning's session. Edward Driscoll was hovering near the front running through his notes one last time. He looked up and saw Brian Saunders.

"Ah Saunders, glad to see you back with us. I trust you're fully recovered."

"Yes, Sir. All my bits are working and I'm raring to go."

"When you're getting out of the aircraft, Saunders, you probably should open your parachute – save another injury." A knot of men nearby guffawed

"Very funny, Perkins. I'll look forward to having a laugh at your expense soon."

"No offence intended old chum. Just couldn't resist it."

There was a sudden hush when Lizzie walked through the doorway. She greeted Edward Driscoll and he spoke briefly with her. She was aware of sotto voce comments being exchanged amongst the crew, speculating on her presence at the briefing no doubt, until Driscoll called the hut to order and they took their seats.

"Right chaps. Let's run through the exercise this morning."

Before he could go further, a hand was raised and Perkins spoke up without waiting for permission. "Sir, where's

Flight Lieutenant Dearing this morning?"

"Flight Lieutenant Dearing is assisting the Police with some matters. That's all I know and that's all you need to know. He won't be joining us for this morning's exercise." Driscoll stifled further questions with a steely look, something foreign to his usually gentle expression. "Fortunately, we have Second Officer Barnes from the ATA with us and she has kindly agreed to take charge of another Wellington so Flight Lieutenant Dearing's crew from yesterday will fly with her. That will be in the new Wellington she delivered on Monday, though, so we can give it a spin."

"Sir, I heard that one was damaged...had some holes in the tail."

"It has all been repaired and is as good as new, Perkins, so you've no need to worry." Driscoll turned towards the boards behind him on which a large map was pinned. Our mission is to fly to the target area - RAF Holbeach - in the Wash," he pointed to the specific area on the map, "as today we will be operating over the sea. The first thing to do when you get on board therefore is to check that you have a lifebelt near your position in case you need to bail out or ditch in the sea."

A silence fell on the room, each man digesting the possible risks should anything go wrong. A few nervous glances were exchanged and some were directed furtively at Lizzie who sat on a chair at the front of the room but to one side. She looked over the men with what she hoped was a pleasant, relaxed countenance. Confidence was everything in training and she realised that she had something to prove. She would confess to some nervousness if asked as she had never taken charge of an aircraft and crew before, nor had she been asked to train anyone. She was courageous, resilient and resourceful, she reminded herself and this would be no worse than the numerous challenges she had faced before.

"There is a barge moored in the target area. On the first run, we will drop flour bombs and your pilot will circle back so you can see if you landed any on the target. When both aircraft have completed that, we will have a run at the barge again for the forward gunner to try to hit the targets that are standing on the deck. These are returned to the vertical remotely after each run so the second aircraft will have a full set of targets to hit. As always, co-ordination between pilot, bomb aimer and forward gunner are crucial. We will swap positions and then do the whole thing probably twice more so that all gunners who did not get the chance yesterday will get it today. My aircraft will lead so that we do the exercises first. We'll hang around then and both aircraft will return together."

"Sir, I think I'm ok with bomb aiming over land but isn't it quite hard over sea – I mean you've got no visual reference points below you."

"That's exactly why we're doing this exercise today, Saunders. I don't think it's a secret that Wellingtons may be transferred to anti-submarine duties now that the bigger Lancaster is taking over the main bombing role. Consider this the start of training for that. Any other questions at this point?" Driscoll looked around the room. "Ok. On your briefing paper, you have the co-ordinates and the other information you need. Check them before you leave this room. Now Miss Barnes will brief us on the weather."

Lizzie stood up and several men sat up from their slouched positions. "Good morning gentlemen. You'll have noticed that it has turned a bit colder this morning. The wind is light, some eight knots, but it is from the East and thus brings a hint of Siberia."

"That's been sent over by Hitler I bet."

"I don't think even Hitler can command the weather, Saunders."

"Nice one, Miss." Perkins grinned at Saunders who flicked a V at him behind his back.

Lizzie resumed. "We will take off from the hangar end of the runway of course and we'll have headwind out to the target area. The gunners will need to be very vigilant. There is always the possibility that enemy aircraft will be trying to penetrate our defences from that direction. If we encounter enemy aircraft, we must be ready to defend ourselves."

"If it's fighters, we'll not stand much of a chance."

"Nowadays, it tends to be lone fighters that come over. Such a plane would certainly attack but with three guns on each of our aircraft, we've got a very good chance of a kill. Stay vigilant, that's the main thing."

"Was that what you encountered on Monday?" Lizzie looked in the direction of the voice: Brian Saunders; there was no trace of his customary mockery however.

"It was, Saunders. I took a few bullets as has already been mentioned but was able to throw him off the scent. But remember, I had no guns armed and no gunners. Today we have three in each aircraft."

Chairs clattered as the men stood and left the room. The straggling line trailed along the row of huts and the two brick buildings to the hangars in front of which the two aircraft waited. Lizzie followed them with Edward Driscoll.

"Nervous?"

"Not really but keen to get on with it. Are there any members of my crew that I need to watch out for?"

"No, they're all sound. Saunders likes a joke but he's a good trainee – takes it seriously beneath the banter."

"I've met him already. I can deal with him no problem."

The desk sergeant looked up when he heard the door swing open and steel tipped heels striking the concrete floor. A glance showed him that the visitor meant business: dark overcoat with velvet lapels hanging open to reveal a crisp, pin-striped suit, gold-rimmed glasses and silver hair impeccably groomed, an expensive briefcase held firmly in the right hand and a face set into the sternest expression he had seen for some while.

"Jeremy Postlethwaite KC. I'm here to see my client, Flight Lieutenant Ronald Dearing."

"Of course, Sir. Would you mind taking a seat for a minute and I'll fetch Inspector Fletcher."

"Make sure it is only a minute. I don't take kindly to having to come out into the sticks because some country policeman is playing detective."

"Of course, Sir. Do please take a seat." The sergeant gestured to the chairs against the wall and bustled off to warn Fletcher who was in his office with Sergeant McBane. "Blimey," the desk sergeant breathed when he had been called in, " the Gestapo has arrived - Dearing's lawyer – introduced himself as KP Jeremy Pistolgrip or something. He looks like trouble to me. I think you'd best not keep him waiting, Sir."

Fletcher smiled. Such a warning only encouraged him to take his time but he and McBane did rise to their feet. "Ready, Sergeant? Sounds like we might have a difficult customer here."

In the foyer, Fletcher walked towards the lawyer and held out his hand. "Inspector Fletcher and this is Sergeant McBane from the RAF Police Special Investigation Branch."

"Jeremy Postlethwaite KC." He stood and gave Fletcher his hand in the briefest fashion possible, withdrawing it as if he may become contaminated by contact with the detective. "I want to see my client immediately. Where is he? I understand that you have kept him here overnight without charge. I am appalled and should warn you that if you do not have sufficient evidence I will see that there are suitable repercussions."

Fletcher remained absolutely calm, almost enjoying the provocation. "Flight Lieutenant Dearing would probably have been released yesterday evening after interview but he refused to answer more questions until his lawyer was present. He brought his stay in our facilities upon himself."

"A senior officer in His Majesty's Air Force does not expect to be hauled off to a police cell like a common criminal."

"Until we have interviewed him thoroughly, Sir, we do

not know whether he has committed a crime or not. This is a murder investigation," Fletcher added in a steely voice, looking the lawyer straight in the eye.

"Take me to him."

Fletcher nodded at the desk sergeant who led the lawyer through the locked iron- barred door to the cells. The corridor was painted in the same shiny green and yellow paint as the interview room and Postlethwaite's shoes clicked loudly on the concrete floor, the sound ricocheting ominously along the length of the corridor.

Whilst he was in with Dearing, Fletcher warned Robbie McBane that they would probably have to release him. "What I want to do though is to try to rattle him enough to get some admission from him." The two men discussed the way the interview would be conducted and, when Postlethwaite emerged from Dearing's cell, led a solemn procession to the interview room.

Fletcher began the interview. "Yesterday, Flight Lieutenant, my colleague Sergeant McBane took you through the evidence which suggested that you were in the room where…"

"Suggested, Inspector? You'll have to do better than that. You need to present evidence not suggestions." Postlethwaite fixed Fletcher with a hostile eye.

"As I was saying, Sergeant McBane presented you with evidence that suggests you were in the room where the girl's body was found. You were shown a tortoiseshell comb. Is that comb yours?"

Dearing opened his mouth to respond but Postlethwaite spoke before he could. "There are doubtless hundreds of tortoiseshell combs in this country. What makes you think it belongs to my client?"

"Because he has a tortoiseshell grooming set in his room but the comb is missing. A hair was found in the teeth of the comb which had pomade on it; it was the same colour as your client's hair."

"There are several men on the base with similar hair colour. That proves nothing."

"We have two witnesses who say they saw you, Flight Lieutenant, in the vicinity of the hut, that's Hut Fifteen, at the time the pathologist believes the young woman was killed."

"My client might have been going for a walk. He'd had a few drinks and needed to clear his head. The fact that he was walking by the hut does not prove he was inside it."

"Three girls were brought onto the base that night and, we believe, twice a week for some time – we're not yet sure how long. The other two girls have admitted it was for the purposes of prostitution. Did you use the services of any of those girls Flight Lieutenant?"

Postlethwaite turned to Dearing and shook his head but Dearing was clearly fed up with the process and fed up with being told to keep silent. "Yes I did," he said defiantly. "I used the services, as you put it, of the girl who is dead but I did not kill her."

With a look of alarm on his face, Postlethwaite leapt in to try to rescue the situation. "As far as I know, Inspector, there is no law against a man and a woman having sexual intercourse by agreement. My client has therefore committed no crime and, unless you have evidence clearly showing that he has, he is to be released immediately."

Robbie McBane made no attempt to hide his contempt and he could see it did not escape Dearing's notice. "There's no need to look so high and mighty, Sergeant. Sex…it's part of being a man, the drive to procreate… but perhaps you wouldn't understand that."

"Oh I do, Sir, but with a young woman you don't know… it's what animals do."

Dearing's face twisted into his characteristic snarl. "Animal am I? Maybe. But what's a man to do, stuck out here in the middle of nowhere with a bunch of men and the only women guarded by that dragon in Sick Bay? I've done my bit, put my life at risk flying raids over enemy territory, no chance of meeting a nice girl and settling down in a nine to five existence. It's not like that for those of us who fight."

Robbie McBane could feel himself boiling with anger at Dearing's jibe but Fletcher laid a hand on his arm. "People serve in different ways, Flight Lieutenant, and right now, Sergeant McBane is engaged in finding a murderer. That's a worthy task too. There's enough killing going on in the World without a young woman losing her life too."

Robbie McBane spoke quietly, causing the three other men in the room to look at him intently. "When you have lost someone close, really close, you understand how valuable life is."

"Maybe...but she was just a prostitute."

Fletcher exploded. "There's no 'just' about it. She was a young woman with her life in front of her, exploited by men who should know better. Her life was every bit as valuable as yours Flight Lieutenant."

# CHAPTER 27

The men hovered under the wing, waiting for the instruction to board. Lizzie called her crew around her. "I realise that some of you may be wondering what experience I have that enables me to take command of this exercise. I have very many hours flying several different aircraft and have encountered most situations...even attack by enemy fighter as I've mentioned. I trust by the end of the flight, you will have no doubts. Now do board please and take your positions."

Lizzie instructed Perkins to take the pilot's seat for the first part of the exercise. He would take off, fly to the target area, make the first runs and then hand over to Saunders who would do the others, bring the aircraft back and land. The engines were fired up and Lizzie once more felt butterflies of excitement in her stomach at the deafening sound, like a drum roll. Slowly the large machine followed Driscoll's aircraft onto the taxiway to the end of the runway. Perched on a fold-down seat across from the navigator and slightly behind the pilot, she watched as the first aircraft trundled along the runway, slowly gaining speed before rising into the air. The instruction came over the radio from the tower clearing them for take-off.

"Ok Perkins?"

"Ok, Miss."

Their aircraft rolled forward again and turned tightly to line up with the runway. Perkins opened the throttles and the sound inside became deafening. Slowly they gained speed until the ground was a blur beside them.

"I'm going up now."

Lizzie peered at the speed indicator in alarm. "Not yet Perkins. You need a bit more speed." She could see the tension in Perkins's cheek as the end of the runway became clearer.

"You need at least 120 mph."

Perkins' eyes flicked from the windscreen and the sight of the disappearing runway to the needle creeping slowly round the speed dial. At last the needle hit 120 mph and he pulled back the joystick. The heavy aircraft lifted her nose and the rumbling of the wheels on concrete stopped. They were airborne. Perkins let out a huge breath.

"Keep her climbing. She'll pick up speed now we're clear of the resistance from the wheels." Sure enough, the needle continued to edge around the speed dial as the aircraft left the base behind and the wheels were retracted.

The flight was uneventful, the navigator, who doubled as bomb-aimer, giving occasional directions to Perkins over the intercom. Lizzie once or twice asked the gunners to report any sightings of enemy aircraft. She could see a great deal from her position but she wanted to remind them. It was easy to allow your mind to drift away when sitting for a long period with nothing to do, listening to the drone of the engines. One of them started to sing 'We'll Meet Again' but Lizzie stopped him. It was not a good idea to allow distractions and levity whilst on a mission, even a training mission over home soil.

With so much flat ground in the East of England, the sea came into view in the distance but it was a thin, indistinct line on the horizon, almost merging with the cloud cover.

"Can you give an exact heading now, navigator?"

"Yep. Just maintain the current heading – sixty-five degrees – and you'll be spot on the target."

"I hope you're right, Simpson." Perkins sounded unconvinced. Lizzie realised it was just the pressure on the trainee pilot to get a clean approach. As they approached the shoreline, Simpson, the navigator, left his position behind Perkins and dropped down carefully into the bomb aimer's well beneath the pilot. He put on the intercom set and settled himself in a prone position with his eye on the sighting instrument.

"Ok we have visual on the barge. Can you see that

Perkins?"

"Can do, Miss. Altitude is five hundred feet and we're heading straight for it so if you can't hit it Simpson, you need glasses."

Even though it was a training mission, tension grew amongst the whole crew. This was a joint enterprise. The success of the first part of the mission was down to pilot and bomb-aimer and they waited in anticipation for several minutes to hear the words.

"Bombs away," shouted Simpson and then he was clambering back to the navigator's seat.

"Let's go round Perkins and see what damage we've done."

"There were already two hits from the first aircraft so we mustn't let Simpson count those." Perkins chuckled as he put the Wellington into a long turn that would take it almost back to the shoreline and out over the barge again. He reduced height further to three hundred feet and flew to one side of the barge. Only two white marks were on the barge. "You missed it, Simpson. I don't believe it. Bloody great barge, we're right over it and you missed it."

"That'll do Perkins. That's why we do training. Don't worry Simpson, you'll get it next time."

"Yeah, If Perkins was the target, I'd drop it right between his eyes."

The training exercise continued with the gunners and then roles were swapped. Brian Saunders took hold of the joystick and waited for Perkins to squeeze out of the pilot's seat before slipping into it. The new bomb aimer scored two hits and then each of the other two gunners took the forward position to fire at the standing targets. There was some success and much joshing at the failures. Lizzie let some of it go but she wondered why it was that men felt a need to ridicule the failures of their colleagues. Women did not operate in that way. They gave each other encouragement and support when things did not work out.

At last, she instructed Saunders to set course for home and spoke briefly on the radio with Driscoll. The two planes flew in close formation for much of the way and the crew settled down to scanning the sky for enemy aircraft. They passed over Bedford, some forty miles from home, and Lizzie privately congratulated herself on running the exercise well. She maintained her concentration, however, and checked the dials in front of the pilot. A frown crossed her forehead and she leaned forward to double check. There was no mistake, the port engine was running hot, very hot.

"Saunders, the port engine is running hot. Can you see anything?"

Brain Sanders turned his head to port and straight back. "Nothing, Miss. What should I do?"

"Close it down...now."

"But...but I've never flown on one engine before. How am I going to land?"

"Close it down now before it blows up or seizes," shouted Lizzie releasing her harness and springing to her feet. She lunged over Brain Saunders and shut off the port engine. His face was white and he was clutching the joystick as if hanging on to it to save his life. The plane began to tilt to port and Lizzie could feel it turning. If it was not corrected, there was a risk it would turn turtle and plunge downwards.

There was silence in the room while Fletcher regained his composure. The lawyer looked embarrassed and clearly wanted to get out as soon as possible. "Please release my client now Inspector."

Fletcher did not respond directly. "Thank you for your... eventual honesty, Flight Lieutenant. That is helpful. It does establish that you were with the young woman and, you will realise, that gave you the opportunity to murder her. It would not be the first time that a young woman has been seriously hurt or murdered by a man who did not get exactly what he wanted."

Dearing was sullen. "I got what I wanted and so did she."

"And presumably that was payment?" Robbie McBane asked.

"Yes…she was a prostitute…of course she was paid."

"Directly by you, Sir, or through a third party?"

Dearing looked at his lawyer who shook his head in a barely perceptible manner.

"I mentioned that we have witnesses who saw you in the vicinity of the hut. One of them said you were seen leaving. That was Corporal Davies."

"Davies?" the one word was an angry snarl. "Bastard." Dearing sat forward. "Alright it was Davies who organised everything…brought the prostitutes in. I paid him and he paid them, taking a cut of course."

Postlethwaite sighed quietly and raised his eyes.

"Thank you for confirming that, Sir. We have established that already and Davies will be arrested later this morning…as soon as we get back to the base. But Flight Lieutenant, it would be helpful if you can tell us anything that might corroborate your account that the girl was alive and well when you left her. Did someone else use her… services… after you for example?"

"I've no idea. I left and went back to my quarters. But, by the way, I did not take her identity card and I still believe I have been framed."

"And I will be taking that up with your superiors…both of you." Postlethwaite was back on the offensive but neither Fletcher nor McBane responded.

Inspector Fletcher suddenly left the room, leaving the door ajar. Within moments he returned and placed a cardboard tube, about four inches in diameter, on the table. The tube was plastered all around with plasticine. "This may allow us to eliminate you from our enquiries, Sir, if you are willing to carry out this exercise." He watched Dearing's face as client and lawyer looked at each other.

"I'd like a word in private with my client."

Fletcher and McBane left the room, the latter closing the door softly behind him. "D'you think he'll bite, Sir?"

"It's a quandary for them isn't it?" There was a hint of triumph in Fletcher's smile. "If the lawyer advises him not to co-operate, he knows Dearing will remain under suspicion. He has to be sure that Dearing is telling the truth to advise him to carry out the test otherwise it could condemn him."

"Clever, Sir, clever."

Fletcher tapped his nose. "Experience, Robbie, experience."

"Can we get fingerprints from it?"

"We can from the plasticine but there's no point as we can't get anything from the girl's neck – the bruises are not that precise."

The door opened and Postlethwaite said they were ready to resume. "Now, Sir," said Fletcher in a business-like manner, "I'd like you to reach forward with both hands and grasp this tube as if you were grasping someone's neck. Please be sure to squeeze it gently so the imprint of your fingers is left in the plasticine. You can wash your hands afterwards if you wish."

Dearing glanced nervously at his lawyer then slowly reached forward. He took the tube in both hands and squeezed as instructed. "Happy?" he said leaning back in his chair.

"Thank you, Sir." Fletcher lifted the tube carefully keeping his fingers well clear of the marks Dearing had made. He examined it for a full minute.

"My client has done what you requested. Now you either charge him or let him go."

Fletcher's voice was reasonable, calm. "Thank you, Flight Lieutenant Dearing for your help. I will, as your lawyer requests, release you but you understand that we will have to report your conduct to your commanding officer. There may be consequences for you in bringing the service and your rank into disrepute and in allowing an operation such as Davies has been running to continue without reporting it."

"We'll deal with that if it arises. Come on Ronald, let's get you back to base." Postlethwaite was on his feet already and the two men had left the room and the building before Fletcher had the chance to ask anything else. The two detectives left the interview room and Fletcher dropped into his office to collect his coat before addressing the desk sergeant on the way out.

"We're heading back to RAF Silverstone. Have the arrest officers left already?"

"Yes, Sir. Gone in the Black Maria, Sir."

Fletcher nodded and led the way out of the swing doors into the cold February morning.

"Is he our man, Sir?" asked McBane as they walked to Fletcher's car.

"No Sergeant, he is not. Did you see how he grasped the tube? His right hand was above his left hand because that is how a right-handed person would grasp a neck to strangle someone. The finger marks on our victim showed the left hand being higher. Secondly, his hands are too big. We are looking for someone with smaller hands but strong enough to strangle."

"Davies? Andrews?"

"Perhaps. Dearing is right about one thing. Someone planted that identity card in his pocket to frame him, someone who is either protecting himself or wants to put Dearing away...or both."

# CHAPTER 28

AC Webster watched the black Fordson van approach the gate slowly. Its long radiator grill and two small headlights mounted on the front mudguards gave it a lugubrious expression – appropriate he thought for its purpose. Above the cab, the word 'Police' was displayed in large, sober letters and, raised to be clearly visible, the blue light, which was not flashing, was proudly prominent.

Webster walked slowly forward to the driver's window which was sliding downwards as the van coasted to a stop in front of the gate. A short interchange occurred with the driver before Webster signalled to Smith to make the entry in the log. They'd had it drummed into them by Lovell that entries must be made every time and had been warned there may be disciplinary action against them for not writing down all movements. Smith stepped inside the gatehouse to make the entry and Webster lifted the barrier. He pointed towards the hangars with his right arm, indicating where to turn off the perimeter road. The van drew forward slowly and the sentries watched it drive a short way along the perimeter road before turning as instructed.

Webster closed the gate, adjusted the position of his rifle on his left shoulder and stepped across to Smith. "Why a police van?"

"Dunno. Bit worrying though ain' it?"

"Said he was looking for Davies. D'you reckon they're onto him?"

"Maybe. May just want information from him." Smith seemed unconcerned as usual. "Davies will make sure he's alright. Blame us probably."

"He bloody better not."

The van moved out of sight as it disappeared between two of the hangars. It drove slowly across the front of one hangar and came to rest at one end of the vast opening. One police officer climbed out of the back, putting his helmet on as he did so. He strolled into the hangar and spoke to an airman, Langford, whom he found working at a bench. The latter looked up at the question and pointed to the office huddled against the side of the hangar towards the rear. The police officer's pace was quicker as he returned to the van and jerked his head towards the darker end of the building. Two more officers joined him, one a sergeant, leaving the driver at the wheel; they walked abreast about a yard apart towards the office.

As they drew closer, they could see a stocky man inside, eyeing them suspiciously. His dark hair was ruffled and accentuated the scowl on his face. He did not, however, come out of the office.

The sergeant tapped quickly on the door and opened it immediately. "Corporal Davies?"

"What's up?"

"Are you Corporal Davies?"

"What d'you want?"

The sergeant became irritated by the evasion. "Yes or no, that's all I need."

"Yes, I am."

"Corporal Davies, I am arresting you on suspicion of procuring young women for prostitution and for stealing government property for sale. That's for starters anyway – there may be other charges. You do not have to say anything but anything you do say may be taken down and used as evidence."

Davies backed against the wall of the office. "Now steady on, steady on. I don't know what you're talking about. You must have the wrong man."

"No. You're the man we want. Turn around, face the wall and put your hands behind your back."

Davies did not move and the other two officers stepped forward grabbing him roughly by the arms and turning him around. His arms were pulled behind his back and handcuffs swiftly fitted.

"I know nothing about this. It's not me you want. It's Andrews."

"Yes we do want AC Andrews as well. Where can we find him?"

"He'll be in the admin block...upstairs."

Davies was pulled away between two officers and marched towards the police van. As they neared it, the metallic voice of the tannoy rang out across the apron. "Action stations. Aircraft returning on one engine."

"We've got an emergency. I have to get the fire tender out."

"No you don't. Someone else can do it."

As the sergeant spoke, Langford was running past them, not even pausing to notice the handcuffs on Davies. The drone of aircraft engines grew until it filled the air. Davies looked up and saw the first Wellington, the port propeller turning slowly, driven by the airflow over its blades. It flew past the airfield and began to turn back for a landing. The second plane was making a wider circle.

"That aircraft's in trouble, look. Only one engine working. It's all hands needed in case it crash lands and bursts into flames. For God's sake let me out of these things so I can supervise the fire team."

The officers holding Davies looked uncertainly at the Sergeant but he spoke with decision. "Someone else'll have to do that. You're coming with us."

The arrest party halted as the first Wellington dropped down, down onto the runway. Immediately, a fire truck, siren blaring, was racing after it from the hangar furthest from them. They watched as the big aircraft gradually slowed and the fire truck caught up, both now smaller due to distance. There was an expectant hush, but no flames burst from the aircraft.

"There you are. You were not needed. Not so important as you think are you?"

Davies scowled at the sergeant but said nothing. When they had pushed him into the back of the Black Maria, the sergeant and one of the officers walked swiftly to the admin block. Some five minutes later, they re-appeared with Andrews in handcuffs. He was bundled into the back of the van to join Davies and two officers climbed in with them. "Right. No talking, you two. Not a word. Got it."

"This is ridiculous..." Davies started to protest but the officer cut him off.

"Shut it. It's our rules in here."

Andy Staples stopped his van on the drive, climbed out slowly and rang the front doorbell. He stepped away, whistling nonchalantly, hands in pockets. Surveying the garden, he thought it would be great to have a property like this, lawns bordering the graceful sweep of drive which curved like a river to the gate. Alright for some!

The door opened. "Ah, Mr Staples, so good of you to come. Your wife said you might return home for luncheon and she could give you a message."

"No problem Madam. Always happy to oblige a good customer. Now what can I do for you? Not a problem with the new bathroom I hope?"

"No, no...not problem there. I had telephone call today and it was mentioned that there is leak at the base...the Sick Bay. Would you be kind enough to go there first thing in the morning...tomorrow?"

"Of course. No problem. I wonder why they didn't phone me direct. I'm sure they've got my number."

She shrugged. "I think it came up in my call and I said I

would you contact."

"Oh that's very kind of you. Thank you."

"So you can be there at 8.30 am at the latest?"

"Course I can. Always work Saturdays these days. What with so many younger lads being off at the fighting, us old chaps have to keep busy to keep up with the work."

"Of course. Well thank you. I won't keep you...unless you like a cup of tea?"

Staples glanced at his watch. I think I've got time for a quick one. Thank you very much."

"Please come in."

He hesitated on the doormat, rubbing his boots vigorously. "Perhaps I should take these off?"

"Yes, perhaps that would be good idea." She smiled at him, a warm smile, a smile of indulgence. When he had removed his boots, she took him by the arm and led him into the sitting room. His eyes roamed around, the expensive furnishings, the soft comfort; he'd not been in here before. "Please make yourself comfortable." She gestured to the sofa and her soft lips closed as her eyes sparkled at him.

"Sabotage?" Lovell had leapt out of his chair at the word.

Lizzie stood in front of him, undeterred and unbowed. "Yes, Sir. I am absolutely sure. Langford is adamant that the drain plug was tested on both engines when they were checking over everything after I delivered the aircraft."

"When you delivered this aircraft, you brought it in on just the starboard engine. I hope this is not some attempt on your part to impress people with your flying ability."

"I find that offensive Group Captain," Lizzie shot back at Lovell. "Do you really think I would risk the aircraft and the lives of the crew when I had been given the chance for the first time to do some training?"

Lovell did not reply but looked for confirmation at Langford who stood beside Lizzie.       "I checked it myself, Sir. It was tightened to the correct torque. We always check them carefully, Sir, as that was a fault with the early version of the Merlin X engine. The bolt had been loosened enough for the vibration of the engine to cause it to come undone slowly. Eventually, the vibration would have loosened it enough for the coolant to start leaking. We found the bolt at the bottom of the engine cowling with a small puddle of coolant that had not evaporated. If the engine had not been shut down when it was, it would have got so hot it would have either seized or blown up. The bolt on the starboard engine had also been loosened, Sir, but not enough for it to have come out. It was not at the correct torque setting and I know that I checked that one too."

Lovell sat down slowly. "Sabotage. I can't believe anyone on this base would deliberately sabotage an aircraft and risk killing the crew."

"It was a clever way of doing it, Sir." Lizzie softened the tone of her voice. "Had the engine blown and the aircraft been lost, it could have been put down to mechanical failure or pilot error and no one would have suspected foul play."

"We're looking for someone with some knowledge of aircraft engines then." Lovell spoke almost to himself. "A member of the ground crew...must be." Lovell looked at Langford again. "When did you do all these checks on that Wellington?"

"Tuesday and Wednesday, Sir...as well as repairing the damage to the tail."

"The base was closed to all visitors apart from the police from the middle of the day on Tuesday so it must be someone on the base."

Lizzie began to pity Lovell. He appeared to live in a world of 'The Boy's Own Paper' that her brother used to read when younger, a world of heroes and villains, right and wrong, simplistic judgements. The World they all now inhabited was not like that; it was complex, where accepted moral certainties were daily tested. "I'm afraid so, Group Captain."

"Who brought the plane back after the port engine had been shut down?"

"I did, Sir. Flight Officer Saunders has been off sick and this morning was his first day back on duty. I'm afraid he rather froze, Sir. Completely understandable if you haven't dealt with that sort of situation before."

"Quite so."

"As soon as I landed, I questioned AC Langford and felt sure that the drain plug must have been loosened deliberately. We came straight over, Sir."

Lovell nodded and looked vacantly out of his office window at the base, lying peacefully under gently drifting grey clouds. He almost forgot the two figures standing in front of his desk as he thought of the discussion that would now inevitably occur with Air Commodore Mitchell. It would be his fault again of course...poor judgement, inadequate checks that sort of thing. Lovell could see him now, his squat form and the head lowered like a bull about to charge. He sighed and at last spoke. "Right, thank you. I will need to discuss this with Sergeant McBane and Inspector Fletcher. Please make sure AC Langford that the Wellington is fit to fly as soon as possible. We cannot afford to lose more training time."

"Sir." Langford saluted and, turning smartly, marched from the office. Lizzie also saluted and turned to leave.

"Miss Barnes...it seems your quick thinking may have saved that aircraft and its crew." Lovell looked down at his desk and his next words were rather mumbled. "Well done and thank you."

"Flying so many different aircraft, one develops an instinct for trouble I suppose." She was going to add something more cutting to remind him of his initial attitude towards her but the creases on his brow, his drawn face and the stoop of his shoulders made her swallow the remark.

Before she could leave the office, there was a knock on the door. Robbie McBane entered with Inspector Fletcher a pace or two behind.

"Good morning Group Captain," McBane said cheerily.

"Is it?"

"In one way yes, Sir. You will be pleased to know that we have eliminated Flight Lieutenant Dearing from the murder investigation but I do have to report to you that he did, on Monday night, use the services of the dead girl who was here for the purposes of prostitution."

Lovell sank into his chair and put a hand to his head. "Prostitution," he repeated wearily.

Fletcher took over. "My men have, this morning, arrested Corporal Davies and AC Andrews who have been running a prostitution racket, bringing girls onto the base a couple of times a week and selling their services to some of the men."

"In addition, Davies is likely to be charged with selling government property on the black market." Robbie McBane could not help feeling triumphant. "I discovered it by the discrepancies in the fuel tank log and the gaps in the truck log. They were taking fuel into a garage in Brackley twice a week and then picking the girls up for the return journey. Quite a lucrative enterprise. I knew there would be a connection," he added with satisfaction.

"But, if Dearing did not murder her, who did?" Lizzie's voice startled all three of them.

"We cannot say as yet, Lizzie. Maybe one of the men we are arresting this morning." Fletcher, however, did not sound convinced.

Lovell pulled himself out of the stupor that had overcome him. "There's been another development. It appears that the Wellington commanded by Miss Barnes this morning was sabotaged. It could have caused the loss of the aircraft and the death of the crew had it not been for her quick thinking. So gentlemen, as well as a murderer, you are looking for a saboteur."

# CHAPTER 29

"My God, Lizzie. How did you get it down safely?"

"If you remember, I've done it before, when I delivered the aircraft here on Monday though, of course, the reason I had to shut down the port engine was different. Lovell you know had the gall to suggest I did it deliberately to show off my flying skills."

"As if anyone would do that. I hope you put him straight."

"You can be sure of that."

Lizzie and Patricia were waiting in the nurses' staffroom for the lunch to be brought over. Lizzie had started to calm down. It had not been fear that had caused the agitation but the state of intense concentration, readiness for action, that had stretched every fibre of her body like the strings of a harp.

"You say Fletcher and McBane have cleared Dearing."

"Of murder but he had sex with the dead girl. She was working as a prostitute - I suspected that early on...as were the other two girls." Lizzie felt a burst of anger swell her chest. "What's the matter with men? Is sex all they can think of?"

Patricia laughed. "It is surely...that's the way they're made."

But Lizzie did not join her laughter. "I've had enough of it already."

The smile faded from Patricia's face and she looked at Lizzie carefully. "There are some men who respect women, wouldn't do anything like that."

Lizzie smiled weakly. "I know...I shouldn't be so down. You're one of the lucky ones who's found a proper man. There aren't many Edwards in the World though."

"Come now Lizzie, there must be loads. What about that hulk of a man, Robbie McBane. He's a nice chap surely?" Lizzie did not respond to the teasing and Patricia sensed something deeper troubling her. "Did something happen…in your past?"

Lizzie flushed. "Perhaps…but I don't think about it."

"You know, Lizzie, 'tis always best to talk about things, 'confront your demons' my mother always says." She waited but Lizzie did not respond. "You don't have to be tough all the time, Lizzie. Strength is sometimes seeking help. I'm here if you ever…" The look on Lizzie's face stopped her mid-sentence and instead Patricia put her arms around her and hugged her tightly. When she released her and stepped back, Lizzie's eyes were watery.

"Some day maybe but not now, Patricia. You can't let your armour down in a war."

Patricia turned away and sat down at the table. "You say they've cleared Dearing. Who's the suspect now?"

"I think they're looking at Davies. He seems to have been the ring-leader, organised it all, arranged for the girls to be picked up, took the money, paid the girls, that sort of thing."

"But why would he kill her if he was making money out of her?"

"Perhaps she demanded more, threatened to tell someone and he killed her to silence her. It happens. If he was capable of running a prostitution racket, he was capable of murder."

The door was flung open and Matron stomped into the room. "No lunch yet?"

"I s'pose 'twill be over soon, Matron."

The older woman humphed and sat down heavily at the table. Her face, always severe, contorted like a bulldog. "I heard the word 'murder' as I came in."

"We were just talking about it. Dearing's been released without charge." Patricia looked out of the window and did not see the scowl break into a snarl of anger on Matron's face.

"They've released him? But surely he was to blame?

Who else could have done it?"

"I was just saying, Matron, that perhaps it's Davies." Lizzie joined the other two at the table.

"Davies...yes could be. Bunch of animals all of them."

"Come now, Matron. They can't all be that." Patricia was not quick to take offence but Lizzie could see she resented Edward being included in such a sweeping statement. He was a gentle, thoughtful man who would never knowingly exploit or mis-treat another person.

The door opened again and a cheerful member of the kitchen team pushed the trolley into the room. He wished them 'bon appetite' with a horribly anglicised pronunciation and left whistling, letting the door slam behind him.

"There's another one. No manners, no respect. He might as well have thrown the food at us." Lizzie began to protest despite her reservations about the male sex but Matron cut her off. "Just serve it up."

Fletcher and McBane had interviewed Andrews first, guessing he would be the easier of the two to crack. He was. Words spilled from his mouth, telling them in detail about the whole operation including his part in it but stressing all the time that Davies was the master mind. He even admitted that, at Dearing's suggestion, he and Davies had cut the fence to support the theory that the girl and her murderer had come onto the base that way. Langford, he also admitted with some guilt, had been coerced into the operation by threats of harm to his girlfriend.

Davies was, as expected, a tougher nut to crack. He sat back in the chair with his arms folded defiantly in front of him, a posture that Robbie McBane remembered well from his interview two days before.

"I've told you several times already. I know nothing

about that murder, nor about any prostitution. I've never met the girls you're talking about, I've never met Wallace. You've got the wrong man."

"Curious that. The two girls have made statements giving your name as the contact and the person who pays them. Mr Wallace was absolutely clear that, though you do not deliver the petrol, you were the one who arranged it with him in the beginning." Fletcher did not seem inclined to argue the point as the evidence of their witnesses was plain enough.

"They must be mistaken."

"Who is it then if not you?"

" I dunno. I know nuthin' about it, alright."

"When my officers arrested you, why did you say," Fletcher paused to look at the notes he had been given, "where is it? Ah...'It's Andrews you want.' Why say that if you know nothing about it?"

"Just a guess he must be involved. He always knows what's going on with him being up in the admin block most of the time."

"Yes he probably does know. Which is why he has told us that you were the brains behind everything, you organised it all, you collected the money and paid the girls."

"That's just like him...try to pin the blame on someone else. It's him and maybe Langford."

Robbie McBane leant forward. "Langford. Glad you raised that. You secured his involvement in your crime by threatening violence to his sweetheart. That could be a further charge I think Inspector?"

"Definitely. Frankly Davies, I'm not interested in your lies. You're in it right up to your neck. We have statements that prove you organised everything. The matter we now need to deal with is the murder of that poor girl."

"Nothing to do with me."

"So you keep saying. But let's imagine the scene. Business is finished for the night, you've collected all the money and the girls come to you for payment. Two of them are happy with what they've been given – it's what they usually get I suppose – but Jenny decides she'll try to get a bit more. When you refuse, she threatens to report you so you have to silence her."

The defiant look did not leave Davies's face. "She would never have reported me...she'd get herself in trouble, wouldn't she?"

Robbie McBane and Fletcher exchanged a grim smile and concern replaced defiance on the face of the suspect. McBane spoke. "So you were organising prostitution....you have admitted as much."

Davies shifted in his chair, unfolding his hands and resting his forearms on the table as he leaned forward. "Well alright...I have arranged a bit of pleasure for some of the men. It's not a problem is it? I mean the chaps have to have some release and no one suffered. The girls got money, they came willingly and the chaps had a good time. Everyone's a winner."

"Especially you."

"I've got to get something for my trouble."

"Your trouble? You seem to be overlooking the fact that a girl has been murdered. Her parents lost their son on the beaches of Dunkirk - you wouldn't know that of course - and now they've lost their daughter. They have no other children." Fletcher finished quietly.

"I didn't kill her. When I paid her and the others, she was laughing and joking and very pleased with the money. They left the office I was in and that was the last I saw of them."

"How is it that two of the girls were taken back in the truck and Jenny was not?"

"No idea. I knew nothing about that until the body was discovered on Tuesday. Langford was driving the truck to take them back and Andrews banged on the back to give the signal. God knows why they didn't realise there were only two girls." Davies had another thought. "Why didn't the other two say something?"

"Because they thought she was staying longer with 'the

posh bloke' by which we assume they mean Flight Lieutenant Dearing."

Robbie McBane stood up to stretch his legs. "Did you used to play rugby, Corporal?"

"Of course…I'm a true Welshman," he replied, squaring his shoulders.

"You're quite strong I'd guess looking at you."

Davies smiled proudly. "Built like a bull my Ma used to say. Not tall, but big enough and strong enough to be a prop forward."

"Certainly strong enough…and powerful hands."

Davies looked at his hands and flexed them, opening and closing the short fat fingers like clamps. "S'pose I have. What of it?"

McBane did not reply but pushed a pad of paper and pen across the table to Davies. "Would you please write your name on that."

"Why? Are you still on about the fuel log?"

"Just humour me."

Davies looked at the pad with suspicion and slowly picked up the pen. "Just my name?"

McBane nodded and watched as Davies took the pen in his right hand. He finished his name with a flourish trailing from the final letter. McBane retrieved the pad, turned it and without speaking pushed it towards Fletcher who looked at it and nodded.

"Right Corporal Davies, we are going to take you to the desk sergeant who will charge you with procuring girls for prostitution and running a black market operation in goods stolen from His Majesty's Government." Fletcher's usually serious expression became yet darker. "I have to say, Davies, that you disgust me. There are men and women dying to defeat Hitler, there are others who are exhausting themselves in that endeavour and you…you abuse your position to make money. You have helped Hitler, Davies, and I hope you have plenty of time in prison to think about that."

"It's not that bad. Plenty have done far worse."

"The same old excuse that every criminal makes – there's others who are worse. Well it's bad enough for us to keep you here at Towcester until you can be tried for those crimes and perhaps also the crime of murder. You are, I'm sure, aware of the penalty for that."

"Murder? I've told you, I did not kill that girl. She was alive and well when I last saw her."

"Save it for the judge. Come with us."

The trainee officers were assembling in the mess for lunch with the usual babble of voices, still chewing over the near loss of the plane. The word 'sabotage' had spread like spilt fuel ready to ignite because of Langford's protestations that the engines had been completely checked, especially the coolant drain plugs. Driscoll was reassuring Saunders that his inability to deal with the port engine over-heating was not something he should be ashamed of.

"You're in training. You can't be expected to know what to do in every situation as yet. Plus it was your first day back on duty."

"Yeah but, Sir, I had to be helped by…you know…"

"By a woman I think you were about to say. Why is that a problem? She was the instructor and that was her job."

"I know, Sir, but it's embarrassing."

"Miss Barnes is a superb and experienced pilot, Saunders. She did what I would have done and today you learnt something new. There is no shame in it at all and definitely not because of the gender of the instructor. Put it out of your mind and focus on the next steps."

Saunders did not have time to reply. The door had opened and a hush fallen on the room when Flight Lieutenant Dearing strutted in. Although his gait suggested confidence, his eyes betrayed nervousness, flicking from left to right under lowered lids. He headed for the bar where Stevens was drying glasses.

"Double scotch with ice."

Stevens put down the glass he was drying, flipped the tea towel over his shoulder and put his hands on the bar widely spaced. His podgy face turned pink. "It's not usual to drink at lunchtime..." It was a tradition that alcohol was not drunk at lunchtime when there was flying to be done.

"Well I'm not flying this afternoon so it doesn't matter to me."

"I'm afraid, Sir, I've been told...um...not..."

"By whom?"

The room was still silent watching the developing confrontation, poor Stevens trying to do his job in the face of Dearing's arrogant aggression.

"Group Captain Lovell, Sir. He told me I was not to serve you with anything alcoholic."

"What at lunchtime?"

"At any time, Sir. I'm sorry but those are my orders."

"Good God. Can a man not have a drink now?" Suddenly Dearing spun round. "And what are you lot looking at? Carry on your conversations...you've usually got plenty to say."

Everyone knew of course that he had been taken yesterday for questioning, had been kept overnight and now had been released without charge. But mud sticks and Dearing now had the unmistakeable aura of guilt. Edward Driscoll felt it behoved him to prevent any further embarrassment to a fellow officer and he approached him slowly.

"Come on old man. Let's go into lunch."

Dearing glared at him with open hostility. His voice was low, savage. "I don't need your pity Driscoll. I've done nothing wrong – just what a real man would do – fuck a whore."

He spun round towards the dining room and marched in, not waiting for Driscoll. He took a table in the centre of the room and stared fixedly out of the window. Edward Driscoll knew his company at the table would be unwelcome so he sat with Saunders and a couple of the other trainees.

Tragic he thought how a good pilot had become a bitter monster, keeping himself going with drink and haughty disdain.

# CHAPTER 30

The dining room at home was silent apart from the occasional clink of cutlery on plates. Charles Lovell chewed a chunk of meat thoughtfully. Presumably it was beef though these days one could never be sure. He looked across the table to his wife, Marjorie, who was eating voraciously, her usually impeccably groomed hair looking slightly wayward. Should he say anything? If he did, how should he broach it? She would be cross of course, probably make some comment about him failing again. But perhaps it was better to give her some warning now because the outcome for him was inevitable and she would have to know at some point.

Conversation was never easy with Marjorie so he started with something innocuous. "How are you getting on with that new pen I gave you, Dear?"

"Very well. It's remarkable. And you never have to fill it with ink, you say?"

"No, you just put a new tube of ink in. It has a little ball instead of a nib and that collects the ink which transfers to the paper. Brilliant invention…designed for our chaps to use in the air. They sent me some for us to try." He chuckled. "Just think, there's only a few people in the World who have one."

"Very nice."

He decided to take the plunge. "You know, Dear, I was wondering with this restriction on leaving the base, how you feel about this posting?"

She looked up, putting her fork on the plate to bring a strand of hair under control. "Why that question now?"

"Well I realise that being on the base does rather restrict your movements, I mean this ban has set me thinking and I wondered if you sometimes feel it would be better if we were posted elsewhere."

She took another mouthful of food and Lovell waited until she had swallowed it. "I am stuck out here in the middle of nowhere with precious little to do. There are no other officer's wives here so I have no company unless I get involved with the WI in Brackley or Buckingham. There is a branch in the village apparently but I suspect it will be full of little housewives talking about jam. So, yes Charles, I would prefer to be somewhere else, provided it isn't somewhere even more remote."

"Yes...I see your point, Dear. I'm afraid I didn't realise we would be so isolated up here in rural Northamptonshire. I could try to have a word with Mitchell and see what else might be available."

"But what about you? I thought you were keen to stay here for the duration."

"I was, yes, but it is rather dull. Oh I know the base will get bigger very soon but training people is a long way from the action."

"You're not proposing to fly missions again surely?"

"No, no, of course not but there are roles in the command structure and maybe...perhaps Mitchell might... consider that."

"From what you've told me of that man and of your dealings with him, I doubt very much whether he will be willing to grant your request. But there's no harm in asking." She bent her head again to her food.

"Quite so. I'll do that when I have an opportunity." Feeling cheered by her ready agreement, Lovell became conversational. "Another problem arose this morning on the training flight. One of the aircraft had an engine overheating which had to be shut down... came back on one engine. Turns out a drain plug was loosened deliberately...sabotage. We can do without that on top of everything else."

"Sabotage? Do you mean someone on the base is sabotaging the aircraft?"

"That's what it looks like."

"Good God!"

"I've ordered all three planes to be grounded and thoroughly checked this afternoon. They'll have to do this afternoon's training flight tomorrow. What a mess!"

Marjorie Lovell said nothing. When they had both finished, she cleared the plates from the table, walked in her characteristically regal manner into the kitchen and set the kettle to boil. Lovell looked through the French window at the garden. He wasn't much of a gardener but he had entertained hopes of making something of it, creating a place to relax with a drink on a Summer evening, listening to bird song, inhaling the drowsy scents of lilac and roses. Stability was not something a career in the armed services gave a man...nor his family for that matter.

Ten minutes later, Marjorie placed a cup of coffee in front of her husband, jolting him from his reverie.

"The Police released Ronald Dearing this morning," he ventured. "No longer under suspicion for murder thankfully. I suppose that's one piece of good news. I told them they were mad even to think of it. I mean as if he would...father a judge and everything."

She looked over the rim of her coffee cup as she sipped delicately at the hot liquid. The faintest wisp of steam rose around her nose. "But if he didn't do it, who did?"

"Still no closer to establishing that but they've arrested Davies and Andrews. I can't believe it. Davies has been running a racket, in fact two rackets. He's been taking fuel - at least not him directly but he arranged it all – from the storage tank and selling it on the black market."

"And the other racket?"

"That girl...there were two others...they were being brought onto the base twice a week, apparently for...you know...um..."

"You can say it Charles. I'm not a child."

"No quite, dear. For prostitution."

"Were all the men using their services?"

"No of course not but...but...Dearing did on Monday. He knew all about it but failed to report it. I've had to stand him down from duty. He'll be court-martialled of course at some point, may lose his rank. It's the fact that he allowed it to happen and said nothing I find so difficult to believe. Why would a man throw away his career like that?"

"Perhaps he's decided like you that training people is dull. Perhaps he's had enough or, perhaps, like many men, he just can't keep his equipment in his trousers."

Charles Lovell looked away and hoped she wouldn't notice the embarrassment that he was trying to cover.

Robbie McBane and Inspector Fletcher had driven their own cars back to Silverstone from Towcester Police Station, leaving Davies and Andrews to the tender mercies of the desk sergeant. They parked by the administration block and walked around it. The airfield had an uneasy calm. The three Wellingtons were in their respective hangars with cowlings off the engines and ground crew clambering around on scaffolding towers, checking every nut and bolt. They walked past the sick bay buildings and on past the long line of huts. Through the windows of Hut Five, Driscoll was visible addressing the trainees.

"I bet he's been fielding some questions," Robbie McBane remarked.

"Indeed. I just can't see the answers at the moment."

It was going to be a long slow afternoon, sitting despondently in Fletcher's incident room, chewing over possibilities. "We're sure it's not Davies nor Andrews?"

"Well Sergeant, you saw they both wrote with their right hands but that's not conclusive. Davies is certainly strong enough, has the right size hands, could have had a motive but would he have left the body there? Wouldn't he have made sure it left the base and was not found at least for quite some time?"

"I take your point. Perhaps whoever killed her did not realise she was dead when they left her."

"Possibly, but if you applied sufficient pressure to someone's neck to leave those bruises, you would assume she was dead surely?"

"Aye. You're right. Clutching at straws." Robbie McBane sighed. "Perhaps though, there is another way of an outsider getting onto the base," he mused. "If you were to approach it say from the trees where there's good cover, you could put a ladder up at night and no one would spot it."

"Isn't the perimeter patrolled?"

"Aye it should be. But if you're a long way inland and on a training base, I'd be happy to bet that those patrols are not as diligently performed as they should be."

"I did have it checked the other day but I suppose something may have been missed."

Inspector Fletcher lifted the phone and waited until the operator in the admin block answered. "Hello, Could you please get me Northampton 201?" There was another short wait before Towcester station responded. "Sergeant, can you get some officers down here to Silverstone base. I want the perimeter fence checked all the way round for any signs of entry. May not be a break in the fencing, it might be evidence of someone climbing over…you know…crushed vegetation… something dropped…holes that the legs of a ladder might have made." He listened. "I know it's already been checked but I want it examined again and thoroughly. Right away please Sergeant. We need to eliminate completely the possibility of an intruder as soon as possible."

When the handset had been replaced, Robbie McBane spoke. "I suppose we ought to go through all the statements again to see if we've missed anything."

"Good idea, Robbie." Before McBane could lift the box of statements from the shelf and divide them into two piles, however, Fletcher announced he needed to get back to Towcester. "You go through them and let me know if anything strikes you."

The door swung closed behind the Inspector and Robbie McBane, with a shake of his head, opened the box. Perhaps he should have kept his mouth shut. He settled to the task, reading each statement carefully as it came off the pile and stacking them afresh. From time to time, he looked at his watch and sighed but he forced himself to concentrate, knowing that this was probably the best hope of finding a new lead. It was extraordinary, even given the conspiracy of silence they had faced, that a young woman could be murdered and no definitive clue as to her killer be left.

At last, a statement given by one of the airmen caught his eye. He said he had seen a figure hurrying away from the area of Hut Fifteen at about twenty-two hundred hours but he could not identify the person. It may of course have been Dearing who had already been seen in the vicinity or one of the men who had used the services of one of the girls. The statement went on to say that the figure slipped between the huts and disappeared, presumably walking behind the line of huts. That was suspicious – someone who did not want to be seen and was perhaps making his escape over the fence somewhere.

He looked up, thinking of the pieces of evidence they had found. Dearing's comb, Davies's cigarette case, the identity card found in Dearing's coat pocket – almost certainly planted there – and of course that tiny scrap of flesh beneath the girl's fingernail. All but the identity card and the flesh had an explanation. The faintest mark had been discernible, though barely so, on Dearing's cheek but Lizzie had explained it had probably been caused by her slapping his face. He had not seen anyone else with a scratch anywhere though of course they had not carried out body checks. It could have been a scratch on an upper arm, shoulder, torso, anywhere in fact other than a face. By now it may have healed. If only there was a way of discovering from the scrap itself where it came from.

Then he remembered the envelope, crumpled and discarded in the waste bin of the office where he now sat. He unlocked the desk drawer where he had placed it for safe-keeping. It surely was of no significance, just an envelope which may have been dropped there weeks before. He took it out of the bag in which it had been stored and placed it on the desk in front of him.

```
By hand

New Swan Stone
7 Acacia Avenue
```

'By hand.' That was curious. If it had been delivered by hand to the base why was it addressed elsewhere? Was it to be taken to that address but was no longer needed because… because its contents had been removed? It was a fairly large envelope and could have contained several fullscap sheets of paper folded in half. But why would someone put something into an envelope and then remove it before it was delivered? Then he held the envelope close to his eye; the lettering was indented – no one would press so hard on a fountain pen. What kind of pen had written it?

Another thought entered his mind. It was Lizzie's observation that there was no sign of Jenny's handbag. 'Find that handbag' she had said. Where was it? Had the killer taken it? Questions, questions but still no answers.

Robbie McBane's deliberations were interrupted by the sudden harsh jangle of the telephone. It was Fletcher. "No sign of any intruders anywhere on the perimeter. We need to keep the focus on those already on the base."

McBane replaced the handset slowly, glancing at his watch. Almost seventeen hundred hours. It must be one of the airmen – that figure who had been seen. If Davies was telling the truth, the murder must have occurred very soon after he paid Jenny, perhaps while the other two girls were giggling and being helped into the truck by Andrews or someone, its engine idling with a quiet chugging sound.

He pictured the scene...a dark night, a strong wind billowing the skirts of the girls, the men enjoying the glimpse of leg, maybe some flirtation with Andrews or other men hovering nearby, catching their last glimpse for a few days of young women. The girls are tipsy. Does one say 'Where's Jenny?' The other says, 'She's with the posh bloke.' They clamber into the back, one of them bends and gives Andrews a last kiss. He bangs the back of the truck; Langford pushes his foot on the clutch and slips it into gear with a clunk. The truck moves slowly forward, the distinctive whining sound growing as it picks up a little speed.

The group watch it pass the line of huts and disappear from view. The remaining men thank Davies for organising a good evening. He clamps his hand on the shoulder of one and they bend forward into the wind as they make their way back to their respective huts. Does one of them linger, wait until the others have gone, return to Hut Fifteen for more. She refuses. Fuelled by drink, he gets angry and grabs her by the throat.

Likely or not? The key thing was to find an explanation of why Jenny did not leave with the others. She met someone but why did that person want her dead? Was there someone with a grudge against Jenny, someone who did not get what he wanted or, perhaps, chillingly, some twisted mind that enjoyed the power of killing?

# CHAPTER 31

The afternoon was dragging. After the stresses of the morning which, now the danger had passed, seemed exciting, Lizzie was helping Patricia on the ward. They had just two patients, one of the trainees who had gone down with a nasty stomach bug, causing sickness, giddiness and exhaustion and an airman from the Turweston base who had concussion resulting from a very large, heavy spanner being dropped on his head by a colleague whilst servicing an aircraft. Both were drowsy and not yet in the mood for merriment. The ward was quiet apart from the occasional ticking of the big heater in the centre of one wall.

The two women were having a good clean and tidy-up, freshening the unoccupied beds with clean sheets. "You're sure you're alright...after this mornin' and all?" Patricia asked smoothing the bottom sheet over the mattress.

"Of course. I was absolutely fine. It's just part of the job. Crises occur...you deal with them."

"I don't think I'd be able to look at it like that."

"Well I bet you do things that would turn me to jelly – you know when there are bad injuries. I couldn't deal with lots of blood and bones sticking out."

"It's not usually that bad here though I've certainly seen some horrific injuries. London in the blitz was terrible. Sometimes we'd have to go out with the ambulance crew to pick up the injured and the dead. I remember once, we went to a street where a bomb had landed. Two houses were completely destroyed. The men were searching in the rubble and one of them shouted for a nurse. I went in. There was a child, a little girl in a faded floral dress, lying on her side covered in dust, clutching a ragged doll, a wooden beam pinning her down. I knelt beside her and leaned over to check her breathing and her heart. There was nothing. I..."

"There's no need to think of that now, Patricia," Lizzie said gently, placing a hand on her arm noticing the single tear that rolled down her cheek.

"I can't help it, Lizzie. I can't forget it and sometimes, at night, she comes to me. She's asking me in this quiet, small voice if I'd go with her to Heaven." Deep lines formed on Patricia's face as she tried to suppress the tears that threatened to destroy her professional calm. She shook herself and wiped her face on her sleeve. "Now we'll not need these sheets," she said with sudden brusqueness. "Would you take them back to the linen store please?"

Lizzie realised that Patricia needed a few moments to recover her composure. After placing her arm around Patricia's waist and giving her a squeeze, she picked up the sheets and slipped through the double doors out of the ward and into the corridor. The door to Matron's office was not quite closed and, through the opening, she could see Matron on the phone, twiddling a thin blue pen in her left hand. As Lizzie passed, she heard the telephone handset clatter onto its cradle. Walking as quietly as she could, she came to the linen store. She was not sure why she was being so quiet but something told her she did not want to alert Matron to her presence. Holding the sheets against her body on one arm, she opened the door with the other hand and entered the gloomy store. It was always warm in there as pipes carrying hot water ran around the bottom of the walls to ensure the sheets were aired.

Closing the door behind her, she strolled towards the ward, placing her feet carefully on the wooden floor. As she approached Matron's door, she heard very faint singing. She stopped before the door so she could not be seen from inside and listened. Snatches of song, a song that was not familiar to her but the language... the language was surely German. Lizzie had a smattering of German which she had learnt for a holiday the family had spent in Bavaria when she was fifteen.

It sounded like a children's song…she listened hard to hear the words and could only just make them out.

The song began again, quietly, happily. 'Alle leut', alle leut' geh'n jetzt nach haus.' She fumbled towards a translation, scouring the recesses of her memory for the words. 'Everyone, everyone is going home.' It's not the song that's important she told herself. It's the language. Why was Matron singing what seemed to be a German children's song?

Lizzie stepped quietly and speedily towards the ward and very close to Patricia. "I need to tell you something," she whispered, "but not here, later."

"Mysterious. I can't wait," mouthed Patricia.

The next hour was an agony of indecision for Lizzie. Should she tell Patricia now and confront Matron? But what could she confront her with? Singing a German song was not a crime and proved nothing. She herself knew 'Frere Jacques' and could just as easily be singing that absent-mindedly as she worked. It just so happened that Matron knew a German children's song. She kept meeting Patricia's eyes, who wore a quizzical expression on her face, seeking some clue as to what she wanted to say.

At last her whirling mind was stopped, suddenly, by Matron appearing in the doorway and announcing she needed to sort something out upstairs. Lizzie listened for her heavy footsteps fading down the corridor and then she motioned with her head for Patricia to follow her. They left the ward and as soon as they were through the double doors, Lizzie turned to Patricia.

"She was singing a German song…Matron…a German children's song, something about going home." Lizzie hissed.

Patricia was puzzled by Lizzie's agitation. "So what?"

"Speak in whispers. Why does she know a German children's song? Why was she singing it?"

Patricia shrugged. "Some people might sing a song from a German opera. What of it? What are you trying to say?"

"Perhaps she's German. Perhaps she's the saboteur."

"Now Lizzie, I think this morning has affected you more than you realise. She's a nurse for goodness sake not a mechanic. Probably doesn't know one end of an aeroplane from another."

"Maybe, maybe but…it's something that needs checking. I've got to tell Robbie." Lizzie left Patricia standing in the corridor, shaking her head.

She grabbed her flying jacket from the hook in the staffroom and, leaving the building, ran lightly down the line of huts to the end. Once inside, she knocked on the door of the incident room and burst in. Robbie McBane had his greatcoat on and was clearly about to leave.

"Robbie, Robbie," she gasped, "Matron, you've got to check her background."

"Hold on, just slow down and get your breath. Start at the beginning."

Lizzie breathed for a few seconds and then explained what she had just heard. Like Patricia, McBane was not convinced that there was any significance in Matron singing a German children's song. Bur Lizzie persisted.

"We should not leave any stone unturned."

"We?"

"You then. Get onto that contact you have who checked Driscoll's background."

"Right away Ma'am." Robbie saluted and clicked his heels together, grinning at Lizzie.

"Robbie, I know you think I'm being melodramatic and overbearing but I have a strong feeling that something is not right with Matron."

"You mean that same sort of feeling you had about Dearing?"

"Ok I was wrong about him, though he is an unpleasant man capable of being violent towards women. I know that to my own cost. Just do it Robbie, to keep me quiet if nothing else!"

McBane sighed and sat down heavily in the chair at the

desk. He picked up the telephone handset and while he waited for the operator said, "Leave it with me Lizzie but at this time on a Friday afternoon, I'm not going to get an answer right away. I may not be able to do anything until Monday if they've all gone home."

"Monday? I hope that's not too late."

"What's her name anyway? I think of her only as Matron."

"Agnes Fisher."

When the operator's voice answered, Robbie McBane waved his free hand as a goodbye to Lizzie and she returned the gesture before slipping out of the office, closing the door quietly behind her. She needed to speak to Patricia again.

Lizzie had left her room door slightly open, the light off, and she lay on the bed fully clothed listening for the faintest sound of movement. The luminous hands of her watch crawled slowly around the dial and she felt sleep pulling her away from her vigil. When she drifted, her thoughts became confused, images forming and fading, memories merging. One moment, she saw the leering face of Dearing, heard his words 'That's all you're fit for', and the next, the pilot in the Shrike removing his goggles and radio mouthpiece to reveal the face of Matron.

She shook her head and sat up to bring herself to full consciousness. Swinging her legs off the bed soundlessly, she stepped across to the door in her stockinged feet and listened. Nothing. She returned to the bed and sat on it. At least that little bit of movement had brought her fully awake. How long should she wait until she decided that Matron was not venturing out? She did not know but sleep would eventually claim her.

At last, the faintest sound. Lizzie sat up straight,

straining her ears. Footsteps, definitely footsteps, very faint but approaching. She did not move, waiting until they passed her room and then she moved swiftly. She stood at her open door inside the room for several seconds and then, very carefully, eased the opening wider. Letting her head move forward she looked towards the stair and, sure enough, a figure in a greatcoat and what looked like a woollen hat was disappearing down the lower flight, sinister in the little light that spilled from the corridor below.

Lizzie glanced at her watch again. Thirty minutes to midnight. Matron was certainly a creature of habit. She stepped lightly to the stairs and down to the half landing. She heard the outside door below close and was confident that Matron – if it was Matron – had left the building. She ran back up the stairs and past her own room to Patricia's where she knocked quietly on the door. There was no answer so she eased the handle round and opened the door. Patricia was lying on her side fully clothed on the bed, fast asleep. She's tired thought Lizzie, compassion dispelling any irritation she might have felt. She put a hand on Patricia's shoulder and shook her gently.

"Patricia, Patricia, wake up."

Patricia groaned and rolled onto her back. Lizzie shook her again and Patricia opened her eyes. "What is it? Who is it?"

"It's me...Lizzie. Wake up. She's on the move."

Suddenly Patricia was awake and sat up. "Right, let me get me shoes."

"It's quieter in stockings. Come on."

Patricia followed Lizzie out of the room and down the corridor to Matron's door. Even though Lizzie was sure Matron was not there, they stopped and listened, Patricia pressing her ear against the door. They could sense rather than see each other, the darkness being so thick. Lizzie put her hand on the door knob and turned. It yielded and she pushed the door very slightly inward. They waited, breath held and then let out slowly, quietly. Lizzie opened the door further and crept in, her every sense alert.

She could see nothing and dared not put on a light. Patricia was behind her. "Wait here," Lizzie breathed.

She started to feel her way along the wall to get to the side of the room where she was certain there would be a window. Her hip bumped against something and she felt it carefully. An armchair. She worked her way around it and continued, slowly, until she felt the corner and the wall at right angles. She followed that and at last felt curtains. Carefully, she pulled one aside; the moon speeding through broken clouds and the apron floodlights outside created a shadowy world inside the room.

Patricia glided into the centre of the room. "Come away from the window, Lizzie, just in case"

Lizzie did as Patricia suggested and huddling close together, they agreed which items of furniture each would search.

"What are we lookin' for?"

"Anything that might tell us who she is or what she's up to."

Lizzie pointed to a door that led off the room. It was slightly open. "What's in there?"

Patricia walked softly towards it, took a deep breath and pushed the door wider. She breathed out and returned to Lizzie. "It's her bathroom. Nothing to search, no cupboard just a shelf."

The two young women worked quickly, deftly going through drawers. In any other situation, Lizzie would have held up a pair of Matron's giant knickers to give Patricia a laugh but not now – there was no time for frivolity. She did lift a framed photograph from the bedside table. Difficult to see in the dim light but it looked like a young man, quite handsome, fair-haired perhaps, well-built, smiling by a tent.

Lizzie held it up. "Matron's lover?"

Patricia stopped her check of the wardrobe, looked at the photograph and smiled. "Bit young for Matron I'd have thought." She resumed her search and pulled out from the bottom a very large carpet bag, carefully sifting the contents. "This looks like a going away bag," she whispered, "all packed and ready."

"She can't go anywhere at the moment. That's for sure."

Patricia turned to the wardrobe again and lifted a spare blanket from the bottom. Under it, was a small clutch bag, the sort a lady would take out for the evening. It was pink, shiny, leather – stylish. Patricia eased the clasp and pulled the two sides apart. Purse, lipstick, compact, some papers. She shuffled through the latter, peering closely in the dim light to read each: an old ticket for the cinema in Banbury, a receipt from a dress shop in Brackley and a library ticket. She lifted the latter out and checked the name, her heart beginning to pound.

"Lizzie," she hissed, "Lizzie look at this."

Lizzie glided the few steps to Patricia, hearing the urgency in her voice. She looked at the ticket held up for her inspection.

There it was, the name, Jennifer Sumser.

The two women looked at each other, unable to speak for a moment. "It must be her," breathed Lizzie. "I told Robbie McBane right at the start that he needed to find her handbag."

Patricia nodded. "Will we bring this with us?"

"No, no. Put it back exactly as you found it. I'll tell Robbie in the morning and he can do a search of her room and find the evidence."

"Where d'you suppose she is now?"

"At the hangars, sabotaging the aircraft. We need to stop her. How long have we been in here?"

"Minutes only."

"Put the bag back and let's go. I'll close the curtain - we need our coats and shoes."

# CHAPTER 32

Patricia shivered and moved closer to Lizzie. They had both put on capes, Lizzie borrowing one from the nurse's staffroom; Patricia was wearing a dark woollen hat while Lizzie had put on her leather flying helmet. "We look like bank robbers," Lizzie had quipped before they left the Sick Bay building. The moon was nearly full, its cold light casting occasional shadows when it darted between the rapid clouds.

They hovered outside the looming shape of the first hangar. The small personnel door towards the back was open. They hesitated, Lizzie fearing a confrontation with Matron if she was inside damaging the aircraft. She was dangerous; she had almost certainly murdered Jenny.

Lizzie stepped through the open doorway, not moving the door in case it made a noise. She stopped, listening for any sound that might indicate the whereabouts of a saboteur. Patricia followed her silently and they stood together inside the vast empty space. A solitary lamp at the front of the hangar, fixed to the side, threw light onto the aircraft and a vast shadow of it against the far wall. The scaffold used earlier to check the engine was still in place under the port wing, a green, metal structure with steps leading to the platform.

There was no sign of anyone.

The Wellington was a silent giant, its internal structure of intersecting diagonal spars discernible through the fabric covering. Everything about it looked huge in the confined space, much bigger than when it was outside: massive, fat tyres on wheels supporting strong hydraulic legs, impossibly large wings reaching out. It seemed inconceivable even to an experienced pilot such as Lizzie that it could ever leave the ground. It was 'her' aircraft, the one she had delivered on

Monday. Monday…it seemed an age away and yet was only the start of the week.

The two women moved towards the front of the hangar, slowly, senses alert to the slightest sound or movement. The smells of grease and oil were heavy. One step at a time they inched forward. Nothing. They reached the wing, passing under its tip and turned in towards the nose with its two guns projecting from the front gunner's position. As they passed under it, Lizzie took a step towards the body of the aircraft, looking up cautiously through the bomb-aimer's window to see if anyone was inside.

Nothing.

The crew door in the underside was closed. They stopped, listened again before moving on into the shadow to circle the aircraft. At the tail, Lizzie motioned with her head to Patricia that they should leave.

Outside, they both breathed deeply. "Let's try the next hangar," whispered Lizzie.

"D'you think this is wise Lizzie? I mean, should we not just wait until the morning and have Robbie arrest her, search her room."

"It's not just about arresting her. She could sabotage one of the aircraft again and, like last time, we may not know until it's too late. We need to stop her or catch her in the act."

Lizzie began to tread as lightly as possible behind the hangar and Patricia reluctantly followed her, keeping close. There was some light spilling from the gate and, when they turned to look, they could see the sentries; neither seemed very alert. One was lounging in the box, the other lolling against the gate post gazing into the sky. Neither were looking in their direction.

"They'll probably not see us and almost certainly will not have seen Matron," whispered Lizzie.

The second hangar was almost identical to the first. The door towards the rear was not open however, and Lizzie tried the handle carefully, slowly applying pressure and praying it would not screech. The handle didn't but there was a creak as she pushed open the door. She froze instantly, the sound seeming to scream in her brain. They stopped and waited but could hear nothing.

Again they stalked around the aircraft, eyes trying to pierce the shadows but there was no movement, no sound. But as they passed under the tail, Patricia drew in a sharp breath and stopped as still as a statue. Lizzie had heard the sound – it came from the back corner of the hangar. Lizzie laid a reassuring hand on Patricia's arm but her own heart was pounding in her chest. She turned towards the sound, trying to see what it was.

Silence.

And then it came again, a faint scratching. Slowly, Lizzie moved towards it, trying unsuccessfully to keep her breathing steady and quiet. She drew closer and closer. Sometimes the sound would stop and then Lizzie stopped too. Like a game of musical chairs. Her eyes were becoming accustomed to the gloom and she could make out what looked like pallets stored at the side of the hangar, a small oil drum, some pieces of machinery decorated with cobwebs as if they had not moved in a long time. She was beginning to be sure that it could not be a person, there was so little space behind the pallets.

Suddenly she strode forward and, grasping the oil drum, tilted it onto its bottom rim and rolled it aside. There was a rapid scurry, a fleeting glimpse of a small, dark body and Lizzie let out her breath. She returned to Patricia, smiling.

"A rat…that's all it was."

Patricia did not look entirely convinced, the worry visible on her face even in the poor light from the lamp. "Let's get out of here." She almost ran to the personnel door and slipped through it, breathing in the cold night air in great gulps.

"Are you ok?"

"Just about. We'll go back now will we Lizzie? She's not here."

"I want to check the third hangar. You go back if you like…I'll be fine on my own."

"I'm not going anywhere on my own if there's a murderer about. If you're determined to go on, I'll come with you but I'd rather we just went back to our beds."

The situation was the same in the third hangar which contained the aircraft Dearing had commanded. The two women took the same route, walking slowly along the lit side of the plane first. They were passing under the nose, Lizzie checking the crew door and trying to see inside, when there was a click behind them. They both froze for a moment; Lizzie started to turn around ready to face Matron.

"Stay still, raise your arms slowly over your heads," a strained male voice shouted, nervousness or excitement in its high pitch.

Lizzie and Patricia complied and Lizzie tried to speak but her voice would not come.

"Now, when I tell you, very slowly turn around and face this way."

Lizzie's brain was in turmoil. This was not Matron. Perhaps this was the real murderer, one of the men from the base. Was this to be their end? He had murdered once and presumably would do so again. He won't shoot though will he? The sound will give him away. Bayonet…stabbed through the heart, a slower death, more painful. A burst of anger vented like a volcano somewhere deep within her and Lizzie knew that she would not die without a fight. No man was going to take her life without resistance. And if she could not save herself, she could perhaps at least save Patricia. As soon as they turned, she would gauge the distance and then lunge at him, try to get the gun off him.

"Ok, one at a time. You on my left, nearest the hangar door, turn slowly to face me." Lizzie could sense Patricia trembling as she turned.

"Now the other one…slowly."

Lizzie readied herself mentally to rush him, grabbing the

gun and forcing it upwards so, if he did fire, the bullet would not hit Patricia or herself. She turned on the balls of her feet and in the same motion leapt forward. Her sudden attempt to stop left her in a heap on the ground. "Langford. It's me...Lizzie Barnes."

He stood, pointing the gun at her, his mouth open. "Not you...surely not..."

"Oh God, I hope it's not you. I thought much better of you." Lizzie blurted.

"What d'you mean? I'm on guard duty to make sure nothing happens to the aircraft. We don't want more sabotage. What are you doing here?"

"This is nurse Patricia from the sick bay. We came here because we think it might be Matron...you know... the one who sabotaged the aircraft and murdered that girl."

"Matron?" the disbelief was evident in the one word. "You can't be serious."

"Have you seen her tonight?"

"I've seen no one."

"Are the aircraft guarded every night?"

"No, but Lovell wanted them guarded after the incident with your engine so I'm on stag now and someone else will be taking over soon."

"That's good. We can be sure there'll be no damage done."

"My orders are to arrest anyone prowling in the hangar, whoever they are, or shoot if necessary."

"Arrest?" Patricia's face, pale in the lamp light, was as horrified as if she had seen a ghost.

"That's right, Miss. You'll have to come with me I'm afraid."

"But we were following Matron – she's almost certainly the murderer and the saboteur."

Langford looked unconvinced. "You'll need to sort that with the powers that be – Group Captain Lovell or Sergeant McBane."

"But...but while we're with you, we can't check up on Matron. She's probably hiding somewhere waiting for a chance to do some damage."

"I can't help that, Miss. My orders are clear." He motioned with his rifle towards the personnel door by which they had entered and the two women moved towards it. Lizzie was cross but could see no way of persuading Langford to let them go. She thought of making a run for it as she was sure he would not shoot but he would simply raise the alarm and other men would search until they found her. Where could she hide? Nowhere on the base. Reluctantly, she walked with Patricia, conscious of the rifle behind them.

Langford issued instructions and they entered the administrative building. He took them along a corridor behind the Officers Mess and opened a door to a room. When he switched on the light, Lizzie realised it was a cell. One small window high up on the outside wall – it must be on the gate side of the building as the Officers Mess looked out over the airfield. Lizzie looked at the room: bare walls, no other furniture except a bed and something that looked like a chair without a back. It had a lid which she lifted and realised it was a commode. A heavy door was slammed behind them and she heard the key turn in the lock.

"I want to see McBane as soon as he arrives. Please arrange that," Lizzie called.

"Ok Miss." Langford's reply was muffled and they heard his steps receding along the corridor.

Patricia had her arms crossed, hugging herself. She sat down heavily on the single bed, little more than a bench with a thin mattress. A sob shook her body.

Lizzie swiftly sat beside her and put an arm around her shoulders, pulling her close. "It'll be alright, Patricia. He had no choice but to follow orders. We've got proof, remember, that it's Matron. We just have to tell Robbie in the morning."

"I wish I'd stayed in me bed. Should never have listened to you."

Lizzie felt a twinge of guilt and pulled her close. "I'm sorry Patricia. We'll sort it out in the morning. Let's try to get some sleep now." Lizzie reached for the blanket which was at the foot of the bed and encouraged Patricia to lay down. She covered her with the blanket, turned off the light and lay beside her, not attempting to get under the blanket. The bed was really too narrow for two but she wanted to be near Patricia to give her comfort.

They lay in silence for a minute or two. Patricia's voice was soft in Lizzie's ear. "Finding that bag does not prove anything, Lizzie. She could have found it somewhere and picked it up. She may be a thief but it doesn't prove she's a murderer."

"Not on its own but there's something else that might be evidence. When Robbie and I went to see the body, one of the things we found was an envelope crumpled in a waste paper basket in one of the offices. On it was an address. I remember it clearly 'New Swan Stone, 7, Acacia Avenue'. Now I don't know where that is but it was the way it was written, the pen had indented the paper. Fountain pens don't do that but Matron's pen does. Lovell has the same sort of pen; I saw it in his office. Maybe they're in it together.

"But the envelope doesn't prove that she murdered the girl."

"It may prove that she was in that hut. Anyway, I feel it in my bones."

"Could she strangle someone? I mean she's a nurse. Our calling is about helping people get better, tending the sick and injured, not murdering people."

"That's true. I think we'll have to wait for Robbie McBane." Lizzie gently stroked Patricia's hair. "Now let's get some sleep. It's been a long day."

She knew she would not sleep, her mind churning over possibilities, wondering if Langford was somehow involved. But why would he sabotage an aircraft? Was he in league with Matron too? Her thoughts became more and more extreme until, eventually, she knew she had to stop thinking about it. She listened to Patricia's quiet breathing, the regular intake and exhalation. How could anyone stop the breath of a young woman? What could be the motive?

# PART 6: SATURDAY 20TH FEBRUARY 1943

# CHAPTER 33

R obbie McBane looked with satisfaction at the boiled egg in front of him. A real fresh egg was certainly a treat. There were some compensations for living in the country. He tapped his spoon around it and carefully removed the top. The smell of the fresh yolk and its deep yellow colour verging on orange cheered him. The white was firm and the yolk still liquid but thick: just how he liked it, perfectly cooked. He took a spoonful and closed his eyes as the rich taste and smooth texture filled his mouth. Then a mouthful of hot buttered toast. For a short while he put aside thoughts of the case.

Outside, he heard the heavy thump of an engine approaching. Motorbike. He glanced to the window and, through it, could see a blood red sun balanced on the rim of the field staining the high ribs of cloud crimson. The sound died right outside the inn but the silence was soon broken by a banging on the door. He looked towards it and then back at the egg. He really didn't want to let it go cold. Fortunately, the landlady bustled into the bar.

"Who can that be at this time of the morning?"

Robbie looked at his watch. Seven fifteen hours. The landlady unbolted the door and pulled it open. He heard a man's voice. "Telegram for a Sergeant McBane. I thought they must mean the new base but it's definitely The Silver Swan,

Silverstone."

"Thank you. Early morning ride for you today then?"

"Yep but I'm on nights at the moment. Last job for me this then it's home to bed."

"Well go carefully and thanks for this." She waved the envelope in her hand and shut the door. It was clear as she approached Robbie's table that she was bursting with curiosity. "Well whatever can this be about so early in the morning? Must be urgent…probably important. It's not about an invasion is it?" Suddenly the pleasure changed to alarm.

Robbie had risen from his chair. He took the envelope. "I don't think I would get a telegram about that. I'm not important enough." He sat down again and began to open the envelope. The landlady hovered expectantly by the table. "Thank you Mrs Rogers."

"Oh right…I'll be getting on then." She half turned and then added, "If it's bad…you know…bad news, we'll do what we can, just let us know."

"Thank you, Mrs Rogers. You're very kind."

He waited until she had retreated to her sanctuary through the door behind the bar before pulling the telegram from the envelope. He read it carefully once and then again. Deep in thought, he replaced the telegram in the envelope and put it in his jacket pocket. He finished his egg, toast and tea hurriedly and rushed upstairs to ready himself for the day; he needed to act quickly.

Lizzie and Patricia were awake before the dawn light had penetrated the room. They lay squashed together and fully clothed on the narrow bed. Lizzie had worn the borrowed cape as she had tucked the blanket around Patricia; she had been grateful for its warmth in the dark emptiness of the night.

Patricia's voice was soft. "Lizzie, you said something

happened in your past. Is it something…d'you want to tell me? I'm a good listener. Something to do with men it was I think."

Lizzie did not respond immediately, wondering if this secret she had suppressed for so long could ever be told. What was the point? It had happened, she had moved on…except she had never really done so. It had affected her whole life, always there, influencing her attitudes to people, men especially. It had made her hard, she knew, but that was no bad thing. Perhaps that had enabled her to survive in a job dominated by men. But, there was no doubt, it had limited her, always on guard, always keeping people at bay, unable to love.

"If I tell you, it must not go further than this room."

"Of course not. But, Lizzie, only tell me if you think it'll help."

Lizzie said nothing for another minute and then came to a decision. It was perhaps time to try an alternative approach; suppression had not worked. "I think I was about eight when it started. He was a friend of my parents, a family friend I suppose you'd say. They lived somewhere else so they would stay with us and we would stay with them. I used to play with their children - a boy and a girl. The girl was a little older than me and the boy a little younger. I was hardly aware of the start but looking back I think it was when I fell over in their garden one day. He was there and he picked me up, carried me inside, put me on a chair and was massaging my knee. It wasn't cut and didn't even hurt that much and I remember thinking he was making more fuss than necessary."

Patricia lay in the dark not daring to speak, not wishing to intrude on Lizzie's memories.

"He lifted my leg and rubbed it gently, making soothing noises. I think he was looking up my dress but I can't be sure. They sent their children to boarding school so I only saw them in the holidays but he and his wife would come to visit us or we would visit them." Lizzie shuddered. "On one of those visits, he came into my room, to say goodnight he said. He kissed me, not on the cheek but on the lips, a lingering kiss, nothing like my parents had ever given me and then his hand went slowly under the bedclothes down my body to my...private area."

Patricia felt her own body tense with the horror of what she knew was coming, no idea what she would say when the revelation ended. She could feel the tension in Lizzie's body too as they lay close together.

"Each time they visited us or we visited them, his hands would wander more freely. He would whisper to me that I was lovely, that this was a very special thing we shared that I would be in trouble if I told anyone. I should have said something to my parents of course. I realised that when I was older. But when you're only eight or nine.... Then one time, he took my hand and he put it on his trousers. The buttons were undone and he worked it inside. I could feel it swelling, his breathing becoming more rapid. He was moving my hand against it until he suddenly jerked and his underpants were wet."

Again there was silence in the cell as a grey light seeped in the high window, bringing blurred definition to the commode, the door, their two figures on the bed. At last Patricia whispered softly. "Did it get worse?"

"Of course. He seemed satisfied with that but on my tenth birthday, he said he wanted to give me something very special. He raped me, that was his special gift to a ten year old girl."

Patricia wriggled her arm from beneath her and, sliding it around Lizzie's shoulders, pulled her close. "My God, Lizzie, and you've carried that with you all these years."

Lizzie sobbed then, her body convulsing, her face buried in Patricia's shoulder. "I knew it was wrong but he told me I'd get in trouble if..."

"There, there. You're safe now. I've got you." ·

"All the time I was thinking was it something to do with me? Was I being punished? Was I wicked? Did I deserve it?"

"It was not your fault, Lizzie. You cannot blame yourself."

"Oh I know that...intellectually, rationally...but it's not

how I felt…not how I feel. It was the shame, I still feel it but now there is anger there. Anything that a man does that threatens me, belittles me. Oh I cover it up by making light of it, pretending I'm amused but really I'm seething."

They lay silent for several long minutes, Patricia holding Lizzie tight, before she said, "And how did it end?"

"I was sent to boarding school when I was thirteen. I was so happy when my parents told me because I knew he could not get at me there though of course school holidays would be a problem. But after a few weeks at boarding school, I began to wonder if I'd jumped from frying pan to fire."

"Why so?"

"Bullying. There was a group of girls, one in particular – Abigail Weston. They were vile, criticising everything about me, my hair, my clothes, the way I walked, jeering, taking my pens or breaking pencils, anything to make me miserable."

"Girls can be such little bitches."

"Some can, yes."

"And did that go on all the way through school?"

"No, Miss Bakewell, my English teacher, noticed it. And the way she dealt with it was superb. She understood that the only way to deal with bullying is for the victim to stand and face them. She told me to think, that's all, just think."

"Did she not have words with them?"

"Not as far as I know. But I thought about it and realised that I needed to find something that would stop them. So I did some digging about Abigail and discovered that she had been sent to school because her parents had split up. It was a thing to be ashamed of in those days. One day, I let her know that I knew and that I could easily tell other people." Lizzie gave a short, bitter laugh. "The bullying stopped immediately. It taught me the only way to deal with a bully is to face them down, somehow, whether it's humour or defiance, anything but never let yourself be bullied." Lizzie thought about what she had just said. "It's the same with this war but on a much larger scale. Hitler's a bully and we have to stand against him."

"You're absolutely right." Patricia paused, seeking a way to enable Lizzie to finish her account. "So what about the holidays...with the fella?"

"The first holiday I had at home when he and his wife visited was Christmas. Their children came too. He came to my room as I knew he would and as soon as he approached my bed, I sat up and clicked on the bedside light. I can still remember the surprise on his face. I looked him straight in the eye and said, 'You've got three seconds to be out of my room or I'll scream. If I scream, I'll tell them what you've been doing.' He was out so fast, I hadn't even started counting. They never visited us again and they always came up with some reason why we couldn't visit them. That suited me of course."

"Did you never tell your parents?"

"Never. They would often wonder why they no longer saw their friends but I never told them. They still don't know. I don't suppose they'd believe me...just put it down to my over-active imagination. That's the way it is."

"Lizzie, I'm so sorry." Patricia paused again. "So you've never had a gentleman friend, never been courted?"

"I've had plenty of offers but never accepted them."

"There are some good men, Lizzie, men like Edward and Robbie McBane."

"I'm sure there are but I'm not ready to give up my career and take the risk of just being some man's nightly entertainment, a skivvy, nursemaid and the rest of it. I'm doing a worthwhile job for the war effort and that's how I intend to stay."

"I understand, Lizzie, but...but what about when you're older? What about when the war ends? God sure, you don't want to end up like Matron now do you?"

"The war will end soon and I can decide what to do when that happens."

That seemed to close the conversation and Patricia, though keen to persuade Lizzie not to cut herself off entirely from male society, realised that it would be indelicate to continue probing. She felt honoured that Lizzie had been able to confide such a deeply held secret to her. They both lay on the bed, lost in their own thoughts while gradually the creeping daylight banished the darkness.

Footsteps along the corridor followed by a banging on the door made them sit upright. A key ground in the lock and the door was flung open. An airman they did not know brought in a tray with two large mugs of steaming tea and a plate with two pieces of dry bread. He dumped it on the floor, left the cell, pulled the door closed noisily behind him and turned the key in the lock. Not a word was spoken. Lizzie and Patricia looked at each other and reached for the mugs.

Patricia slurped noisily. "God I needed that." She bit into a piece of bread. "Come on Lizzie, eat, drink. We don't know when we'll get anything else."

Some thirty minutes later, footsteps again echoed in the corridor but the sound was confused – more than one person. "Let's hope this is Robbie," Lizzie muttered. Again the key ground drily in the lock and the door was flung open but it was not Robbie McBane who strode into the room.

# CHAPTER 34

Robbie McBane swung his car into the lane that ran along the perimeter wire and put his foot down. The car surged forward and, after one change of gear, he braked hard and turned into the base entrance. The car stopped just before the barrier and sank back on its rear wheels as if with a sigh. AC Smith approached the car and McBane wound down the window.

"Group Captain Lovell would like to see you in his office, Sir...as soon as you arrive...like now, Sir."

"Ok, thanks. Is Inspector Fletcher on the base?"

"No, Sir. No sign of him today as yet. Mind it is Saturday, Sir."

"Quite. I've just got to make a quick phone call and then I'll see the Group Captain."

Smith lifted the barrier and, with a wave, McBane revved the engine, letting in the clutch so the car lurched forward. He drove at speed in front of the buildings to Hut Fifteen. With remarkable agility for such a big man, he slipped from the car, slamming the door behind him. In a few long strides, he reached the outer door of the hut, unlocked it and, once inside, unlocked Fletcher's incident room which had the phone. Lifting the handset, he pressed the cradle repeatedly until the base operator answered. His fingers drummed on the desk top as he waited for the call to be put through and answered.

"Morning. McBane here. Is Inspector Fletcher in?"

"Not yet, Sir. He doesn't usually work on Saturdays."

"He needs to do so today. Please get a message to him. It's urgent. He needs to come to Silverstone Base immediately. Tell him I have been given important information that will lead to us discovering the guilty person."

"Right you are, Sir. I'll send a PC to his house now."

"Please stress the urgency."

"Will do, Sir."

Robbie McBane replaced the handset and caught his breath. How much should he tell Lovell before he told Fletcher? He would judge that depending on how Lovell was reacting. Still thinking about that, he strode towards the administrative building, the rush of adrenaline produced by the telegram still coursing through his body. When he reported to Lovell's office, he was asked to wait; he was assured the Group Captain would not be long. McBane paced the corridor outside Lovell's office, muttering about the delay.

❖ ❖ ❖

Lizzie and Patricia gaped at Lovell. It was not the fact that he was there but the belligerence with which he had stamped into the cell. He gave them no time to speak.

"So, it was you all along." He glared at Lizzie, contempt evident in every part of his body. "You were in the hangars last night, no doubt attempting to repeat your efforts at sabotage. Tell me pray," he continued with heavy irony, "is this solely in order to impress us with your ability to fly or is there a more sinister purpose? Working with the enemy perhaps?"

All the anger that had been brought to the surface in the discussion with Patricia now erupted in Lizzie's chest. "How dare you suggest that I sabotaged the aircraft and for such a dishonourable reason as to make myself look good."

Lovell shouted loudly, the sound filling the small cell. "How dare you answer me back in such a disrespectful manner. While you are on this base, I am your commanding officer and you'll speak when I give you permission."

"I'm not…"

Patricia pulled Lizzie's arm, turning her away from

Lovell. "No, Lizzie. That'll do no good at all."

"And you Nurse O'Flynn. You're part of the plot are you or has she just put pressure on you, coerced you into acting with her?"

Both women were shaking, Lizzie with anger, Patricia with fear. Patricia took a moment before replying. "We were following Matron, Sir. We believe her to be the saboteur."

"Do you realise how ridiculous that sounds? A respected figure in authority over you who spends her days tending the sick and injured and you think she prowls around at night in aircraft hangars wielding a spanner in order to wreck aeroplanes and kill the crew."

Lizzie jumped in. "But she was singing..."

"I don't care if she was dancing a jig. The suggestion is ridiculous. But your involvement Nurse worries me. I thought you might have better judgement. But perhaps you have a motive. Are you working with the Irish rebels who think Hitler will give them a united Ireland? Is that it?"

Circumstances often change people. Patricia took a slow breath and looked Lovell in the eye. Her voice was quiet but icy. "That is not it at all, Group Captain. I have no such connections nor sympathies."

Lovell grunted, subdued by her composure, the new sense of assurance she displayed. He turned back to Lizzie. "So what have you got to say for yourself, Miss Barnes?"

Lizzie took her cue from Patricia, fighting to control the anger that seethed in her. She wanted to say something curt, savage, about Lovell's inadequate leadership but knew she needed to restrict herself to the issue. She looked at him, and realised why she reacted to him as she did. Some of his mannerisms reminded her of that family friend, the way he stood, his attempts to be intimidating. "I think it best, Sir, if I say nothing more until I can speak with Sergeant McBane or Inspector Fletcher. I have information to give them which will help the enquiry."

"And so do I, Miss Barnes, so do I. Your antics last night

make you the prime suspect. After all, there were no problems until you arrived on Monday afternoon. That girl was murdered on Monday evening. Quite a coincidence wouldn't you say?"

Lizzie said nothing and Lovell, turning on his heel, stamped out of the cell, the door banging shut behind him.

The two women looked at each other and both let out long breaths. Both had been tensed, quivering, one with fear, the other with anger. Lizzie could see that Patricia was going to cry and she put her arms around her. "I'm sorry Patricia for dragging you into this but...but it will get sorted as soon as Robbie gets here."

The corridor that Robbie McBane was pacing felt cold. It was not just the temperature but the plain paint on the walls, the absence of pictures. There were three windows which looked out over the entrance. Smith and Webster were on duty again – they seemed to be getting a lot of gate duty - probably part of their punishment for failing to log all movements. He could see the lane he had driven up earlier, the bare fields on the far side, ploughed and awaiting the seed that would transform them into green lakes that rippled in the breeze. What would it be, he wondered, wheat, barley, oats?

His eye was drawn to a vehicle approaching slowly. As it drew nearer, he saw it was a van and the legend 'Staples Plumber' became clear. He watched it turn into the entrance and stop in front of the barrier. There was a conversation between the driver and Smith and the barrier was lifted. Robbie McBane watched the van pull forward and travel along the perimeter road a short way before turning towards the airfield and disappearing from view between the two main buildings.

Curious, he thought. The instruction that no one should

leave nor come onto the base was still in force, yet the plumber had been let in with no trouble. Something to investigate later.

Footsteps stamped on the stair and then the sharp sound of tipped heels striking the concrete floor drew his eye. It was Lovell, his face twisted in an angry snarl.

"McBane. You've not been waiting long." It was a statement as if to forestall any impatience.

"No Sir."

Lovell swung the door of his office open, barked "Come" over his shoulder and strode into the room. Robbie McBane followed him in and closed the door quietly. Lovell had stopped at the window overlooking the airfield; he whirled around.

"Well we've found the culprit. I knew we would sooner or later. No need for all that detective nonsense."

"Culprit...who...?"

"None other than that young woman whom you've been treating as above suspicion." Lovell stopped, smiling sickly at the look of shock on McBane's face. "Oh yes, none other than Miss Barnes, she of the ATA."

"But how...what has...?"

"Found by one of our sentries in one of the hangars with that Irish nurse, clearly about to sabotage an aircraft again."

"Again, Sir?"

"Oh yes. I thought it was odd that she knew all about the way the aircraft she flew the other day was sabotaged. What I don't know is whether it was simply to prove what an able pilot she is or whether she's on the side of Jerry. That's for you to discover of course but we've got them locked up so they can do no more harm."

"What have they said...I mean about being in the hangar?"

"Some cock and bull story about following Matron... Matron for God's sake! They could have picked someone more likely."

The colour drained from Robbie McBane's face. "I think you should read this, Sir." He pulled the envelope from his jacket pocket and thrust the telegram towards Lovell.

Lovell read slowly, his eyebrows lifting higher and higher. When he had finished, he stared at McBane. "But...but what....what does this mean?"

"I believe it means, Sir, that you've got the wrong people locked up. Miss Barnes suggested to me yesterday afternoon that I needed to get information. I phoned immediately and received this telegram less than an hour ago. I need to speak to Miss Barnes right away. She may have more information."

"She and Nurse O'Flynn were creeping around the hangars last night, McBane. That's evidence enough that they were up to no good."

"I'm afraid there's no time to discuss that at the moment, Sir. I need to speak to her now." With that he took the telegram from Lovell's fingers and turned smartly towards the door without saluting nor further words. He ran along the corridor, down the stairs and found the cell at the end of the corridor.

A voice followed him. "You can't go in there, Sir, there are prisoners..."

"I can and I will. Unlock it immediately."

The guard decided not to argue. After all this was a sergeant from the RAF Police. He took a clanking ring of keys from his belt and unlocked the door. McBane was inside the cell so quickly Lizzie and Patricia were still rising from the bed.

"Are you alright?"

"We're fine," answered Lizzie. "Probably don't look our best but we're alive."

"I've got some information but tell me what you've got first."

Lizzie responded to the urgency in his voice, talking rapidly. "We waited last night until we heard Matron leave her room. We searched it and found Jenny's handbag hidden in the bottom of the wardrobe. We then came over to the hangars as we thought she might be sabotaging the planes again. But Langford arrested us – as he'd been instructed."

"Matron had a large bag packed in her wardrobe too… looks as though she's planning to go away," added Patricia.

"We left Jenny's bag there so when you search the room, you'll find it. But another thing. That envelope we found in Hut Fifteen in the office next to Jenny's body. The writing puzzled me as the pen had indented the paper – not like a fountain pen at all. I've just remembered Lovell had an unusual pen and I think Matron has one too. You need to find that pen in Matron's office and check how it writes."

"I need to get onto that. Come with me. Lovell thinks you're to blame for everything but we can sort that out later."

"Another thing…the address on the envelope…the name of the house. Do you know where that is?"

"No but perhaps Fletcher or his men do."

"The house was called New Swan Stone. I realised during the night that it's a translation of the German name Neuschwanstein. It's a castle in Bavaria built by mad King Ludovic. There must be a connection with Matron. If she wrote that envelope, as I suspect she did – you can prove it by the writing – then whoever lives at that house is probably a contact."

# CHAPTER 35

Inspector Fletcher turned into the lane leading to the base entrance. He would normally be cross at being denied his Saturday morning recreation but, if it meant the culprit was apprehended, it was worth it. A vehicle was approaching from the gate, lumbering slowly towards him. It was a small green van. He gave it plenty of room and as the two vehicles passed, he just caught the name 'Staples' on the side.

As he waited for the barrier to be raised, he saw McBane striding towards the gate with two young women in tow. He drove onto the base and stopped the car alongside him.

"Morning Sergeant. You have information for me."

"Aye, lots to tell you but first, do you know a house called New Swan Stone. It's number seven, Acacia Avenue but not sure where that might be. We think it's local because it was written on that envelope we found in Hut Fifteen which was marked 'By hand'."

"No…don't think I've come across it."

"Can you find out where it is? It's important. We think it may be a contact of Matron."

"Matron?"

"Yes, Sir. No time to explain. We've got to check a couple of other things and then we'll meet you at Hut Fifteen."

"I'll make some phone calls."

Before he had let in the clutch, he saw McBane and the two women dash into the Sick Bay. He turned the car onto the apron where the ground crew were putting chocks on the wheels of the three Wellingtons that had been towed out from their hangars ready for the morning's training flight. The car purred along the buildings and he parked it by Hut Fifteen. Inside the office, he picked up the telephone and asked to be put through to Brackley Police Station.

Arthur Sumser used to like weekend shifts as things were much quieter, fewer trains, fewer passengers. He did not look forward to work at all now, since…since Jenny had died. At least he had time to think, to remember, her lively smile, her zest for life. Even from a child it had been evident. Everything was an adventure, exciting, to be enjoyed to the full.

He remembered when they had taken the children to the sea, made possible by the considerable reduction in train fares he was entitled to as an employee of the railways. The children had squealed with delight when they saw the vast expanse of water, the waves rolling lazily up the sand, the sun sparkling on the green sea. George had set about building a sand castle with help from himself. Enid had flopped with a satisfied sigh onto the blanket she had spread on the sand, the lunch bag, towels and so forth marshalled around her. But Jenny, Jenny had run in her bathing costume to the water's edge, jumping up and down, splashing, rushing in and rushing out, screeching as a new wave rolled up against her legs, throwing drops of water on her little body.

Bliss. Who could have predicted that a few short years later, both would be gone, all that youthful energy extinguished?

From the ticket office window, he could look across the station. The lines and platforms were at a much lower level than the office. Stairs led directly down to the up-bound platform – Number One – and the bridge which started at the same level as the ticket office led across the tracks to stairs which led down to Platform Two, the line for London and stations on the way. He always had to explain that he worked at the top station. There was another station in Brackley, owned by a different company which ran East to West from Banbury, through Brackley to Buckingham – all the Bs.

As he looked out of the window, he could see Sidney in the signal box almost on a level with himself but at the end of Platform Two. When he saw Sid look up, he gave him a wave and a smile. Sid was a good man, quiet, reliable. When he had heard about Jenny, he had said very little but he had put a hand on his arm. 'Anything, Arthur…just let me know.' Those few words and that gentle touch had been enough. Even in this mad World, there was goodness, feeling for the grief of others.

His reveries were interrupted by a figure approaching the ticket hatch, a woman whom he recognised. She was dressed in a black beret which sported a narrow bow on top and was at a slight angle on her head. Well-groomed fair hair swayed beneath it on each side of her face as she walked. She wore a well-cut black overcoat that was nestled around the contours of her figure. Her eyes were confident, perhaps arrogant and she held a leather purse in her hand which she had taken from the large bag hanging on her arm as she had approached the counter.

"Two tickets for London, I like please. I have friend coming."

Arthur Sumser was surprised at the way she spoke, the order of words in the sentence – he'd never noticed it before. He glanced up at the clock. Six minutes to nine. "I'm afraid there are some delays this morning Madam. The nine fifteen to London is not expected until nine thirty. I had a call this morning. There are some problems on the line."

She looked angry and as she passed some notes under the window, he heard her utter an expletive under her breath. It sounded like 'Shisa' or something. Definitely not an English word. Sounded more like German. He completed the transaction, passing the tickets under the window.

"The London train leaves from Platform Two, Madam. Just along the passage there…"

"I know. I've been here before," she replied curtly and then whisked away, clutching the tickets in her hand.

Curious. Arthur Sumser watched her retreating figure.

Sergeant Bailey also liked Saturday duty – during the day at least. 'Money for old rope' he would say to his wife. Nothing much happened on Saturday morning which gave him a chance to catch up with any paperwork and, if the truth were known, daydream a little about the massive robbery he would foil or…or the murder he would solve that would bring him promotion to inspector.

His mood dropped when the telephone rang. He picked up the handset wondering if this was some idiot with a lost cat or… something really serious that would require him to expend energy. His spirits sank when he heard Inspector Fletcher's voice. He listened and then brightened.

"Well as a matter of fact, Inspector, I do know where that is. I had occasion to visit number seven Acacia Avenue earlier this week when I needed to speak to Staples, you know the plumber, Sir. It's quite a posh house up at the top of the town, Sir. Very well dressed lady lives there - not sure if I should mention this as it was just an impression – but, though she looked very middle class and home counties… you know … the way she was dressed, Sir, she did speak a bit funny."

"What do you mean funny? Was she making jokes?"

"No Sir, I don't mean funny like that. No, it was the order of the words she used…not quite like the way a British person would say things. I mean I didn't think much of it because I thought maybe I was just imagining it."

"Thank you, Sergeant," and the phone went dead. Frank Bailey held the handset away from him and looked at it as if he could see Fletcher in it. Then he replaced it, wondering why Fletcher was interested in that address. He had been musing only a minute when the telephone's jangling bell startled him again.

Once more he listened, with increasing intensity, sitting forward in his chair. Then he said, "It's the order of the words in her sentences that makes you wonder then? Is she quite a smart looking woman, perhaps well-to-do would you say?" Frank Bailey listened to the response. "Top station. Right I'll be up there as fast as my old legs will take me. Don't let her leave on the train. Hold it up, don't let it leave the station."

The handset clattered as it was dropped onto the cradle and, with an agility that surprised himself, Sergeant Bailey was on his feet, reaching for truncheon, handcuffs and his cape. It wasn't raining but that wind was still cold. Facing the hill of the High Street yet again was not a proposition he relished but… maybe this was the break he was looking for. As he wobbled away on his bike, he thought of the headlines: 'Local Police Sergeant Arrests Spy' or perhaps, 'Brilliant Bailey of Brackley.'

He thought of several more as he was labouring up the High Street and it was only as he reached the top where the road levelled off that he started to think about what he might face. He had his trusty truncheon but what might a spy have?

Sergeant McBane, Lizzie and Patricia marched into Fletcher's incident room, but before the Scotsman could speak, Fletcher held up a hand.

"I've just spoken to Sergeant Bailey at Brackley. He went to seven Acacia Avenue earlier this week when he needed to speak to Staples. So what's it all about?"

"I've just searched Matron's room. There's no sign of her but I found this." He placed Jenny's small clutch bag on the desk. "It belongs to Jenny Sumser. Whilst I was doing that, Lizzie and Patricia checked Matron's office near the ward to find a sample of her writing. Lizzie."

"She uses a new type of pen which has a tiny ball at the

tip instead of a nib. I used it once. When you write, you have to press hard and it makes an indentation in the paper. More than that, her handwriting matches that on the envelope we found. I know Lovell has a pen like that but I've not seen any others. Almost certainly, she wrote that envelope. She is connected to that address - New Swan Stone – which is a translation of the German Neuschwanstein, a castle in Bavaria...Hitler's favourite part of Germany."

Inspector Fletcher made the connections quickly. "Bailey just said that the woman at New Swan Stone spoke strangely, not like a British person would do. Perhaps like a German. There's a link there alright. But he also said he went there to speak to Staples. I just passed Staples' van leaving the base not even ten minutes ago. I wonder."

"She's with him in the van." Lizzie blurted. "He's taking her to Brackley to that woman."

"Why was he let onto the base? I was going to check that with the gate sentries. No time now. We need to get after them." McBane was already reaching for the door handle.

"That van of his will not make good speed. Let's go."

All four rushed out of Hut Fifteen and towards Fletcher's car. Suddenly, the metallic voice of the tannoy blared across the base. "Action Stations, Action Stations. Incoming enemy aircraft. Man the anti-aircraft guns. Fire crews ready." There was panic in the voice which they all recognised as Lovell's.

"I need to stay...there may be casualties." Patricia's eyes were wide with shock and sudden fear.

"I must stay too. We need to get the Wellingtons in the air."

"Let's go, McBane." Fletcher did not wait for an answer but yanked open the driver's door of his car. The engine roared into life as McBane flung himself into the passenger seat and the car leapt forward even before he had his legs inside and the door closed. Fletcher swung the big car round and pushed his foot hard on the accelerator, hardly slowing as they turned between the administrative building and the sick bay, the tyres screeching in protest and McBane clinging to the edge of his seat as his body was forced against the door.

As they approached the barrier, McBane threw open the door and leapt out, shouting at the sentry, "Get that barrier up now." He ran to the gatehouse. "Why was Staples on the base this morning?"

"Staples, Sir?" the startled airman repeated blankly.

"Yes Staples, man, Staples. Look in the log."

The sentry turned to the log book lying open on the desk. "Um…I remember now…said he had been called to fix a leak in the sick bay, Matron's bathroom I think he said."

"Clever." Robbie McBane ran to the car which had been driven through the open barrier and was waiting for him, passenger door open wide. He dived in, slammed the door and Fletcher took off, the bonnet of the big car lifting eagerly like a big cat rising for the final spring.

The two young women had watched the car speed away for a moment and then turned to each other. They hugged briefly but closely and looked into each other's eyes. The moan of the siren, starting low and quiet but rising in pitch and volume with each second to a piercing wail struck fear and urgency into both. Then Patricia was running for the Sick Bay and Lizzie was beside her. She crashed through the door into the admin building and took the stairs two at a time. She could hear voices in the corridor upstairs, Dearing and Lovell. She reached the top of the stairs and ran towards them, hearing Dearing's voice, strong, insistent.

"We need to get the Wimpeys into the air, Sir. They're sitting ducks on the ground. You must let me back on duty."

"Ok Dearing go. Get Driscoll and whatever crew can be spared. See what you can do."

"What about the third one, Sir?" None of the trainees are ready to fly in this sort of sortie." Dearing's voice was urgent, unlike his usual drawl.

Lovell's eyes fell on Lizzie for the first time. "What the

devil are you doing here? You should be locked up."

"No time for that now, Sir. I'll fly the third Wellington."

"But you should be…"

"She must fly it, Sir, or we'll lose that aircraft." Dearing turned to Lizzie, looking her in the eye. "Sure you can do this?"

"It's better that I try than the aircraft is smashed to pieces by a bomb."

"Agreed. Let's go." Dearing turned, leaving Lovell waving his arms and trying unsuccessfully to get some words out against the deafening keening of the siren.

# CHAPTER 36

Arthur Sumser strode over the footbridge and down the steps onto platform two, his feet hardly resting on the treads, his hand sliding down the rail. He did not run along the platform as he did not want to alert her but he walked with long, purposeful strides. The woman was pacing back and forth along the platform her eyes flicking to the footbridge and stairs when facing north, searching for someone, the mysterious friend. He smiled at her as he passed her but there was no smile in return. He climbed the wooden steps to the signal box and opened the door.

"Mornin' Sid. Got a bit of a situation here."

Sidney raised an eyebrow and leant his forearm on one of the huge levers that controlled the points and signals. He said nothing, waiting for Arthur to explain.

"Got some suspicions about a passenger on Platform Two. You can just see her, look. Anyway, Sergeant Bailey from Brackley Police is on his way and he wants us to hold the train until he gets here. So do not let the train go until I tell you to. Nobody else…just me. Got it?"

Sidney smiled. "Aye, aye Skipper."

"I reckon she's a jerry…maybe a spy…you never know these days."

"Maybe…on the other hand, she may just be a lady going to visit her sister in London."

"Maybe, but let's be sure before we let her go. London train's running late I'm told."

"Yep and will be running even later if Bailey doesn't get here soon." Sidney looked out of the window. The signal was in the horizontal position to stop the train at the station. "Train's going nowhere until you say, Arthur."

"Great. I'm going to have a word with her, tell her it's running even later." Arthur Sumser re-traced his steps and stopped by the woman who had ceased pacing and was focused on the footbridge, scanning its length for the umpteenth time. He coughed. "I'm afraid, Madam, we've just heard that there is a slight problem further down the line so the train has to be held at the station here until we get the all clear."

She spun around and glared at him. "What kind of service this is? Inefficient huh? Ticket costs fortune but train is late, always it is late."

As she spoke, Arthur Sumser could see the train approaching in the distance, blowing clouds of steam and smoke into the clear morning air. The woman had her back to the approaching train but she turned to watch it until the engine passed her and, snorting steam like a monstrous beast, came to a halt, carriages creaking and couplings clanking. She raised her arm and consulted her watch.

"It is twenty minutes past nine. This train should leave now and it will leave now. Kindly arrange that."

"It can't and won't leave the station whilst the signal is against it Madam," Arthur replied calmly and with a feeling of satisfaction.

"I realise that a porter little authority has but you will tell the signal man to let the train go."

Arthur Sumser was not one to stand on his dignity but the woman's manner made his hackles rise. "I am not a porter, Madam. I am the Assistant Station Manager."

"Well whatever it is you are, just make it move."

"The train stays here until it is safe for it to move."

Her hand suddenly reached into the capacious handbag on her arm and was withdrawn. Arthur Sumser found he was staring into the barrel of a pistol. "I said make the train move now." Her voice was crisp, threatening, malicious.

But Arthur merely smiled. He felt no fear, only a great calm sweeping over him. "You can do nothing to me," he said. "I've lost my son to your lot and now I've lost my daughter too. There's very little left for me in this life. Your gun does not scare me...you can do your worst. But I'm the Assistant Station Manager at Brackley Top Station and this train does not leave until I tell the signalman, in person, to change the signal. You can shoot me, but the signal will definitely not then be changed and the train will go nowhere." He squared his shoulders and lifted his head, presenting himself for the bullet that he was sure would come. His voice was an inaudible whisper as he said, "Forgive me Enid but know that, when I was called, I answered and did my duty."

◆ ◆ ◆

Dearing and Lizzie burst from the administrative building and ran around it towards the hangars. As they careered onto the apron at full tilt, Edward Driscoll with all the trainees met them.

"Spread yourselves amongst the aircraft and get them up as soon as possible." Dearing waved an arm at the few ground crew left – the others had gone to their action stations. Those remaining had frozen, not sure whether to get the aircraft out of sight in the hangars or prepare them for take-off. "Chocks away, get ready for take-off. Are they all fuelled by the way?" he shouted.

"All full, Sir," Langford shouted back.

There was a scramble for flying helmets and parachutes and then they rushed for the two furthest aircraft, as the trainees had mainly flown in them. Brian Saunders and Perkins another trainee headed for Lizzie's plane. She realised it would take too long to arrange others to join and saw Langford who had just removed the chocks from her aircraft. "Langford, come with us."

"Miss?"

"Grab a flying helmet and parachute and come with us."

"But Miss...I'm ground crew."

"Yes but now you're air crew. Do it."

As soon as the engines had been started, Dearing's aircraft led the short distance to the end of the runway on the western side of the airfield. Over the intercom, Lizzie checked the positions of her crew. Saunders had taken the centre turret and Perkins the rear turret. Langford was clutching one of the struts behind Lizzie.

She whipped her head around. "Langford," she shouted over the thunderous roar of the engines, "take the forward gunner position."

Langford staggered closer to Lizzie, hanging on to whatever was conveniently placed. "I've never used these guns, Miss."

"It's about time you did. They're machine guns – just like the ones you've been trained on for use on the ground. Release the safety and press the buttons when we're lined up with the enemy. Don't forget to put on the intercom headset." She looked at Langford as he gingerly lowered himself from the cockpit to the bomb aimer's position. His face was white with terror. He crawled forward and disappeared from her view. She waited a minute and then spoke on the intercom.

"Langford, can you hear me?"

"Yes Miss. I'm in position."

"Strap yourself in. This might be a rough ride."

Despite the drama of the moment, Lizzie smiled to herself as she heard Langford's quiet voice in the intercom. "Holy shit."

The radio burst into Lizzie's headphones. "Dearing here. Report in. Everything ok?"

Driscoll reported everything was fine as did Lizzie though she explained she had only three crew.

"That's all you need...one on each gun. Now when we get airborne, we'll head south and then east. Main thing is to gain height as soon as possible. We need to be able to attack the enemy from above. Don't bother with fighters, we'll not do any damage to them. Go for the bombers."

"This is very strange. What are they doing attacking in the morning? They normally come at night." Driscoll's voice was calm, measured.

"God knows."

The three Wellingtons took off in turn and veered to starboard following Dearing's plan. Gaining height was a slow process but soon they were passing through the small white clouds. Dearing then leaned to port and headed eastwards. The other two aircraft followed suit. It was not long before they saw three aircraft in the distance on their port quarter. Two which were larger were flying at a lower altitude than them and a third was higher well clear of the clouds.

"Looks like two bombers and one fighter. Very strange. Keep an eye out for others."

Dearing's aircraft dipped its port wing and turned towards them. "Ok. I'm going to come down on the closest bomber – looks like a Junkers JU88."

Lizzie could make out the two engines of each bomber and then heard Driscoll's voice on the radio.

"You're right. You can see the bulge under the front fuselage for the bomb aimer. They're fast and very versatile but we have surprise on our side. We need to watch for our own fighters. I don't know why they've let them get this far in land."

"Surprise I suppose. No one was expecting them in daylight."

The nose of Dearing's aircraft pitched down and Lizzie could imagine the scream of the wires as it gained speed. From her position as the third aircraft, Lizzie could see that Dearing was aiming straight for the first bomber. For several seconds, with gathering alarm, Lizzie thought Dearing's plan was to crash into it. She stared in horror at the disaster she was expecting. Spits of fire were shooting ineffectually from the guns of the German plane – there was no central gun turret and neither forward nor rear guns could swivel far enough to hit a target approaching from the flank. As Dearing's plane plummeted closer, the German bomber seemed to shudder and she realised that Dearing's forward guns were blasting the port wing.

Just when she thought the aircraft would collide, Dearing's plane pulled up and to starboard, to head east and well to the rear of the German aircraft. Suddenly there was a massive explosion and burst of light from the port wing of the German bomber. Black smoke trailed from it and the plane began a spin towards the ground, pieces of its port wing falling like confetti.

"You got him, Dearing, you got him," the usually calm Driscoll shouted excitedly over the radio. "I'm going for the second."

As Driscoll's plane began its charge, Lizzie could see the fighter swooping down upon it. She recognised it as a Shrike, a Focke-Wulf FW 190, the same type of aircraft that had tried to destroy her on Monday when she had delivered the Wellington. "Driscoll, fighter approaching from five o'clock."

Driscoll's plane immediately veered away eastwards and the Shrike changed course. It was up to her now. "Right chaps. We're going for the other bomber. We'll do what Dearing did...head straight for it and when I say, Langford, let rip. Aim for the wing and port engine."

Lizzie put the plane into the steepest descent she dared and the Wellington gathered speed. She could feel the whole aircraft shuddering as it reached a speed it had not really been designed for. She gritted her teeth. Closer, closer until she thought the guns would do enough damage.

"Now," she yelled, "let 'em have it Langford."

She heard the forward guns juddering angrily and saw holes appearing in the port wing of the Junkers before she pulled back on the joystick and turned to port. As she roared over and away from the German bomber, she heard the rear guns take up the fight. She looked back. There was no explosion.

"Damn," she said quietly and continued to turn the

Wellington westwards as the momentum of the descent lifted them above the Junkers again. "We'll try again. This time, go for their starboard wing Langford and I'm going to drop below them so Saunders, fire at either wing from below as we pass under. Perkins, you try when you can as we leave them behind."

Lizzie was surprised that the Junkers took no evasive action, so determined, she supposed, the pilot was to reach the target. She completed the Wellington's turn and dived downwards at the Junkers. Again she yelled for Langford to open fire and kept the joystick pushed forward so the Wellington plunged beneath the German plane. She heard Saunders fire his guns from the centre turret and then Perkins from the rear. She knew they had succeeded even before she had turned to see the ball of fire that was falling from the sky, pieces of metal cascading around it.

All four of them were cheering. "Well done everyone. Can any of you see the Shrike, or our other aircraft?"

All three reported seeing no sign of any other aircraft. A wave of nausea swept through Lizzie and settled in her stomach. They had destroyed two enemy bombers and probably saved the airfield but at what cost?

# CHAPTER 37

Robbie McBane hung onto the edge of his seat with one hand and braced himself against the dashboard with the other. He liked to drive fast, or at least he thought he did, but Inspector Fletcher was flinging the car alarmingly around bends in the road. The big Wolseley bucked and rolled like a wild horse galloping over the fields. Hedges, trees flew past and he was conscious of the deep drainage ditches at the sides of the road. His ears were filled with the clanging of the bell.

But he could do nothing except resign himself to Fletcher's driving skill. It gave them the best chance of catching Staples before his passenger – assuming she was in the car – made an escape. The tyres squealed as they turned left onto the A43 in Silverstone village, heading for Brackley. At least on the main road, there were fewer bends and they were much less severe. There was as yet no sign of Staples' van but Fletcher was determined they would catch them before Brackley. He was muttering to himself, his hands gripping the wheel, his eyes intense on the road ahead.

Lizzie had called on the radio several times for Dearing and Driscoll, repeating that the second Junkers had gone down. At last Dearing's languid voice came on the radio.

"We're heading back to base. No sign of the Shrike. Over."

Then Driscoll's voice. "Sorry for the delay in responding. Playing games with that wretched Shrike but he seems to have gone now. Last seen heading westwards. Probably going to strafe the airfield, do as much damage as he can before heading home. We're heading back to the airfield now. Over."

"Roger. I have the base in sight. I'm going to fly past to see if I can see Staples on the road."

"Staples? Why Staples?" Edward Driscoll asked.

"Long story. Tell you when we land. Out."

Lizzie followed the road from the base to the A43 and within minutes saw the police car racing southwards. With so little traffic on the road, she was able to see the van less than a mile ahead, crawling at a sedate pace. She flew low over it, and dipped her wings to port and starboard. She swooped up and around, looking down on the van. It was still pottering along. Once more she passed low over it, this time flying northwards straight towards it. She was trying to intimidate Staples into stopping but it had no visible effect.

She swooped upwards again and banked the aircraft around like a hawk preparing to stoop. Flying south once more, she scanned the road ahead. There was a long straight stretch coming out of Brackley where the ground either side was level with the road and only hedges lined it – no trees. She made up her mind.

She flew to the edge of the town and turned the aircraft to head north towards the van. Gritting her teeth, she began to descend and then lowered the wheels. If she had to, she would land on the road and stop the van. As she got closer and closer, perhaps fifty feet above the road, Langford's voice stammered in her headphones.

"We're going down Miss. You've got to pull up."

"I know. Brace yourselves to land everyone. We may hit some telegraph poles on the way."

"But, but…it's a road. You can't land on a road."

Lizzie realised it must look terrifying to Langford, positioned as he was right in the nose of the aircraft. "Sit tight Langford. We may not have to."

Lower and lower, Lizzie carefully reduced height until the wheels of the big plane were some fifteen feet above the road. That meant, she reasoned, that the wings would be at least twenty-five feet above the ground and hence would miss any obstacles. It should be enough to clear the telegraph poles.

"For God's sake Miss, pull up."

"Langford. Keep quiet."

Arthur Sumser stared unflinching at the woman whilst his mind raced. He thought he saw the gun shake at one point but could not be sure. He knew he had given her an impossible decision and he was pleased with himself for doing so. If she shot him, the train would not leave the station because Sid in the signal box would not change the signal until he and only he gave the word. If she did not shoot, she would have to persuade him to tell Sid to change the signal…and nothing she could say would bring that about, not at least until Sergeant Bailey had dealt with her.

The footbridge from the ticket office and station entrance was behind the woman and in Arthur's sight. He and she stood like that for what seemed an age but was in fact only seconds.

"Tell him the signal to change or I shoot."

"As I've already explained, if you shoot me, the signal will never be changed. It's only me the signalman will listen to."

"He'll listen to a person with a gun."

Arthur smiled. "So you'll shoot him and then what?" Do you know how to change the signal? There's a lot of levers up there."

He detected a brief moment of uncertainty, the smallest crack in the ice of her face.

"What in God's name is he doing?" Fletcher's eyes were

292

flicking from the road to the Wellington and back, tracking its flight first south then north and south again. The speeding police car came over the brow of a hill, devouring the road even more rapidly as it descended the slight incline of a long straight stretch of road. They could now see Staples' van, still ambling along, the driver presumably oblivious to the chase. Fletcher silenced the bell and the roaring of the Wolseley's engine filled their ears.

Robbie McBane was watching the Wellington. It was now well south of the Staples' van and he could see it lean over to make another turn to the north. Something told him it was Lizzie at the controls. He watched the big aircraft descending, becoming larger with every second. The wheels appeared from beneath its belly and McBane understood what the pilot was about to do.

"She's going to land on the road and block Staples."

"She?" Fletcher flicked a glance at McBane and understood. "She can't land on a road. She'll never make it."

"Well it certainly looks as if she's going to try."

The pursuing car was now only a few hundred yards behind the van. "I'm going to have to get off the road. If that thing lands it'll make mincemeat of Staples and us. I don't fancy getting chopped up."

Suddenly the fleeing van juddered to a halt, swerving onto the grass verge. The driver's door opened and they could clearly see a man jump out. His hands were in the air in the universal gesture of surrender. The nose of the Wellington lifted, just a little, and then the aircraft swooped over the van and, a second later, themselves. Both McBane and Fletcher ducked instinctively, deafened by the roar of the plane's engines.

"Blimey! That was close."

"Far too close for my liking, Sergeant, but it looks as though the van's been stopped. Very handy that, saves us having to force a stop."

Fletcher slowed the police car as it approached the van.

There was suddenly a burst of blue smoke from the van's exhaust and it was off, bumping over the verge until it had regained the carriageway. Staples was standing in the road, his hands still in the air, watching his van accelerating away from him.

"Who's driving it now?"

"Must be the woman - damn and blast her." Fletcher's foot pressed hard on the accelerator and one hand flicked the bell switch.

Staples, alarmed by the clanging of the bell, turned towards them, the expression on his face turning to relief; his arms fell to his sides and his shoulders sagged. But Fletcher swerved around him, not slowing at all. Robbie McBane twisted in his seat and saw him standing open-mouthed in the middle of the road, becoming smaller as they sped after the fugitive van. They were not far behind but it was definitely driving more quickly than it was with Staples at the wheel so they were gaining on it only very slowly.

The first houses of Brackley flashed past the windows and suddenly the van veered off to the left opposite the Bronnley soap factory.

"She's heading into the station," shouted Fletcher as he yanked the wheel over causing the car to sway dangerously and the tyres to protest. "We've got her now."

A slight movement on the bridge caught Arthur Sumser's eye. He did not look directly at it so as not to give it away but followed it in his peripheral vision. It was Bailey. He needed somehow to indicate to him that the woman was armed. Sergeant Bailey turned at the top of the footbridge and began to descend the steps to the platform. In any other circumstances, the sight of the burly policeman trying to tread silently in his heavy boots would have been comical.

Bailey advanced along the platform, quietly, not rushing, his truncheon in hand, walking directly behind the woman so she would have to turn around completely before she would see him. Arthur's view of Bailey was obscured by her but he could still see his helmet above her head.

Suddenly Bailey rushed forward and shouted – no words just a bellow of anger. She  began to turn, the arm holding the gun swinging dangerously towards the train as she spun round to aim at this new assailant. But her arm did not complete the turn. Sergeant Bailey's truncheon came down sharply with great force on her forearm and the gun dropped from her hand as an anguished cry of pain broke from her lips. The gun clattered on the paving and slid towards the train, stopping some inches from the edge of the platform.

Arthur Sumser lunged forward to hold her but there was no need. Sergeant Bailey flung one huge arm around her, pinning her arms against her body while she clutched at her right forearm with her left hand, strangled noises gurgling in her throat. Bailey did not need to hold her. He dropped his truncheon on the platform and whipped handcuffs from his tunic pocket. They were on her wrists in seconds.

"You're under arrest. Anything you say may be used in evidence. Come along with me."

She was gasping, her words coming in fits and starts. "Why…why you arrest me? I've done nothing."

"Aiming a gun at a station official at point blank range is not nothing, Madam. I daresay, that's just the tip of the iceberg. You're coming with me."

"Thanks Sergeant. You got here just in time. She could have pulled the trigger at any moment…but I told her, if she did, the train would not leave."

"You did very well, Sir, spotting her unusual way of speaking. I noticed it when I met her earlier this week but didn't think too much about it." Turning to the woman, he said, "Mrs Chalmers isn't it? I don't suppose that's your real name but we'll find that out soon enough."

"I don't care. You can do what you like. Germany, under our great leader the Fuhrer, will win this war and you English, you will be slaves."

"Save it for the judge. Come along now." Sergeant Bailey turned back to Arthur Sumser. "You can let the train go now. I'll need somewhere to lock her up here until I can telephone for a van."

"I'll just give the word to Sid to change the signal and then I'll show you."

◆ ◆ ◆

The van swerved slightly as it skidded to a stop in front of the entrance to the station building. It was Matron right enough who swung her legs out of the open door and, leaving it wide open, ran into the building, clutching a substantial carpet bag.

Fletcher and McBane were close behind but they knew she could only evade them if she was able to board a train that was leaving.

On the platform, Arthur Sumser had just turned towards the signal box but, before he had taken two steps, a clattering on the footbridge made him turn back. A stout woman, probably in her forties, was rushing down the stairs, so intent on watching her feet, she was unaware of Bailey holding Mrs Chalmers. When she looked up at the bottom of the stairs, her headlong rush faltered momentarily but then she strode forward, reaching with her left hand into her bag. When she withdrew it, she held a pistol and aimed it at Bailey.

"Let her go now. We're leaving on this train and I'll shoot you both if you try to stop us."

"I assume you know this woman, Madam. She's not going anywhere except to prison and nor are you." Frank Bailey, still one arm clasping Mrs Chalmers, pulled himself up to his full height and pushed out his chest defiantly.

Arthur Sumser had frozen but he eyed the pistol laying where it had landed near the platform's edge. "Alright. I'll just open a door for you." He walked slowly towards the train, watching the new arrival carefully. He reached out his arm as if to open a door but suddenly dropped and, picking up the gun, whirled round pointing it at Matron. "Drop your weapon or I'll shoot."

Again time stopped. It was a battle of nerves. Arthur Sumser reasoned that he could take a shot now but she may be able to fire before his bullet disabled her. It was an impasse and he had no idea how it might be broken. The eyes of the woman he faced flicked continually between himself and Sergeant Bailey.

From the corner of his eye, Arthur Sumser detected movement on the footbridge and then on the stairs. There was no sound as two men, one of whom he recognised as Inspector Fletcher descended the stairs from the bridge. The other was in RAF uniform. They stopped on the platform. They looked at each other and then back to the scene in front of them.

Suddenly, soundlessly, the RAF officer raced forward and, leaping from behind at the woman with the gun, knocked her left arm upwards as he crashed into her, bringing her to the ground with him on top.

The Inspector walked forward slowly, eyeing the writhing bodies on the platform. "All that rugby training came into use at last, McBane."

# CHAPTER 38

"Blimey, I thought we were goners then."

Lizzie made no reply; she was turning the Wellington to starboard so she could see what was happening on the ground. When she was facing south again, the van was visible entering the edge of Brackley with the police car close behind it. "Ye men of little faith," she said quietly and added, "Looks like the van got away again but there's nothing we can do whilst it's in the town. I'm sure Fletcher and McBane will catch it. We'll head back to base."

Yet again, Lizzie turned the aircraft and headed back up the A43 until she had reached Silverstone village. She turned to starboard and followed the lane towards the base. She would have to fly over it to make sure the runway was still intact and then circle to make her approach from the west into the easterly wind. She began to relax. White clouds were drifting from the east, sailing over a cold blue sky. Perfect flying conditions. If only she could fly for longer, back to White Waltham preferably, her own base. But there needed to be a debriefing and she had to return the Wellington and her crew to Silverstone.

The rattle of the rear guns startled her. "Shrike descending on us at eight o'clock." It was Perkins, his voice shrill with adrenaline.

Within seconds, Lizzie was aware of the other aircraft alongside her own, its speed reducing until the two cockpits were in line and level with each other. She looked across. The pilot of the Shrike took off his radio and smiled, the same supercilious expression she had seen before. She did not remove her radio. He saluted, the same British style salute as before but she did not return it. The smile faded, he returned his mouthpiece to his face and then he was climbing away from them, banking to port. The wings of the enemy plane dipped to starboard and then to port and Lizzie watched it diminishing as the distance grew between them.

"One day that pilot will try to be too clever and I hope I'm there to take advantage," she muttered to herself.

"Have you met him before?" Saunders asked.

"Yes. When I delivered this plane on Monday. He tried to take me out."

"Take you out. Romantic meal for two was it? I bet he hasn't got a Rolls though."

Lizzie smiled. Some humour was welcome after the tension of the last thirty minutes. "No, probably not. But then, nor have you Saunders."

"How d'you know? I might be from a very rich family – my dad's a Lord."

"What Lord Haw Haw?"

"Shut it Perkins."

"Both of you shut it please and check the airfield as we fly past. We don't want to pitch into a big hole in the runway."

Fletcher and McBane stood in the stark corridor of Towcester police station watching Mrs Chalmers being led away to the cells.

When she and her guard had turned the corner and were out of sight, Robbie McBane spoke. "I made that phone call – much more in Matron's background than I imagined. Still hard to believe that she lived so long amongst our people yet is such an ardent supporter of Hitler."

"Early loyalties, Sergeant. They're the strongest. Let's see what she has to say for herself."

It was only a couple of paces to the door of the second interview room where a constable stood, a face of stone; Matron was sitting at the table inside. It was the same room where they had interviewed Davies and Dearing. Robbie McBane looked again at the drab institutional green paint on the otherwise blank walls.

"Not sure what we should call you," Fletcher began, "but let's say Miss Fisher and you can take that as your assumed name or your real one."

"It took you long enough to find out, didn't it?" She stared at Fletcher with defiance and contempt. She had been required to remove her make-up and a line was visible on her cheek.

Fletcher ignored the provocation. "Did you kill that girl, Jenny Sumser?"

For a moment, her eyes opened in outrage and her mouth began to form a violent no but then she seemed to change her mind. "I had no choice. She was going to report me. Anyway, she's no loss. A slut that's what she was. A few weeks in the Hitler Youth would have sorted her out. She's not important."

"She was to her family," snapped McBane.

Matron shrugged.

"Why was she going to report you?"

"I gave her a letter to deliver and the stupid girl opened it. It had some... information... some drawings."

"The letter was for Mrs Chalmers no doubt – not her real name of course – your contact in Brackley, living at seven, Acacia Avenue."

Matron nodded and Fletcher continued. "You do realise that spying is a capital offence...punishable by hanging?"

Matron let out a brief, harsh laugh. "By the time your justice system gets round to a trial, the Fuehrer will be in charge of this little island and I will be a heroine. And if not, I would happily die for the Fatherland."

Inspector Fletcher turned to look at Sergeant McBane who met his eyes. There was nothing one could do with such fanaticism. Fletcher sighed. He wanted to go home, read a good book, anything to take him away from the ugliness of this war. "How can you, an experienced nurse, be so callous about the death of a young girl?"

"She shouldn't have opened a private letter."

An uneasy silence fell in the room as Fletcher wondered whether to continue with the interview. It was broken by Robbie McBane. "Did you sabotage one of the Wellington bombers?"

"Of course. I'd have done all three if I'd not been interrupted."

"Why did you decide to leave this morning? Did you realise we were on to you?"

She smiled. "You had no idea who it was did you? I made sure you suspected Dearing. So easy to do. I left this morning because I had arranged for the base to be destroyed."

"You mean…you were able to instigate the raid this morning?"

She nodded and smiled again. "My nephew, my sister's son, is a fighter pilot in the Luftwaffe. I passed information to him through my contacts and he arranged to come with two bombers." Her face distorted with anger and she spat the next words. "Why the bombers did not make it, I don't know."

"Because they were destroyed by our Wellingtons from Silverstone…not fighters but our bombers. Impressive flying I'd say." Fletcher made no attempt to keep the triumph from his voice.

"And what part did Staples the plumber play in all this?" McBane leaned forward over the table, his eyes boring into Matron's.

"He's nothing. He took some envelopes to the house in Brackley, that's all. He had no idea what was in them and had the sense not to find out. Yesterday, I phoned my contact to send Staples to fix a leak in my bathroom and I made him take me in his van. I was going to get on the train with my contact. We'd be leaving this wretched country this evening if …" she turned away, her mouth clamping shut.

"You'll be staying in this country for the rest of your life, Miss Fisher…what's left of it that is."

Her dark brows closed together. "You've no hope of stopping us. If I die, it does not matter. There are hundreds of us all over this country."

"I understand loyalty to one's country but you seem to have a bitterness, a resentment that is vengeful. What caused that?"

The hostility in Matron's eyes intensified and she stared into Fletcher's own. Her voice was quiet but steely. "Do you know what it is to lose your only child, murdered by foreigners? No of course not."

"Yet you took the life of someone's else's only child and show no remorse for it."

"An eye for an eye."

"Mr and Mrs Sumser had already lost their son in Northern France."

She sat back, shrugged and folded her arms. Robbie McBane was intrigued. This revelation was in addition to what he'd already been told.

"I'd like a few more words with the prisoner, Sir."

"As you wish Sergeant." Inspector Fletcher stood up, his chair scraping noisily, opened the door and signalled to the young constable to enter. "To the cells when Sergeant McBane has finished," he said.

It was almost sixteen hundred hours and Air Commodore Mitchell stood, sturdy legs apart and arms folded in Lovell's office. "Quite a mess I'd say, Lovell."

"Yes Sir."

"There's many things I don't understand about all of this, Lovell, but one thing I'm sure of. You've dropped the ball again haven't you?"

Lovell knew the attack was coming but was still flustered. "Well Sir, I mean I can hardly be expected to know that some of the staff I was given are rogue."

"If you had a proper set of checks on everything, you would know. That's the point. You seem to think you just have to sit in your office and everything will take care of itself. Things need managing, Lovell, people need managing. If they get even a hint of slackness at the top, they'll take advantage."

"There's a lot to sort out at a new base, Sir."

"I know that, Lovell. Kindly remember that I have run air bases before and busier ones than this. Which of your men let the side down?"

"The Police have rather taken over all the investigation, Sir, but I've been told that Corporal Davies and AC Andrews are the prime movers in the racket."

"Anyone more senior?"

"I'm afraid Flight Lieutenant Dearing has rather disgraced himself, Sir. I mean I can't believe it. His father's a judge."

"Huh! That's no recommendation. What's he done?"

"He apparently used the services of one of the girls Davies had brought onto the base."

"Not the behaviour we expect from an officer. Anything else?"

"I think he might be a little too fond of a drink, Sir. His bar bill does rather mount up."

Mitchell said nothing for a while, staring out at the airfield. "It's a tough job flying missions over enemy territory. It does things to a chap. But we can't let that go on...too dangerous when you're flying."

Lovell turned his eyes to the airfield. The three Wellingtons stood unscathed on the apron and no damage to speak of had been done by the enemy planes in the raid, just a few bullet holes from the Shrike here and there. Dearing and the others had done a good job preventing the enemy bombers reaching the base. He decided not to make that point, however, but try to have a discussion about his own future. "Actually, Sir, I have been thinking that perhaps this posting is not the best thing for my wife. She does rather miss a more active social life."

"We are not running the Air Force to provide an active social life for wives, Lovell. Godammit man there's a war on." Mitchell glared at Lovell.

"Quite so, Sir. I didn't mean that but perhaps a posting... you know...where there are more married officers on or near the base might make life..."

"As it happens, Lovell, I've already decided you're not staying here. The chaps here will not have confidence in you so I'm going to move you somewhere I can keep an eye on you."

"I don't think, Sir, I'm fit for...active service, Sir."

"You're damn right you're not fit for active service. I'm not moving you to a squadron, you're going to come to High Wycombe, to Bomber Command. You'll work in the bunker tracking the enemy and our planes. There are always several officers doing that so you can't make a cock up of it...at least I hope not."

Lovell's expression brightened. "Well thank you, Sir, that sounds perfect."

Mitchell dropped his arms and took two paces towards Lovell so his face was close to his. The voice was low and cold. "This is not a promotion, Lovell. Just remember that. It's a face-saving exercise. We cannot allow anyone to think that we have incompetent senior officers...even if we do."

"Sir."

There was a knock on the door. "That'll be everyone arriving for the de-briefing. I just hope everything is explained. The whole thing is damned confusing," grumbled Mitchell.

# CHAPTER 39

Chairs had been arranged in a rough circle around Lovell's office. He introduced each person to Air Commodore Mitchell as they filed into the circle and sat down. Mitchell shook hands with each man but, Lizzie noticed, simply nodded at herself and Patricia. He dropped heavily into Lovell's usual chair behind the desk; Lovell seemed shrunken, a mere cardboard cut-out of the authoritative leader he had tried to appear. So is the hawk diminished by the presence of an eagle.

"I'm sure Inspector you will provide a written report in due course but I need to know immediately what has gone on – the whole lot please. Don't worry if you think I might know some things…I need to get it straight so I can report up the chain of command."

"I don't know everything, Sir, so I will ask the others here to chip in if they can elucidate at any point."

Mitchell grunted and the Inspector started. "On Monday evening, we believe at about nine-thirty pm, a young woman – a girl really, she was only nineteen - called Jenny Sumser was murdered in Hut Fifteen. She was strangled. It was clear from the bruising on her neck that her assailant's left hand had been placed higher, suggesting we were after a left-handed person. Her clothes were in a state of disarray. There were two initial questions: who was she and what was she doing on the base?" Fletcher paused. "I'll let Sergeant McBane explain why he came to be here on Tuesday morning."

Mitchell's searchlight glare turned to McBane. "As ye'll know, Sir, I am in the Special Investigation Branch of the RAF Police based at RAF Burnham. I had been asked to check use of supplies, especially fuel on various bases including this one… as it was new. I noticed a much higher use of both petrol and food supplies than one would expect for a base with this number of personnel. My boss, Flight Lieutenant Belding, suggested I should look into it. I found discrepancies in the storage tank records and vehicle logs."

Mitchell nodded.

"Thank you Sergeant." Lizzie admired Fletcher's business-like manner. "On Monday afternoon, Second Officer Barnes of the Air Transport Auxiliary delivered a Wellington bomber to the base for use in training. On the way, she had been attacked by a ...Shrike you call it?"

"Yes, Sir, A Focke-Wulf 190 fighter. They sneak in to make daytime raids."

"Yes Miss Barnes, I am familiar with current German tactics."

Lizzie disliked his superior tone, his deliberate contempt for her; colour flushed her cheeks. "Of course, Sir, but others in the room may not be."

Lizzie felt a little cheated that Fletcher forestalled the possible row by resuming. "The storm overnight Monday and into Tuesday prevented her from returning to her base so she volunteered to help in the Sick Bay. Whilst walking with an injured trainee, they stopped to rest in Hut Fifteen and Miss Barnes discovered the body. Group Captain Lovell informed Sergeant McBane who informed us – the local police. On inspecting the murder scene, Sergeant McBane and Miss Barnes found various objects which suggested that Flight Lieutenant Dearing and Corporal Davies had been in that hut. Naturally, they came under suspicion."

Mitchell's thick neck swivelled to look at Dearing who avoided his eyes and said nothing. He was sprawled in his chair in his customary careless attitude. Lizzie wondered how he could appear so unconcerned in front of a very senior officer.

"Our enquiries in local towns revealed a missing girl and we were quickly able to identify the victim as Jenny Sumser. Further investigations in Brackley and on the base here revealed that three girls, Jenny being one, were being brought onto the base to supply sexual services to some of the men. This was organised by Davies though he was careful to use other people to do the driving. He was giving sweeteners to them and the sentries on the gate so that these trips were not recorded. To cut a long story short, the Brackley police also discovered one of the garages was being supplied twice a week with petrol from the base, again organised by Davies."

"Quite the racketeer then this Davies."

"A thoroughly disreputable and disloyal man, I'm afraid, Sir. Naturally, he and his side-kick AC Andrews have been charged. They will serve time at His Majesty's pleasure."

"Quite right too. And you didn't know anything about this Lovell?"

"N...no, Sir."

"And which men were using the services as you put it?"

"Perhaps best not to go into that at this point, Sir... ladies present."

"Quite so."

Lizzie looked at Dearing. He remained lolling in his chair, that amused smile on his face, completely unperturbed by the possibility of being identified as one of the clients. It looked as though he was proud of it. Perhaps he felt it made him a real man.

"We were able to eliminate Flight Lieutenant Dearing as a suspect with a little test that I had devised and we thought Davies was not the murderer as he is not left handed either. It was Miss Barnes who identified Matron as a suspect. She heard her singing a German song to herself. She alerted Sergeant McBane who instigated a background check. Sergeant."

"Early this morning, I received a telegram which I have in my pocket still. It revealed that Matron Agnes Fisher came to this country from Germany as a child. Her name was Agneta Fischer, the surname having a 'c' in the centre - the German spelling. She was born in 1900 and came to England to live with an aunt when she was eight after her parents died. In interview earlier today, she told me that when she was sixteen, she became a nurse and was soon after posted to a field hospital in Belgium where she had a liaison with a German POW whose injuries she had been treating. When she became pregnant, she returned to this country but it was decided her son, Johannes, should be brought up by her sister in Germany - a brother to her sister's own son - as she had no means of supporting the child. Both boys joined the Luftwaffe and Johannes was killed over Kent in the Battle of Britain. That's where her bitterness came from – she wanted revenge."

Fletcher added, "She was very forthcoming in the interview, defiant actually, certain that Hitler will prevail and she will be honoured as a true servant of the Third Reich. The same applies to Mrs Chalmers who was her contact."

"So what was this Matron up to?"

"She had hoped to be posted to a squadron flying combat sorties but she decided to do what she could to help Hitler from her posting here. She was to gather intelligence about our activities, the aircraft, whatever she could get and pass it to Mrs Chalmers. She usually did this using Staples the plumber."

Lizzie was surprised. "So he was involved too?"

"Yes he was, Lizzie, but unwittingly. Matron would simply ask him to take an envelope to Mrs Chalmers who was a regular customer of his. If he had not been on the base, she would use Jenny as her courier and pay her to take the envelope."

"And let me guess. This Mrs Chalmers lived at number seven Acacia Avenue?"

"Correct. Miss Barnes and Sergeant McBane had found a large opened envelope in the waste paper basket in one of the offices in Hut Fifteen. It had the house name – new Swan Stone – and 7 Acacia Avenue on it as well as the words By Hand."

"Something had struck me about the way it was written," Lizzie said, "…the letters were indented in the paper as it was written with a new type of pen. I saw Matron with one. I have only seen one other like it – Group Captain Lovell's.

Having heard her singing in German, I made the connection with the writing. We checked it this morning." Lizzie sneaked a look at Lovell. He had coloured and was looking intently at the floor.

"The pen you mention is being called a 'biro'. We are testing it with aircrews – much easier than a fountain pen when flying. Have you distributed them Lovell?" Mitchell growled.

"Not yet, Sir. It's just my wife and I are trying them as yet."

"So where did Matron get one?"

"Oh...perhaps I asked her to test one too...I don't remember."

Mitchell's brows furrowed.

Fletcher continued. "As Staples had not been at the base, Matron asked Jenny to take it. But, apparently, Jenny was suspicious about the bulkiness of the envelope and opened it soon after Matron had handed it to her. She followed Matron and confronted her, saying she was going to report her."

Inspector Fletcher paused. "She is a strong woman, Matron, not tall, but strong, a bit of a barrel you might say. She may have had training in unarmed combat or she may simply have a natural savagery that enabled her to strangle the poor girl. She then dragged her back into the bedroom and arranged her clothing to make it look as though she had been killed during the act of sex."

"A tiny piece of flesh was found under Jenny's fingernail. Was that from Matron?"

"She was required to remove her make-up – you'll know that she wore a lot of face powder. A scratch on her cheek was clearly visible but of course hidden under the make-up. I'm sorry that it didn't occur to me before." Fletcher looked around the circle of faces.

Suddenly Dearing spoke with unusual belligerence. "So how come the girl's work pass was found in my greatcoat pocket?"

"Matron planted it there at some point to incriminate you...not sure when."

Patricia started, blushing."I think it may have been the other afternoon. She left the ward saying she had to do something in one of the residential huts. I thought nothing of it but the trainee we had – Brain Saunders – followed her and said she had gone into the officers' hut. He's a bit of a joker is Brian so I took no notice I'm afraid."

Mitchell looked at her with curiosity, realising at last why she might be in the meeting. "So the petrol theft is sorted and is not connected to the girl's murder?"

"The only connection, Sir, is that Davies was running both rackets. The truck delivered fuel in the late afternoon and picked up the girls on the way back." Lizzie noticed Robbie McBane looking pointedly at Lovell.

"Quite so. In summary, Matron, a German by birth, was intent on disruption, sabotage and spying. She was passing information to her contact, this woman Chalmers."

"Correct, Sir." Fletcher confirmed.

"How on earth did she manage to sabotage the aircraft...I mean how did she get past the guards, how did she know what to do?"

Lizzie noticed the colour drain from Lovell's face. Fletcher answered. "The hangars were not guarded until after the sabotage was suspected. We must assume she had been told what to do and how to do it by... Chalmers."

Mitchell shot a look of contempt at Lovell before continuing. "This girl, Jenny Sum...or whatever she was called...was very brave to tackle her. Despite her occupation or pastime," Mitchell's distaste was obvious, "she was loyal to her country."

"So it seems, Sir."

"The raid on this base this morning was presumably unconnected with any of this. I have to say they took our boys completely by surprise. We don't usually get bombers coming over in broad daylight and I've never known just two to come

– stray fighters, yes, but not bombers. I don't understand why they came right over here...I mean there are better targets closer to the coast."

"Actually, it was connected, Sir. It turns out that the pilot of the Shrike is none other than Matron's nephew. Matron had a sister who was sent to another aunt in Germany when the parents died. The Shrike pilot is the son of that sister. Through Chalmers, Matron had arranged for the attack. It may not have been sanctioned by the Luftwaffe at senior level and I guess the pilots were trying to make names for themselves but it was deliberate. That's why Matron had arranged to get away before they arrived here. Didn't want to be shot by her own nephew."

"Good God! But why attack a small training base?"

"The more the Germans can disrupt our Air Force, Sir, the better. Had they destroyed the Wellingtons, killed some of our crew, it's fewer pilots and planes to bomb them."

"Yes, I suppose so." Mitchell looked thoughtful. "Damned good thing that you chaps stopped them before they could do any real damage."

Edward Driscoll sat up. "I would like to say, Sir, that Flight Lieutenant Dearing showed great leadership and skill. He suggested we get the Wellingtons airborne and he showed us the way to destroy the bombers." He stopped suddenly, seeming to Lizzie surprised to hear his own voice in defence of Dearing.

"Group Captain Lovell has told me about your antics, Dearing. Not what we expect from our pilots but perhaps you have redeemed yourself this morning to some extent. I think maybe you're in the wrong place. We need men like you flying combat duties."

"I think, Sir, that might be best for me. I thought I had done my bit but I miss it, Sir. I need action, direct action."

Mitchell looked at him carefully, assessing this statement. Dearing had survived many combat missions but Mitchell knew it became like a drug for some, a drug they could not do without. He was a decisive man and he came to some decisions. "Group Captain Lovell is being transferred to Bomber Command at High Wycombe. You Dearing will be posted to a squadron but you'll need to reduce the drinking. Driscoll, I'm making you Acting Wing Commander and you will run the base here. If it goes well, it will become permanent." For the first time, Mitchell addressed Patricia. "Nurse O'Flynn, you will become matron for the time being and run the hospital. We may have to send more injuries your way when the campaign against Hitler steps up."

"Thank you, Sir." Driscoll cleared his throat. "I'll need at least two more flying instructors if Dearing is leaving. We were already short. I've not spoken to her but perhaps we should consider Second Officer Barnes."

Mitchell looked startled. "What? A woman training men to fly planes. Don't be ridiculous Driscoll."

"But, Sir, she is…"

"The answer's no Driscoll. I'll send you two people."

Edward Driscoll looked at Lizzie and she smiled back, suppressing her natural urge to challenge such bigotry. "I want to go back to my job with the ATA anyway but thanks for thinking of me."

"The one question that remains in my mind is how this woman Matron could be so determined to damage the very people and country who gave her shelter for so long." Mitchell looked around the circle but no one offered an explanation.

After a silence, Lizzie spoke quietly. "We are never free of our past, Sir. For good or ill, it conditions us, influences our actions, our very thoughts and feelings, our loyalties. She was a child of Germany and lost a child at the hands of our forces. Which of us can ever free ourselves from our childhoods, from our past? Jenny's parents will carry the past to their graves."

No one spoke. Lizzie could feel all eyes on her; in Patricia's was concern, love, in Robbie McBane's a gentle wonder.

At last, Inspector Fletcher stood up slowly. "Thank you

for reminding me, Lizzie. There is one more thing." He looked around the circle of expectant faces. "Jenny Sumser's parents lost their son at Dunkirk. They've now lost their daughter. They do not need to know what she was doing at the base on Monday evening. I will be telling them that she was here to see a young man she'd met at the dance in Silverstone Village Hall last Saturday. I think that's the least we can do so they can preserve the memory of their daughter as the vivacious, pretty and loving girl she was."

Murmurs of assent greeted this statement; Fletcher's words had brought back the tragedy that had taken place, the life of a young girl with everything to live for, cut short.

# EPILOGUE: MONDAY
# 1ST MARCH 1943

## CHAPTER 40

S hafts of sunlight stroked the ground, breaking between rolling clouds of dappled white and grey, finding the occasional daffodil opening tentatively in defiance of the March winds. The sun was bright, hard, after months of Winter dullness - the first intuition of Spring, thought Lizzie. She, Patricia and Edward walked slowly and in silence along the gravel path through the churchyard towards the doors in the west end of the church which were open invitingly.

An old man, from the funeral directors no doubt, stood in the doorway in a black overcoat. He had a suitable face, long, drawn, solemn. His eyes did not meet theirs as he handed them the order of service, a foolscap sheet of paper folded once in the middle to make a little booklet. It had been arranged that Edward would drive her and Patricia from Silverstone to the funeral. Her boss, Commander Trueman, had allowed her to fly a Bristol Beaufighter up for the day as she had not flown one before. It was fast and exciting to fly, the twin Hercules engines providing huge thrust, though Lizzie had not been in the mood to enjoy it fully.

The old parish church in Brackley was large and the congregation so far assembled did not fill it by any means. There was the unmistakable, musty smell of an old building, the occasional shaft of sunlight penetrating the stained glass, revealing the dust dancing in the air. The organ was playing quietly, Mozart's Ave Verum Lizzie thought, the organist invisible somewhere at the side of the Chancel. She missed the bells which, as in all churches, had been silent since the start of the War. Soon after they had sat down, Robbie McBane joined them in the pew, sitting beside Lizzie.

"I'm glad we came," she whispered.

"Aye. So am I. Having spent several days investigating her death, I feel a strong connection to her. Fletcher seemed able to remain distant but then I suppose he's seen it all before."

"But not uncaring I think... Fletcher that is."

"Definitely not."

"It's strange...I don't even know his forename. I just called him 'Inspector'."

Robbie turned to look at Lizzie. "Same here. I'd not thought of it before. He kept himself at a distance, but he was not overly formal."

Robbie McBane glanced behind and saw Inspector Fletcher entering the church with a uniformed police officer.

Robbie leaned close to Lizzie. "Make it casual but look at the polissman that's just come in with Fletcher."

Lizzie looked behind and saw Fletcher wearing his overcoat as usual. The officer with him looked rather self-important, shoulders pulled back and strutting like a cockerel. His rounded stomach filled his tunic and he wore sergeant's stripes on his arm. His shoes were brightly polished and he carried his helmet pressed against his side with one great hand.

She stifled a giggle. "I see what you mean but perhaps he's just very conscious of maintaining the dignity of the force."

"Aye...or maybe he's not used to being at funerals. It's Sergeant Bailey – he arrested that Chalmers woman."

They returned to silence, surveying the backs of other members of the congregation sitting in front of them. Two young women, girls really, were sitting in the pew immediately in front. One was very tall. They looked uncomfortable, sitting still and mute, perhaps unused to the solemnity of being in church. The front pew on their side was empty, waiting for the closest family. She scanned the congregation but there was no sign of Lovell nor Dearing. She was glad; their attendance would have been in bad taste.

She did wonder about Dearing. What was it that made a man so arrogant, so dismissive and unpleasant to women? He had obviously been that before the war so combat could not be blamed. Something nagged at her mind. Was she being unfair? The image of Dearing's Wellington streaking down onto the German bomber could not be displaced. Was it his disdain for others, perhaps for his own safety, that enabled such an act of courage? And he had not boasted about it; all in a day's work it seemed. Perhaps in wartime there was a place for haughtiness and even brutality but neither should be countenanced in a social setting. What life would he lead when peace was restored?

Lizzie glanced at her watch. It was approaching mid-day. A loud voice rang out from the back of the church. "Please be upstanding." The organ stopped leaving a brief moment of silence like an empty space which was quickly filled with the shuffling, coughing and rustling of the mourners rising. The sombre opening notes of Nimrod from Elgar's Enigma Variations crept around the church, seeping into the high roof arches, trickling around the pews, stealing into every heart. Lizzie knew even before the coffin came into her view that she would not be able to hold back some tears. It was not so much the coffin, carried at a very slow march by four men in dark suits, that caused the traitor tears to squeeze from her eyes but the sight of the man and woman that followed it. Mr and Mrs Sumser.

Mr Sumser was dressed in uniform, presumably that of his job while Mrs Sumser wore a long black coat, a black hat and a black veil over her face. Neither looked to right nor left and maintained dignified, statuesque faces. What torment must it be to be burying your daughter, a girl who had not yet really lived, and your only child? What suffering to be enduring this again after the loss of a son?

Lizzie's thoughts wandered from the immediate. How would her parents act if they were attending her funeral? Would they be devastated by her death? They had never shown much emotion, nor even affection. She never knew whether it was because they were incapable of feeling or whether, perhaps, they suppressed their feelings behind a mask of social correctness. It was not 'the done thing' to show emotion. Lizzie thought of that conversation when she had announced her intention to join the ATA. Her mother had raised the possibility of her dying but, Lizzie felt, was more concerned at what friends from the golf club or hunt might say. That would always be a sadness in her heart and, she had to admit, she did blame her parents for what had happened to her in childhood though she realised it was unfair to do so.

Lost in such thoughts, she sang the hymns and said the prayers when required without thinking but was brought back to the present when the vicar mounted the pulpit. He gave an address in which he spoke of the horrors of war, the loss of the young, the life that Jenny would not live and her loveliness as a daughter and a girl. Lizzie was glad. That was the image she wanted Jenny's parents and friends to cherish in their memories.

The vicar stepped cautiously down from the pulpit and announced the funeral would now move to the graveyard for the committal and burial. The coffin was lifted once more and the bearers shuffled slowly around to turn it through one hundred and eighty degrees. Mr and Mrs Sumser stood as it reached them and the congregation followed suit. The grieving parents stepped into the aisle and followed their dead daughter. The congregation filed in turn from each pew and joined the line.

The chill air of the graveyard was welcome, refreshing, and birds chattered in the ancient yew trees. The vicar paused at the side of the grave, the coffin on the ground, while the mourners shuffled into positions around it. Prayers were said. Finally, as the coffin was lowered into the open grave, the words that were so familiar.

"We have entrusted our sister, Jenny, to God's mercy and we now commit her body to the ground: earth to earth, ashes to ashes, dust to dust: in sure and certain hope of the resurrection to eternal life through our Lord Jesus Christ."

All heads were bowed. Standing so close to each other, Lizzie could feel Robbie McBane shake. His hand was on his face, gripping his jaw as if to hold it still. A tear was squeezing from one eye. Lizzie felt the sting of a tear in her own and her hand reached for his.

Slowly, reluctant to leave that young body to the hard usage of the cold ground, the mourners drifted away from the grave. Mr Sumser's arm was around his wife who sniffed into a handkerchief. He steered her towards the lych gate where they waited to thank everyone who had attended the funeral. Whilst they waited their turn with Edward and Patricia, Inspector Fletcher and the rotund policeman approached them.

"I don't think you've met Sergeant Bailey. He was crucial to this investigation, finding out key information and at the end arresting Mrs Chalmers at the station. He disarmed her using only his truncheon and did not flinch when Matron pointed a pistol at him."

The Sergeant listened, shuffling his feet and protesting feebly in embarrassment. "Just doing my job, Sir."

"Yes Sergeant, but what you did was beyond the call of duty."

Sergeant Bailey's eyes twinkled mischieviously. "Would have been quicker if we'd had a car, Inspector."

Fletcher smiled. "I've got the message, Sergeant. I'll do what I can." Bailey beamed and pulled his shoulders back even further. Fletcher turned to Lizzie. "I wondered if I could persuade you to join the Police. We need people with your qualities in the detective team."

"Now hold on Inspector. I think the RAF Police Special Investigation Branch has a stronger claim on Miss Barnes."

Lizzie smiled. "I'm very flattered but I'm happiest when I'm leaving the ground behind in an aircraft."

"Well...if you change your mind, you know where to find me." Fletcher shook hands with each of them before strolling towards the lych gate with Sergeant Bailey strutting beside him.

Patricia and Edward Driscoll followed them. Lizzie had taken only a couple of steps beside Robbie when he stopped. "You know in that meeting you said about the past staying with us, influencing us." He looked back briefly towards the grave. "I found that service difficult."

Lizzie turned to face him, seeing his eyes which did not meet her own and creases on his brow. "I think everyone did but perhaps there is something that makes it especially so for you."

"There is. I...I lost the girl I was due to marry." His lips pressed tight together.

Lizzie laid her hand on his arm. "You don't need to say any more if you don't..."

"No...no. I want to tell you...if you don't mind?"

"Of course not. Shall we sit on that bench over there?"

He nodded and they walked slowly to the old wooden seat at the side of the graveyard. "It was a bombing raid...in Glasgow. She was staying at her aunt's house. Everyone in the house was killed...it was completely destroyed. That's why I came South...change of scenery, change of job...you know..."

"So many people have been lost in this war. Life can never be normal after it."

"Why I wanted you to know, Lizzie, is because I... otherwise...I have a great admiration for you and...and fondness." He stopped for several seconds and when he continued, his voice was strangled with anguish. "But I can't... I'm not yet free...."

"Shhh. I understand. Thank you anyway. I'm not ready

yet for anything either…with a man I mean…."

"But one day perhaps…d'you think…?"

She laughed and her eyes sparkled. "Oh yes, one day… who knows?"

They sat in silence for a while as other mourners sidled along the path to wait their turn with the Sumsers. "What's your story, Lizzie…if you want to tell me that is?"

"One day maybe but not now. We must hope, mustn't we…hope for better times to come?"

He nodded. "Aye…we must never lose hope."

# METEOR

## *Book II of Lizzie's War*

If you have enjoyed New Swan Stone, you'll love the second book in the series. Lizzie is assigned with Alice, a young navigator with the ATA, to take some important personnel to Cranwell airbase in Lincolnshire. The mission is top secret and Robbie McBane is assigned to provide additional security. Can they find out who is leaking information to the Germans? Can they identify the killer of a young airman on the base?

It's a real page-turner with plot twists and surprises, a cracker of a story with the same elements that make New Swan Stone such a good read: Lizzie's observation, instinct and her huge capacity to respond to human suffering.

Meteor is due to be published in May 2024 and will be available on Amazon as an e-book or paperback.

# THE DRESDEN TANGO

*Kevin's debut novel*

It is 1889. A ship is bound for Buenos Aires, Argentina, laden with Irish migrants escaping the poverty of their homeland. Rose is nineteen, a seamstress whose hopes of a better life are dashed when she finds herself trapped in a brothel, forced by the ruthless Madam to endure daily abuse by clients. Patrick is a young priest, ambitious to do great deeds, but the demands of leading hundreds of migrants in a barren land nearly breaks him.

When the two meet again in Buenos Aires, they recognise in each other the despair that fills them and the need for their self-worth to be restored. Can Rose trust Patrick to take her out of her hell? Can Patrick find in her the love that will give balm to his damaged soul?

Please see below for cover image and where to obtain The Dresden Tango

The Dresden Tango is available on Amazon. Simply type the title and Kevin O'Regan into the Amazon search box.

# ABOUT THE AUTHOR

Kevin O'Regan

Photo by Dominic O'Regan

After obtaining a degree from Exeter Univeristy and a PGCE from Southampton, Kevin taught English in maintained secondary schools for many years, becoming a headteacher and, afterwards, an educational consultant. He left his career in education early to develop his vocation as a musician and writer. Kevin is an award-winning singer-songwriter who performs across the UK and abroad, solo, as a duo and with his band.

Kevin's first book, The Dresden Tango, was published in November 2022 to critical acclaim. The second book in the series, Lizzie's War, is due for publication in 2024.

To learn more about Kevin and where he is appearing, please go to his web-site: www.kevinoregan.co.uk

Printed in Great Britain
by Amazon

27344442R00188